Every Reason We Shouldn't

SARA FUJIMURA

**TOR
TEEN**

A TOM DOHERTY ASSOCIATES BOOK

NEW YORK

EVERY REASON WE SHOULDN'T

Copyright © 2020 by Sara Fujimura

A Tor Teen Book
Published by Tom Doherty Associates
120 Broadway
New York, NY 10271

www.tor-forge.com

Tor® is a registered trademark of Macmillan Publishing Group, LLC.

The Library of Congress Cataloging-in-Publication Data
is available upon request.

ISBN 978-1-250-20408-0 (trade paperback)
ISBN 978-1-250-20409-7 (ebook)

Our books may be purchased in bulk for promotional, educational, or business use. Please contact your local bookseller or the Macmillan Corporate and Premium Sales Department at 1-800-221-7945, extension 5442, or by email at MacmillanSpecialMarkets@macmillan.com.

First Edition: March 2020
First Trade Paperback Edition: March 2021

Printed in the United States of America

0 9 8 7 6 5 4 3 2 1

Praise for *Every Reason We Shouldn't*

"A rich, emotionally layered story . . . Wonderful."   —NPR

"This book is like a warm hug filled with all the things I love.
I started smiling from page one and couldn't put it down."
—Courtney Milan

"Whether your first ice-skating romance was *The Cutting Edge* or
Yuri!!! on Ice, you will absolutely love this book. Full of complicated family relationships, sparkling friendships, and a completely
delicious romance, *Every Reason We Shouldn't* is an uplifting love
song to everyone who's ever lost their way and then had the
courage to find it again."   —Lindsay Ribar,
author of *Rocks Fall Everyone Dies*

"Sure to take the gold."   *—Kirkus Reviews*

"Readers will enjoy the well-developed characters, witty dialogue,
and cringe-worthy romantic fumbles right through to the awfully
neat, but very happy ending."   *—School Library Connection*

"Compelling . . . An obvious choice for fans of classic love stories
that play out on the ice, but also for readers looking for a nuanced
story of self-discovery."   *—Booklist*

ALSO BY SARA FUJIMURA

Faking Reality

To the wildly talented and wonderfully unique people I watched grow from little girls to young women as part of my Girl Scout circle and beyond: Ally, Jona, Kira, Katie, Natalie L, Natalie S, Savannah, Zoe, Jeannie, Allison, and Carly. You opened my world in many different ways, invited me into your individual zones of genius, and gave me the bonus gift of friendship with your equally awesome moms. With love and gratitude.

Every
Reason
We
Shouldn't

Chapter 1

I roll into the parking lot of Ice Dreams and swap my in-line skates for mint-colored Chucks. I've got fifty-one minutes before my lesson. *If* she shows. So far this month Hannah has called out four times. Cramps. A cold. "Bad fish tacos." Sore quad. I don't know how she expects to make it to Nationals, much less the Olympics, when she can't even handle the slightest twinge of discomfort. I medaled in the World Junior Championships with a fractured toe when I was her age.

WELCOME TO ICE DREAMS! Olympic gold medalists Midori Nakashima and Michael Kennedy—aka Mom and Dad—greet me as I enter our rink. I bring my fingertips to my lips and slap a kiss on Mom and Dad's poster as I pass in front of them.

"Put your hands together for OH-LIV-I-AHHH 'ICE SCREAMS' KENNEDYYYYY!" Mack says in a let's-get-ready-to-rumble voice when I get to the snack bar. She flips her magenta-streaked blond braids over the back of one of the hundred roller derby T-shirts she owns. Today's choice says: EAT. SLEEP. SKATE. REPEAT.

"Ice Screams?" I grab my official Ice Dreams jacket off its designated hook and pull it over my plain T-shirt.

"Ice Dreams. Ice Screams? Eh, I'll keep working on it." Mack squirts some cleaner on the glass box hanging on the wall. My parents—still wearing their baby-blue skate costumes and gold medals—smile back from their Wheaties box inside.

"Is my mom at physical therapy?" I hop up on the counter, even though I know it's a health code violation.

"Yep." Mack hands me a pretzel that has the consistency of a doggie chew toy. "Either you eat it, or we throw it away. I've already had three. It's your turn to take one for the team."

I gnaw on the pretzel, praying I won't chip a tooth in the process. "I need the energy. Hannah's coming in at four. Maybe. If she doesn't have a hangnail or Ebola or some other life-threatening problem today."

"Nah, she quit this morning."

A stab of guilt punctures my gut. Hannah may be my least favorite Olympic wannabe, but I also like to eat. Every day, in fact. We need Hannah's tuition money to keep the lights on. Literally. Open Skates on Sunday afternoons keep the water turned on.

"You missed all the drama," Mack says. "Hannah's mom stormed in here this morning all high and mighty about how her little sparkle pony was no longer getting the quality training they expected from a former Olympian and her staff. That Hannah had been pushed onto a lesser coach, and that you weren't teaching Hannah the skills she needs for Olympic-level competition."

"She's twelve! I'm not going to teach Hannah how to do a triple loop until she can do a double loop consistently. Mrs. Taylor is delusional."

"That's what Midori said too. Only at a much lower decibel. Eh, goodbye and good riddance." Mack flicks her hand toward the door. "Especially now that we have a new client."

"We do? Is she a preschooler, or can she at least lace her own boots?"

"*He* is neither."

"He?" I've never taught a boy before, but I've partnered one. How hard could it be? "Well, he couldn't be any worse than

Hannah unless . . . Oh no. Am I going to be partnering somebody whose head will be squarely in my boobs?"

"He's not your charge, princess. His dad wrote a big fat check to buy rink time from three to five p.m. Monday through Thursday, and some Sunday mornings. Midori skipped out the door to physical therapy. Your mom. The boss lady. Her bad back. Skipping. Oh look, here they come now."

I turn back around to see an Asian guy carrying a pile of tiny orange plastic cones heading for the ice. A middle-aged man, who I'm guessing is his dad, follows a few steps behind him.

"*That's* our new client?" I say.

"Yep. Short-track speed skater on deck." Mack smiles so big that her lip ring clinks against her bottom teeth. The guy slides off an oversize sweatshirt to reveal a form-fitting speed-skating top. "Enjoy the view, princess. He's too young for me, but we may have potential prom date material for you."

When I reach out to smack Mack upside the head, she grabs my arm and pulls me into a headlock. Meanwhile, the guy steps out onto the freshly Zambonied ice and hands his blade covers to his dad. He skates around the rink, dropping orange cones until an oval path forms. His dad yells to fix them a little here, a little there.

"Wait. What happened to my ice?" I say as another cone splashes into the puddles of water covering the ice.

Mack puts her nose in the air and says in an uppity voice, "When one skates short track, the ice must be wet." Mack rotates her shoulders. "I got in an extra workout today thanks to all the buckets of water I had to lug out onto the ice. The things I do for you guys."

"You know you love it."

"There are worse jobs. Here, this came today." Mack hands me a UPS box. "You get to put it together. The party is at seven tonight, so this needs to be done ASAP. Midori said to start deodorizing the skates after that."

I miss Hannah. I take the box over to Table #1, the one closest to the snack bar, and open it. I groan. It's a Skater Barbie piñata. It's always Skater Barbie. I am Ice Dreams' reigning Piñata Queen. I can also make simple balloon animals and do the Hokey Pokey on the ice. I'm a multitalented girl. I've barely gotten the mass of papier-mâché out of the box before I notice the guy's dad standing in front of me.

"Hey, I need to take this." The man waves his cell phone in my direction. "Can you keep count for me?"

"Excuse me?"

"Can you count laps for my son? He needs to do twenty-five." The man places a clicker in front of me. After reading my name off the front of my official Ice Dreams jacket, he turns back to the ice and yells, "Jonah! Olivia here has the lap counter. I'll be back in a few minutes. Eat if you get done before me."

Jonah nods. His dad plunks down the skate guards, oversize sweatshirt, and a soft-sided cooler in front of my UPS box before walking away. Meanwhile, Jonah takes off in a slow, counterclockwise, oval path around the rink. When he gets back into prime viewing—right in front of Table #1—I click one on the lap counter. Jonah is on lap #12 when Mack comes over.

"Do you want me to bring you a napkin for the drool?" Mack squeezes in across from me, blocking my view of the ice.

"Ha-ha. I can't keep an accurate count with you here."

"Why? Because your brain is melting?"

"No, because your big head is in the way." I push Mack to the side.

She crams candy into Skater Barbie as I watch Jonah sail around the ice in an easy flow. Each stride during the straightaways is smooth, controlled, and completely even. He takes each curve at a perfect seventy-degree angle.

"He looks bored out of his mind." Mack slides to her feet with a grunt. "You know what he needs? A little GNR."

"Guns N' Roses? Isn't that kinda last century?"

"It's what the derby girls do drills to. He'll love it."

"Sure, if he's secretly a fortysomething suburban mom."

"You'll see."

I count off lap #14 as Mack enters the sound booth. The PA system crackles to life.

"Hey, new guy," Mack's voice booms around the empty rink. "Here's my lap music. Enjoy."

A few seconds later, "Welcome to the Jungle" blasts through the PA system. Jonah trips but immediately regains his footing. It takes him a solid lap to get his timing back, though. Mack gives Jonah a thumbs-up as he whizzes by a second time. He nods back. As the song goes on, Jonah's speed picks up to match it. Even his crossovers are on the downbeat. I watch him fly, the wind pulling his longish black hair straight back. Axl Rose is in his final wail as Jonah completes lap #25.

"Hey, that was twenty-five," I yell.

Jonah catches my eye, nods, and slows his pace. He arcs around and heads for my table. I busy myself stuffing Skater Barbie with candy. Jonah leans over the wall. He grabs his water bottle from the cooler and chugs.

I want to say something. Anything. But what? I look at him. He looks at me.

Mack appears at my elbow. "Olivia Kennedy. Jonah Choi. Jonah. Olivia."

"Hey." Jonah nods at me.

"Hey." I nod back.

"Thanks for the inspirational music . . . um . . ." Jonah says.

"Annabelle MacIntosh, but my friends call me Mack." Mack

flips her braids over her shoulders. "And the derby girls call me 'Mack Truck.'"

"Mack is an aspiring roller derby queen," I say, and Jonah looks confused because obviously this isn't a roller skating rink.

"Ice. Roller. In-line. Honey, I can do it all," Mack says.

"My mom likes to run to that song," Jonah says.

"See!" I say to Mack.

"Whatever, hatertot." Mack gives me a playful shove. "You wanna skate with the Surly Gurlz, you skate to a lot of GNR."

"You do roller derby too?" Jonah raises an eyebrow at me.

"No," I say as Mack says, "Not yet."

"Your dad wants you to eat." I push the cooler toward Jonah. "No eating on the ice, though. My mom is super strict about that."

"Gotcha." Jonah grabs his skate guards off the table and heads to the exit near Table #3, or as I like to call it, the bronze exit. Jonah waddles over to Table #1 and slides in across the table from me. There's something different about him. He's definitely Asian, but maybe he's biracial too? But you don't exactly lead with that.

"Candy?" I say instead, and offer Jonah a Tootsie Roll from the stash.

"Nah. Simple carbs are crap," he says.

"Well then, I will be cleaning the Slushee machine if anybody needs me." Mack snatches a handful of candy off the table and crams it into the pocket of her Ice Dreams jacket.

Jonah pulls out a container of hard-boiled eggs and peels one. He holds it out to me. "Want one?"

"Thanks, but I'll pass." I unwrap a mint—crap carbs and all— and pop it into my mouth to counteract the egg smell wafting across the table.

Jonah's on his third hard-boiled egg when his dad gets back.

"You didn't let him cheat, did you?" Mr. Choi smiles and grabs an egg for himself.

"No, sir. He did all twenty-five," I say. "And ate three eggs."

"I like you, Olivia." Mr. Choi gives Jonah a pointed look. "See, this is going to work out fine."

"For now." Jonah slams the lid of the egg box firmly closed with his fist. "Then I'm going back to Arlington. For good."

"One skate at a time, son." Mr. Choi wipes his hands together to get rid of any egg cooties. "Now, give me your pants and go stretch."

"I'm cold. I'll take them off later."

"Jonah." Mr. Choi holds out his hand.

Jonah looks at me and then his dad. "Later."

Mr. Choi finally puts two and two together. "Son, this a professional skating rink. I'm sure boys skate in tights, yoga pants, whatever all the time. Act like a professional, Jonah."

Jonah unzips the sides of his warm-up pants and yanks them over his skates. He shoves the pants into his dad's chest.

"Stretch." Mr. Choi's voice has a warning tone. He hands Jonah a piece of blue fabric. "We do sprints in five."

When his dad is out of earshot, Jonah leans toward me. "They are not *tights*. It's a skinsuit."

"Oh-kay," I say to Jonah's back.

I bet Skater Barbie never has to put up with salty speed skaters. Mack chuckles as she pushes the broom around the snack bar area. When she gets to my table, Mack leans over my shoulder.

"You could crack walnuts with that butt," Mack whispers in my ear, which of course makes me look.

I've watched enough Olympic speed skating on TV to know that your typical skinsuit leaves nothing to the imagination. Though the rest of his body is willowy, this guy has thighs larger than Mack's. And, yes, he could crack walnuts with those glutes.

Mr. Choi returns from the locker room with Jonah's helmet, so I make my eyes scan a little farther north. Jonah ties the folded royal-blue bandana around his forehead. Once his helmet is securely on, Jonah plows over to the starting line, which also happens to be right in front of Table #1. He crouches down into launch position with his left foot out front. He pounds his right foot into the ice at an eighty-degree angle. His left arm bends across his chest. His right elbow cocks back. Silence floods the rink and he waits. And waits. And waits some more. Is he going to skate or do the Chicken Dance?

I almost fall off my bench seat when an air horn pierces the quiet of the rink. Meanwhile, Jonah bursts off the start line like a runner. It only takes a few steps before he's coming into the turn. Jonah drops into a seventy-degree lean until his left fingers graze the ice. He's flying. Chicken Boy has turned into a phoenix. He pumps around the back stretch, the sound of blades cutting ice echoes around the rink. He loops another couple of times before he stands up tall and stretches his right foot forward over the imaginary finish line—Table #1.

"Too slow," Mr. Choi says as Jonah whizzes past him.

Less than a minute later, the air horn goes off again.

"Too slow," Mr. Choi says again. "You're holding on to it too tightly, son. Find your balance. Feel the ice."

Jonah loops around until he's at the starting line again. He shakes out his tree-trunk thighs and resumes the chicken position. The air horn blares. Jonah explodes off the starting line.

"Whooooooa," Mack says from behind me. "This kid's got some serious moves."

Yes, he does. An hour sprints by, and I still haven't finished filling the piñata. Jonah's eyebrows furrow in frustration as once again his dad pronounces his time "too slow." It takes more than a minute for him to reset this time. He is gasping for air and his face is flushed. I know that feeling. When the lactic acid builds up so high that your legs feel like they are on fire. When you're body screams that you can't go any farther. When all you want to do is go home and sit on your couch with a bag of frozen peas for the rest of the night. And yet, you do it again. Jonah shakes out his legs and takes the position. And this, Hannah, is what a *real* Olympian looks like.

Jonah comes into the first turn in his usual deep lean. It's the second turn that goes sideways on him. Literally. Jonah's inner foot goes from 70 degrees to 180 degrees. A thunk echoes around the rink as Jonah hits the ice and slides out of control. Followed by the crack of him colliding with the painted wooden wall—the boards—in front of my table. I jump to my feet.

"Are you okay?" I peer over the top.

Jonah is curled up, his hands cradled around his helmet. Air hisses through his clenched teeth. Mom is going to kill me if our new client dies on his first day at the rink. I hop over the wall and nearly bite it on the ice myself. I squat down. Jonah's eyes are squeezed tight, his face contorted in pain. Mack arrives seconds after me and plops the first aid kit on the wall. Somehow, I doubt a Hello Kitty Band-Aid and an ice pack are going to help a possible skull fracture.

"He's fine, ladies." Mr. Choi jogs up to us. "Happens all the time."

Mr. Choi puts his hand over the side, but Jonah doesn't take it. I put my hands on Jonah's upper arm to pull him to a stand. He jerks away from me.

"If this were a *real* training facility like in Arlington, they'd have freakin' safety padding on the boards." Jonah grabs the wall and scrapes himself off the ice.

"That's what safety helmets are for." Mr. Choi taps the top of Jonah's helmet. "And watch your language."

Jonah snatches the skate guards off the table and limp-skates away. An unflattering wet mark spreads from his butt up the left side of his skinsuit, thanks to the excess water on the ice.

"Take five, and we'll go again," Mr. Choi yells after him. "And use the hairdryer to dry your suit some."

Five minutes pass, but Jonah doesn't reappear from the men's locker room. After fifteen minutes of Mr. Choi over-helping me hang Skater Barbie in the party area, he finally goes to investigate. A minute later, Jonah—now dressed in jeans, royal-blue Chucks, and a NEED FOR SPEED T-shirt—bursts out of the locker room with his dad two steps behind.

"Ladies, I think we are going to call it a day," Mr. Choi says as Jonah storms out the front door of Ice Dreams without even acknowledging our presence. "See you tomorrow."

"I hope," I say when the door closes behind him.

"What a drama king," Mack says, coming out from behind the now-pristine snack bar. "Derby girls skate without safety padding on the boards. Sheesh. He needs to man up. The girls would kick his walnut-cracking ass."

"I hope he doesn't have a concussion. I heard his head hit the boards. He may have scrambled his brains a bit."

"Speaking of scrambling, the Chois forgot their cooler."

My phone buzzes as I go back to retrieve the cooler.

Mom: Hurting from PT. Going home until 6:30. Will return for the party so you can leave. Can Mack stay a little longer or does she need to go pick up Fiona?

I relay the message to Mack. Sure thing. Granny MacIntosh has Fiona but Mack needs to leave for derby practice at 6:00 tonight.

I'll be in at 6:00 then. Stay safe. Love you.

"Since Drama King left his cones on the ice, and we have the afternoon to ourselves . . ." Mack holds up her pair of hockey skates and nods her head "yes" as I shake mine "no." "Come on, just for thirty minutes. I need the workout. I'll even help you deodorize the skates after."

"Okay, but just for you."

"Liar. You're doing it for you." Mack shrugs. "That works for me. Go put on your *fancy* skates and meet me in five."

I pass several more vintage posters of my parents as I jog over to the skate counter and pull my skates from their designated spot. Mack ribs me about my skates all the time—they did cost more than her car, after all—but today after losing Hannah's tuition and maybe the Chois' business too, they feel so extra at our little rink. But I love them, and it's not like I will be getting another pair anytime soon.

"C'mon, princess, let's go," Mack's voice booms over the PA system, followed by Guns N' Roses, yet again.

Mack does a little air guitar as she comes out of the sound booth. She makes a large, easy loop around the rink as she swings her braids around and sings along. She's made a couple of passes by the time I hit the ice.

"Seriously, we have to get you up to this decade," I say when I skate up beside her. "This century, at least."

"Whose workout is this? Mine. Therefore, we skate to my music."

"When's the next Surly Gurlz tryout?"

"This training cycle ends in six weeks, then I might be eligible for a spot on a team. Six weeks to work on this." Mack pats her belly. "Easy to put on in nine months, next to impossible to get it back off again. But the derby girls told me not to give up. I'm almost there. Gotta keep training."

"Training. Something I'm good at. Well, used to be good at."

"Ride my ass about this, Olivia. I need this. I know my life went a little sideways after high school, but this will help me get it back together." Mack looks over at me, her blue eyes teary.

My stomach clenches. Instinct says I should hug Mack, but Mack doesn't do hugs. So I punch her in the arm instead.

"C'mon, Mack Truck. Catch me if you can." I'm only at 50

percent, but I'm leaving Mack in the dust. "Move it! Move it! Move it! You call that skating?"

Mack growls at me. I flip around in front of her and skate backward. I yawn for emphasis. It works. Mack picks up speed. I flip back around and fall in behind her. My heart rate goes up, but I could still skate circles around Mack if I wanted to. I slide off my jacket and tie it around my waist like a skirt.

"Tag, you're it!" I slap at her braids as I pass.

"You're going to get it now," Mack wheezes.

Mack's got brute strength, but her endurance sucks. At least she stopped vaping. I have to thank the Surly Gurl "Barnacle Barb" for that one. I zigzag in front of Mack, humming the cancan song. At the end of my off-key rendition, I flick my jacket-skirt up in the back with a "woo!" Mack smacks me on the butt.

"Ow! Okay, I need a break," I say more for Mack's benefit than mine.

"No. Not yet. Not until. I almost. Puke. Only queasy. Keep going."

I take it back down to 50 percent until Mack can find her breath. I stop at one of the orange cones and assume the Chicken Dance position.

"Let's race," I say.

"You're on." Mack lines up beside me and squats down. "On three. One . . . two . . ."

And Mack takes off.

"Cheater!" I dig my skates into the ice and explode into motion. Within seconds, I catch up with her. When I go to pass her on the inside, she slides to the left to block me.

"Nope," Mack says over her shoulder.

Fine. I wait until we are out of the curve to try passing on the right instead.

"Nope." Mack blocks me again.

I drop back. As we come into the next turn, I see an opening on the inside. I wait until Mack is two strides into the sharp curve and struggling to stay balanced when I duck under her arm and pop through the other side. Except Mack's blade catches mine. We both stumble forward. Mack's arms windmill, but my muscle memory kicks in. I pull my arms in and sit back, lowering my center of gravity. Mack crashes into the ice with an audible thunk, but I stay on my feet.

"That's going to leave a mark," a voice echoes across the rink.

Jonah stands next to Table #1 with a slip of paper in his hand. Mack scrapes her wet butt off the ice and limp-skates to the boards. With a groan, she climbs up on top of them and swings her legs over. Mack pulls down the waistband of her jeans a few inches on one side to expose the top of her hip bone.

"Yep. One more battle scar." Mack presses on the red mark and winces. "Such is the life of a derby girl."

I climb up beside Mack since Mom isn't here.

"That was kinda impressive," Jonah says, nodding toward the ice.

"Kinda? What d'ya mean kinda?" Mack says. "That was freaking awesome. Did you see Olivia here trying to sneak by me? Nuh-uh, honey. Not on my watch."

"I saw how you waited until she was in the turn to make your final move," Jonah says to me. "Short track is as much a mental game as a physical one."

"Short track? Pfft," Mack says. "Honey, this is practicing for derby life. I'm training to be a blocker. My job is to keep the jammers—today played by the lovely Olivia—from slipping by. But you're right. This is as much a mental game as a physical one. Being the biggest or the fastest doesn't mean squat if you lose your balance, even for a second."

Mack pulls at her clothes again. The red welt on her hip is already taking on a blue-black tinge.

"Don't I know it." Jonah pulls up his T-shirt. He's got a matching bruise peeking out the top of his waistband over his left hip too.

"Nice six-pack, kid," Mack says with an appreciative nod.

"Told you, simple carbs are crap. Eggs, salmon, and seaweed. Fuel of champions." Jonah pulls his shirt back down. "Gives you long, lean muscles."

"Speaking of eggs, you forgot your cooler. I'll go get it out of the fridge for ya." Mack slaps on her skate guards and waddles toward the snack bar.

"How's your head?" I say.

He shrugs, but I can see the red mark on his left temple. "So, you work here? Like, every day after school?"

"Olivia practically lives here," Mack yells over, her butt sticking out of the refrigerator. "You will be seeing a lot of Ice Dreams' reigning princess. A lot."

"Cool. I gotta go." Jonah holds out the slip of paper to me. It's a check folded in half. "Can you give this to your mom? Dad will email her the specifications for the safety padding tonight."

"You're such a wuss, Choi." Mack playfully shoves Jonah's cooler into his chest until he takes it. "Derby girls don't use padding." Mack snorts. "Well, at least not on the track. Other places? Yep. Some very much so."

I take the check. "See you tomorrow, then?"

"Junior Championships are in ten weeks. I can't waste any more time." Jonah slides the cooler strap over his muscular shoulder and rocks back and forth on his heels. "So, I guess that's a yes."

I nod. A new energy crackles around the rink as Jonah makes a less dramatic exit this time. That, plus the amount of zeroes on this check, makes our dying rink spark back to life.

Chapter 2

"So, is this the designated Asian-kid table at this school or something?" a voice comes from behind me the next day during lunch.

OMG, it's Jonah Choi. I thought I saw him in the hall before first period but figured my brain was playing tricks on me.

Brandon looks up from our science homework. "Hey, you're the new guy from PE this morning. I can't remember your name, though."

"Jonah Choi," I say, and three heads snap my way.

"Korean?" Brandon says.

"Mostly," Jonah says.

"Mostly?" I say.

"Three-quarters Korean. My mom is half Korean-American and my dad is full." Jonah answers the question I've been wanting to ask since yesterday.

"Close enough." Brandon holds out his fist for Jonah to bump. "Represent."

Jonah gives Brandon a half-hearted tap with his fist. I move my backpack so Jonah can sit between Brandon and me.

"Seriously, where are all the Asians?" Jonah pulls two plastic boxes from his backpack.

"For the sophomore class, you're pretty much looking at 'em. I'm Brandon."

"Naomi." She waves at Jonah. "And this is my cousin, Erika."

"Hey." Erika nods at Jonah.

Jonah does a double take because Erika is obviously white. "Cousin?"

"Yep. My last name is Ito too." Erika brushes her light brown hair over her shoulder. "Because my biological dad is a complete waste of carbon. Naomi's uncle has been my dad since I was two years old and legally my father since I was ten, when Mom and I took his last name."

"Well, that's . . ." Jonah says.

"Extra?" Brandon offers.

"I was going to say interesting."

Brandon leans in front of Jonah. "Can I see your chem lab, Liv?"

"Here, I'll help you," Naomi says, pulling the packet to her side of the table. She has a huge crush on Brandon, not that he's noticed. Not that she has the guts to tell him either.

As we always do, Naomi, Erika, Brandon, and I do our homework during lunch. Meanwhile, Jonah watches YouTube videos while eating his brown rice with salmon and broccoli. I guess I could do my homework at the rink now since the Chois have eaten up what was once prime private lesson time. Granted, I've only been doing traditional school for two and a half months now, but this seems to be the norm, at least at our lunch table and the ones around ours. Everyone seems to forever be going to club meetings, private music lessons, volunteer events, and whatever "normal" high school students do that causes them to post #stressedout selfies at midnight. With a filter, of course. Because nobody wants to see your stress acne and the bags under your eyes for real, you know. The bell rings, and we pack everything up.

"You're welcome to sit with us anytime, brother." Brandon holds out his fist to bump again.

Jonah gives it another half-hearted bump. I can read his expression. *What a bunch of losers.*

Hey! I am not a loser. I'm the US Junior Pairs Figure Skating gold medalist. Okay, I was. I pop the last bite of my peanut butter and jelly sandwich in my mouth as everyone else clears out. Only Jonah lags behind.

"What is up with Fist-Bump Dude?" Jonah says when we are alone.

"His name is Brandon Park."

"Boyfriend?"

"Lab partner."

"Is he always that annoying?" Jonah says.

"No. Yes. Sorta. He doesn't have a filter. Ignore him."

"Your friends are very studious." The way Jonah says it, it doesn't sound like a compliment.

I shrug. "We have a lot of the same classes. Everybody is busy after school, so we use the divide-and-conquer method of getting homework done."

Also, if Brandon hadn't insisted that I join him for lunch so we could work on our lab paper the third day of school, I would probably still be eating my sandwiches solo in the girls' restroom. The fact that he routinely brings homemade baked goods from his "Test Kitchen" for us to try more than makes up for his occasional awko-taco moments like today.

"What do you have now?" I say, and Jonah shows me his schedule. I read down the list. "I have the same class. I can show you."

"Thanks. I already walked into the wrong class once this morning." Jonah slides his backpack over his shoulder. "This school is enormous. I need GPS to get around it."

As we walk toward honors English, I look up at Jonah. He still has a small red mark on his left temple from yesterday.

"Were there a lot of Asians at your old school?" I say.

"Yeah. Mostly Koreans. Filipino. A few Vietnamese. A lot of biracial kids. Arlington is much more diverse than Phoenix."

"Why'd you move here, then?"

It takes a few beats before Jonah answers. "My mom got a huge promotion at work. Unfortunately, it required her moving to Phoenix. Then Dad was laid off, so here we are."

"Did you skate a lot in Arlington? You're really good."

"Yes."

"Phoenix isn't exactly known for ice sports. I think you moved to the wrong state."

"Yeah, I did."

"Well, at least you came to the best rink in the state."

"Do they pay you to say that?"

"No. It is the best rink."

Jonah shrugs. "It'll do. For now."

This isn't the first time people have talked smack about our rink. I've seen the Yelp reviews. Mom won't let me feed the trolls who call us all "washed-up, figure-skating has-beens" and say that our rink is "dying a slow, painful death." They've announced loudly about moving to Gold Medal Ice—our biggest competitor—up in Scottsdale. They've trashed my parents. Criticizing Dad for "selfishly leaving his family to relive his glory days as part of the Olympians on Ice tour," and calling Mom a "tragic has-been who can barely skate, much less teach anymore." And then there was the review left by Hannah's mom yesterday. I shouldn't have looked, but I couldn't stop myself. Paragraph two was all about me and how much I suck. I know I'm not the best coach. I got the job purely because Mom didn't want to give Crystal any more of her students and the money that comes with them. Also, it's not like I had anything better to do. Still, her last dig was a low blow.

I guess the old adage is true. Those who can't do, teach. Need proof? Watch "Coach" Olivia's latest Skate Detroit competition with her partner Stuart Trout. Sad. Must be hard to be washed up at sixteen. Why they made her a coach is beyond me. *If you want a *real* coach for your talented child, go to Gold Medal Ice in Scottsdale instead.*

Hannah's mom must have asked all the Gold Medal Ice skater moms to vote on her review because now it's at the top of the page for everyone to see. Fabulous. Like we need more bad publicity. Pretty soon all we're going to have at Ice Dreams are the baby skaters and the Red Hat Society ladies who do Zumba on Tuesday mornings in the barre area. I look up at Jonah. I don't expect him to make it more than six months at Ice Dreams. Maybe one month, based on yesterday's tantrum.

"Well, hopefully, you'll be leaving Phoenix soon and going back to wherever." That may have come out a little more acidic than necessary based on Jonah's wince. I point to the door. "We're here. Honors English."

Thankfully, the only open seat available is at the back of the class next to Brandon, who gives Jonah another awkward fist bump as I pass them. Whatever. Jonah can be Brandon's problem for the rest of the day.

Unfortunately, I get Round 2 with the Ice Prince after school. A navy-blue BMW pulls into Ice Dreams right behind me. Mr. Choi steps out of the car and tucks his fashionable shades into his pocket.

"I thought that was you, Olivia," Mr. Choi says. "Would you like a ride tomorrow, so you don't have to skate over from school?"

"No, thank you." I slide my in-line skates off. "It's part of my training."

"See, son, now that's a work ethic," Mr. Choi says as Jonah gets out of the car, grumbling something under his breath. "When's your next competition, Olivia?"

Crap.

"I'm not sure yet." Possibly never?

"Were those your medals I saw yesterday hanging in the box behind the skate counter?" Mr. Choi says as I slip on my Chucks.

"Some of them. The rest are Mom and Dad's. Well, except for the Olympic gold. Those two are in the bank box."

Mr. Choi lets out an impressed whistle. Jonah looks bored. Or he's still pissed about having Brandon inflicted on him during honors English. Whatever.

"The two of you will have to share training tips. Jonah could sure use some of your discipline."

Jonah slams the car door with unnecessary force. "Dad, we're on the clock."

I follow Jonah and Mr. Choi into Ice Dreams. I bring my fingertips to my lips and slap a kiss on Mom and Dad's poster. Jonah looks back over his shoulder at me. I don't have to explain myself. This is *my* rink.

Mom—the three-dimensional version—greets us with a huge oh-thank-God-I-can-pay-the-mortgage-this-month smile.

"Mr. Choi! When you have a minute, I wanted to go over the specs for the safety padding," Mom says, and then tells her 2:00 p.m. Olympic-hopeful goodbye for the day. Bella isn't going to the Olympics. Not this year. Not any time in the next ten years. Not ever. But her parents keep fueling that golden dream with a steady cash flow for private lessons and top-of-the-line equipment and airline tickets to competitions around the country. I give thirteen-year-old Bella another eighteen months before she gets a reality check. Then she'll find something else to fill her time. Like a life. I'm still working on that part myself.

I never finished the boots yesterday, so I go straight to the skate booth. When I squat down to throw my backpack under the counter, I find a flier with a note.

Free Saturday at 7 p.m.?

My stomach flips for a second, until I keep reading.

The Surly Gurlz vs. The Destructo Kitties
7 p.m. Saturday

I kneel on the floor so Mom can't see me on my phone and text Mack. Got derby flier. Yes! Can you give me a ride?

Mack texts back immediately. Yes. Come to my house at 5. Bring something fierce.

Fierce?

FIERCE! If you show up in jeans & T-shirt, I'm sending you home.

"Fierce?" I say, standing back up.

I let out a yelp when I find Jonah standing on the other side of the counter. He jumps back.

"Are you asking me out?" Jonah holds out an identical flier. "I found this taped to my locker."

"Um, no. That was all Mack."

"Oh." Jonah cringes. "She's not really my type."

"Why? Because she could probably kick your ass?"

"No," Jonah says too quickly. "Though you have to admit, she is a little . . . intimidating."

"Mack is almost twenty. She's not interested in dating *high school* boys." I pull the flier's twin out from underneath my backpack and show it to him. "Mack and I go to roller derby bouts on Saturday nights sometimes. She was being nice since you're new to the area and don't have any friends."

"Oh. Okay. Maybe." Jonah looks at the flier a little closer.

I shrug. Whatever. "Did you need something? I've got work to do here."

"Do you ever feel like your parents are watching you?" Jonah nods at the line of giant posters of my parents in various skating costumes that extend from the snack bar area to the skate booth and beyond.

"You get used to it."

"Is this you?" Jonah points at the framed picture closest to his side of the skate counter.

"Yeah. And my partner, Egg."

"Egg?"

"Stuart, but I call him 'Egg.'"

"Do I want to know why?"

"Stuart is a triplet. His brothers are identical. He is the single," I say, and Jonah looks confused. "He got his own egg."

Jonah still looks confused.

"Look, I'm not explaining reproduction to you. Pay attention in biology or google it or something. I started calling him Egg back in the beginning, and it stuck."

"Oh, okay. Were you any good?"

"Well, there is a medal around my neck in that picture. And in this one. And this one. And, oh look, in this one too."

"Then why'd you quit?"

"Who said I quit?"

"You said you weren't sure when your next competition is. The Olympics are in February. Shouldn't you be out convincing the Olympic Committee to pick you instead of making plans to go to a roller derby bout?"

I step back like Jonah has punched me in the face.

"C'mon, Jonah. We're on the clock." Mr. Choi slaps Jonah on the back and then pushes him toward the locker rooms. Mr. Choi doesn't realize how much his voice carries in our now-empty rink. "I know you're lonely, son, but we're here to train, not to find you a girlfriend. Focus."

Mom snickers as she hands her well-worn skates over the skate counter to me. "He's here to train, Olivia. Don't be a distraction."

"He came over here to talk to me, not the other way around. It's not my fault he has focus issues."

"True." Mom tucks a piece of hair behind my ear and smiles. "And Mack needs to keep a professional distance too. We don't want to give the Chois anything else to complain about."

Subtext: *We can't afford to lose another client.*

I think we're both relieved when Mr. Choi is the official lap counter for the day.

When I take a break later—after Jonah takes his egg-eating break—I pull out my phone and text Egg at Virginia Tech.

How's it going?

Less than a minute later, he texts me back a GIF of a dumpster fire.

Overly dramatic much?

I wish I was exaggerating, Livy. College life as the third wheel of the Trout Triplets Freak Show got old about Day 3. People are like, "Oh, you're the brother who DOESN'T play football." And then they give me a pitying look.

We were the freakin' World Juniors Pairs Champions!!!!

Yeah, that doesn't help me at parties. AT
ALL.

> Come back to Phoenix then. I'll let
> you scrape the gum off the tables at
> Ice Dreams with me and everything.

Normal life going that well for you too?

I don't know how to answer that. Our last disastrous performance together at Skate Detroit is still fresh in my mind.

> I'm fine. School is fine. Mack is fine.
> The rink is fine. My mom's back . . .
> not so fine. As always.

Mack says you have a prom date.

I drop my phone.

> What?!?! We met yesterday. I wouldn't
> go to Sonic with him for a Slushee,
> much less prom.

Tell Matchmaker Mack that she can't marry
you off yet. I need your help soon.

> Boy, bye. To both of you. What do you
> need?

Your dad sent me an email about openings
in the corps next summer with Olympians
on Ice. I need to make an audition video
over winter break.

> Are you sure about this?

Yeah. If it means escaping from Football-is-King Land, I would gladly skate with a snowman costume on, be a tree, carry your dad's luggage . . .

No, I meant skate with me.

Yes! That's why I want to shoot a completely new video instead of piecing together a highlights reel from our past performances. I want to get out of the shadow of our last couple of competitions. I want them to see the new-and-improved version of me. The more mature, artistic version of Stuart Trout.

My heart clenches. I look at the picture that Jonah admired earlier. *World Junior Pairs Champions Kennedy and Trout.* Back when we were on top. Back when leveling up to seniors was the natural choice. Back before my body betrayed me and my whole life came crashing down around my skates. The USFSA rep's words after Skate Detroit still shred me.

This is the senior level, sweetheart. Raw talent is no longer enough.

What if it's not enough?

It has to be. I'm not going back to Tech next fall, so I need a plan B. We can do this, Livy. Or should I call Britney instead?

I send a series of No, Nope, and Oh hell no GIFs to Egg.

Okay, then get off your ass, make me look good, and redeem yourself. And you should definitely wear the phoenix costume. The

adult one not the little kid one. I'll send you
all the deets as soon as I have them. Gotta
run. Bye!

The Ghost of Bad Skates haunts me all during Jonah's skate time. It doesn't help that Mr. Perfect just broke his personal record according to his dad, who is yelling that piece of news to everybody in the nearly empty rink. I run my fingertips over the laces on my skate boots. I can't wait until Jonah's practice is over. I want my ice back. I want my normal back. My favorite little skater, six-year-old Lina Kitagawa, comes in at six thirty but that still gives me time to practice solo for a bit. Lina is my favorite because she doesn't care about being an Olympic skater. Her mom doesn't question my coaching techniques. Lina can't do anything more complicated than a waltz jump and a scratch spin, but she loves it. You can see it on her face. I want to find that skater in me again. Then maybe I can be the new-and-improved version of me.

Mr. Choi's whooping interrupts my brooding. "That's it, son. One more time. Just like that."

I can see Jonah's smile all the way over here. He gives himself a fist pump and a "Yeah!" I know that feeling. I miss that feeling. Is it 5:00 p.m. yet? I want to go find some of that.

Chapter 3

Taking Brandon up on his invitation, Jonah gloms on to our lunch table again the next day. He slides in across from me and my tuna-and-cucumber sandwich. I prefer PB and J, but I have to squeeze back into the phoenix costume in a few weeks.

Jonah looks me in the eyes. Challenging me. "Stuart is dizygotic, while his brothers are monozygotic."

Brandon, who sits next to me, flips his lab paper over. "Where does it ask that? And how do you spell it?"

"It's not on the homework, Brandon," I say.

"Then why are we discussing it? What's the answer to number four?"

"Are you guys talking about the Trout Triplets?" Naomi pulls out her lunch, a bento box with rice on the bottom and some fried chicken pieces, cherry tomatoes, and kiwi slices on top.

I nod. "Yes, I was explaining to Jonah yesterday why I call Stuart 'Egg.' When Stuart was . . . er . . . conceived, he got his own egg. Steven and Scott's egg was fertilized and then split in two. So technically, those two are twins, but Stuart is as genetically different from the two of them as their older brother, Patrick."

"Are we really going to talk about reproduction at lunch?" Naomi says with a nervous giggle.

"We can talk about sex all you want," Brandon says with all the social grace of a sledgehammer.

"Lord, help us," Erika says to the ceiling, as she tends to do at least once a week at lunch.

"I almost forgot." Brandon digs in his backpack and pulls out a small plastic box filled to the brim with cookies. "In today's Test Kitchen: Decadent Double Chocolate Chip Cookies."

Naomi and Erika squeal in tandem and take two. Brandon swings the box toward Jonah.

"I don't do simple carbs," Jonah says.

"They're really good." Brandon wiggles the box. "I used both milk and dark chocolate chips."

"No, thanks."

"Those look amazing." I put one on my napkin.

I break off a chocolate chip and let it melt on my tongue. It's all I can do not to wolf down the rest of the cookie along with several others. I can't remember the last time somebody made me cookies. Certainly not my mom.

Show some self-discipline, Olivia! You are a professional skater. Sort of.

I take one bite and then make myself put it back down.

"And taste amazing. Thanks, Brandon," I say, and Brandon beams. "I'm going to save mine for later."

I wrap up the cookie in a napkin. I'm going to have to find a trash can on the way to English class to discreetly drop it into. My body is changing too quickly now that I'm only training a few hours each day. My butt, in particular, has gone rogue. Maybe Mack is up for some Goodwill shopping this weekend. I need more jeans.

"Are the Trout Triplets coming back into town for Thanksgiving?" Erika takes another cookie.

"No, Virginia Tech is in some big bowl game or something Thanksgiving weekend, so now Mr. and Mrs. Trout are going to Virginia instead," I say, remembering Egg's epic text rant about this archaic tradition being forced upon him. "Egg is coming back for winter break though."

"Ah, the talented Trout Triplets," Erika says wistfully. "Scott and I are still friends, but he never comments or likes any of my posts anymore. Meanwhile, Steven totally ghosted me. I'm like, dude, don't make me post pictures of you from my second grade birthday party. It's like they are on this whole different plane of existence now."

"They're skaters like Stuart?" Jonah says.

"No, football players," Erika says.

"Professional?"

"Not yet. Tech gave them both a full ride though, so they must be important."

"Virginia Tech gave Stuart a full ride too," I say in Egg's defense.

"I hope they come back for winter break. You let us know, Olivia, since you have an in with Stuart. He might have the four-one-one on a party or something."

"Sure," I say, though I have no intention of doing so.

"So what's the answer to number four?" Brandon waves his chemistry packet at us to refocus our attention. "I've got PSAT prep class tonight. Gotta get this junk done."

Just like yesterday, the rest of us work on homework while we eat. Meanwhile, Jonah picks at his lunch of chicken breast with brown rice and broccoli, his headphones on, never cracking a book. And again, it's Jonah and me who are last at the table after the bell rings. He pushes his blue, top-of-the-line headphones down around his neck and closes his plastic lunch container.

"Am I the only one not impressed by the Trout Triplets' fame and glory?" Jonah says under his breath. "They're just college *football* players. How special is that?"

"Egg doesn't play football." Since Brandon already left for English, I leave the cookie behind on the table.

"Still." Jonah shrugs. "Is Stuart coming back in December to be your partner again?"

"No. I'm helping him with an audition for a skating job." I slide on my backpack and head for the door.

"But you are looking for a new partner, yes?"

"Yes, but it takes a while. Football players are a dime a dozen. Competitive-level male skating partners are harder to find than unicorns."

Which is why Britney Freakin' Xiao has tried to "buy" Egg out from under me three times now since he and I became a pair. Most recently after watching our crash-and-burn performance at Skate Detroit this summer. Skate Detroit. The tuna sandwich in my stomach threatens to come back up.

"You two have so much potential, but you can't seem to get your footing at the senior level," the USFSA representative said after our performance. And, as she had previously threatened to do, added, "The USFSA regrets that we will not be able to fund your training this season. I'm sorry."

I cried for a solid week after Skate Detroit. Egg told Tech he changed his mind about deferring a year, and my parents signed me up for high school. Meanwhile, Dad hit the road with Olympians on Ice for a reunion tour. He's still a big draw after all these years. Dad is boy-next-door handsome and funny and does great "back in the day" interviews at every tour stop. Middle-aged skater moms who dreamed of being his partner once upon a time routinely throw themselves at him. Gross.

"Don't worry." Jonah holds the cafeteria door open for me. "You'll be back on the ice again soon with a new partner."

I'm glad one of us is confident about that. "It is kind of nice to talk to someone who gets it. Our weird lifestyle."

"We're not weird. We're special. Everybody else is boring."

A warmth spreads in my stomach. "Yeah, we are. You and your carb phobia are extra though."

"Says the girl who drooled all during lunch and yet only took one bite of one cookie before leaving it behind."

Busted.

"I've been lax with my training recently. Time to get serious again."

"Speaking of which, thanks to you, Dad told me to start skating to Ice Dreams after school now. It's mid-October. Why is it still so hot here?" Jonah might be complaining, but there is a smile across his face.

"Welcome to hell, aka Phoenix, Jonah. This is nothing. Wait until July. That's a whole other level of hot. Meet me in Room 102 after school today. Morinaka-sensei lets me store my rollerblades in her class during the day."

"You take Japanese?"

"Yes. Not that I ever have a chance to practice it. Mom's Japanese is about on the same level as mine. We try to speak Japanese with my grandparents, but it's so frustrating, we usually end up switching to English after about five minutes. Do you speak Korean?"

"Nope. I went to Korean Saturday school for a little while during elementary school, but then I started skating. I didn't have time for both. If I think about it, I might be able to spell my name. Maybe count to ten. Dad has a couple of favorite words he says when I'm skating. Those might be swear words, though."

I look up at Jonah. When he smiles down at me, little parentheses form at the corner of his mouth. The warmth spreads from my stomach to my chest.

I snap my head back to face front. "Where'd you leave your in-lines?"

"In my gym locker."

"You take PE? On purpose?"

"Of course. I might as well get in another workout during the day since school starts so stupid early here. Once the sun starts coming up at six, I'll run a couple of miles in the morning too. What?"

"You are hard-core."

"No, I'm elite, just like you are. Were?"

"Are."

"Are. You never had six a.m. practices?"

I wince.

"We own the rink. Why do I have to train at five thirty?" I had whined last season before I realized that it was going to truly be my last season.

"Because we are professionals," Dad had snapped. *"That's what we do."*

"If you're not going to do this at a hundred percent, Livy, then why are we doing it at all?" Mom had said and then gave me an extra mile on the treadmill to "test my commitment" to skating.

"Five thirty," I say to Jonah. "But now that I'm a 'normal teenager,' I get to sleep in until six thirty."

"So, if you aren't competing right now, what are you currently obsessing about? School? I bet you have a 4.0 GPA."

"No." Then I add sheepishly, "Because I've only been back in traditional school since August. Honors English—got it. Japanese—got it. Chemistry—mostly got it. History and Financial Apps—could sleep through them and get an A. Remedial geometry—no clue, and that's with Mack tutoring me. But I'm going to get an A in this class if it kills me. And it might."

"Like I said. Elite. Being number two is not an option. We have to be the best."

I stop in the middle of the hallway. He does get it. More so than Naomi, Erika, Brandon, and even Mack combined.

"You know we're not helping the overachieving Asian stereotype," Jonah says, pulling me back into motion.

"Yep. We should have our own elite hand sign."

Though I was being sarcastic, Jonah puts out his fist for me to bump. After I bump it, he flicks his index finger out to make a #1 sign.

"Yikes. And, no." I can't help but laugh, though.

"You got something better?"

"Let me think about it. I know I can come up with something better than that."

"You are so extra."

"Whatever."

We walk into English class together just as the bell rings and straight into one of Mr. Balducci's infamous pop quizzes. The class groans. The quiz is easy, though. We grade them in class. Erika draws smiley faces in the zeroes of my 100 before we pass them all forward to our bowtie-wearing teacher.

"How'd you do, Olivia?" Brandon asks as we herd out the door fifty minutes later. Jonah falls in behind us.

"Aced it," I say.

Jonah puts out his fist. I know what's coming. I bump his fist anyway. I get the same stupid #1 hand sign after.

"Yeah. Represent." Brandon bobs his head.

I don't bump his extended fist.

"C'mon, the new kid gets a bump, and I don't?" Brandon says.

"You wouldn't understand. You're not an elite skater." Jonah turns to me. "How long does it take you to skate to the rink after school?"

"About ten minutes," I say.

"Okay. Today, we're doing it in eight. Try to keep up."

Today, I make it to Ice Dreams in seven minutes and thirty-seven seconds, and I almost hurl tuna-and-cucumber sandwich afterward. I lean against Mack's ancient, weather-beaten Toyota

Corolla, examining my fingernails, when Jonah rolls into the parking lot at eight minutes and seven seconds.

"Tomorrow. Keep up," I say, though my heart is still threatening to explode.

"Cheater." Jonah tucks sweat-dampened locks of hair behind his ears as he pretends like he's not dying too.

"Am not. I took. The shortcut."

Jonah can't catch his breath enough to argue with me. He puts out his fist, and I bump it. This time, I'm the one who makes the #1 sign afterward. He laughs.

"Ahhhhhh," we say in tandem when Jonah opens the door and cold air rushes over our skin.

I enter the rink first. As it should be. I bring my fingertips to my lips and slap a kiss on Mom and Dad's poster as I pass in front of them. It's weird, I know. I'm not about to stop doing it, though.

Mack is wiping down the snack counter when we come in. Her eyebrow pops up.

"Put your hands together for OOOOLIIIIVIAAAAA 'ICE KILLPADES' KENNNNNNEDDYYYY!" Mack says in her usual let's-get-ready-to-rumble voice.

"Ice Killpades?" Since Mom can see me from the ice, I don't jump up on the counter.

"Eh, I'm still workin' on it." Mack's magenta-blond hair is down today, and she's cut her bangs into a severe Bettie Page look.

"I don't get an intro?" Jonah says, distracted by the Wheaties box on the wall next to his head.

"When you become a potential derby girl, honey, I'll give you one. Until then, all you'll get is: Hey, Choi. What's up?" Mack hands him a cup of water. "You look like you're about to pass out."

Jonah chugs the water. He's done before Mack locates my designated cup.

"Thanks." Jonah holds his paper cup out for Mack to refill. "I don't know how you stand it here. I feel like I'm dehydrated all the time. My body can't run like the fine-tuned machine it is when it's dehydrated."

I roll my eyes at Mack and take a big swig of water from my bedazzled *O* cup.

"Hey, look what I brought for a snack today." Mack pulls a margarine tub out of the refrigerator and pops it open. Two hard-boiled eggs sit in the bottom. "What was the other thing you said to eat when you are training?"

"Seaweed." Jonah holds out his water cup for a third refill.

"Seaweed? Where do I get that? We live in the desert."

"The Asian grocery store at Warner and Dobson. That's where we go," I say.

"Great. Thanks." Mack takes a bite of her already peeled egg and makes a face.

"It takes some getting used to." Jonah chuckles and slides the salt shaker down the snack bar. "Put a little salt on it."

"I talked to Midori," Mack says through a mouthful of salted egg. "She said you could come with me on Saturday. Have you found something fierce to wear yet?"

"Fierce?" Jonah says.

"Fierce. This look . . ." Mack gestures at me. "Unacceptable."

"What am I supposed to wear?" I say. "Leather and chains?"

"Do you have any?" Mack is actually serious.

Jonah's eyebrows rise. "Where are you going again?"

"Roller derby bout. Didn't you get the flier I put on your locker?" Mack says.

"Yeah, he did," I say. "But he's too busy to hang with us."

"That's too bad." Mack leans over the counter and pulls my hair out of its usual low ponytail. She fluffs my hair around my shoulders and collarbones. "C'mon, let me cut it. You don't have to wear it up anymore, so what's the point? You'd look fierce with short hair. Maybe a little color?"

"Mom would kill you and me both."

"Not permanent color. Wash out. At least until Midori gets used to it. Then we'll make it permanent."

"Jonah, why are you standing around?" Nobody noticed Mr. Choi coming in behind us. "Get changed, son. We're on the clock." He tips his head at us. "Ladies."

Jonah chugs the last of his water and dutifully follows his dad.

"Fuchsia," Mack says when Jonah enters the men's locker room. "Your prom dress. It should be fuchsia. It's a good color on you. And I bet Choi cleans up nice."

"Stop!" I grab my Ice Dreams jacket off its peg and head to the skate counter. Fuchsia, the color of my face.

Chapter 4

By Saturday night, both my ripped shirt and my hair are fuchsia.

"Now, *that's* a proper boutfit," Mack says when I come out of her bathroom wearing the Goodwill outfit she insisted on buying for me this afternoon.

"I don't know, Mack." I run my hand through my now nine-inches-shorter hair. It's practically a pixie cut. "Mom is going to freak."

Mack adjusts six-month-old Fiona on her hip. "No, she won't. Okay yeah, she will. But you're a teenager. You're supposed to disappoint and annoy your parents. You didn't hear that, Fi. Don't worry, Liv, Midori'll come around. Eventually."

"Or she may ground me."

Mack and I laugh. That's what *normal* parents might do, but Midori Nakashima and Michael Kennedy haven't exactly figured this whole parenting thing out. Then again, Mack's parents were a textbook example of helicopter parents, and look where she is now.

I adjust my black pleather skirt over my leggings and boots. "I should probably change before I go home, though."

"Fine. One thing at a time." Mack holds up her daughter in front of me. "See, Fi. Doesn't Auntie Olivia look awesome?"

Fiona's face crinkles and she howls in fear. Yeah, she doesn't recognize me either.

"Aw, c'mon, sweetie. It's me, Auntie Olivia." I stretch my arms out toward Fiona.

She screams louder.

"Gran!" Mack yells over top of Fiona. "Gran, we gotta go. Can you come take Fiona?"

Mrs. MacIntosh shuffles in from the living room and holds her arms out. "Come to Granny."

"Tyler is supposed to come by tonight," Mack says, and Mrs. MacIntosh scoffs. "I know, but he promised, Gran. He's bringing diapers and formula. The good kind."

"I'll believe it when I see it." Mrs. MacIntosh bounces up and down a bit until Fiona settles down. "Don't be out too late. Be safe. And no drinking."

"Yes, Gran." Mack leans in and kisses the top of Fiona's head and then her grandmother's wrinkled cheek.

Mrs. MacIntosh looks at my boutfit and shakes her head.

As we slide into Mack's Toyota, she looks me over one last time. A Cheshire Cat–like smile pulls across her deep purple lips.

"What?" I look in the rearview mirror and try to remove some of the four inches of black eyeliner Mack put on me. At least I'd talked her out of the magenta foil eyelashes—this time.

"Just own it." Mack fires up the engine.

Ten minutes later, we pull into Arby's for our pre-bout tradition. Mack's friend from high school is working tonight. As always, she sells us large root beer floats for the price of smalls.

"Here's to being fierce." I hold my root beer float out to Mack.

"To being fierce." Mack clinks her cup against mine, and we both take a noisy slurp.

When we head back out, there's some guy leaning against

Mack's ancient Toyota. I look at Mack. She laughs at my expression.

"Did I forget to mention that Choi is meeting us here? His schedule was suddenly free." Mack stops to burp loudly. "Remember. Own it."

Jonah squints at me. "Olivia?"

I try to play it cool, though part of me wants to run in the opposite direction. I give him a nod.

Jonah's eyebrows knit together. "I thought we were going to a roller derby match, not a Halloween party."

"First of all, it's a bout, not a match. Second, you're the one who is going to look out of place, Choi." Mack messes up Jonah's hair. "Nothing a little guyliner can't fix though."

"No." Jonah flattens his hair back down and tucks it behind his ears.

"Fine. Get in the car, kids."

"Shotgun," I say, and Jonah opens the door for me.

Mack pops a cassette tape—a *cassette tape!*—into her Toyota's ancient sound system.

"Do you listen to anything besides Guns N' Roses?" Jonah leans forward, resting his right arm on the top edge of my seat.

"No, Mack. Just, no." I pop the tape out.

"Then you two pick something." Mack takes a hard right.

My body shifts left, causing my exposed left shoulder to brush against the back of Jonah's hand. I look back. Jonah's face is so close to mine that I can see where he cut himself shaving. All five of the facial hairs he probably has. He smells good. The root beer bubbles in my stomach.

"God, Choi, you smell like somebody smacked you with a pine tree." Mack rolls down the windows. "Spritz, don't douse, next time, honey. My eyes are watering."

Jonah sits back. The bubbles dissipate.

The Ability360 Sport and Fitness Center parking garage downtown is packed. I wish Ice Dreams had this kind of traffic on a Saturday night. Or any night.

Mack is only partially right about Jonah looking out of place. A middle-aged couple with arms full of tats parks next to us. On the other side of us, a young couple who look like they stepped out of a Target ad attempts to get a squirmy toddler into his stroller. I look down at my boutfit. I am so extra.

Like she can read my mind, Mack says, "It's roller derby. Lean into the theatrical side of it. Own it. Choi, you sure you don't want to borrow one of my derby T-shirts? There's a clean one in my workout bag."

"Nah."

"You know, *most* teens go through experimental phases with their hair and clothing, right? It's like a rite of passage or something." Mack looks at Jonah in the rearview mirror. "Look at Olivia. She's not afraid to experiment with her look."

Well, that's not true, but I'm not going to correct her.

"I think she looks hot, don't you?" Mack's icy blue stare challenges Jonah.

The question hangs in the air. I want to die, but not before I strangle Mack first.

"Okay, do it. Guyliner me." Jonah catches my eye in the mirror. "Just don't let me forget to take it off."

"Awesome. You do it, Liv. My hands shake too much."

I give Mack a pointed look. She smiles until her lip ring clinks against her bottom teeth. I flip on the overhead light in the car and dig around in my purse for my eyeliner pencil.

"I see a friend of mine." Mack hands Jonah her keys. "Lock up when you guys are done. I'll meet you inside. Take your time. No hurry at all."

You're killing me, Mack. Killing me.

"Can you come up here?" I ask Jonah.

Jonah slides into the driver's seat and turns his body toward mine. Our kneecaps touch and the root beer bubbles up again.

"Tip your head up." My left hand flutters around, trying to find somewhere to land. "Stop moving."

"I'm not moving."

"You are." I put my left hand on Jonah's face and tilt it toward the light more. The skin on his cheek feels smooth against my fingertips. His warm breath washes across the palm of my hand. A sizzling sensation travels up my arm. "Close your eyes."

My right hand hovers over Jonah's left eye. I will it to stop shaking. I do a couple of narrow swipes on his eyelid above his lashes. I stop, look at my work, and use my pinky to smear out the color a little. I have to push the hair out of Jonah's right eye before I can line the top of that one. Jonah's hair feels thick, stiff on my fingers.

"What do you use on your hair?" I say. "Mack used her gel on my hair, but I don't have white-girl hair. I don't think it's going to hold."

"Secret Korean stuff. Only people who are seventy-five percent Korean get to know." Jonah's lips brush my palm, making my hand quiver even more.

When I pull my hand away, Jonah opens his eyes and looks in the mirror. He yelps. "I look like my mom!"

"I'm not done yet. I still need to do the bottom lids." I grab Jonah's wrists to keep him from wiping off the eyeliner. "I promise. You'll be K-pop idol material by the time I'm done."

I have to remind myself to let go of him. I tip his head back toward the light. Jonah's lips are only a few inches away from mine. I wonder what they feel like. I could lean in and . . . I clear my throat to end the train of thought that is sending electricity to the pit of my stomach.

"Look up," comes out more like a squeak than a command.

I gently pull the lower lid of his right eye down, line it, and smudge the color out with my pinky. When the other eye is done, I lean back and let Jonah inspect my work. This time, he nods.

"If you're not going to do it at a hundred percent, then why bother?" When Jonah leans between the two front seats to dig through Mack's workout bag, his chest presses into my arm. He looks up at me with kohl-rimmed eyes. Challenging me. Little parentheses etch the corners of his mouth when I don't move my arm.

"Ah-ha." He pulls a piece of black cloth into the front seat. It's Mack's DON'T BE A HATER, BE A SKATER T-shirt. "On brand, if a bit big. It'll do."

Jonah pulls off his plain, royal blue, long-sleeved T-shirt. Maybe I should look away. But, as Jonah says, if you aren't going to do it at 100 percent, then why bother? The smell of pine makes me feel light-headed. He slides the derby girl shirt over his finely tuned body.

"You know if this whole speed skating thing doesn't work out"—Jonah messes up his hair and gives himself a seductive pout in the mirror—"maybe I could be a K-pop idol."

"Wow." I shake my head.

"What? I work out. I have a sexy American accent. I can sing, sort of. I'm sure Korean girls would be screaming 'Oppa!' and falling all over themselves to get to me."

I shake my head again and put the eyeliner pencil in my purse.

"'Cause, God knows, they don't give me the time of day in Phoenix," Jonah says.

"Korean girls?"

"No, girls in general."

"That's not true. I've seen girls staring at you in English." Okay, one of them was me.

"Because I'm new. And I'm one of two Asian guys in the tenth grade. Once the novelty wears off, I'll start blending in with the cinderblock walls again."

"Hey, Jonah."

"Yeah."

"It's six thirty-seven." I put my fist out for him to bump. "Try to keep up with me tonight."

And he does. We barely make it past the food truck outside selling churros without me caving to its cinnamon-sugar goodness. The lobby of Ability360 is so packed that Jonah is practically standing on top of me. Somebody jostles us, and Jonah puts his hand on my hip to keep from colliding with me. It stays there longer than necessary. And I am totally okay with it.

I look around, trying to find Mack. Usually, she sticks out like a beacon, but tonight she blends into the kaleidoscope of colors. I finally see her in the derby girl prep area. She's surrounded by women of all colors, shapes, and sizes in fishnet stockings and sexy pirate boutfits.

"Would you like a drink?" Jonah nods at the tiny, makeshift concession stand at the gymnasium's entrance.

"Sure. Pepsi, if they have it." I catch Mack's eye, and she waves me over. "I'll be back in a minute. Mack is hailing me."

I've been to enough bouts with Mack over the last year that I recognize several of the women's faces, even if I can't remember all their names—their real ones or their over-the-top derby girl ones.

"Here she is." Mack throws an arm around my shoulders. "My accountability partner. I teach her geometry. She teaches me self-discipline."

"You're going to come skate with us sometime, aren't you, Olivia?" Up close, I realize this woman with the spiky blond hair, Barnacle Barb, is probably the same age as my mother. Maybe even a little older. "We need some more young blood. Are you eighteen yet?"

Though I am flattered, I think these women would eat me alive. "No. I'm sixteen."

"Oh." Barnacle Barb looks genuinely disappointed to hear this. "Do you want to join our new junior derby? We're actively recruiting."

"Nah, her parents won't let her," Mack answers for me. "They're afraid she'll get hurt."

I cringe. Mack's right, but she didn't have to make me sound like such a baby.

"That's understandable. A shame, but understandable. Parents want to keep their babies safe." Barnacle Barb pats my shoulder. "Even when they are almost grown."

I'm not sure if roller derby is really for me, but the one time Mack brought the idea up with my parents, Mom immediately shut it down with an uncharacteristic "Oh, hell no!" And, for once, Dad backed her up. Parenting. What a concept! The one good thing about being a "normal" high school student now is that I'm expected to hang out with friends on the weekends. Mack might be an odd choice for a BFF, but when my parents question it, I remind them that I could be going to parties instead of bouts. Parties like the one the Trout brothers threw while their spare kidney—and their parents—was out on the road competing with me at Nationals. Mack looks like an angel compared to them.

"You keep training with Olivia, Mack Truck." Barnacle Barb puts on her helmet. "Your speed is coming up, but you're not quite there yet. And work on your endurance."

"I stopped vaping," Mack says.

"That's a good start," Barnacle Barb says.

"Now to lose some of this." Mack pats her soft stomach.

"Mack Truck, look around. Do we look like a bunch of size-zero supermodels? If you're going to fall—and you will, repeatedly—

you want a little extra junk in the trunk for cushioning." To illustrate her point, Barnacle Barb sticks out her booty, which is barely covered by the striped pirate-wench skirt, and smacks it. "Speed trumps size. Balance trumps both. I gotta go. The bout is about to start."

Barnacle Barb squeezes us in a double-armed bear hug before putting in her mouth guard and skating off. She passes Jonah on his way over to us. His eyes follow her.

"That's a costume," Jonah says when we meet up with him.

"It's part of the show." Mack looks Jonah over and gives him an approving nod. "I like your look, Choi. See, I told you you'd look good with guyliner. Makes you look older too."

Jonah stands up taller. "So, roller derby is like WWE?"

"No. It's not staged. All the fights are real."

"Well, this should be interesting."

"I'm teasing. Fighting is not allowed."

Jonah hands me a bottle of Pepsi. He looks at Mack. He holds out his bottle of water to her. "Here. Since you're in training. Simple carbs are crap."

"Thanks, Choi." Mack takes the bottle. "Let's go get a seat. The bout is about to start."

We slide through the crowd and over to the short set of bleachers closest to the track. Mack picks the bottom row. Ten feet away from us, two ovals of pink tape on what's normally basketball flooring delineate the track. Jonah sits down last in our row.

"Shouldn't we move up a few rows?" A concerned wrinkle creases Jonah's brow.

"Nope," Mack says.

"But there isn't a safety barrier between the skaters and the crowd."

A wicked smile pulls across Mack's deep purple lips. "I know. Live dangerously occasionally, Choi."

"Okay, then." Jonah sits back, but I can tell he's planning an escape route.

All the skaters come out onto the track to warm up. They travel in a swarm around the track. The opening guitar riff of "Welcome to the Jungle" blasts through the speakers and the crowd goes wild. Her weird music taste validated, Mack looks down the row at us, makes a rock-on hand sign, and bobs her head along with the music.

Meanwhile, Jonah keeps eyeing my Pepsi. I offer it to him. He shakes his head but continues to stare at it. I offer it again. Jonah grabs the bottle, wipes off the lip with his shirt, and takes a tiny sip. And then another larger one. And then a chug.

"Hey, Mr. Carbs-are-Crap, may I have my soda back?" I say.

"Yeah, sorry." He wipes the lip of the bottle before handing it back. The parentheses appear again. "Now I remember why I gave soda up three years ago. It tastes too good."

"When all you eat are eggs and seaweed, no wonder your body craves something sweet. You think I'm obsessive about stuff." I take a swig of my soda. "At least I know how to have a good time."

"I know how to have a good time. I'm having a good time right now. I'm sitting in the danger zone. I'm wearing guyliner." Jonah takes my soda, and without wiping the lip, takes a chug. "I'm even consuming high-fructose corn syrup. How much wilder can this night get?"

I have a couple of ideas, but I clamp down on them. I take another drink of my soda, purposely not wiping the lip of the bottle either. Jonah notices.

When the emcee comes out to the middle of the floor, the crowd goes wild. The derby girls line up around the track. As he introduces each player by their number and derby name, they skate out and wave to the crowd. Mack screams for each of the Surly Gurlz like they are all her BFFs. When he introduces team captain Barnacle Barb, I stand next to Mack and yell loudly for her too. Jonah stands a beat later and claps politely.

I don't know if it is the energy and blood lust of the sport, the guyliner, or the Pepsi, but as the night progresses, Jonah comes to life. By the end of the night, he's on his feet yelling as much as Mack is.

"Inside! Inside! Inside! NO! What?! She was clear!" Jonah yells before flopping down on the bleacher.

"Tell us how you really feel," I tease.

The corner of Jonah's mouth pulls up. He takes my soda and chugs the rest of it.

"Hey!" I yell when he passes the empty bottle back to me.

Jonah says something, but I can't hear him. Or read his lips.

"What?" I yell over the crowd.

Jonah leans into me, putting his hand on my lower back. His long hair tickles my shoulder, and his warm breath washes across my ear and neck. I inhale his piney, sweet scent. All the nerve endings in my body spark and threaten to shut down the whole power grid.

"I said, do you want another one?" Jonah yells in my ear before sitting back up. His warm hand continues to rest on my lower back.

I shake my head since the muscles in my mouth are completely misfiring. The whistle blows, and the final jam begins. Mack and Jonah—and his hand—jump to their feet. The Surly Gurlz win. Mack jumps up and down, pumping her fist like it's her win too. She and Jonah high-five each other over my head.

"I'm going to go congratulate Barnacle Barb and the Gurlz. I'll meet you guys at the car." Mack hands Jonah her keys but gives me a pointed look. "Give me five minutes. Maybe ten. Yes, definitely ten."

I give her a hard look back, but Mack just smiles. She rushes over to the oval where, in a few minutes, all the skaters will take a lap to high-five fans standing on the outer loop.

"Shotgun," Jonah says when we get to Mack's car.

I groan. Jonah unlocks the rear driver's side door—Mack's ancient car doesn't have power anything—and opens it for me.

"That was awesome," Jonah says when we're both inside. "I'm glad Mack texted me this morning."

A weird twinge replaces the bubbly feeling in my stomach. I don't know Jonah's phone number, and I spend seven-plus hours in the same building with him every day.

I lean forward and put my right arm on the top of Jonah's seat. "I'm glad you came with us after all."

Jonah leans toward me and my eyes instinctively close. Warm fingertips brush the side of my neck and finger my hair. I wait. And wait. I open my eyes again.

"Your earring was caught in your hair." Jonah leans back, and my face burns. "Dippity-do."

"That's a stupid roller derby name."

"It's not a derby name. It's hair wax. And it's not Korean." Jonah runs his hands through my deflated hair, trying unsuccessfully to spike it back up. Meanwhile, his hair still looks as perfectly and intentionally messy as it did at the beginning of the night. "Now you know my secret."

"Hey, Jonah."

"Yeah."

"It's eight twenty-two."

Jonah's laugh launches a swarm of butterflies in my stomach.

"So, do you want to come with me—me and Mack—to the next bout?"

"Yeah. If I can. Remind me not to drink soda, though. I've got a serious sugar buzz going. I'm not going to be able to sleep tonight."

He rubs his eyes and smears his guyliner.

"Oh, don't forget to take that off."

Though I was referring to his eye makeup, Jonah takes off Mack's shirt instead. I hand him his long-sleeve T-shirt from the back seat. Slowly. Admiring the fine-tuned machine in the process.

"Mack usually has baby wipes in her car somewhere. That'll take your eye makeup off." I dig around in Mack's workout bag. Along with her derby-regulation roller skates, there's a diaper, some toy keys, a baby blanket, and a pacifier in a plastic baggie. I finally find the box of baby wipes. "Here. One for me. One for you."

I scoot up closer so I can see myself in the rearview mirror. My forearm drapes over both the seat and Jonah's muscular shoulder, but he doesn't move. My face is so close to his. If he would only turn his head. A smear of black eyeliner comes off on the baby wipe.

"You have beautiful eyes." Jonah catches my eye in the rearview mirror. Challenging me.

I take Jonah's baby wipe from his hand and bring it up to his eyes. He closes them.

"You do too." I wipe the makeup gently away. His eyes stay closed after I'm done. I am so close to him. My lips are two inches away from his, max. The caffeine in my blood buzzes to my toes and back. I lean forward to close the space. Challenge accepted.

And then the door opens.

"Damn, kids." Mack slides into the driver's seat. "I leave you two alone for ten minutes, and you're already fogging up the windows."

The cool air extinguishes my flame. The only heat left is what's coming off my face.

Mack chuckles, pleased with herself. "Where do you live, Choi? I'll drop you off first."

"Oh." Jonah sounds as disappointed as I feel.

"Unless you want to continue living dangerously for a little while longer, of course," Mack says with a mischievous smile.

"Yeah. I do." Jonah pops in the Guns N' Roses cassette tape and cranks it up. "Just nothing stupid. I gotta skate tomorrow morning."

As we pull out of the parking garage, Mack drums her fingers on the steering wheel. "What could we do? Something to fully initiate Choi into Phoenix life."

"We could climb 'A' Mountain in Tempe," I say.

"What is up with you two and exercising all the time?" Mack says.

"According to my student Lina Kitagawa, using a black light and collecting scorpions is fun. That's a very Phoenix thing to do."

Even in the low light, I can see Jonah's grimace. "That's a hard no from me. I'd rather go mountain climbing."

"Spoiler alert, Mr. Extra. 'A' Mountain is really just a butte," I say. "It's only a one-mile hike, but it's steep. Dad used to make me run up it for conditioning."

"That sounds like fun." Jonah looks over his shoulder at me. "Maybe we could do that together another time when you have better shoes on?"

Did he just ask me out? The butterflies alight again.

"You two." Mack shakes her head. She gets on the freeway headed toward Tempe. "Wait. I got it. You don't mind getting a little dirty, do you, Choi?"

Jonah's eyebrow quirks up. "Depends."

"Shh," Mack says as she pulls the side of the chain-link fence back enough for a person to slide through.

Jonah shifts the three blocks of ice wrapped in less-than-clean workout towels and T-shirts onto his shoulder. "Isn't this considered trespassing?"

"No." Mack uses her phone's flashlight to look around us. "Okay, yes. But Granny's friend owns this land. If he happens to bust us, I'll talk our way out of it, I promise."

"I don't know," I say, and Jonah nods in agreement.

"C'mon, guys! This is the kind of stuff I did in high school, and I was kind of a nerd. So this is like low-level normal teen behavior."

"You were a nerd?" I say, because I have a hard time seeing Mack as anything but sassy Mack Truck.

"Yes. And I played it safe. Too safe. Let's be dangerous." When Jonah starts to complain, Mack cuts him off. "Not the reckless, stupid kind of dangerous. The pushing the envelope, feeling alive kind of dangerous."

"One time. Then we go," I say as doubt grips my gut.

"And you, Choi? You wanna be initiated into the Ice Dreams family tonight?"

"You don't have to. You can stay here and be lookout for us if you want to play it safe." I look him in the eye. Challenge him.

Jonah is the first one to squeeze through the gate. And the first one to the top of the steep, grassy hill. And the first one to park his butt on a thick, cookie-sheet-size slab of ice. Mr. Extra to the end.

"So, how do we do this?" Jonah says when a wheezing Mack gets to the top of the hill.

"It's not rocket science, Choi." Mack plops down on the slab of ice next to Jonah. "It's physics. The friction coefficient of ice is—"

"Less talking. More doing!" A squeal rips out of my throat as I tip my body back and take off down the hill.

I hear Jonah's panicked "Ahhhhhh!" as he slides down behind me. Wind rushes through my deflated hair, and my heart soars. My butt cheeks might have frostbite after this, but it's totally worth it. That is, until I hit an unseen gravelly patch and the piece of ice stops but I don't. I slip off the top and tumble down the rest of the hill. Jonah obviously hits the same patch, because a moment later we both find ourselves face-planting into the grassy patch at the bottom. Mack cackles from her perch at the top of the hill. Jonah groans and blows a lock of hair out of his face. I spit out a clump of dried grass. We look at each other. Even in the low light, I can see Jonah's pained expression melt into a smirk. A laugh bubbles out of my chest despite the pain coming from my elbows and knees where—based on the current stinging sensation—I am now missing several layers of skin. Jonah's chuckle turns into a full belly laugh as we pull ourselves to our feet. I yank my pleather skirt back down and turn it to face the right direction. At least the new holes in the knees of my leggings will still be on trend for the next derby bout, after I get all the grass out of places where nobody should ever have grass.

"Outta tha wayyyyy!" Mack says as she barrels down the hill toward us.

"Watch out for the . . . Oh, ow," Jonah says as Mack hits the gravelly part.

Mack's stop is just as graceless as ours. If I laugh any harder, I'm going to pee myself.

"That was epic," Jonah says when he finally catches his breath.

"Welcome to Phoenix, Jonah." I put out my fist for him to bump. We flick out our #1 signs. "You are now officially initiated into the Ice Dreams family."

"You two are so adorkable," Mack says.

"Let's do it again." Jonah surveys the rip across the right knee of his jeans. "Only let's find a different path first."

Jonah insists we drop him off at the front of his subdivision. I don't think he wants his mom to meet us. Honestly, in the same shoes, I wouldn't either. I don't know how he's going to explain the rips in the knees of his jeans, much less the huge muddy grass stain on his butt.

Jonah leans down next to my open passenger side window. "Thanks for tonight. I haven't had that much fun since . . . I don't even remember."

I look up at Jonah, and my heart feels like I'm still ice blocking down the hill.

"Stick around, kid," Mack says. "This is only the beginning of the hijinks and shenanigans that you are about to experience in Phoenix."

We watch Jonah—and his wet butt—walk down the street to the first house on the right. Once he disappears inside, Mack fires up the engine.

"So, can we revisit the fuchsia prom dress idea now?" Mack says.

"Mack!" I smack her shoulder.

"What? Just because my love life is one step up from a dumpster fire, doesn't mean yours should be. Have some fun, will ya? I'm telling you, this adulting thing is not what they promised it would be."

It's almost midnight by the time I finally get back to my house. I sneak in the front door, my derby girl clothes hidden in my backpack. The lights and TV are on, but my mom is passed out cold on the couch. Her bottle of muscle relaxants is on the coffee table. Her heating pad has slipped off her back onto the floor. I turn everything off and tiptoe into the kitchen to hang up my keys—my signal to Mom that I'm home so she won't have to climb up the stairs to check. There's a note hooked to my key peg.

> *Livy—DON'T let me oversleep. I have to*
> *open the rink at 9:00 a.m. for the Chois.*

When I get upstairs, I cram the bag with my sweaty, dirty, grassy derby clothes in the back of my closet and set my clock for 8:00 a.m. After I make sure Mom is out the door, I plan to sleep until at least noon. It's close to one by the time I get most of the fuchsia dye scrubbed out of my hair. I face-plant into bed, but my brain won't shut up. It keeps replaying the evening, down to the tiniest details. The smell of pine. The taste of Pepsi. The buzz in my stomach when Jonah's lips moved against the skin of my palm. Warm fingers brushing the side of my neck. The sound of Jonah's laugh at the bottom of the hill. Sleep slowly pulls me under, but not without a parting shot of Jonah's beautiful face, his eyes closed. His lips available. And this time, Mack doesn't interrupt us.

Chapter 5

Mom—You rest. I'll let the Chois in. I'm on at 11:30 anyway. ~O

It's after nine thirty before the Chois arrive. Mr. Choi bursts through the front door and stomps inside. My heart hiccups a little when Jonah drags in behind him, rubbing his temples. I sit at Table #1, pretending I'm doing homework. I've read the same paragraph three times now. Mr. Choi walks by my table, nods at me, and then pulls up short. My hair. I run a hand through it, trying to flatten some of what's left of the fuchsia spikes. Jonah catches my eye, and his face lights up.

"Good morning, Mr. Choi." I pretend like I've gotten more than thirty minutes of quality sleep. "I was wondering if you guys were coming in this morning after all. You did say nine, right?"

"Yes, I did. I wish Jonah had your work ethic, Olivia." Mr. Choi turns to Jonah, and the smile on Jonah's face extinguishes. "I can tell you what, though. You won't be hanging out with that Brandon kid again if this is how you're going to be the next day."

Jonah shoots me a panicked look. He doesn't need to. Does he think I'm going to blow the chance for a repeat?

"Is there anything you need, Mr. Choi, before you guys start your training?" I give him a big smile, trying to distract him from Jonah, who has slinked off to the locker room to change.

"No, we're fine. Thanks."

I'm bummed that Mr. Choi doesn't ask me to keep count today during the warm-up. Now I have to keep making myself look at my homework instead. Meanwhile, Jonah skates like Egg did the time he had food poisoning the night before our competition in Anaheim. Jonah is slow. His crossovers are sloppy.

Mr. Choi mutters what is probably a Korean swear word and throws his clipboard on top of the nearest table. "What are you doing, son?"

"Skating!" Jonah yells back.

Jonah glides over to the wall in front of his dad. I can't hear what they are saying, but from the look on Jonah's face, his dad is ripping him a new one. Mr. Choi snatches the clipboard off the table and storms toward me. I drop my head and reread the same paragraph for the hundredth time.

"Olivia, do you have any coffee?"

"No, sir. I don't have a food handler's license to work in the snack bar." Also, I have no clue how to make coffee.

"Jonah!" Mr. Choi gestures at him to come to our table.

Mr. Choi flips through the papers on his clipboard until Jonah slides into the seat across from me. Jonah strips off his gloves. Some of last night's dreams steam into my brain as Jonah unzips the top of his skinsuit several inches to release some of the heat trapped underneath. A small cross on a fine-chained gold necklace sits over his breastbone. It pulses as Jonah tries to catch his breath.

"Eat some eggs, and then get back out on the ice." Mr. Choi smacks the clipboard down between us like a chaperone. "I'm going to Starbucks. *Do not* waste your training time while I'm gone."

After Mr. Choi stomps out the front door, I slide the soft-sided cooler to Jonah.

"I'm going to hurl if I eat those." Jonah pushes the cooler back to my side of the table. "I have got the worst sugar-caffeine hangover ever. I feel like there's an elephant standing on my chest. Why'd you let me do that last night? Maybe I'm dehydrated from the caffeine."

"Jonah. It was one soda. Half a soda at that."

"I know, but I still couldn't sleep last night."

I unzip the cooler and hand Jonah his water bottle, accidentally brushing his hand at the same time. It sends a crackle of lightning up my arm. "We were that fun?"

Jonah chugs half the bottle before answering, "Yes."

"So, I have to know exactly how 'hanging with Brandon' resulted in your jeans getting ripped and muddy."

Jonah bites his bottom lip. "We were goofing around with Brandon's dog in the backyard, and I tripped over a sprinkler head or two. And it went downhill from there. Yeah."

"I hope you delivered that with more conviction than you just did, especially as I don't think Brandon has ever mentioned owning a dog. Dude, you kind of suck at being a normal teen."

Jonah reaches his hand across the table. His long fingers hook underneath the cuff of my Ice Dreams jacket and tug.

"Then come be extra with me." Jonah's fingers fan out around my wrist. Surely he can feel the spike of my pulse. "Skate with me. For a little bit." He pulls me to a stand. "Please."

"Challenge accepted."

I put my skates on in record time. Jonah's already back on the ice making a slow loop when I skate up next to him on the outside. I dip low and mimic his skating.

"So . . . how's it goin'?" I say, matching his slow, even strokes.

"Today? Not so great. I have a qualifier coming up, and Dad is freaking out."

When Jonah leans deep into the curve, I do too. I can't get as close to the ice as he can. At least not going forward.

"What about you?" I say on the next straightaway.

"What about me?"

"Are you freaking out?"

"No," Jonah says, but it's too clipped to be the truth.

"That's why you can't sleep?"

Jonah makes a noncommittal noise. The curve comes up again and we lean into it.

"You're pretty good at this." Jonah smiles at me. "Wanna switch sports?"

"Boy, please." When I stand up, Jonah does too. "Besides, I can actually get lower than you do in the lean."

"Not with those skates."

"Watch me," I say, and Jonah comes to a stop.

I flip around and do a few backward crossovers until I build up enough momentum. I squat down and lean into a hydroblade on my backward inside edge, stretching lower and lower to the ice until I look like a perfect *4* on its side. I reach my arms out and let the tips of my fingers graze the ice as I loop in tighter and tighter spirals.

"Wooooow," Jonah says when I come back up.

I curtsy. "Want to try it together?"

"Speed skates aren't really designed to go backward."

"You don't have to. Just lean like you normally do, then hold it and try to sink lower instead of coming back up. Watch." I grab Jonah's outside hand and pull him into motion.

This time as we come into the curve, Jonah and I act as counterbalances to each other. Neither of us go very low, but as our spiral gets tighter, our smiles get bigger. We stumble a little getting back up, but otherwise . . .

"That was awesome," Jonah says, without releasing my hand. "Can we do it again?"

I don't release his hand either. "Of course. We definitely can do better."

This time, Jonah pushes me into motion.

"Ready?" I say, and Jonah nods. It takes us a little longer to find our counterbalance, but we do get lower the second time. We even rise back out of the move with minimal bobbling.

"Third time's the charm?" Jonah quirks up an eyebrow.

"Let's see what you've got."

This time, we find our counterbalance within seconds. As we spiral, we ease farther and farther into the ice until both of us can glide our hands on top of it.

Jonah looks over at me. "We got—"

And my foot slips. I fall out of the move and slide across the ice, pulling Jonah with me. We both end up belly down. When we finally stop sliding, I push up on my skinned elbows and laugh. Instead of laughing like last night, though, concern wrinkles Jonah's brow.

"It's okay, Jonah. We fall all the time." Though I'm thankful we crashed on the dry interior ice and not on Jonah's sopping ice track which Mr. Choi creates before each practice.

"Yeah, so do we, but we also wear Kevlar skinsuits during races for a reason." Jonah pushes to a stand and gives me a hand up. "I don't want to accidently cut you with my blade."

I don't release his hand. "Then don't fall."

Jonah pulls me toward him until I'm standing between his feet. He looks down at me. Parentheses etch the corners of his mouth.

"Will you skate with me again sometime?" he says.

"Anytime, Ice Prince."

We stand there looking at each other. Waiting. Wondering.

Jonah blinks first. "I should probably get back to work. Dad is already in a mood this morning."

I skate backward until he releases my hand. "Yeah. Sure. And I've got . . . homework to do."

I can feel Jonah's eyes on me as I skate away.

Just as I slide into Table #1 with my Chucks back on, Mr. Choi—and his giant cup of coffee—returns, grumbling under his breath. Jonah takes off around the rink at top speed, but Mr. Choi isn't buying it, especially as Jonah's gloves are still sitting on the table in front of me.

"Tell me, honestly, did he skate at all while I was gone?" Mr. Choi puts his Trenta coffee with all kinds of detailed instructions scribbled down the side on top of my book.

"Yes, sir. He skated." Like I would throw Jonah under the bus even if he hadn't. "Very well, in fact. He was doing balance work."

From the ice, Jonah gives his dad a thumbs-up. Mr. Choi still looks skeptical but walks toward the ice with his stopwatch, clipboard, and Jonah's gloves. As the pair discuss split times and whatever people who skate around in ovals care about, I stare at my history book and fantasize about what I looked like skating with Jonah. Though Mack would have given me crap about it for the rest of my life, I wish she would have been here to take a video or at least a picture. My eyelids are so heavy. I gaze into my textbook until my fantasy melts into a dream.

The air horn goes off just as Dream Jonah's lips are about to touch mine. I jolt awake. I hate that thing.

"Yes!" Mr. Choi yells as Jonah's skates eat up the ice. "You're on fire now, son."

Jonah flies down the back straightaway. Something has changed. His upper body is strong, but no longer tight. His crossovers in the final turn are even and powerful. Mr. Choi whoops as Jonah passes the finish line.

"Now that's some skating!" Mr. Choi's voice echoes around the rink. "You shaved two-tenths of a second off your best time."

Jonah does a cooldown loop before stopping in front of Table #1. He reaches over the wall for his water bottle, but it is just out of range. Instead of scooting it across the table, I bring the bottle to him.

"Way to go," I whisper and put out my fist. This time Jonah makes the still stupid #1 sign after he taps me. "I'm going to make a figure skater out of you yet."

"*Pfft.*" Jonah hands his water bottle back to me and whispers back, "I plan on holding you to your promise."

"Anytime, anywhere, Ice Prince."

"Challenge accepted."

Never has our near-empty rink seemed so crowded. Especially when Ernie comes in at 11:00 a.m. to Zamboni the ice before Ice Dreams' Open Skate. Usually the 'boni's hum makes me feel weirdly happy and peaceful. Today, it makes me sad and agitated. My time with Jonah is done.

"See you at school tomorrow, Olivia," Jonah says as he passes by me in street clothes after practice ends.

I watch him walk away. At the front door, he looks over his shoulder one last time. My heart melts a bit. And for the first time ever, I look forward to going to school.

Chapter 6

There's some kind of drama going on when I arrive late to lunch on Monday. It must be juicy because whatever is playing on Jonah's phone is more important to everyone than homework. That music sounds familiar. Egg and I did a routine to it once. Oh my God. It *is* our routine.

Four sets of brown eyes bore into me as I look at the screen. It's a little grainy and jumpy, so I know it must be one of the videos that Mom took with her phone and posted up on the Ice Dreams YouTube page. At least it's not the phoenix number or our last Skate Detroit number. Thank God.

"How many of these have you guys watched?" I slide into the table next to Jonah.

"Just the one. So far," Brandon says, and a panic stabs my heart.

"You were so good!" Naomi squeals and squeezes my arm.

Were?

"Stuart is hot," Erika says as the shaky footage zooms in on Egg.

I look down at the video. I know what's coming up next in the choreography: the arabesque spiral. Jonah leans in as Old Olivia slides to Egg's left and lifts her outer leg into arabesque. I fly around the rink in a spiral with long airplane wings. Then Egg comes into arabesque and pulls me back until I'm tucked under him in our continued spiral. Mom zooms in on our faces. Egg—

his braces freshly off—has a huge smile. Erika squeals when then-sixteen-year-old Egg lifts me above his head. My legs make a perfect *V.* In our red—again—costumes, Egg and I look like a flaming arrow twirling around the ice. Mom focuses in on my huge, thirteen-year-old, brace-face smile as Egg lowers me gently back onto the ice. Egg and I do one last easy jump combination before sandwiching ourselves together for a final spin combo. As the song comes to an end, Egg scoops me in his arms and dips me backward. My arms reach back until my spine makes a dramatic arch. As the last measure of music echoes around the rink, Egg folds over me in a final embrace. Unfortunately, from Mom's camera angle, it looks like Egg has his head buried in my non-existent boobs. I assure you, Egg did not. Erika squeals and grabs my forearm. Meanwhile, Egg pulls thirteen-year-old me back up to a standing position and gives me a brotherly bear hug like he always does.

I look over at Jonah. The Ice Prince's eyebrows furrow.

"How come you never told us about . . . this?" Brandon gestures at the phone.

"I told you I skated." I pull out my tuna-and-cucumber sandwich and pretend that Jonah outing my secret isn't a big deal. "Probably on the first day I met you guys."

"Yeah, you mentioned that your family owned the skating rink and that you skated. But not that you like, *skated* skated."

"She has medals and everything." Jonah leans back and crosses his arms.

"Really?" Erika says.

"You've never been to her ice rink?" Jonah says.

"Well, no. We don't skate."

"You're missing out. Ice Dreams is where all the action is." Jonah puts out his fist to me. We bump and #1. Still dorky, but whatever.

"Maybe we should try it sometime," Naomi says.

I suddenly *don't* want them to come into my world. I want to stay there with Jonah, alone. Okay, maybe with a little color commentary from Mack on the weekends, but honestly just me and Jonah.

"Where's your next race, Jonah?" I say before somebody makes concrete plans to invade my world.

"Denver. If the rumors are true, I can beat my biggest competitor's time. Of course, there's no guarantee everybody is going to stay on their feet. One lapse of concentration and the person in front of you can fall and take you out too."

"Gotta stay balanced." My mind slips back to our skating yesterday.

By the look on his face, Jonah's thoughts are there too. Everybody else has returned to their homework though. For once, I don't join them.

"You could try pairs skating as a kind of cross-training," I say to keep Jonah from putting on his headphones and slipping away. "We spend a lot of time learning how not to get hung up in each other's skates."

"Eeeh." Jonah shrugs, but he leaves his headphones off. He also leaves his left forearm on the table as he picks at his lunch with his right.

I look around. Everyone else is focused on homework, or waiting for Naomi to tell them the answer. Ahem, Brandon. I put my right forearm on the table next to Jonah's. After a few beats, I curl my fingers under the cuff of Jonah's shirt sleeve and tug.

"Skate with me today, Ice Prince," I whisper at him.

Jonah smiles and nudges me with his shoulder. A line of fire travels up my arm like a match on a trail of gasoline.

I daydream through English class, superimposing Jonah's face on Egg's body throughout our phoenix number. Maybe Jonah will let me teach him some new, easy moves. Moves that require a lot of hands-on work. Hands definitely on. I look across the room. Jonah has his head propped up on his hand, his hair acting like a curtain on one side, Mr. Balducci's side. From my side, I watch as Jonah's eyes fight to stay open.

Does he ever take notes or do homework?

Most professional skaters' educations can best be described as "spotty." My parents both have GEDs. Online school and tutors are the norm for us. Egg didn't get into Virginia Tech because of his SAT score, that's for sure. Meanwhile, my math skills are so far behind the curve that the school talked my parents into making me a sophomore instead of a junior.

"Excuse me, Mr. Balducci," a crackly voice booms over the room's intercom. Jonah and I both snap to attention. "Please send Jonah . . . uh . . . Chewy to the front office to check out."

Snickers echo around the room, especially when some smart-ass in the back makes a Chewbacca noise.

"Settle down, people," Mr. Balducci says. "He's on his way, Ms. Walters. Jonah, finish reading chapter fourteen and do the corresponding questions in the packet. And don't forget your essay is due tomorrow."

Jonah nods but doesn't bother writing anything down. Why should he? It's not going to help him become a better skater. Jonah gives me a nod when he catches my eye. As soon as he hits the door, someone makes the Chewbacca noise again. Jonah doesn't look back but closes the door with unnecessary force.

I rollerblade solo to Ice Dreams. Mack's car is in the parking lot. At least she'll make doing inventory—my task of the day—a little more entertaining. I bring my fingertips to my lips and slap a kiss on Mom and Dad's poster as I pass in front of them, but I don't get my usual derby girl introduction when I arrive at the snack bar. Instead, I hear bad singing from the back of the rink. I grab my Ice Dreams jacket from its peg and throw my backpack onto Table #1. Mack obviously has earbuds in, because she's singing something at the top of her lungs. Unfortunately, it is so off-key that I can't make out what it is.

I do a double take when I get to the barre area. The barre is still there, but now there is a state-of-the art treadmill along with a rack of barbells, a thick cable coming out of the back wall, some kind of Slip 'N Slide thing on the floor, and a massage table. Where are the Red Hat ladies going to shake their Zumba booties now?

"Won't ya take meeee!" Mack sings as she thuds along on the treadmill. That is until she catches my reflection in the barre mirror. Mack and her singing abruptly stop. Unfortunately, the treadmill does not. Mack flies off the back, her earbuds ripping out of her ears.

"Shit, what time is it?" Mack stumbles back to the machine and slaps the stop button. "Are the Chois here?"

"Not yet."

Mack grabs a towel out of her bag and quickly wipes down the expensive-looking machine. She catches herself in the mirror. Mack gives her face and pits a quick wipe down too.

"I was . . . testing them out." Mack tosses her towel and phone back in her workout bag. "I think Mr. Choi will be pleased with his latest purchases."

We used to own this same treadmill. Two, in fact. They paid September's mortgage. Though I'm not supposed to say that. "We're making room for the Zumba class" was Mom's official answer.

"Must be nice to have a money tree in your backyard." Me, jealous? Not at all.

"Tell me about it. I could use one too. Think they'll let us play with their toys?"

"Maybe." I look into the barre mirror and refluff my deflated hair. Maybe I should buy some of that Dippity-do stuff.

"If you want to put on some eyeliner before His Royal Highness gets here, I'll let you borrow mine."

"*Pfft.* I'm not putting on eyeliner for some guy."

"Jonah Choi is not *some* guy. He's *the* guy. He's like the male version of you."

"No, he's not. I'm half Japanese. He's three-quarters Korean."

"Not your ancestry, dork. The raw talent that oozes out of your pores. Your obsession with being number one."

"But I'm not number one."

"Well, not now, but you were."

Thanks for plunging that knife deep in my chest, Mack.

"And you could be again *if* you got off your ass and took it back." Mack slings her workout bag over her shoulder. "A little something to think about as you do inventory. Well, I gotta get back to the snack bar. The Slushee machine vomited all over your mom this morning. Guess who gets the privilege of taking the damn thing apart and cleaning it out? The things I do for you."

As Mack walks away, her words reverberate in my head.

If you got off your ass and took it back. But what if it's too late? What if that was my one shot? What if I'm a has-been at sixteen?

I swing my right leg up onto the barre and fold over until my forehead brushes my shin. Holding on with both hands, I let my leg slide down the barre until I have a line of about 170 degrees. I can't even blame it on my jeans being too tight, because I'm wearing leggings today. I press into the split until the muscle fibers feel like they are ripping. I get to maybe 175 degrees. Pitiful. And that was my good side. I swing my leg down and walk over to the tiny cleaning cubby in the barre area. I spray the mirrors in front of Jonah's new state-of-the-art treadmill with Windex and wipe away the sweat splotches that Mack left behind from her workout.

I used to dread the five-mile conditioning run Mom made me do every morning when she was my coach. Back when she was still functioning most days. When Egg was here. When I was a competitive skater. When I was #1.

I look in the barre mirror at the girl with the pink-tinged, chopped-off hair and rapidly expanding ass. I have no idea who she is.

My phone buzzes in my back pocket, breaking me out of my trance.

It's my first ever text from Jonah unless you count the #1 finger emoji he sent me earlier when we swapped numbers after lunch: Need a rain check on our plan. Not skating today.

I text back: Why? Are you dying from Ebola or something?

Nah

                                                                    Ok

Rain check?

                                                            Of course.

"Hey, I fixed the Slushee machine, so I'm knockin' off early." Mack interrupts my mirror cleaning. "I want to spend some time with Fiona before I leave for derby training tonight. What time are the Chois coming in? You know your mom doesn't like you to be here by yourself, especially after dark."

What am I? Five?

"Soon, I'm sure," I lie. "It's fine. I'm sure Fiona is missing her mommy."

"Yeah. Granny said Fiona cried for a good ten minutes after I left this morning. It breaks my heart. I miss my baby girl."

Mom texts me while Mack babbles on about Fiona's new

Cheerio habit: Can Mack give you a ride home tonight after the Chois leave? I'm going to bed.

It's not even 4:00 p.m. Glad Mom misses *her* baby girl so much.

> Sure. See you tomorrow morning. Get some rest.

Thanks, baby. Love you.

> You too.

"You should get going" comes out sharper than I mean it to.

It's not Mack's fault that Midori Nakashima and Michael Kennedy won't be winning any gold medals in parenting. I practically push Mack out of the barre area.

"Okay, okay, so you don't want to hear about the contents of my daughter's diaper after strained peas. Got it." Mack punches me lightly in the arm. "See you tomorrow, Liv. And think about what I said."

I nod. If I open my mouth, I'm going to vomit all my thoughts about being a normal teen all over Mack like our temperamental Slushee machine. Instead, I clean and reclean the mirrors in the barre area until Mack finally leaves.

I don't want to do my homework. I don't want to count cups for the snack bar. I don't want to clean the bathrooms. I don't want to go home. I throw the cleaning supplies back into the cubby and slam the door closed.

I want to skate with Jonah. Or maybe I just want to skate.

It's after nine before I rollerblade home. I'm not quiet when I pass behind the couch Mom is snoring away on. Some sick part of me wishes Mom were waiting up for me, demanding to know where

I've been and with whom for the last six hours. That she would threaten to ground me for such dangerous behavior. But I don't have a normal mother. And I am not a normal teen. A normal teen doesn't bust her ass falling out of a triple salchow, get up, and repeat it twenty-three more times. I pull down the waistband of my leggings. The bruising has already started. The constant bruising high-level skaters have. The bruising that earns you a visit from CPS after a routine visit to the pediatrician. The bruising that is hard for a scared seven-year-old to explain to the CPS lady who makes your parents stay away from you for a little while. The bruising that some sick part of you actually likes because it means your double salchow is about to become a triple salchow if you've got the guts to push through the pain. *If* you get off your ass and take it back.

I open the freezer and pull out a bag of peas. I briefly contemplate eating them, but my hip needs them more. I open up the refrigerator. I can't make much with ketchup, soy sauce, bottled water, butter, and moldy tortillas. I grab an apple out of the fruit bowl and cram it in my mouth like a stuffed pig. I drop a second and third apple in my backpack. Lunch for tomorrow. Done.

My muscles scream as I climb the stairs. A thirty-minute shower doesn't even make a dent in the pain signals flooding my brain. For a hot second, I contemplate sneaking downstairs and swiping one of Mom's muscle relaxers. But one, it would require me to climb the stairs a second time. And two, it would probably make me comatose for the next sixteen hours, and school starts in less than nine. Instead, I rub Tiger Balm into my skin and hope it will appease—or even better, smother—the demons who keep telling me I can't skate. I hobble to my bed and snuggle down with the bag of half-frozen peas. Just like the old days. Now, this is Olivia Kennedy. This is my normal.

Chapter 7

"Put your hands together for OH-LIV-I-AAA 'TRIPLE AX-KILL' KENNNEDYYYYYY," Mack announces my arrival to Ice Dreams on Wednesday afternoon.

I swap my in-lines for Chucks without a word. Mack takes my silence as commentary on her name choice.

"Liv and Let Die? Livin' on a Prayer? C'mon, Kennedy, work with me here."

I roll my eyes.

"Fine." Mack sprays down the snack counter with cleaner. "Oh, by the way, the Chois aren't coming in today."

"Again?" I pull my Ice Dreams jacket off its peg and slide it on. I toss my backpack onto Table #1. "Jonah wasn't in school again today either. But if he's missed three days of training in a row, maybe he does have Ebola."

"He does not have Ebola." Mom hobbles out of the supply closet with a sleeve of paper cups. "I'm sure Jonah's simply preparing for his big competition coming up. Getting extra coaching or something. You remember the drill. That's why we finally had to pull you out of public school after fifth grade. You were absent too much."

I give Mom a gentle hug, but she still winces.

"You mean Jonah hasn't texted you about it?" Mack says pointedly, and I shoot her a dirty look.

"You and Jonah text each other?" The corner of Mom's mouth pulls up. "He is a cutie."

I pull away from my mom. "Can we not?"

"What? I'm interested in your life."

"Jonah is a friend. Just a friend." A friend I like to skate with. And eat lunch with every day. And put guyliner on. And occasionally dream about.

"I think her prom dress should be fuchsia," Mack says, like this is a done deal. "We should re-dye her hair to match."

"Yes on the dress. No on the hair." Mom tugs gently at a wayward lock that decided to stick out from the side of my head this morning like a slightly pink horn. "My little girl, going to prom."

"Mom, I'm not going to prom."

"I never got to go to prom. Shoot, I never got to go to high school. Or do any of the things high schoolers do."

"Believe me, you didn't miss anything," I say.

"I have to agree with Olivia on that one," Mack says. "Sometimes, I wish I could go back and do high school all over again. I would definitely do things differently."

"You'd study harder so you wouldn't be working at an ice rink making minimum wage?" I regret that as soon as it's out of my mouth. Mom's bony elbow in my ribs doesn't make me feel any better about it.

"What she means is, maybe you would have been more focused," Mom says.

"Lack of focus wasn't my problem. I was too focused on all the wrong things." Mack attacks a stain on the counter that has been there since before she came to work at Ice Dreams. "Sometimes I wish I could get all that wasted time back."

Mom wraps her bony fingers around Mack's wrist to make her stop scrubbing. "Annabelle, everybody has things they wish they could have a redo on. We can't change the past. We can only get up and keep skating."

Mack shrugs but doesn't look up. "Give me five more minutes to get stuff put away, and then I can take you to PT, Midori."

"Mom, Mack is not your chauffeur." *She's also not your daughter.* "How am I going to get my full license if you never let me practice?"

Mom shoots Mack a panicked look.

"C'mon, Midori. The kid has a point. She's a good driver. I swear. The last three times I've taken her out, she's done great."

My mom has *never* taken me out. Everything I know about driving, I learned from Mack.

"Okay. Crystal is coming in at four to do a makeup lesson with one of my students." Mom pulls the keys out of her purse.

"You don't have to pay Crystal to do it. I can do it." An indignant fire burns in the pit of my stomach. Don't get me wrong. Crystal is a good skater, but there's a reason why she doesn't have a picture in the skate booth area.

"Then who would take me to physical therapy?" Mom places the keys in my palm and squeezes my hand closed. She's got me there. Part of me wonders, though, if Mom has read the latest negative Yelp review about my coaching style and doesn't trust me with her precious student. "While I'm gone, Annabelle, can you fix locker twenty-two in the men's locker room? It's jammed again."

"Sure thing, boss lady. You take care of you." Mack gestures around the rink. "I'll take care of this. We need to get you better so you can reclaim your title as Ice Dreams' reigning queen."

Mom's eyes turn watery. "Annabelle, I don't know what we'd do without you. You are a godsend to me. I wish I could pay you even half of what you are truly worth. I know someday someone is going to swoop in and offer you a better-paying job that you'll have to take, but this will always be your home. You will always be a part of our family."

"Thanks." Mack turns on her heel and suddenly becomes obsessed with the cleanliness of the nacho cheese machine. I look back over my shoulder as Mom and I head out the door. Mack wipes her eyes on her forearm, leaving behind a smear of black.

"Mom, I missed them by a mile," I say when we pull into the physical therapist's parking lot fifteen minutes later.

Mom releases the death grip she has on my right shoulder. I rotate my shoulder, wondering if I'm going to have five oval bruises there now. I hop out of the car and come around to the other side. Mom slides her body as one unit to the side and uses my arm to pull herself to a stand.

When did Mom turn into Obaachan? Seriously, my grandmother moves better than my mom at this point.

Mom has been going to Sandy the physical therapist for as long as I can remember. We shuffle past the new, expensive-looking SUV in Sandy's reserved parking space. It replaced the new, expensive-looking SUV Sandy bought less than two years ago.

"So nice to see Livy's college fund being put to good use," Dad said the last time the three of us came to PT together.

While Mom checks in at PT, I text Dad. I don't expect a reply for a while. He's working. I don't even know which city's civic center he's lacing up his skates in right now.

> Break a leg tonight, Dad. And I mean
> that figuratively because I'm at PT w
> Mom right now. We don't need to buy
> Sandy a Ferrari next.

To my surprise, Dad texts me just as Sandy calls Mom back to the treatment room.

Thanks, Livy! If I don't get a Ferrari,
Sandy sure as hell doesn't get one. Miss
you, baby.

                                        Miss you too.

How's Mom doing?

                        Not good at all. Crystal took all her
                        private lessons this week. And Mack
                        is getting overtime.

There is a long pause before my phone buzzes again.

Will call you both this weekend. When is
your spring break? I'll be in CA mid-March.
Maybe we could meet up in LA or San
Diego.

                                        YESSSSS!

Don't make plans yet. It depends if Mom's
back can handle it.

                                        : (

We'll talk this weekend. Gotta run. Love you.

                        XOXOXOXO

I'm already planning our trip to Disneyland when I hear the unmistakable sound of Mom sobbing. It's quickly muffled. Sandy comes out a minute later.

"What happened?" I shoot to my feet.

"Everything is okay, sweetie," Sandy the Torturer says in a sickly sweet voice like I'm four. "Let's give your mom a few minutes to work through her pain."

Mom is not fine, but Sandy never tells me anything. So, I use my secret weapon. I pull out my phone.

"Oh, okay." I smile like I believe her BS and put my earbuds in.

Sandy walks over to the receptionist and doesn't bother whispering. "Carol, can you see if Dr. Jaeger has any ortho consults available this week? I think we've done about all we can do for Mrs. Kennedy. And start totaling all her outstanding charges."

I bite the inside of my cheek to keep my emotions inside and my face neutral. Sandy catches me looking at her, so I nod my head like I'm getting my jam on.

When I look back down, Sandy continues, "Make a note in the referral that Mrs. Kennedy is extremely stubborn. He's going to have his hands full trying to convince her to get the surgery."

I drop my phone on the floor. It pulls my earbuds out.

Sandy plasters her fake smile back on and comes over. "Olivia, sweetie, I'm going to try a little more therapy on your mom today, but she's going to be very sore for the next few hours. Do you think you could take care of yourself tonight? Don't bother her with laundry or cooking or anything. She's going to need to take some medicine to help her rest. Can you do that for your mom, sweetie? Can you be a good helper?"

Fire races through my veins. I want to throat punch this woman. It's a wonder Sandy's head doesn't spontaneously burst into flames from my glare.

"Okay, then," Sandy the Torturer says when I don't answer her. She turns on her heel and goes back into the treatment room. "Let's try again, Mrs. Kennedy. Okay, sweetie?"

Mom's sobs echo around the waiting room. I dig my fingernails into my palms. Hot tears burn behind my eyelids. I crank up my skating music and try to disappear into it.

I yelp when a hand squeezes my shoulder.

"Are you okay?" Jonah's lips say.

Before I can answer, the treatment door opens, and Mom shuffles out. Her eye makeup is smeared down her cheeks. Her dark brown eyes are bloodshot and swollen. Mom drops her head in shame when she sees Jonah. I cram my phone and earbuds in my pocket and rush over to grab her arm. I want to push past Jonah and tuck Mom into our car like we're avoiding the paparazzi, but Mom's steps can be measured in inches.

As we pass Jonah at the speed of snails, he offers the box of tissues that lives on the waiting room coffee table. Mom grabs a handful before giving Jonah a grateful smile.

"Olivia, sweetie, come here. This is very important, so I need your listening ears on, okay?" Sandy stands behind the receptionist's desk with some papers in her hand.

Mom leans on one of the reception room chairs as I go to fetch the papers. Jonah looking at me is currently the only thing keeping me from leaping over the reception desk and strangling this woman. After overexplaining how to take care of my mother— which I've been pretty much doing for the last three months while Dad has been on the road—Sandy the Torturer urges me to order a pizza for dinner after we stop at the pharmacy for even stronger painkillers.

"Also, I need to talk to your dad about your family's outstanding bill. He hasn't returned any of my prior messages. Can you have him call me, sweetie? *This week.*" Sandy's stern exterior suddenly melts back into her usual gooey one. She gives my arm a gentle squeeze. "You are such a little trooper. I am so proud of you."

I yank my little trooper arm out of her claws and return to Mom. I can't look at Jonah. I want to throw myself into a deep, dark hole. Or have Ernie run over me with the Zamboni. Adding to our mortification, Mr. Choi bursts through the door a second later.

"Mrs. Kennedy?" he says with alarm. "Are you okay? Sorry, a silly question when you are standing in a physical therapist's office. Well, um, I hope you feel better soon."

"Thank you, Mr. Choi." Mom's voice is scratchy. "I'll see you tomorrow."

As Mr. Choi walks over to the receptionist's desk, Mom and I inch through the small waiting room. Will this torture ever end? Apparently no. Jonah sprints over to open the door for us and then insists on following us to the car. He opens the door for Mom. Though it is complete overkill, he escorts me to my side of the car.

"Hey, if you need anything . . ." Jonah digs at his T-shirt collar. "Anything at all. Text me."

I know he's trying to be nice, but I can't stand it anymore. I'm so tired of being a mom to my own mother. I wish she was healthy enough to take care of *me* for a change. I hate myself for even thinking that, but it's the truth. My eyes burn, and my blood boils.

"You know what I need right now, Jonah Choi? A new spine for my mom. Not even a whole spine. Just L1 through L3. Can you buy my mom some new vertebrae? 'Cause God knows your parents buy you everything else you want."

Jonah's body curves from my verbal whiplash. I know I need a filter, but I'm sick of life taking a dump on me today.

"Sorry," I mumble. "Mom's hurting. I need to get her home."

I reach out for the door handle. Jonah wraps his fingers around my wrist.

"Wait. I'm worried about you too," Jonah says. "Let me help you. Or my mom. Or at least Mack. Somebody."

I flash back to the last time my mom had a flare-up like this. Watching Dad carry her to the toilet and bathing her like she was ninety-five was humiliating for everybody involved. Mom was so spaced out on muscle relaxants and painkillers that all that was left of Midori Nakashima was a hollow shell of a former gold medalist. I look through the side window at Mom. Her arms are wrapped tightly across her chest. She's holding in the pain until we get home. Then she can finally take her meds and escape from her crappy life. And disappear from my life too.

The wall around me implodes. A gasping sob sneaks out of my chest, followed by tears I can't keep inside anymore.

"Sorry!" Jonah releases my wrist and takes a step back. "I'm making everything worse."

I take a deep breath and wipe my eyes on my sleeve. It's harder than ever to summon the highly armored version of Olivia Kennedy. The Olivia who can wave and smile at the small crowd even when her brutally low score is announced at Skate Detroit and her skating career crashes down around her in flames.

Jonah takes my momentary show of weakness as an invitation. He steps in and wraps his arms around me. Jonah's hug is not comforting. It's awkward. He pats my back like I'm a stranger.

"Your mom is giving me a weird look through the window," Jonah says into my ear. "Oh wait, now she's smiling."

When Jonah starts to move away, I wrap my arms around him. The Ice Prince slowly melts into me, and his hug does bring me comfort. I hold him tighter. For the next fifteen seconds, the world is all right. For fifteen seconds, I pretend I'm an average high school girl hugging the cute guy she can't admit out loud she has a crush on. For fifteen seconds, I honestly believe I might get through all of this.

"Jonah, sweetie," Sandy the Torturer yells across the parking lot, bursting my bubble. "Can you come in now?"

Jonah turns his head enough to acknowledge Sandy. When he turns back around to me, he pretends to vomit.

It squeezes a chuckle out of me. "I hate her."

"Do you want me to *accidentally* key her car door on my way back in, *sweetie*?"

"As tempting as that offer is, don't."

"Can I at least kick her tire?"

I chuckle. "Sure. Sorry, some friend I am. I hope your dad is going to be okay."

Jonah looks confused. "Dad's fine. Oh. Yeah. That. No, the appointment is for me."

"You? Something is wrong with the finely tuned machine?"

"Dad's overreacting. I pulled a muscle Sunday afternoon during dry land practice, and he's freaked out. He put me on bedrest for the last two days."

"That's where you've been." I step away from Jonah and look him up and down. "Where? You look fine to me."

"My . . ." Jonah digs at his shirt collar and mumbles ". . . groin."

Though I heard him just fine, I say, "Where?"

"My groin." Jonah's face colors.

"I'm sorry. Especially when you have a big competition coming up." I can't stop the snicker that sneaks out. "I'm sure it's going to be an interesting PT session, *sweetie*."

Jonah groans. "I better go. Text me if you need something. Anything."

"Thanks."

Now, I can tell he's injured, maybe even worse than he's letting on about. His normal even stride—when he skates and walks—is off. When he gets to Sandy's car, he stops and kicks the tire. I laugh and some of the knots in my stomach release.

I finally get Mom home, drugged up on new painkillers, and tucked into bed when the doorbell rings. I grumble back down the stairs and throw open the front door, but nobody is there. Halfway down my street, a familiar BMW speeds away. At my feet is a large cardboard box. Inside it is an assortment of disposable plastic boxes containing baked chicken breasts, steaming brown rice, broccoli, seaweed salad, and cut-up fruit. I burst into tears.

Thank you, I text Jonah later while digging into my feast. I even sit at the kitchen table instead of eating in my room.

You're welcome. It was all Mom being . . .
momly. Also, the next time you're at PT, key
Sandy's car for me. SWEETIE.

Ha. Are you ok?

So-so. No skating until Mon.

Noooooo! How will you survive?

Maybe I can lift weights instead?

That was sarcasm. You can come w
M & me to Sat's bout now, though
we'll have to pass on the ice blocking
this time.

Tempting.

Guyliner, derby & Pepsi vs Quality
1-on-1 time on the couch w bag of
frozen peas. Your choice.

???? & you use frozen peas too?

Doesn't everybody?

Tiger Balm?

Of course.

Moleskin w duct tape as back up?

Duh. I was a competitive skater for 8
years remember?

Skate w me.

You can't skate. Come to the bout w
me instead. Rain check on the skating tho?

Deal

I don't feel guilty about having seconds. Mrs. Choi's food fills—
at least temporarily—the gaping hole in my life. And for the first
time in a long time, I think everything might turn out okay.

Chapter 8

Saturday night, Mom drops me off at Mack's house. Mom's knuckles are white from her death grip on the steering wheel. I know why she hasn't taken any painkillers in the last twelve hours. I also know why she insisted on giving me twenty dollars tonight.

"Tell Dad 'hi' for me. And don't forget to talk to him about spring break. I want to go to Disneyland." I regret that as soon as it comes out of my mouth. If we can't afford Mom's outstanding medical bills, how are we going to afford a vacation?

Mom pretends like we aren't up to our eyeballs in debt.

"That would be fun. We'll see," Mom says to the steering wheel because she can't turn to look at me. "You and Mack have a good time tonight at the bout. You both deserve a girls' night out. And don't let her pay for you this time."

"Okay." I give Mom a quick peck on the cheek. I don't mention that Jonah is coming with us. Especially as I don't think his parents know either.

I ring the doorbell twice before letting myself in. Music blasts from down the long hall.

"Go, go, go!" Mack's voice echoes out into the hallway.

"Whatcha . . . oh." I skid to a stop in the doorframe of Mack's cluttered room.

Jonah is sprawled out on Mack's not-so-gently-used weight bench, holding at least two hundred and fifty pounds over his chest. The muscles in his chest strain the fabric of his black, fitted T-shirt. Jonah looks over at me with kohl-rimmed eyes and artfully messy hair.

"I thought we were picking you up at Arby's?" My voice sounds weird, even to me.

Jonah clunks the weight bar back onto the catchers with a grunt and wiggles out from underneath it. He's added a leather cuff bracelet with blunt spikes on it and a chain wallet to his boutfit.

"Jonah has been kicking my ass all afternoon long." Mack stands beside the weight bench braiding her wet hair.

"You said you wanted a professional workout, so I gave you one." Jonah removes some of the weight disks and puts them on the floor. "Speaking of which, you still owe me another set."

Mack sighs dramatically but slides underneath the weights. Jonah stands at her head and helps unrack the weights over Mack's chest.

"Last set, Mack Truck. You can do it."

Jonah puts two fingers from each hand underneath the bar like they are playing Light as a Feather, Stiff as a Board. I hear girls play this game at slumber parties. I wouldn't know. I've never played the game. I've also never been to a slumber party. In fact, I haven't even been invited to a birthday party since fourth grade.

"That's one." Jonah's fingers guide the weight up and down.

There is no other place to sit in Mack's cluttered room besides her bed, so I stand in the doorframe.

"I'm going to go change in your bathroom," I announce to the room. *Crickets.*

"That's two. Slow and steady, Mack."

My heart clenches. Get a grip, Olivia. They're friends. Just friends.

I can still hear them counting as I dig my boutfit out of my giant purse. I smooth the clingy fabric over my small-but-growing curves. I bend over and shellac my hair until it's as spiky on the outside as I feel on the inside. Mack's black eyeliner on the counter helps create a thick shield to complete my look.

"I am fierce. I am number one," I say to my reflection. I fling open the bathroom door and strut back into Mack's bedroom. "I am . . . what?"

Mack lies facedown on her bed with Jonah sitting at her hip. His hands are on her back.

"Ow. Ow. Ow. God, Choi, easy. You're making it worse," Mack says.

"Stop being such a baby." Jonah presses his fingers into her shoulder blade. "You gotta hold it for about a minute to get the muscle to release."

"What the hell?" a male voice says from behind me.

Mack's head snaps up. "Hey, honey."

I'm not sure whose feet hit the floor faster, Mack's or Jonah's. I step to the side and let Tyler shoehorn into the room with us. I can count the number of times I've hung out with Tyler on one hand. I try to avoid him as much as possible. I wish Mack would too. Even if he is her baby's daddy.

"Who the hell are you?" Tyler growls and looks down his nose at Jonah.

Jonah gulps.

"Tyler, this is Jonah. Jonah, Tyler." Mack jogs over to Tyler and wraps herself around one of his beefy arms. "Jonah's the boy from the rink I was telling you about. This kid is gonna go all the way to the Olympics, I know it."

"Mack wanted to learn some of my training techniques." Jonah glances around the room as he says this, obviously looking for a potential escape route.

The vein in the side of Tyler's pale neck throbs. "Didn't look like training to me."

And for once, Mack is silent. The same Mack who once got kicked out of Walmart for defending a cashier with a speech impediment from some nasty high school boys. The same Mack who will tell you, yes, those jeans do make your ass look big. The same Mack who will tell you that you could be #1 again if you got off your ass and took it back. That Mack is suddenly silent. Or maybe silenced.

One match and this room is going to explode. I strut over to Jonah and wrap my arm around his waist.

"Jonah's been cross-training with me too," I tell Tyler while squeezing myself tighter against Jonah's rigid torso.

"Why don't you kids go grab a soda in the kitchen?" Mack gives me a pleading look. "I'll be out in a minute."

"C'mon, *sweetie*, let's give them some space." I let go of Jonah's waist and lace my fingers through his icy ones. I pull him into motion.

Tyler doesn't move. He glares down at Jonah as we squeeze by. The door slams closed behind us. Jonah doesn't breathe again until we get to the kitchen.

"I don't know what Mack sees in him," I whisper.

I open up the fridge and dig around. When I close the door again, Jonah's face is still pale. I hold out a can of Pepsi to him.

"She had a cramp in her back. I was releasing the muscle." Jonah pops open the can and takes a big chug. "Did it look that bad?"

"No. Well, okay, yes."

"I'm dead." Jonah runs a hand through his hair. "I am so dead."

We hear Mack's bedroom door burst back open, followed by heavy feet coming down the hallway. Jonah falls into a kitchen chair and pulls me onto his lap like a human shield.

"Oh, hey." Jonah tightens his arms around me. I play my part by nuzzling his neck. Jonah's voice breaks when he says, "So, are you coming to the bout with us tonight, Tyler?"

"Nah. I've got stuff to do." Somehow Tyler—wearing khaki pants and a white polo shirt with the name of the electronics store he's a drone at—manages to take up the entire kitchen.

"C'mon, honey. Granny'll watch Fiona." Mack slips her arm around Tyler's waist. "I'll ask her. She won't mind. They should be back any minute now."

"Nah. I don't want to watch that shit." Tyler snakes his arm around Mack's back, letting his hand rest on her butt. "Come home with me instead."

Mack squirms. "I don't know."

"Derek will get us a six-pack or two. We'll hang and stuff." Tyler pats Mack's butt. "My mom doesn't care if you sleep over. Long as we're quiet."

"But I promised Liv and Jonah . . ."

"You kids don't mind, do you?"

"*I* mind." Mrs. MacIntosh pushes between Mack and Tyler into the kitchen and places Fiona, asleep in her car seat, on the kitchen table. "I have Bunco tonight, Tyler. So you are on Daddy Duty in about . . ." She looks at her watch. "Fifteen minutes."

"But, Granny, Tyler was going to come to the bout with me tonight. Right?" Mack nods at Tyler.

"No, he's not. Tyler's going to man up and take care of his daughter tonight." Mrs. MacIntosh goes to the cupboard and pulls out a canister of formula. "I'm going to take a shower. Your daughter should be awake any minute now. She will expect both dinner and a clean diaper."

Tyler grumbles and runs a hand through his already receding, deep brown hairline. "I have shi . . . stuff to do tonight."

"Not tonight, you don't." Mrs. MacIntosh gives Mack a pointed look. "Annabelle, the derby girls are expecting your support tonight. Get going."

Tyler gives Mack a wounded-puppy face. Pathetic.

Mack starts to cave. "Maybe I should stick around."

"No. You made a promise to Olivia and her ... um ... boyfriend, and we MacIntoshes *honor* our commitments even when they are inconvenient or not what we want to do." Mrs. MacIntosh crams the canister of formula into Tyler's chest until he takes it. "You've worked every day this week, Annabelle. You deserve a break. Speaking of work, isn't today a payday? Pony up, Tyler. Your daughter has almost outgrown all her clothes."

"You see, this month I'm a little tight." Tyler shrinks several feet.

"Unacceptable. If you have enough money for a brand-new truck, then you have enough money to take care of your child." Mrs. MacIntosh steps forward, and Tyler takes a step back. "Do I need to call your mother? Do we need to have another meeting about this? Do I need to get a lawyer involved this time?"

For someone who is barely over five feet tall, there is no doubt in my mind that Granny MacIntosh can—and will—open a can of whoop-ass if you cross her family. Tyler has suddenly managed to shrink to half his original size.

"No, ma'am," Tyler mumbles.

"Well then. If you have a car seat *correctly* installed in your truck, then you may take my great-granddaughter to your house. If not, you will stay here with her until Annabelle gets back from the roller derby bout with her young friends."

"We're gonna go now, Granny." Mack leans over to kiss Fiona, who has somehow managed to sleep through the increasing decibels of the room. Mack yanks me off Jonah's lap and toward the door. "Let's go."

Jonah stumbles two steps behind us. He doesn't even stop to introduce himself to Mack's grandmother or clarify that he's not my boyfriend. He doesn't even call shotgun when we get to Mack's car.

Jonah falls into the back seat. "You have a baby?"

"Yes, that's what can happen when you have unprotected sex." Mack's voice is frequently sarcastic, but for once, it's acidic too. "Who did you think the baby paraphernalia around my house belonged to?"

I punch Mack in the arm.

"Sorry, Choi." Mack takes a deep breath. "Things are a little . . . awkward between Tyler and me right now. And Granny isn't helping."

Jonah scoffs. "I think Granny kinda kicks ass."

"Yeah, she does. Speaking of awkward, what was that in the kitchen?"

Jonah shrugs.

"Self-preservation," I answer for him.

"No," Jonah says too fast. "Okay, maybe a little."

Mack groans. "I want to forget about Tyler and all the other garbage going on in my life right now. I hope Barnacle Barb knocks some heads together tonight. Wish I could be out there with them."

"You'll get there." Jonah puts a hand on Mack's shoulder and squeezes it. "Be patient."

"You know what, Choi?" Mack looks at Jonah in her rearview mirror. "I'm glad you moved to Phoenix instead of Seattle. Your mom was completely right, ya know?"

Jonah and Mack share a laugh. They don't bother to explain their in-joke to me. Before I can ask about Seattle, Mack cranks up Guns N' Roses so loud, the glass in my window vibrates.

Tonight, Jonah sits between Mack and me, so the two of them can compare strategies and complain in tandem about the referees' calls.

"Do you want to share a Pepsi?" I ask Jonah, interrupting his in-depth analysis of the last jam with Mack.

"Nah, I'm good. I shouldn't have had what I did at Mack's. Especially since I can't do a full workout again until Monday," Jonah says before turning back to Mack.

I roll my third-wheel ass all the way to the mini pop-up concession stand and back without them even noticing. By the end of the bout, I have a plan.

"Mack, can I have your keys?" I reach my hand across Jonah, letting my lower arm rest on his thigh. "We'll wait in the car while you congratulate the girls."

Mack puts her keys in my palm. "Sure. Give me about ten minutes."

I push through the crowd toward the door, my plan solidified in my mind. When I get to the front door, though, Jonah is no longer behind me. I backtrack to find him standing next to Mack, high-fiving all the derby girls as they take their final lap. The Pepsi in my stomach turns to acid.

I wait in the car by myself. I don't take my eyeliner armor off. A few minutes later, Jonah slides into the car on the driver's side.

"Hey, you left without me," Jonah says. "Mack'll be here in a minute."

If I'm going to win, I need to pass on the inside. "Do you want to go to the movies tomorrow?"

Jonah's eyebrow pops up. "Wait. Are you asking me out?"

"Yes. I have to work eleven to five tomorrow, but I'm free after that."

Jonah's face falls. "I promised Barnacle Barb I'd train with the Surly Gurlz at the park tomorrow night from six to eight."

"You can't skate."

"I know. I'm going to talk them through a dry land workout. Maybe look at some of their old footage and discuss strategies.

Though if my dad asks, I'm working on a school project at Starbucks with Brandon."

"So, you don't want to hang with me, then?"

"I didn't say that."

"Then come hang with me."

"I can't. I promised. Please don't be mad."

I shrug like I don't care. I hope my act is convincing.

Mack yanks the door open. "Back seat, Choi."

I add *uh-huh*s and noncommittal shrugs to their conversation
as we head for home. We stop at Arby's so Jonah can take his eye
makeup off and change. I come out of the ladies' room to find
Mack sitting with her high school friend, picking at an order of
curly fries. The woman nods, making all fourteen or so earrings
she has tinkle together like wind chimes.

"So, what are you gonna do?" Mack's friend says.

"I don't know. Maybe Granny's right. Oh, hey, Liv. I gotta go,
Shel. Thanks for the fries."

"Hang in there, girl." Shel squeezes Mack's hand before heading back behind the counter.

"Thanks for tonight, guys," Mack says when Jonah returns to
the table in his semi-normal teen form. He hands his boutfit back
to Mack, who tucks it in her backpack. "My house is a little complicated right now."

I steal one of Mack's fries. "Mine too."

I hope my parents have miraculously figured everything out
this evening while I was gone. I doubt we are going to Disneyland,
but I pray things aren't worse than I originally thought.

"Want some fries?" Mack pushes the tray toward Jonah.

He shakes his head. I eat his share.

Jonah calls shotgun when we get back to the car, so I have to
get out of the car again when we stop at the front of his subdivision. Jonah closes his car door before I can get back in.

"I know you're mad at me," Jonah says.

"I'm not mad."

"Okay, disappointed."

I shrug. Disappointed. Dejected. Denied.

Jonah puts his hand on my upper arm. "You still owe me a skate."

Though I want to throw myself into his arms, instead, I say, "Let me know when you have time. Maybe sometime next month? This summer? Next year?"

"Before then. Way before then, I promise." Jonah squeezes my arm before backing away. "This week."

Yeah, I know the likelihood of that happening. I will never be #1 in Jonah's life. I look over at Mack. But can I at least be #2?

Chapter 9

"No fair," Brandon complains at lunch. "My parents never pull me out of school."

Jonah sits at our table, propping up his head with one hand and shoveling chicken and broccoli into his mouth with the other. If he can eat in ten minutes, then he still has time for a power nap on top of his backpack before class starts again.

I slide in on the skater side of our table. I pull out two rice triangles with a strip of seaweed around them.

"Onigiri. Getting in touch with your Japanese side today, Olivia?" Naomi nods with approval.

"Yeah." I hold one up. And it has *nothing* to do with the fact that Japanese sticky rice is the only thing we have left in our house right now. Mom hasn't been anywhere except Sandy the Torturer's this week. I eye Jonah's lunch like an alley cat. Maybe he'll be too tired to finish it.

"Dad is pulling me out before lunch tomorrow so we can get to Denver early," Jonah says. "That way I can get in a practice on Friday before Saturday's race."

"Well, good luck, man. Represent." Brandon puts out his fist to bump.

"Thanks." Jonah bumps him back.

"I guess we'll have to skate together another time." The rice sticks behind my breastbone, intensifying the ache that was already there.

"I'm sorry. Soon. I promise." Jonah plumps up his backpack and puts his head down.

I shrug like I don't care. Jonah quietly snores while I choke down the rest of my lunch. He doesn't even wake up when Erika slides into the table in a complete tizzy.

"O-M-G, I need an intervention here. Should I do the PSAT this spring or wait until junior year next fall?" Erika acts like this is a life-or-death question. "My freshman scores were okay, but that was kind of a throwaway. Just a practice for the real test."

Naomi reads off her phone. "The experts say that you should take the ACT in February and the SAT in March of your junior year."

"Great. Then I don't have to start thinking about it until, say, January of next year," Brandon jokes, but I'm the only one who laughs.

"Lord, help us," Erika says heavenward, though I think Brandon has the right idea.

Naomi taps Erika's arm to get her attention and points at her phone. "You need to take the PSAT next fall if you want to be in the running for the National Merit Scholarship. Maybe do another practice one this spring?"

"I don't know. I'm not a good test taker." Erika chews on her cuticles. "Maybe I should take another prep class over the summer."

"Don't you think you're making too big of a deal about this?" I ask genuinely, but Naomi and Erika both recoil like I dropped an f-bomb.

"Some of us plan to go to a *good* college." Erika looks down her nose at me.

Naomi elbows her cousin. "What she means is that we have

our sights set on the Ivy League. We can't just be good. We have to be the best."

"And I get that," I say. "But you act like getting into Harvard is the equivalent of winning a gold medal. Trust me. It's not."

"Who wants scones tomorrow?" Brandon interrupts what is about to be a scene. "Which do you like better? Cinnamon or chocolate chip? Or wait, cranberry and white chocolate. Yes?"

Erika and I both cross our arms and clamp our mouths shut.

"Cranberry and white chocolate," Naomi chimes in.

She starts an inane conversation with Brandon about some popular TV show teens watch when they aren't giving themselves ulcers over standardized tests. You want an ulcer? Land a two-footed throw triple salchow after a year of training when there is only two-tenths of a point between you and the gold medal.

Erika and I sit in silence for the rest of lunch. Naomi herds Erika out the door as soon as the bell rings. Somehow, Jonah snores on.

"Should we wake him?" Brandon says. "I feel bad for him. Dude looks exhausted. Plus, it's not like he cares about his GPA."

"Just because we're athletes, doesn't mean we're stupid," I say, and Brandon winces. "Our priorities are different. Maybe going to Harvard isn't as all-important as some people like to think it is."

Brandon puts his hands up in front of him. "No shade from me. I could score a 1600 on the SAT, and it wouldn't matter. My parents have already decided that I'm going to ASU and commuting from home to save money. It's more about the potential scholarship money right now than the colleges themselves. 'Everyone goes to college these days, Brandon. Save your money for grad school. That's what makes you special.' We'll see. Maybe I'll take a gap year." He laughs. "That would make their heads explode."

"Erika and Naomi?"

"No, my parents. But them too."

"Five more minutes, Mom." Jonah wipes drool from the corner of his mouth and turns his head to the other side.

"Seriously. Let's leave him and see what happens." A mischievous spark lights behind Brandon's dark brown eyes.

"Go." I push Brandon toward the door. "And I'm fully expecting cranberry scones tomorrow from the famous Brandon Park Test Kitchen." Mostly because I despise cranberries—raisins too—so it will be the easiest to resist. "I'll wake up Sleeping Beauty."

We are late for English. Mr. Balducci introduces us to another high school phenomenon—the late pass.

"It was five seconds," Jonah complains as Mr. Balducci, a stickler for punctuality, closes the door in our faces. "I've won gold medals in less time than that."

"C'mon." I grab Jonah by the elbow and drag him away.

"I say we take the long way to the office and back since our education isn't nearly as important as everybody pretends it is." Jonah's voice crescendos on the last part. Not that I think Mr. Balducci truly cares.

"Stop. It's not worth it." I purposely go left when we should go right.

Jonah continues to grumble as we take a lap around the school. Meanwhile, Erika's words still grind me. I know I'm right. Probably.

"Are you going to college?" I ask Jonah. "Like, right after senior year."

"Not sure. Depends. I know some people can train for the Olympics and go to college at the same time. I'm not sure that's for me though. What about you?"

"What about me?"

"Are you going to train for the Olympics, go to college, or both?"

What if I'm not good enough to do either?

"Not sure. It depends," I say, and Jonah shrugs, because to him, that's a perfectly acceptable answer. He gets me. Even when nobody else does.

After school, Mr. Choi won't let Jonah rollerblade with me to Ice Dreams.

"Are you sure you don't want a ride?" Mr. Choi says as Jonah slides into the BMW. "It's no trouble."

"No, thanks. I'll see you guys there in a bit." I purposely skate the long way to the rink to give the fire raging in my brain since lunch a chance to burn itself out.

When I finally get to the rink, I find three cars in the parking lot. I don't get my normal derby girl intro when I walk in the front door, because there's a party going on instead. One that everybody forgot to tell me about.

GOOD LUCK, JONAH! GO FOR THE GOLD! the banner reads above the snack bar.

"Olivia, there you are. We've been waiting for you." Mom gestures at me to hurry up.

Jonah looks both flattered and embarrassed standing under his banner.

"Let me take another picture." Mom fumbles with her phone. "I want to put it on our Instagram page. See, only the best train at Ice Dreams."

Subtext: *See, Ice Dreams isn't washed up.*

"Olivia, can you move to the right a bit? You're casting a shadow on Jonah."

"Smile, son." Mr. Choi steps in front of me so he can add a few candid shots to Jonah's professional Instagram page that his dad has complete control over. "Why don't you take a selfie while we're at it? Your target audience loves a good selfie. Turn your head to the left, though. That'll hide the pimple on your cheek better."

"Dad!" Jonah puts a hand to his cheek to check, though. Yes, even the Ice Prince breaks out occasionally.

"Take one with Olivia too," Mack suggests. "Your target audience loves a good secret romance."

"Secret romance?" Mr. Choi and Mom say at the same time.

"Don't tag her though." Mack steamrolls on with her idea despite Jonah's and my panicked looks. "Who's that mystery girl with Olympic hopeful Jonah Choi? It'll be good for business. We should re-dye your hair this weekend just in case the paparazzi arrive."

"Can we not?" I say.

"Seriously," Jonah says.

Our parents share another concerned look between them.

"We'd love to add another medal picture to our collection, Jonah. Competitions are so exciting. I've got butterflies. Just like the old days." Mom is genuinely smiling for the first time in weeks. I don't think she's even on heavy-duty painkillers today. Mom turns to me. "Oh, Livy, before I forget, we have a birthday party tonight at seven. Can you do the piñata first before you Febreze the skates? It's in the skate booth."

"Sure. I've got butterflies thinking about it." I can't keep the sarcasm out of my voice.

"Not right this second, silly. We can celebrate Jonah first."

"I appreciate all of this, Ms. Nakashima, but I need to go get changed." Jonah pops a strawberry in his mouth. "Save me some fruit salad for later during my break."

I ignore the fruit salad even though my stomach lets out a roar in protest. I snatch my Ice Dreams jacket off its peg, throw my backpack onto Table #1, and head toward the skate booth. Jonah follows two steps behind me. When I come through the door and around to the counter, Jonah is standing on the other side looking at my podium pictures.

"I don't get butterflies," Jonah says, not taking his eyes off my pictures. "But I have been known to hurl into a trash can on more than one occasion."

I look at the picture Jonah is staring at. My very last gold medal. The last performance we did as juniors with the old, conservative choreography and the old, conservative costumes. The costumes with the feathers made out of fabric.

"You're not kids anymore," Alexei, Mom's very first partner, said when he became our new coach halfway through last season. "If you want to compete on the Senior Grand Prix circuit with the adults, then you must skate like adults. I'll give you all new choreography. Sexy choreography. And a new sexy costume."

Dad was not on board. "She's sixteen, Midori. I don't want her to be sexy."

I'll admit it. I liked the costume. It was sexy. Fiery. Not really me. The illusion panels and sheer cutouts created a sparkly red X across my no-longer-flat chest. Mom hand-sewed more sequins above the low-cut, attached skirt until my belly button was hidden. Sequin flames licked up my body on a diagonal like I was burning. And I did burn. Crashed and burned. And that was *before* the Skate Detroit fiasco.

"That's some outfit." Jonah breaks into my thoughts. "How many chickens had to die for that costume?"

"Don't you need to go change?"

"Fine. I know when I'm not wanted," Jonah jokes, though he's right at the moment.

Jonah walks off, and I find the UPS box with today's piñata inside. I kick the box over and squat to cut it open. Inside is another Skater Barbie. It's always Skater Barbie. The one with the perfect body. And the perfect boyfriend. And the perfect routine that always wins the gold medal. I slump down onto the threadbare carpeted floor. I hate Skater Barbie. Yet, I desperately want to be

her. I cram cheap candy into her empty head. I want the butterflies again.

Thunk.

I look up. Jonah, wearing his skinsuit, has flopped himself
across the counter and is looking down at me. A navy bandana
keeps his hair back.

"I think you're jealous." A smirk pulls across his face.

"Of what?"

"Me."

"Don't flatter yourself. I have no desire to be a speed skater.
Who wants to waste their life skating in large ovals?"

"No, of my talent."

"I have talent. Look to your left. See all the medals in the pictures."

"Then it must be my drive."

"Get off my counter."

"Did I hit a nerve?"

"The only thing that is going to get hit is your overinflated head
with this Tootsie Roll if you don't leave me alone."

"What made you quit?"

I grab a Tootsie Roll and cock my arm back to throw it. Jonah
reaches down and grabs my forearm.

"Okay, okay, never mind. Don't be mad at me," Jonah says as I
try to rip my arm away. "Everybody else wished me luck. So how
come I don't even get a fist bump from you?"

"That's what you came all the way over here to ask me?"

"Yeah." Jonah's hand slides down my arm. The Tootsie Roll
drops from my palm so that Jonah's hand can take its place. "I
don't even get a handshake? Nothing?"

Jonah gently pulls my hand, and I roll up to my knees. Jonah
looks deep into my eyes. Challenging me. I cup the side of his
beautiful face.

"Good luck. Skate fast. Stay balanced."

As I stretch up, Jonah's eyes close. My lips are millimeters from touching his when Jonah's eyes suddenly fly open.

"Get off the counter this instant," Mr. Choi snaps. "What is wrong with you?"

"Sorry. I was talking to Olivia. Never mind." Jonah hops down and waddles off toward the ice.

My head spins when I stand. The butterflies have returned. Mom might have canceled my official Instagram page in August after the trolls were particularly vicious, but I contemplate restarting it. My skating career might have crashed, but I may have landed a secret romance.

It takes me forever to get the piñata done. Mostly because I'm distracted by the phoenix flying around on the ice. Every time he stops, Jonah looks over at me and smiles. I'm melting. I fantasize about stepping up onto his bladed feet, wrapping my arms around his neck, and kissing him until we're standing in a puddle of water in the middle of the rink.

"Livy, are you done yet? I need you to drive me to PT." Mom bursts into my fantasy. "You can finish the boots later. We need to leave within the next five minutes."

Okay, I strip the fantasy down to a simpler version. Me. Jonah. Supply closet.

That doesn't happen either. By the time we get back to the rink after Sandy's latest torture session, the Chois are gone. I won't see Jonah again until Monday.

Good luck. I hope you bring home the gold, I text Jonah. Before I can chicken out, I add, And I want a redo on our last performance.

What have I done?

Chapter 10

By Saturday night, Jonah's continued silence breaks me. I text Egg.

> Hypothetically speaking, if someone doesn't text you back after 24 hours, can you safely assume that they aren't into you?

Maybe. Or they may have lost their phone. Or have the stomach flu. Or be focusing on their big skating competition in Denver this weekend.

> What did Mack tell you?

Everything. Bwah ha ha! And for the record, I think the secret romance internet ploy is a stupid one. Either date or don't. Don't sneak around.

> I'm gonna kill Mack.

And use protection.

> Stuart Trout, we are not going to have this conversation.

Fine. Then talk to Mack about it. And don't
you dare send him nudes.

                                    I regret texting you.

What? I'm your pseudo big brother. It's my
job. Oh, believe me, Jonah and I are going
to have a *chat* when I'm in town. And he
better not be sending you pictures of his
junk.

                                    Aaaaand I'm done here. Time to get
                                    some sleep. Since Jonah is gone this
                                    weekend, I'm taking his ice time to-
                                    morrow morning.

Good. BTW, how's the triple-double-double
coming?

I shift the frozen peas on my hip and lie. Great.

Awesome. I know we only need a double-
double, but I want us to shine. Show them
who we really are.

I would if I knew the answer myself. Sure thing. See you soon!

Monday rolls around, and Jonah and I are still on radio silence.
The hollowness in my chest that I've been walking around with
all weekend becomes cavernous. I slump into our lunch table first
today. I pull out the English essay I never got around to editing
and pretend to work on it as the rest of the table joins me, babbling
on about some new blockbuster movie they saw this weekend. Part
of me is jealous they didn't ask me to go.

"Hey, thanks for all your help, Olivia." Brandon slides in across the table from me. He smacks his chemistry test down in the middle of the table. Mr. Verne has written in green pen, *Well done, Mr. Park. 100/100* in the corner. "I'm going to put this on the refrigerator when I get home."

"You still do that?" Erika says.

"Of course. But only when I'm trying to talk my mom into buying me a new stand mixer."

A shadow falls across my homework. A second later, an eight-by-ten picture of a finely tuned machine wearing a huge smile and a gold medal lands on top of Brandon's test. A shaft of golden light shoots down through the gray clouds that have been following me around all weekend. I leap up and throw my arms around Jonah. I can feel all the muscles in his core contract to keep us from falling over backward onto the grimy cafeteria linoleum. I'm not sure who is more shocked at my behavior, Jonah or the rest of our squad.

"Yeah, I'm not giving you a hug, but congrats, bro." Brandon holds out his fist, and Jonah gives it a solid bump. "Represent."

"Wow. Way to go." Naomi picks up the picture frame.

"So, details," Erika says, looking closely at the picture. "I knew you skated, but this is a whole different side of you."

"This is a whole lot of you." Brandon takes the photo out of Naomi's hands and gives it back to Jonah. "You got guts, bro."

My heart slams around in my chest as Jonah and I sit back down. He never answered my text from last weekend. I'm not sure what to do with that.

"I wish I could show you the race, but I lost my phone somewhere between Phoenix and Denver." Jonah digs out his usual lunch. "My dad had it last on Wednesday, but it must have fallen out of his coat pocket or something."

"So you never got my text?" I say.

"Nuh-uh. What'd it say?"

Naomi's chopsticks stop halfway to her mouth. "Yes, what did it say, Olivia?"

"Nothing. I don't even remember. Good luck or something."

"Thanks." The pause in Jonah's voice gives me hope, but he doesn't press the issue.

Instead of wolfing down his lunch and taking a nap, Jonah gives us a blow-by-blow account of every race he skated on Saturday. Three minutes into his monologue, the non-skaters' eyes glaze over. But I'm there. I remember how a single performance can be burned into your brain for forever. The good and the bad.

This is the senior level, sweetheart. Raw talent is no longer enough.

I shake the thought loose from my brain and give Jonah my attention again.

"You should have seen it, Liv." Jonah is still on his skater's high. I remember that feeling. "We came around the final turn, and I thought I was done for. Not even a third place. But then number two bumped number one, and suddenly the whole front of the pack was a tornado, people spinning out of control. One guy fell right in front of me, and I had to pull up to slide around him." Jonah puts his hand on my knee and a line of fire races up my spine. "Then number one and I almost got tangled in each other's blades. I ended up backward while he face-planted onto the ice. It was possibly the ugliest finish in the history of speed skating, but there you go. First place. I'll take it."

"See, we should skate together more often." I place my hand over Jonah's and squeeze it.

"Agreed."

Naomi is staring at us again. Jonah looks at his picture one last time before putting it into his backpack.

"So, this Saturday, my mom is throwing a party for me. I hope you'll come." Jonah looks at me first, before saying to the rest of the table, "All of you. Please come, or I'll never hear the end of it."

"To celebrate your win?" I say.

"Birthday."

"Cool. I'm in," Brandon says, and Naomi and Erika agree.

I haven't been to a real birthday party since elementary school. The last social event I went to was Mack's baby shower. Not exactly your normal teenage event. Then again, when have I ever been normal?

"You don't have to work Saturday night, do you?" Jonah puts his hand back on my knee. "I'll get Mom to change the date if you can't come. Or better, cancel the whole thing."

"No, I'll definitely be there."

"Cool."

How do girls do this on a regular basis? I've been obsessing over my clothes, my hair, my nails, and my shoes all week. It's one party. I even watched movies about teen parties to see what they look like. Somehow, I don't think it's going to be the same thing. It's not like Jonah knows a lot of people in Phoenix. Unless some of his skater friends come for the weekend. This is going to be a disaster.

Chapter 11

I look over my shoulder when I get to the Chois' Saturday night and wave. Mack—Mom's stunt double for the evening—gives me a thumbs-up from her Toyota. Mack declined her invitation to the party. Not because it would be weird for her to hang out with a bunch of high schoolers, but because she would have had to bring Fiona with her. Yeah, I'm not sure the Chois are quite ready for that yet. Part of me feels bad, but part of me also says it's every woman for herself. I take a deep breath and ring the doorbell.

"I got it, Mom," Jonah yells from the other side of the door.

My heart feels like I've been skating sprints. *Normal. Be normal, Olivia.*

"You came." Jonah's panicked expression relaxes into a smile.

I follow Jonah into his enormous—but currently empty—house. I slide my shoes off and leave them at the front door next to Jonah's Chucks.

My heart hiccups. "The party is tonight, right?"

"Yes. I just wanted you to come early. Before Mom completely loses her sh— Oh, hey, Mom."

"You must be Olivia. Welcome." A middle-aged woman walks in the room carrying a life-size cutout of Jonah in his skinsuit under her arm. She puts Cardboard Jonah down in the middle of the living room.

Jonah cringes. "No, Mom, no."

"What? I'll put a giant *16* over the ad in your hand." Mrs. Choi swoops out of the room, ignoring Jonah's continuing protests.

Jonah rolls his eyes and sighs. "And it begins."

"Oh, I gotta send this to Mack." I pull out my phone, swing an arm around Cardboard Jonah, and take a selfie.

LOL! Mack texts back a second later. Be sure to take a picture WITH the birthday boy too, ok?

Mrs. Choi returns with a Mylar *16* balloon and a *16* cutout. She ties the balloon around Cardboard Jonah's free arm and tapes the *16* over the info bubble sitting on his two-dimensional palm which reads: OH BOY! GET YOUR TOYOTA SERVICED AT OH'S BIG 5 TOYOTA IN ARLINGTON.

"Mom! We are *not* doing this."

Mrs. Choi throws her hands up in defeat. "Fine. Put him in my office, and I'll take him back upstairs later."

"Since you're here early, Olivia, can you give us a hand?" Mrs. Choi gestures at me to follow her to their state-of-the-art kitchen. "The birthday boy's dry land training went too long this afternoon, and now we're all in a tizzy."

"Correction. *You* are in a tizzy." Jonah follows us into the kitchen. "Dad and I were the ones who were fine with *not* having a party."

"Jonah Choi, you will let me have this sentimental moment," Mrs. Choi teases, but then adds seriously, "Please."

Jonah wraps his arm across his mom's shoulders and squeezes her. "Okay. For you."

I always thought Jonah was a carbon copy of his dad. Up close, though, I notice it's his mom who Jonah resembles more. He has her heart-shaped face and slightly larger nose.

"Thank you. Now, stop standing around and help me." When Mrs. Choi hands Jonah two packages of colored napkins, I notice the boulder-size diamond on her long, artistically manicured nails. I put my hands—with my sloppily painted nails and ninety-nine-cent-store rings—behind my back.

"Arrange those decoratively," Mrs. Choi says before swooping out of the room.

Jonah puts them on the kitchen table in two neat piles. I come behind him and fan them out into two colorful arcs.

"That's better." I poke at the Mylar balloon tied to one of the kitchen chairs. "You guys went all out."

Jonah bops the balloon toward me. "Yeah, especially since there will only be five of us, not the fifty my mom prepared for."

I bop it back. "Be a normal teen, Jonah Choi."

Mrs. Choi comes back into the kitchen. She picks up one arc of napkins and places them on top of the other. "That's better. Now, show Olivia what you got on Friday."

"Mooooom," Jonah says, but slips his wallet out of his back pocket. He pulls out a learner's permit.

"Hey, congrats." I take a look at his license and then hand it back. "Good picture, even."

"Do you drive, Olivia?" Mrs. Choi says.

"I have a learner's permit. I hope to get my full license soon."

"See, Jonah, I told you. All your friends at school are going to be driving soon, and I can barely get you behind the wheel. When I was a teen, we couldn't wait to drive. We—"

"Mom, please. Not today. I promise, after the season is over, I'll put more effort into learning how to drive."

"And your school work. Especially English."

"And *this* is why I don't have people over," Jonah jokes, but I suspect there is a kernel of truth in it too.

"Anyway, he's going to need a little more time, Olivia, but then Jonah can take you out. To a dance. Or to the movies. Miniature golf? And not be so serious all the time about skating."

"Mom thinks I'm obsessive about speed skating," Jonah says.

"Who else would take PE when they weren't forced to?" I say.

"See. Listen to Olivia." Mrs. Choi hands Jonah three six-packs of soda. "Here, set these out before the rest of your friends arrive."

She hands me extra-large bags of potato chips, cheese puffs, and Doritos. I see three serving bowls lined up beside a giant white sheet cake with a speed skater airbrushed on top. I rip open the bag of cheese puffs and pour them into a bowl. When Mrs. Choi goes outside into the backyard, I bump Jonah with my hip.

"So what are *you* eating for dinner?" I say.

"Not this crap, that's for sure." Jonah shoves the cans of soda into the tub of ice. "I gotta skate tomorrow morning."

I rip open the potato chips and pour them into a bowl. I stop to test a few of them. "Where's your dad?"

"Pouting upstairs," Jonah says. "We were supposed to go to Salt Lake City this weekend to train with a former Olympian, but Mom said no. She was determined to throw me a birthday party whether I wanted one or not. She even made me skip practice Friday to go party *shopping*." Jonah shudders. "She's going to make me normal if it kills her. And me."

"What exactly *is* normal?"

"I have no idea."

Mrs. Choi pokes her head back into the kitchen. "Olivia, can you bring the hamburger patties out for me? They're in the fridge. Jonah Choi, I've asked you three times today to take the garbage out. Right now, mister."

"Sure, let me grab my shoes," I say, as Jonah groans dramatically.

I'm relieved the Chois don't wear shoes in their house either. That way I don't have to put my fashionable torture devices back on until the very last second. My mouth waters when I pull the platter of high-grade meat patties out of the refrigerator. I head out the French doors into the Chois' enclosed backyard. A gasp sneaks out of my lips. Fairy lights wrap around the bottom of the palm trees and line the barbeque pit area. There's a colored light show going on in the pool, and the water feature in front of their Jacuzzi bubbles like the yoga soundscape mix Mom meditates to. Little *16* signs and centerpieces dot the area along with baby pictures of Jonah.

"Wow, this place is magical." I place the tray next to their shiny, built-in gas grill and try to remember the last time I've been outside in my weed-infested backyard. Everything is so perfect here. Every little detail. I can't decide if I hate the Chois or want them to adopt me.

Mrs. Choi looks over her shoulder. Jonah is still fussing around in the kitchen with the trash.

"I'm so glad that Jonah has you as a . . . friend," Mrs. Choi says in a hushed girlfriend-to-girlfriend voice. "He gets so hyperfocused on his skating that everything else suffers. Schoolwork. Friendships. His health. And when the skating falls apart"—Mrs. Choi's voice drops even quieter—"then he has nothing."

Something pings in me. I know how that works. How it felt. How it feels.

"I'm glad you guys moved here. I like Jonah. We get each other."

Mrs. Choi's face lights up. She squeezes my hand. "I'm glad we did too."

A wave of sound comes out the back door, followed by Brandon Park, who is hopping around trying to get his Nikes back on. Erika and Naomi are behind him, and Jonah brings up the rear. Brandon sees Mrs. Choi and launches into an elaborate greeting in Korean. Mrs. Choi continues the conversation, but you can tell by the blank look on his face that Brandon has already used up his entire Korean vocabulary. To break the awkward silence, Brandon holds out a paper plate with tinfoil on top. When he pulls back the edge, a wisp of cinnamon-sugar steam sneaks out.

"What are they?" I put a hand on my stomach to stifle the growl.

"Hotteok," Jonah and Brandon say at the same time.

"It's like a yeasty pancake with brown sugar syrup inside." Jonah pulls back the tinfoil some more until I can see the pile of thick, palm-size pancakes on the plate. "Halmeoni—Grandma, Mom's mom—used to make them for me every Saturday morning before practice when we lived in Arlington."

I'm guessing Mrs. Choi is giving Brandon a big Korean thank-you. He keeps bobbing up and down, saying something.

"I'm going to put these inside to keep them warm. You kids make yourself at home." Mrs. Choi crinkles the foil closed again and darts into the house with a big smile on her face.

"Happy Birthday, Jonah." Erika gives Jonah a side hug and hands him an envelope.

"Happy Birthday, Jonah." Naomi also gives Jonah a side hug and hands him an envelope.

"Happy Birthday, Jonah." Brandon hands over an envelope and then puts out his fist. "Yeah, I'm not going to hug you, bro."

"Yeah, not going to happen." For once Jonah bumps his fist with enthusiasm. "And thanks, everybody."

Crap! You don't wrap gifts and hand them to people anymore? I spent two hours yesterday designing and making the perfect mix tape of new skating music for Jonah. Mack even sacrificed one of her Guns N' Roses cassette cases so I could slide the thumb drive inside to make it look more authentic. Now it seems both cheap and stupid. I'll give it to him later. Or never. Can I go home now?

"Dude, this is an awesome sound system, but this music has got to go." Brandon fiddles around with the state-of-the-art entertainment system on their porch. He pulls up the satellite feed for a music channel on their outside TV. Who has an outside TV?!

"Awwww, you were so cute." Naomi picks up one of the picture frames littered around the backyard. "Look how chubby you were."

Jonah colors and lets out a nervous laugh. "Um, yeah. Can I have that, please?"

Jonah flies around his backyard, picking up all the picture frames. I pick up the gold frame on the plant stand next to me.

"Hey! Isn't this the *Dancing with the Stars* guy?" I flip the picture around so the rest of them can see.

"Hey, I remember him. He and Julianne Hough won the mirror-ball trophy their season," Naomi says. "Isn't he an athlete or something?"

Jonah looks like somebody has stabbed him in the chest. "That *Dancing with the Stars* guy has eight Olympic medals in short-track speed skating. That's more medals than any other Winter Olympic athlete. Apolo Ohno is like a speed-skating god."

Crickets.

"One day, Apolo Ohno is going to ask to take pictures with you," I say and the others thankfully agree with me. The party is saved!

Jonah squeezes my hand as he takes the picture frame away from me. When he gets to the door, Jonah stops, trying to balance the pile against his chest while turning the doorknob. All the frames start to slide. I save Apolo Ohno from sudden doom on the pavers below and put the picture next to the high-end birthday cake with my favorite speed skater airbrushed on top.

"Olivia." Jonah reaches for the picture again.

"What? Don't you know that Apolo Ohno is a speed-skating god?" I wrap my hand around Jonah's wrist to stop him. "And the guy standing next to him isn't too bad of a skater either."

A smile cuts across Jonah's face. He leaves the picture alone.

Mrs. Choi comes back out into the backyard while tying an apron around her waist. "Let's get this party started!"

She does a little "raise the roof" kind of dance to whatever pop song Brandon has found. I chuckle at the horrified expression on Jonah's face.

"Mom! Please." Jonah shakes his head.

"Fine." Mrs. Choi still bops around to the catchy tune as she fires up the grill. "Who wants a hamburger?"

The party downgrades from there. Jonah and I both try to be normal, but I don't think he's been to a party since elementary school either. Thankfully, Brandon knows exactly what to do.

"Really? You two haven't seen *Street Fight Race 5*? Not even the first one? Have you been living under a rock?" Brandon stuffs more Doritos in his mouth.

"No. Just training and competing," Jonah says, like this is a valid excuse.

I shrug. "I don't have cable."

"You two are seriously deprived." Brandon plops down on the overstuffed outdoor couch between Naomi and Erika. He swings an arm around each of the girls' shoulders. "*SFR6* opens next month right before winter break starts. We should go to the midnight opener. We may have to stop for Venti Frappuccinos before the movie, but it'll be worth it. Who's game?"

Naomi leans into Brandon. "I'm in."

Erika leans away from Brandon until he removes his arm. "It depends. Exam time always wipes me out."

"Olivia?" Brandon says.

"Um, maybe." If Jonah is going. I'm not going to be all third-wheelish without him, though.

"Choi?"

"Probably not. It depends on how my season is going." Jonah swirls the ice around in his cup of water.

"Well, I'm goin'. I even got my shirt today." Brandon points to the design on his chest. I'm guessing it's the logo for the movie, but it looks like a bunch of nothing, plus a woman with enormous boobs to me. "On sale today at Hot Topic for $19.99. Score!"

Who pays twenty bucks for one T-shirt? My whole outfit—jeans, lacy blouse, sandals, and leather coat—costs less than Brandon's shirt. Granted, I got the jeans, blouse, and sandals from Goodwill, and Mack gave me her old high school real leather coat, but still. I pull my awesome coat tighter around me. It's too big, but it makes me feel fierce.

"So you've never seen *SFR*, you don't go to midnight movies, and I noticed that your ancient gaming console in the living room has dust on it. What exactly do you do for fun?" Brandon removes his arm from around Naomi so he can dive into the Doritos bowl again. Her smile fades.

"I skate," Jonah says.

Mrs. Choi stands at the gas grill, shaking her head.

"Then come over. We'll stay up all night and have an *SFR* marathon." Brandon licks the electric-orange powder off his fingers. "Bring a case of Pepsi and a couple bags of Doritos, and we're set. Insta-fun."

Mrs. Choi stops cooking. Jonah and I exchange a panicked look. Brandon is about to blow our roller derby cover.

So I say the first thing that pops into my head, "The Winter Dance is coming up soon at school. Anybody want to go?"

Jonah shoots me a *what the hell?!* look. I shrug.

"You should all go together." Mrs. Choi puts a heaping plate of hamburgers in front of us, and we all dive in. Jonah removes the buns—too many simple carbs!—from two of the hamburgers and hands them back to his mom. "Jonah is a good dancer. He used to take a hip-hop dance class."

Jonah chokes on his bite of hamburger patty.

"My SUV can carry seven people. I'm happy to drive you all to the dance." Mrs. Choi's face lights up. "Then you can come back

here. Maybe watch a movie? You could have dinner here before
you go. I'll put it on the calendar."

"Mom. *Mom!* We'll get back to you. Besides, I think it's the
same weekend I go to Utah," Jonah says.

"We'll look at the calendar and then decide." Mrs. Choi wipes
her hands off on her apron. "Is there anything else you kids need?"

"We're good, Mom. Really."

We wait until Mrs. Choi is safely inside before we all pounce
on Jonah.

"Hip-hop dance?" Erika says.

"Hey, I've got moves too," Brandon says.

"Have you heard Epic Danger's new single?" Naomi says. "It's
good to dance to."

"I warm up to it," I say, and Naomi gives me an approving nod.
"Did you like their first single?"

"I *loved* it!"

I got this. I so got this. Halfway through the party, Brandon
talks Jonah into dusting off his gaming system and bringing it
outside. While Brandon connects it to the outside TV, Jonah tries
to figure out how to start a fire in the fire pit.

"Here. Let a Girl Scout show you how to do it." Naomi puts out
her hand, and Jonah deposits what's left of the full box of matches
he started with into her palm. Naomi reconfigures the logs and
kindling. She starts the fire with a single match.

"And that's how it's done, my friends." Naomi wipes her hands
off on her jeans.

"Thanks for the fire, cavewoman." Brandon waves a controller
at Naomi. "You have earned the right to be the first victim . . .
I mean, person . . . to have their ass handed to them tonight by
yours truly."

"Don't be so sure." Naomi slides onto the puffy outdoor couch
next to Brandon. "I played this game religiously during fifth grade."

Later, despite Jonah's protests that we don't need to sing to him, Mrs. Choi insists that Jonah and his dad both participate in the birthday cake ritual. We each receive an enormous slice of chocolate cake covered with fluffy white frosting. If Mrs. Choi doesn't stop feeding me, I am seriously never going home. I may slip into a carb coma later, but I enjoy every chocolate crumb of the real bakery cake. When Brandon swoops in for thirds, I notice that Jonah has cut his cake into smaller and smaller pieces, but none of it appears to have made it into his mouth. Meanwhile, it's taking all of my self-control not to lick my plate. I follow Jonah into his house to throw away my plate before I cave. I happily kick off my blister-inducing sandals at the back door next to Jonah's Chucks.

"You know a little frosting won't kill you," I say as Jonah dumps his entire piece of cake into the trash can. "You ate all of your vegetables with your bunless hamburgers. You've managed to stay strong against your archnemesis, Pepsi. How about getting on the normal train with the rest of us? You too could have orange fingers." I wiggle my cheese-puff-stained fingers at him. "And that was possibly the best cake I have ever eaten. You are missing out, my abnormal friend."

"Just because I don't want to eat cake doesn't make me abnormal."

"When it's your own birthday cake, yeah, it does."

Jonah shrugs. I look out the window. Now that most of us have a good sugar buzz going, Brandon has challenged Naomi to a rematch in an attempt to soothe his bruised ego. I don't think they realize we're gone. Then again, that pretty much sums up my entire high school experience so far.

Jonah pokes at the tinfoil-covered plate sitting on the kitchen counter. "Mom, can we eat the hotteok?"

"Sure. Leave one for me, though, and one for your dad," Mrs.

Choi yells over whatever K-drama she's watching in the living room.

Jonah pulls one of the pancake things off the heavy paper plate and hands it to me. I take a cautious bite. A warm syrup of brown sugar and cinnamon covers my tongue.

"This is sooooo good." Some of the syrup dribbles onto my chin. "Maybe even better than the cake."

"Can I have a bite?"

"Get your own."

"One bite."

"Jonah, it's your birthday. Live a little."

Jonah takes a hotteok and slowly eats it, making sure I watch him take every single bite. "Hotteok are really good straight off the griddle with a big glass of milk. Halmeoni's are better, but these are pretty good. If I throw up tomorrow morning from all these simple carbs, I'm blaming you."

"One night, Jonah. For one night, try to be normal."

"Fine." Before I can process what's happening, Jonah leans in and presses his lips against mine. They are soft and warm and everything I hoped they would be. "I found my phone. I got your text."

Jonah looks at me. Challenging me. I accept. I step toward Jonah and relevé up on my tiptoes. Instead of his eyes closing, though, Jonah's eyes get bigger.

"Those hotteok smell so good." Mrs. Choi steps into the kitchen and immediately turns back around. "Aaaand, I will have one later."

Jonah retreats out the back door. I follow, two steps behind him.

"Who wants to play me next?" Naomi shakes the controller above her head triumphantly.

Chapter 12

At 9:00 p.m. everybody's mom shows up, except mine. Not even my mom-stunt-double, Mack.

"I know you didn't say nine," I whisper to Jonah as everyone thanks Mrs. Choi.

Jonah gives me a conspiratorial smile. He leaves to thank people for their gifts again and for coming over and says, "Let's do it again soon," and all the social niceties. Brandon insists on one last selfie with Cardboard Jonah, who magically reappeared in the living room again during the evening.

"Mom, can we give Olivia a ride home later?" Jonah asks when everybody else is out the door. "And can you watch your show upstairs so we can watch a movie or something?"

"Yes, and of course." Mrs. Choi squeezes Jonah's arm, trying to contain her enthusiasm. "Is eleven o'clock past your curfew, Olivia? We don't want to get you into trouble."

"I'm sure it's fine." My mom is probably already passed out on the couch anyway. "I'll text her." Or her stunt double.

As Mrs. Choi heads upstairs, Jonah sits on one side of their long leather couch, and I sit on the other. He turns on the state-of-the-art TV—would there be anything else in this house?—and scrolls through a dozen channels. One of them has an ice dancing competition on, but he doesn't stop.

Jonah looks down the length of the couch. "You can make yourself at home."

"In that case." I lean over and grab the remote control from him and turn the channel back to the ice dancing competition. It's the NHK Trophy live from Sapporo, Japan. The Carter Cousins are up next. My stomach is a jumble of emotions. If we had nailed Skate Detroit and proved to the USFSA rep that we were on our way back up, then Egg and I could have kept our Skate America assignment. Maybe we could've politicked our way into the NHK Trophy this weekend. The camera focuses in on Jonathan Carter's gorgeous face. The face I once famously embarrassed myself on national TV fangirling over even though Jonathan doesn't know—or care—that I'm alive.

"You can put your feet up." Jonah pats the throw pillows beside him, bringing me back to Phoenix and my new reality.

I take him up on his offer. "I usually keep a hot guy around to massage my calves on Saturday nights, especially after I had to teach four . . . count 'em, *four* . . . skater-wannabe private lessons this morning. I also did an hour of conditioning with Mack this afternoon, and the hardest part of all"—I point to my sandals with the three-inch heels that I deposited at the front door after we all came back inside—"I've been wearing those stupid shoes all night in an attempt to look like a normal party girl."

"See, I'm telling ya. Normal is overrated."

I nestle down into the pile of throw pillows on my side of the couch. Though I was joking about the massage, Jonah takes my right heel in one hand and presses my toes back with his other hand until I feel the stretch in my Achilles tendon. Then, he makes little circles with his thumbs, up the muscles from my ankle to my knee. A sound escapes my lips that resembles a purr. I clear my throat.

"I was kidding, but you are hired, effective immediately. Are you available most Saturday nights?"

Jonah laughs and puts my right leg down. I lift my left leg toward him. He continues.

"Ahhhh." I lean back and attempt to tune back into the ice dancing competition, but I can't focus. Who knew there were so many nerve endings in ankles? All of them are firing messages up my legs at a frantic pace.

The announcers bellow first in Japanese and then in English, "On the ice, representing Australia, Melinda Carter and Jonathan Carter!"

Jonah watches their whole performance without comment. Only when the announcers start to pick apart their flawless routine does he remember I'm in the room. "How come they didn't do any big tricks like you and Stuart do . . . did?"

"Because they're ice dancers not figure skaters. There's a difference. Different rules. Different styles. The British are up next. They might not be as technically accurate, but they'll have the crowd."

And, of course, I'm right. The British team doesn't have the wild, Cirque du Soleil-ish lifts and balances like the Australians, but the pair has chemistry. A heat that makes me want to trade Egg in for a British model.

When their scores come up, Jonah is indignant. "What? The Australians were robbed."

"Ice dancing isn't about the stunts. It's more artistic. It's about chemistry. It's hard to have convincing chemistry when your partner is also your cousin."

"Ew. What about you and Stuart? It looked like you had something going on in that video at lunch."

The USFSA rep's words sting me. *This is the senior level, sweetheart. Raw talent is no longer enough.*

Jonah mistakes my silence as a confession. "So is he gonna beat my ass after what happened in the kitchen?"

"What? No. Egg is like my brother. Believe me, we have no chemistry." Which was the problem.

"Do we have chemistry?"

"No, but we do have English and lunch." I sit up and put my fist out for Jonah to bump. He lets it hang in the air. "C'mon, you know you walked right into that one."

Instead of bumping my fist, Jonah's fingers encircle my wrist. He slides me across the leather couch until we're sitting side by side with only the squashed throw pillow between us like a chaperone. He lets go of my wrist and drops his hand back into his lap.

"What chemistry these two have," the male announcer on TV says of the British team. "Do you believe the rumors swirling around that they might be more than just partners on the ice?"

"I don't know, Jim," the female announcer says. "But the way these two melted the ice tonight with this sizzling routine, I wouldn't doubt it."

When the competition breaks for another commercial, I slide my hand over the throw pillow wall and lace my fingers through Jonah's.

"Okay, that is creeping me out." Jonah looks over his shoulder where Cardboard Jonah stands staring at us. He grabs the throw pillow and hurls it at the cutout. Cardboard Jonah takes a header into the floor. "Situation solved."

Jonah pulls me in closer, wrapping one muscular arm around me. And this time, it isn't for self-preservation. I melt into Jonah. His long-sleeved T-shirt is soft against my cheek. He took Mack's advice and spritzed with the piney scent tonight. His fingertips gently slide up and down my bare forearm as the competition comes back on. There is definitely a chemical reaction going on. Especially when he turns his head and his warm lips brush my temple.

"Are you cold?" he says.

All I can say is "Mmpf."

Jonah takes that as a yes and reaches toward the adjacent chair to grab the blanket off it. I feel all the muscles in the fine-tuned machine stretch and contract.

Seriously, he needs a blanket? I'm about to have a core meltdown right here.

"You're cold because you have about two percent body fat," I say, as he flicks the blanket over top of us.

"Twelve percent."

"Not normal."

Jonah snuggles back down on the couch and draws me closer until my head rests on his chest. I tuck my legs up and lean into him even more. Underneath the blanket, Jonah finds my hand again. He laces his fingers through mine and places our hands on his chest.

"Normal," he says.

I bring my other hand up underneath his T-shirt until my palm rests over his heart. Despite our inactivity, Jonah's heart pounds like he's been doing sprints.

"Not normal. I can feel all the muscles under your skin. I can count each part of the six-pack. One. Two." My fingertips slide down his torso, finding each individually defined muscle. Jonah stops breathing. "Three. Four."

Jonah's right hand wraps around my wrist and pulls my hand away from his stomach. Our hands stay out to the side like he doesn't want me to touch him. I decide to pass him on the inside. I press into Jonah and take back what he gave me in the kitchen, and then some.

"Now *that* was normal."

"I can do better," Jonah says.

I tuck the curtain of hair behind Jonah's ear. "Prove it, Ice Prince."

Jonah pushes me gently down on the couch until his whole body presses into mine. A thousand points of contact send electrical bursts up my spine. When Jonah's lips find mine, the blanket becomes completely unnecessary.

"Normal," he says a few minutes later when we both remember to breathe again.

"Chemistry," I say in between brown-sugar-and-cinnamon-hotteok kisses.

Those are the last words we say for a long time. If the floor above us hadn't squeaked, I'm sure we would have normalled all night long. Sometimes I forget that Jonah has parents. Parents who are in his business 24/7/365.

"Jonah, it's almost eleven," Mrs. Choi's voice echoes from the top of the stairs like she's giving us a warning. Which we needed. We untangle ourselves, and I spring to my feet, smoothing my clothes out as I go. "We better get Olivia home. Come out the front door. I'll pull the car out of the garage."

Mrs. Choi chuckles as she passes through the living room a minute later. The scene looks worse than it is. Jonah sits chastely on the couch, his eyes closed, as I scoop decorative pillows off the floor and hurl them back onto the couch. I walk to the front door and squat down to strap on my high-heel torture devices. When I stand back up, Jonah is behind me. He wraps his arms around my waist and pulls me into him until his chin rests on my shoulder.

I fold my arms over his. "Happy sixteenth birthday, Jonah."

"Thank you." Jonah's lips brush my ear and travel across my cheek. "I got exactly what I wanted."

"You didn't think my mix tape idea was dorky?" I had caved when Erika insisted that Jonah open his gifts. I'm the only one who didn't give him a generic Target gift card. I'm not sure if that means my present was better or worse, though. "I thought you'd appreciate some new music to skate laps to."

"Not what I was referring to." Jonah's lips travel from my cheek to the corner of my mouth. "But thanks for that too."

"Oh. Then you're welcome. Very welcome." I rotate in Jonah's arms and loop my arms around his neck.

We perfect our new making-out technique to gold medal standards. At least until Mrs. Choi beeps her car horn. She smiles when Jonah climbs in the back with me instead of calling shotgun. He holds my hand all the too-short way home. He even walks me to my door.

"You know I'm going to skate like crap tomorrow," he says.

"Too many simple carbs?"

"That, and I doubt I'm going to be able to sleep now."

"Why? You didn't even have half a Pepsi."

"You don't get it." Jonah leans in and gives me a short hug because his mother is watching. "But that's okay."

Jonah waits until I'm inside with the door locked before he leaves my doorstep. I wave out the window to them. Mrs. Choi beeps back.

I'll let the Chois in tomorrow. You sleep in. I attach the note to Mom's keys.

Sleep. Right. I spend most of the night replaying our performance on the couch. I give it a perfect score. Then I finally get it. We don't do anything at 50 percent. It's all or nothing.

I'm in deep trouble.

Chapter 13

I skid into Ice Dreams at 9:00 a.m. on the dot Sunday morning. The BMW is already waiting for me. Jonah's at the door before I can even dig my rink keys out of my backpack.

"You didn't sleep much last night," Jonah says more as a statement than a question. "You've got dark circles under your beautiful eyes."

"You do too."

"It was worth it." Jonah holds the door open for me after I unlock it. "Even if I'm going to pay for it today."

I bring my fingertips to my lips and slap a kiss on Mom and Dad's poster as I pass in front of them. As I slide my Ice Dreams jacket off its peg, I watch Jonah walk straight for the locker rooms, his skate bag slung across the body with only 12 percent body fat. The body that was pressed up against mine less than twelve hours ago. The body that ignites mine just looking at it. He glances over his shoulder and gives me a knowing smile. I hang my jacket back up. I definitely don't need it right now.

I clean skate boots while Jonah does his warm-up. I would do homework, but I don't have enough brain cells firing to even hold a pencil in a believable way.

"Okay, that's twenty-five. Come take a break," Mr. Choi yells across the ice.

Jonah skates over to his dad and talks to him. Finally, Jonah nods and comes off the ice. I put the skate I've probably cleaned four times now back on the shelf and decide to take a break too. After Mr. Choi goes into the locker room, I intersect Jonah at Table #1. He slides off his gloves and pulls a box out of his soft-sided cooler. He pushes it to my side of the table.

"No offense, but I can't do hard-boiled eggs this morning," I say.

"Open it."

When I pop open the lid, a cinnamon-brown-sugary smell wafts out. To my horror, my stomach roars.

"Mom was in such a good mood this morning that she got up extra early to make hotteok before my practice, just like Halmeoni used to. I even ate one. Two, actually. She made these for you."

I try to eat one politely and delicately, but I'm starving, and these sweet pancakes are freakin' awesome.

"Oh! These are even better than the ones Brandon made. In fact, if your mom wants to make this a weekly habit, I would be totally on board with that." I snarf down another one.

Jonah looks over his shoulder and then leans across the table to kiss me.

"Good morning," I say when he breaks away.

"Good morning to you too."

"Come with me. Right now."

"What? Where?"

I grab Jonah's hand, and he stumbles after me in blade-guarded skates to the supply closet. As soon as the door is closed, I launch myself at him, our lips connecting like I've wanted them to all morning. As our kiss deepens, Jonah reaches down and pulls me up against him until I'm standing on the tops of his skates. He tilts his upper body back against the door for stability and pulls me in even closer. Cool fingertips glide underneath the back of my T-shirt and up my spine, adding fuel to the fire already burning in my belly. I pull the zipper of Jonah's skinsuit down to mid-chest, and a wave of heat rolls off the bare skin underneath. Jonah's breath hitches when I slide my cold hand underneath the fabric.

"Jonah? Son?" Mr. Choi passes by on the other side of the door. Crap.

I don't open the door until I hear Mr. Choi's feet on the linoleum of the snack bar. I take a deep breath and walk out of the supply closet like the hormonal inferno with his son never happened. I hope my performance is convincing.

"Thanks, Jonah. I didn't want to drop that box of . . . uh . . . cleaning solution on my head while trying to get it down. Glad to have such a tall guy around to help me out." I hope Mr. Choi can't see the stepstool sitting inside the doorframe like I can.

After a few beats, Jonah comes out of the closet, a case of toilet paper in front of him and his skinsuit zipped back up. He waddles over to Table #1 with it, tosses it on the table, and immediately sits down. He grabs his water bottle out of the cooler and chugs.

"Couldn't that have waited until after practice?" Mr. Choi says.

"Nope. She needed me right now," Jonah says.

"True." I give Jonah a look that makes him grab his bottle of water and chug some more.

"Five hundred in 44.7 or less, five times." Mr. Choi sits down at Table #1 with us. "We need to go for consistency. That's what the scout said."

"I can do it." Jonah jumps to his feet.

"Son, please," Mr. Choi says. "We're not in that big of a hurry."

Jonah leaves his skate guards on the wall and takes off for the center of the ice. "I am."

Jonah is at the starting cone before his dad even has a chance to dig the stopwatch out of his bag.

"Who knew?" Mr. Choi says with a chuckle.

"Who knew what?" I say.

"That you were the secret weapon."

"Excuse me?"

"We agreed earlier that if Jonah can do five hundred meters in 44.7 seconds or less five times in a row, then he gets to spend the rest of today's practice 'training' with you. I'm not sure what that entails, but if it motivates him to skate cleaner, good enough."

Mr. Choi's comment cuts me. I'm not some empty-headed, talentless fangirl distracting his son. I can't wait for Jonah to finish so I can show Mr. Choi who I am and what I do.

The rest of the morning flies by, but Jonah doesn't make his goal. He can't get past #4 no matter how hard I pray. I look at the clock. It's 10:45 a.m. Ernie usually Zambonis the ice at 11:00 a.m. And Mack is always early for her shift. The open skating session starts at noon. I look back at the ice where Jonah is crouched down again. I can tell he's tired. My heart sinks. We aren't going to get to skate together. *Again.* The air horn goes off, and I jump.

"C'mon, son, pick it up. You can do it," Mr. Choi yells from the wall. "Little faster. This is #5."

"Go, Jonah! You can do it!" I know Mom told me not to interfere with Jonah's training, but I can't help it. This is as much for me as it is for him.

Jonah flies down the back straightaway like he's on fire. He comes around the second turn, his fingertips dropping to the ice. The same fingertips that traced lines of fire up and down my back when we were in the supply closet.

"Please make it. Please make it," I chant under my breath.

Disaster strikes. Jonah's inner foot slips, and he hits the ice hard. He slides out of control across the ice and crashes into the padding. The thud echoes around the silent rink. I drop the skate I was cleaning and rush to the side of the boards nearest where I think Jonah collided.

"Are you okay?" I say.

"I blew it. Again. Again!" He slams his fists on the ice.

"You okay, son?" Mr. Choi puts his hand over the side, but Jonah doesn't take it.

With a groan, Jonah sits up and takes his helmet off. He rubs his left temple. He chucks his helmet at the boards. It ricochets back at him.

"Tell you what. You worked hard today." Mr. Choi tucks his clipboard under his arm. "Much harder than I thought you would, especially after last night. Let's call it a day."

"No. I want to skate," Jonah says, standing up.

"Don't overdo it, son. We just got you healed."

"No, I want to skate with Olivia."

"Give me two minutes." I sprint to the skate counter.

Mr. Choi obviously thinks we're goofing around because by the time I have my skates laced up, he's playing around on his phone and drinking coffee at Table #1. But that's because he doesn't know who I am. Or what I do.

"Now skating for the American team, Olivia Kennedy! And the crowd goes wild." Jonah makes a fake crowd sound.

Mr. Choi looks up. Just to show off, I skate backward, prepping for my easiest jump—the triple toe loop. I can do doubles in my sleep, so I have no problem landing this one. Jonah whistles when I finish. I slice to a stop next to him.

"Get it, gurrrl!" Mack yells from next to Mr. Choi at Table #1.

Somebody should tell Mr. Choi to pick his jaw up off the table, because we are just getting started.

"Okay, Ice Prince, let's show 'em what you got. Same trick as before."

"But my blades."

"Dude, you know my blades are super sharp too, right?" I step into Jonah and lower my voice. "So, you wanna play it safe and stay away from me, or do you want to live dangerously and be close to me?"

Jonah strips off his gloves and tucks them in the top of his skinsuit.

He takes my hand. "I promise not to fall."

Nobody plans to fall, but I keep that to myself. I pull Jonah into motion. We skate one lap around the rink before I flip around. As we come into the turn, I nod. Just like the last time, we find our counterbalance effortlessly. We ease farther and farther into the ice as we spiral until both of us can glide our outside hands on top of the ice. Jonah looks over at me. His smile must be mirroring mine.

There is definitely a chemical reaction going on because Mack hoots loudly from the side. Egged on, I decide to take a chance.

"You want to learn a new trick?" I say when we come back up. Jonah nods. "Remember the arabesque spiral Egg and I do? The one with the airplane wings?"

"Yeah, but I'm no ballerina. My leg isn't going to do that. And then there is the blade situation."

I sit in my hip and give Jonah a look that says: "Playin' it safe or embracing the danger?"

"Airplanes it is," he says as we push off around the rink.

To his credit, Jonah does attempt an arabesque. It's low and wobbly and threatens to take both of us out. Jonah's bright smile is replaced with a grimace.

"We didn't nail the hydroblade the first time either, remember." I squeeze Jonah's cold hands. "And don't be afraid to lean into me a little bit for support. Let me help you stay balanced."

"You already do."

My fingers might be icy, but my heart is melting.

Our arabesques are still low, but they're solid. The natural curve of Jonah's blade causes us to do a spiral around the rink without even trying.

Jonah tempts fate by saying, "We got it!"

We stay on our feet this time. My heart soars. We don't let go of each other, even after our momentum dies and we stutter to a stop. I wish I could find this with Egg or even another partner. This unbridled joy. This reminder of why I skate.

"Woo, girl. You gotta see this." Mack waves her phone at us from Table #1.

Mr. Choi's jaw is still on the table. We skate hand in hand over to the wall in front of Table #1.

"Did I miss something last night?" Mr. Choi says.

Jonah and I look at each other and smile conspiratorially. *Yes, you most certainly did.*

"Are you planning on switching sports now?" Mack asks Jonah.

"Nah. But I want to continue cross-training with Olivia, Dad." Jonah looks at me with his deep brown eyes, and it threatens to melt me on the spot. "She keeps me balanced."

No, Jonah keeps *me* balanced.

Chapter 14

"Look what I have." For once, Naomi is the last one to appear at lunch. She puts a light blue flier in the middle of the table.

We all lean in to look. The flier announces the Winter Dance coming up in two weeks.

"So, we're going?" Naomi nods at us when we don't immediately answer. "Yes?"

The five of us stare at one another, waiting for someone to make the decision.

Naomi cracks first. "Come on, guys. Show some school spirit."

"Some of us apparently have mad dance moves." I look at Jonah. "Some of us even took hip-hop lessons."

Jonah groans. "Can we please pretend like my mom never said that?"

"Wouldn't it be weird to go without a date?" Brandon pulls the flier toward him.

"Then *ask* someone," Erika says pointedly.

"What if she says no?"

"She won't. And if she does, she's an idiot, and you should come with us anyway." I give Naomi a pointed look too.

"There actually is a competition in Utah that weekend," Jonah says, and my stomach drops.

"We should go shopping this weekend." Naomi grabs Erika's arm. "And make plans to get our nails done."

I want to be interested in their talk of dresses and hairstyles, but my mind is on the ice. I watched Mack's video at least two hundred times. That girl with the softer, curvier body and her lean, strong partner heating up the ice. I look over at Jonah, and my heart threatens to burst out of my chest.

At the end of lunch, it's Naomi who straggles behind. She grabs my arm to keep me in the hallway after Erika and the guys go into English.

"So, are you and Jonah, like, a *thing* now?" Naomi's eyes sparkle.

"Um, maybe?" How can one ambiguous word carry so much weight?

Naomi squeals and stomps her feet. "Then he better get out of going to that competition and take you to the dance. That's what a *real* boyfriend would do."

"Jonah needs to skate. It's an important race for him."

"Jonah needs to give you his attention. You're not going to wait around forever for him."

I suspect we're talking about Brandon now instead of Jonah. "Um, yeah, we'll see. It's only a dance."

"What planet are you on? It's not *a* dance. It's *the* dance. At least for sophomores."

"Sure. Okay."

"I don't know how I'm going to be able to concentrate for the next two weeks." Naomi flutters off, mumbling, "So much to do. So much to do. Hair. Nails. Dress. How am I going to find the time?"

When I walk into English, Jonah stops talking to Brandon as I pass them and smiles. I smile back. *A thing.* None of the others get it, but we do. This is our normal. Even when it sucks occasionally.

Before class starts, Brandon finally gets up the courage to ask the girl in question to the Winter Dance. And Rhea Martinez says, "No." Loudly. Publicly. Emphatically. And in front of Naomi.

A huge black cloud descends over the room, especially when Mr. Balducci calls for everyone to buddy up. Naomi ditches her normal partner, Brandon, for Erika's usual partner, Davina. Erika, in turn, gives Brandon and Naomi both the stink eye as she is forced to walk around the room trying to break up somebody else's pair. Eventually, she's stuck with Brandon anyway. It's so painfully awkward that even Jonah notices.

"If this is being normal, I'm gonna take a pass." Jonah puts his hand on my lower back and ushers me out of class after the bell rings. "In skating, you either win or lose. You shake hands. You move on. None of this unnecessary drama."

Nobody brings up the dance again. In fact, Naomi doesn't talk to Brandon at all for a solid week, which is awkward when they still sit on the same side of the table with Erika between them as a human shield. Thanksgiving break comes and goes, giving me hope that all the drama has burned out. But when Monday rolls around again, life throws another curveball at our squad. I somehow missed that our school has a time-honored tradition right before the dance that involves the giving and receiving of flowers. And people act like their lives depend on it.

"Where's Naomi?" I say on Flower Day when everyone assembles at lunch.

Brandon, who is carrying around a white carnation with a sparkly silver ribbon tied to it, pulls at the neck of his T-shirt. "Yeah. I need to say thanks."

"For what?" Jonah digs into his usual boring lunch with his spork.

"The flower." Brandon winces. "Why didn't you guys tell me that Naomi has a crush on me?"

Erika smacks her forehead. I shake my head in disbelief.

Brandon looks at Jonah. "Bro, you could've given me a heads-up."

"Bro, I've got more important things on my mind than your love life," Jonah says.

I struggle to open the little tub of applesauce that came with my school lunch. My *free* school lunch. The one that Mack talked my mom into applying for. I'm so completely mortified, and yet grateful at the same time. With one final tug, the foil gives way and applesauce explodes all over my shirt. I dab at it with my napkin, making it worse.

"I'll be back." As I stand, a girl with a huge basket of carnations arrives at our table. My heart flips.

"For you, Erika." The girl holds a carnation out to Erika like she's presenting her with a bejeweled scepter. "From Aiden Serrano."

Erika turns beet red, Jonah cringes, and Brandon puts his head down on his homework and bangs it a few times. Meanwhile, I walk slowly toward the door in case the girl wants to pull out another flower. She doesn't. I look over my shoulder one last time as I leave the cafeteria. Jonah is talking to the girl, and she's shaking her head.

I'm standing in front of the drier with my wet shirt when the door to the last stall opens, and Naomi comes out.

This situation wasn't in the *Normal Teen Handbook*, so I go with, "Hey."

Naomi nods back at me. She splashes water on her blotchy face.

"I'm sorry about Brandon. Guys can be so dense."

Naomi's lip begins to quiver. Crap. Jonah's right. Drama is so overrated.

Naomi sniffs. "Did you get a flower from Jonah?"

"No." So much for no more drama. "But I wasn't expecting one."

"But it's Flower Day."

"I don't even know what that means. Remember." I point at myself. "Homeschooled since sixth grade."

"It's one of our school's oldest traditions. Like for the last hundred years. Even my aunt did it back in the day."

I shrug. "Okay."

"It's a big deal."

"If you say so."

"You don't mean that."

"Yeah, I do."

"Really? Jonah not sending you a flower doesn't bother you at all?"

No. Yes. Maybe? What do normal teens do in this type of situation? Deflect!

"Erika got a flower during lunch," I say.

And for a second, curiosity beats selfishness.

"She did? From who?" Naomi says.

"Aiden."

"Aiden? English-class Aiden?"

"Yeah."

"Well, at least one of us is having a good day." Naomi puts on a layer of bubblegum-pink lip gloss and fixes her eyeliner. "You're still going with me to the dance, though, right? Even if our love lives are a train wreck."

I flash back to Jonah's and my last make-out session in the supply closet. My love life might be complicated, but it's definitely not a train wreck. Besides, it's only a stupid flower for some ancient school ritual. Who cares? And yet, something pings in me.

"Sure, I'll still go."

"Come over to my house before the dance on Saturday, and we'll get ready together." Naomi fluffs her shoulder-length black hair in the mirror. "Auntie Jennifer is coming with Erika to do our hair and makeup."

"I don't have much hair to do." I run a hand through what's left of my hair. "It might be closer to five. It depends if I have to teach or not."

"Can't you cancel?"

"I'll see if Crystal will switch with me," I say, though I have no intention of doing it.

When we get back to the table, Erika is still beaming and fondling her flower. Brandon squirms and refuses to make eye contact. Jonah looks from Brandon to Erika to Naomi and finally to me with a *what the hell?* face. I shrug and shovel what's left of the applesauce into my mouth until the bell rings.

"Hey, Dad just texted. I have to run an errand with him right after school, so don't wait for me." Jonah throws his backpack over one muscular shoulder and mine over the other one. "I'll definitely see you at the rink later, though. And if you happen to need my help in the supply closet, all you have to do is ask."

I don't need a stupid flower. Or a date to a dance. All I need is right here.

"Put your hands together for OH-LIV-I-AHHH 'TOE PICK' KENNEDYYYYY!" Mack announces as I walk in front of the snack bar.

"Ehhhh." I shrug and grab my Ice Dreams jacket.

"I'll keep working on it." Mack goes back to cleaning the Wheaties box case that wasn't dirty to start with.

"From Tyler?" I nod at the large bouquet of red roses sitting beside the pretzel warmer.

"Nah. We don't do that kind of mushy stuff."

My heart flips. "Who are they for, then?"

"Your mom. Isn't that sweet? No matter where in the world your dad is or how busy he is, he never forgets about you and your mom."

He never forgets. Yeah, sure. I don't think Mom has forgiven him yet for choosing to stay in Florida for the long Thanksgiving weekend instead of coming home. Even if—at least according to his Instagram account—he really was signing autographs at Rick's Sports Supply stores all over Florida the entire weekend. We need the extra cash, but still.

"It's their anniversary," Mack informs me. "In case you forgot."

Crap, I forgot. "I knew that."

"They are such a cute couple that they make me want to hurl." Mack nods at the giant poster of Mom and Dad from their first tour with Olympians on Ice that hangs near the supply closet. *America's Gold Medal Sweethearts, Midori Nakashima and Michael Kennedy.* My parents are selling it to the cheap seats in this promo picture. Dressed in coordinating white-and-gold costumes, Mom is staring dreamily into Dad's eyes as he dips her back toward the ice. It's both effective and completely gross.

"You're lucky, Liv, to have parents who not only love each other, but actually like each other too."

"Having baby daddy drama?" I hop up on the counter.

"Every. Damn. Day." Mack sighs. "But today's pain in my ass is courtesy of my parents, who are suddenly interested in being a part of their granddaughter's life after the most awkward Thanksgiving dinner in all of recorded history."

"I told you to come spend Thanksgiving with us instead." Granted Mom's and my Thanksgiving dinner was one of Ms. Karrie's homemade pumpkin pies smothered with whipped cream while sitting on the couch watching *The Cutting Edge*, but it still sounds better than Mack's.

"They want me to move back home with Fiona and start going to college full-time again in the spring instead of working here."

"What?!" I startle.

"Don't worry. I'm not going anywhere. At least not for a while. So much fun going on with Clan MacIntosh right now. You have no idea what you are missing out on." Mack's cheeks puff out with air, and she adds, "Do you think it's too late for Midori to adopt me?"

"Probably. She might be interested in a trade, though. Especially after that last Yelp review from Hannah's mom." My stomach clenches. "What are we going to do? Mom's medical bills are piling up."

"I'll tell you exactly what we're going to do." Mack puts her hands on her hips. "We're going to pivot. We're going to go after more high-caliber clients like the Chois. So keep Jonah happy." A sassy smirk pulls across Mack's face. "Not *that* happy, though, Olivia. And stop messing up my supply closet." Mack grabs a sponge and wipes around the pretzel machine. "This rink would descend into complete chaos without me. Now, get off my counter and go work on that piñata."

Sure enough, on Table #1 is a familiar box.

I hop down, and Mack wipes where I was sitting. "Can you check my geometry homework first?"

"Of course." Mack dries her hands off on her jeans and follows me out to Table #1. "Did you talk to the teacher? Did you get those two points back on the test? 'Cause Ms. What's-Her-Butt was wrong. She had the decimal in the wrong place."

"Yep. So now I have squeaked into C territory. It's a C-minus, but I'll take it." I sit and slide my homework out of my backpack.

"It's a C-minus *for now*, you mean."

"Eh. A C-minus is good enough."

"No, it's not. You need to have a strong math foundation before you take physics or you're going to be lost."

"Who said I was going to take physics?"

Mack leans over and messes up my hair. "Me."

I give her the stink eye and flatten my hair back down. "Pretty sure there are plenty of professional skaters who have never taken a physics class."

"True." Mack pulls my notebook over to her side of the table. "But you should always have a plan B."

I pull a pencil out of my bag and use the eraser end as a microphone. "Now that you've defeated your biggest opponent—the ill-tempered Slushee machine—what's *your* plan B, Annabelle MacIntosh?"

I poke the eraser-mic at her. Mack, who has an opinion about everything whether you ask for it or not, is suddenly speechless.

"I don't have a plan B." Mack drops her eyes and bites at her lip ring. "Besides making a derby team, I don't know what to do about anything in my life right now. And that scares the shit out of me."

"You didn't make the team?"

"Nope. My times were too low. Barnacle Barb encouraged me to keep training, though. To not give up."

I lower the pencil and my voice. "I'm sorry, Mack. I know you really wanted this."

Mack shrugs, but I know it's a front.

"Wanna skate?"

Mack looks me dead in the eyes. "I want *you* to skate, Olivia."

"Duh, of course. I'll be your pace partner. It's not like I'm dying to do geometry or make a piñata."

"No, I mean, I want to see you give your skating a hundred percent again. Like Choi. Now that boy's got something. I wish I had what you have."

"You have a crush on Jonah?"

"Don't be an idiot. No. I wish I could go back in time and tell Past Mack to make some different choices."

Before I can press Mack for more details, the front door of Ice Dreams opens, and Jonah jogs in. Mack stands up. She high-fives Jonah on the way back to the snack bar. Jonah sits down across from me and plops a nondescript paper bag on top of my geometry homework.

"Happy Obscure High School Flower Ritual Day." Jonah's eyes sparkle as he pushes the bag toward me.

I cautiously open up the bag and plunge my hand into it. I pull out some moleskin, a little pot of Tiger Balm, and a pair of red skate guards. "Thanks. It's . . ."

"Weird? I know. But they don't sell flowers at Rick's Sports Supply. Can we chalk it up to 'it's the thought that counts'?"

I look behind me. Mack has her back turned, so I lean across the table and kiss Jonah. "It's perfect."

"I have good news. Well, bad news but good news. They lost my registration for the Utah race, and now there's no more slots open, so I can't skate. The good news is that I'm free this weekend." Jonah's eyes drop. "So can we? I mean, be all normal and go to the dance. Together."

I'm not sure why he is so embarrassed all of a sudden.

"*Yes!*" Mack yells from the snack bar. "The correct answer to that question is yes, Olivia Midori Kennedy! Don't make me smack you upside your head."

"You should listen to Mack." Jonah tips his head toward Mack.

"Okay. Yes." I yell over my shoulder to Mack, "*Yes!* I would love to go to the Winter Dance with you, Jonah Choi!"

Mack swings her cleaning rag around her head like a lasso and whoops. "That's what I'm talkin' about. It's about damn time. Now get to work, Choi. That gold medal ain't gonna win itself."

Jonah gives me a kiss before sliding away from the table. He gives Mack another high five before disappearing into the locker room.

Mr. Choi bursts through the door with his phone up to his ear. "Are you sure? Could you make an exception just this one time? Okay, then. Put us on the waitlist. Thank you."

Mr. Choi hangs up and bangs his fist on his thigh, muttering what are probably Korean curses. He stomps into the men's locker room.

I am going to a dance. Oh God, what have I gotten myself into?

Chapter 15

Help! Having a fashion crisis! I send Mack an emergency selfie with the arm that isn't currently stuck up in the air. Zipper bent. Send help.

LMAO.

Not funny!

C'mon, you know it is. Rip the seam and free yourself. I'll take you shopping for a plan B dance dress tomorrow. Fi needs new stuff too.

Crying Thanks.

"You still don't have a dress?" Naomi says in disbelief at lunch. "The dance is Saturday, Olivia. *This* Saturday."

"I'm going shopping today after school. The dress I was going to wear doesn't fit anymore." I look at my tray of high-calorie, low-nutrient foods. I put down my half-eaten slice of pepperoni pizza. Not like that's going to help my ass miraculously shrink by Saturday, but whatever.

"Go to Macy's. That's where I got mine. They're probably all picked over by now, but at least they're on sale. I'm sure you can get a good one for one-fifty easily."

One-fifty? My whole budget is $22.78, and that's including the money from the tip jar Mack insisted I take.

"Good to know. I'll check it out," I say, though Mack has already promised to take me to her favorite Goodwill as soon as Mom comes in this afternoon.

My phone buzzes and my heart clenches. What if it's Mack texting that she can't go? What if I can't get a dress by Saturday? What if this is a total disaster? My phone buzzes a second time. I steel myself and take a cautious peek. It's not Mack. It's Egg.

Change of plans. Coming in THIS weekend.
Need you Friday pm thru Sun pm.

Sure. But not Sat.

I need you all day Sat for rehearsal. Sun we
record.

Okay, but I need to leave at 4.

Please Livy. Can you cancel your plans?

No.

I'm begging you. I need this job. You are the
only person I trust with this.

Now I feel like dirt. I'm sorry. I can't.

Did I mention this is a PAYING gig? I'll pay
you $500 cash for the weekend.

??????

And another $100 if I get a callback.

I admit it. Dollar signs flashed in front of my eyes. Maybe.

I guess I could see if Britney Xiao is available this weekend instead.

Well, that's a low blow. Oh hell no!

If my favorite partner isn't available, then I
have no choice but to find someone else.
And the tea is that Britney is partnerless.
Again.

Britney Freakin' Xiao. Nope. Nope. Nopeity nope.

"Hey guys, bad news," I say after texting my answer to Egg. "I'm going to have to bail on the dance."

"What?" Naomi and Erika shriek in tandem.

"Why?" Brandon says.

"I have a skating thing this weekend."

Erika genuinely looks annoyed at my announcement. "It can't wait until next week? This is a once-a-year event, you know."

Jonah and I share an *are-they-for-real* look.

"No. Egg and I have been partners since I was ten years old. I'm the only one who can help him with it."

Naomi throws down her katsu sandwich. "Well, this totally wrecks all our plans."

"Really. It's fine." As always, Jonah is the only one who gets it. "Nobody wants to see me dance anyway."

The other three people at our table look at Jonah like he's from another planet.

"I'm sorry," I say more to Jonah than anybody else, and he shrugs.

"I'll take a rain check." Jonah puts his hand on my knee and squeezes it. "It's one dance. Who cares?"

"Unbelievable." Erika shakes her head. "You two are so weird."

Naomi elbows her cousin. "Not weird. Dedicated. Very dedicated."

"Well, I hope you two won't look back on your high school life one day and regret it. You only get to do this once."

"Thank God," Jonah says. "I can't wait to finish high school. I would skate full-time tomorrow if my parents would let me take the GED test and be done."

The GED? Erika's and Naomi's heads look ready to explode.

"I guess we have different priorities." Erika's voice matches Jonah's.

"Yeah, we do."

"Save me," Brandon mouths at me when everyone but Jonah pulls out homework and pretends to do it, so we don't have to continue this conversation.

The bell rings, and the silent treatment continues.

Once Erika and Naomi are out of earshot, Brandon says, "How long do you think they would let me live if I suddenly announced that I wasn't going to the dance either? That Choi and I decided to have an all-night *Street Fight Race* marathon instead?"

Jonah bangs the lid of his empty lunch container closed and throws it into his backpack. "How about you three go to this all-important, only-once-a-year dance, and Olivia and I skate. That way, everybody'll be happy."

But I'm not happy. I want it all. And as much as I hate to admit it, Erika does have a point. I don't want to look back and regret anything.

I stop Jonah. "That's it. I'm going to the dance. Pick me up at seven thirty. Egg can make it by himself for three hours. Warning:

My hair and makeup aren't going to be perfect, and I won't have time to do my nails. I will take the time, however, to put on some extra deodorant and inhale a protein bar."

"Deal." Jonah looks me up and down. "And you look beautiful no matter what you're wearing."

"So extra." I wrap my arms around Jonah's bicep and look up at him. "And yet, so working."

Jonah leans into my ear and whispers, "Can we sneak out of the dance a little early?"

My body buzzes. "Definitely."

This is going to be the Best. Weekend. Ever.

Chapter 16

Rock. Paper. Scissors.

"Ugh," I say when Mack's paper covers my rock.

"I'll do the toilets." Mack squeezes my fist. "You get the gum."

"So gross." I slip on my latex gloves, grab the putty knife, and lie down on the linoleum underneath Table #1. This is wrong on so many levels. A curse on the jackass who's been parking their gum underneath this table for what must have been months now. Stupid. I'm the rink owners' daughter. I shouldn't have to do this. I should be warming up. Going through Madame Pichon's pre-workout barre routine. The sound of Jonah's blades hitting the ice in even strides echoes around the rink. I want to be on the ice. With him.

I'm busy daydreaming under an ABC gum sky when a pair of giant hiking boots walks up next to the table. A duffle bag hits the floor next to the boots with an echoing thud. The body attached to the boots squats down and peers under the table at me.

"Hey, Short Stuff."

"Egg!" I slide out from under the table and peel my latex gloves off. "I thought you weren't coming in until tomorrow morning."

"I was able to get an earlier flight." Egg looks me up and down. "Well, look who finally finished going through puberty."

"You too." I point at Egg's five-o'clock shadow. He finally looks like a man. "I feel like I should call you Mr. Trout now, or at least Stuart."

"Nah. I'm still Egg. I'll always be your Egg." Egg throws his arms around me and swings me around.

"Okay, okay. Thank you. I missed you too. Now put me down."

"Hey! Look who's here." Mack puts down the cleaning supplies and strips off her gloves.

They do an awkward side hug.

"I appreciate you letting me bunk at your house, Mack. You won't even know I'm there, I promise."

"Wait, why aren't you staying at Trout Manor?" The whole Tech football team could stay at Trout Manor.

"My parents don't exactly know I'm here." Egg and Mack share a look. "And I'd like to keep it that way. For a little while, at least."

"It's fine, Stuart." Mack claps him on the back. "Everything is going to turn out the way it's supposed to. Sometimes you have to do your own thing, even when nobody else is on board with it."

"Well, *I'm* on board with it and ready to get started." I hand Mack the gum scraper and she groans. "I can't wait for Jonah to get off my ice."

Egg throws an arm across my shoulders. "I'm presuming the guy on the ice—who, if he looks at me any harder, may cause my head to explode—is this Jonah I've heard so much about."

"Mack?!" I say, and she shrugs.

"Go change and meet me in the barre area. I don't have a minute to lose this weekend."

"About that." Time to pull that Band-Aid off. "I'm going to need a three-hour dinner break Saturday night."

"Olivia, we're already going to have to work around the private lessons on Saturday and dodge people during the Open Skates."

"I can skate late at night. I have a set of keys. We can skate until the sun comes up if you want. I just want to go to the dance on Saturday night."

"I don't know. Maybe it's not enough time." Egg chews on his bottom lip.

"For you, maybe, but I've been training for at least a couple of hours each day. Cardio, barre work, as well as back-to-basics technique work on the ice." I put my hand on my sore hip and immediately regret it. I cross my arms instead. "It may not be Olympic gold level, but my skating is solid. You need a professional skating partner, and I want to redeem myself inside Skatelandia, so let's get to it."

Egg puffs out his cheeks in frustration. "Okay, you can take an extra-long dinner break on Saturday."

"Meet you in ten." I jog off to the locker room, feeling at home for the first time in several months.

I pull on my favorite skate outfit—the black unitard with the thin layer of red piping that swirls up my calves like licks of flame. As I check myself in the mirror, I realize how close to home Egg's earlier comment hit. That's why my dance dress didn't fit at all. I did finish going through puberty because I don't remember this outfit straining across my curves quite so much before Skate Detroit. Maybe I'll splurge and buy myself a new skate outfit with some of the money Egg promised. I slip my Chucks back on and grab my skates. I remove my cheetah-print soakers and put the red skate guards Jonah gave me for Obscure High School Flower Ritual Day over my blades.

When I come out of the women's locker room, I find Egg and Jonah in deep conversation next to Table #1. Mack's legs stick out from underneath the table as she continues to scrape away. I put my skates down on the table and slide on my Ice Dreams jacket.

"That powdered soy-based stuff is crap." Jonah, his back to me, gestures at Egg's protein bar with his hard-boiled egg. "Eggs are pure protein. No chemical crap added."

"Yeah, if you like being constipated," Egg says through a mouthful of chocolate and peanut butter. "I need to build and maintain muscle."

"Why? Bulk makes you slow. Causes wind resistance."

"Because I'm not going for speed. You can't do *this* without bulk." Egg crams the rest of the protein bar in his mouth until he looks like a chipmunk and makes a beeline toward me. I yelp when Egg suddenly scoops me off the floor. With a grunt, he deadlifts me from waist level to above his head.

"Throw me a bone here, Livy." Egg wavers a little off-balance. I grumble and lengthen out into a star shape, my left hand connected to Egg's left shoulder. "Not only do I have to deadlift ninety-five . . . okay, now one hundred and five . . . pounds, I gotta keep it in the air, and then skate on top of all that." Egg releases me gently back to the floor. "So, thank you, but I'll stick to my protein bars."

Egg turns to me. "You've gained weight. Your body feels different."

I punch Egg in the arm, even though he's right.

"What? You've always complained about your flat butt. Now you got a booty. Embrace your new curves."

Everybody suddenly looks at my butt. I take off my jacket and wrap it around my waist. Jonah unlaces his skates and slips them off. He puts them on the table next to mine. "Teach me the lift."

Egg scoffs. "Dude, you can't lift her."

And in stupid boy code, that becomes a challenge. Jonah leans over and scoops me up. You know, this would be kind of a romantic moment if my ass weren't made of lead, and Egg and Mack weren't here.

"She's not a barbell. You're not going to be able to get her above your head like that," Egg says.

Which, of course, guarantees that Jonah is going to try. It's a good thing Mack comes out from under the table just in time to break my fall.

"Whoa! Knock it off before you two boneheads hurt Olivia." Mack gives me a hand off the floor. "Dude, it's simple physics. F equals MA."

"Huh?" Jonah says.

"Newton's Second Law. Force equals mass times acceleration," Mack says like everybody knows this. When we give her blank looks, she adds, "Show him. Press lift."

I step back a few paces. When Egg gives the signal, I jog up to him. I lace my fingers through his. Egg presses up as I push off the floor until I am suspended above his head. I spread my legs out into a modest *V* as Egg rotates slowly. My muscles quiver a bit, but overall, this feels right. This feels like me. This is my normal.

"Olivia's jog brings the acceleration into the equation. Her momentum, plus Egg's strength overcomes the drag of Olivia's ass . . . I mean, mass . . . to force her up into the air. F equals MA. Newton's Second Law."

Egg gives me the signal. We gently collapse back down until my Chucks touch the ground.

"That was fantastic. Solid. Just like old times." Egg gives me a bear hug. "I knew I could count on you. You're still my number-one girl."

I know Egg means that in a brotherly way, but a deep groove forms between Jonah's eyebrows. I break away from Egg's embrace and move next to Jonah.

Jonah clears his throat. "How do you know so much about physics?"

"Just because I work at a skating rink and have a baby doesn't mean I'm an idiot," Mack snaps, and Jonah winces. She softens her tone. "I was valedictorian of my prep school. The other kids hated me because I always ruined the curve in physics class. I could've been an engineer. God knows that was my dad's plan for me. MacIntosh & Daughter, LLC."

"I didn't know your dad was an engineer." I realize that though Mack knows my family inside and out, I barely know hers. "Maybe you could go back to school when Fiona is a little older? You could still be an engineer."

"Who said I want to be an engineer?" Mack's voice turns frosty again. "I just said I was freakishly good at physics."

"And English." Jonah digs a tiny envelope out of his cooler. "Mom said to give this to you for editing my English paper. I got a ninety-five. She almost cried."

"Ninety-five? How'd you manage that? It was perfect."

"Exactly. Too perfect. So I misspelled 'lightning' and threw in a couple of typos. I wanted Mr. Balducci to believe I actually wrote it."

"You did write it."

"Kinda, sorta, not really." Jonah pulls at the collar of his skin-suit. "It was my idea, but you improved it. A lot. Whatever. Who cares?"

Mack throws up her hands in disgust.

"Here." Jonah holds the envelope toward Mack, but she pushes it away. Jonah pushes it back. "Take it. Seriously, my mom was thrilled with the ninety-five."

"I can't."

"It's gas money, then. For driving Olivia and me to bouts." Jonah opens up Mack's palm and presses the envelope into it. "If Mom asks, though, it was for the editing."

Mack slides the decorative envelope into the back pocket of her jeans.

"So, now will you show me the lift?" Jonah is not going to let this go. "My feet are freezing."

"No." Egg crosses his arms. "Because I don't trust you. You

drop her on the ice, and she could get seriously hurt like Midori did."

"That's what happened to your mom?" Jonah turns to me. "I thought she'd been in a car accident or something."

My stomach clenches. I was three then and out on the Olympians on Ice tour with my parents. I'm not sure if I remember the accident or just remember Dad telling me about it later, but I was definitely there the night my mom's fall stopped the entire show. I remember being backstage with my nanny, twirling around in my fabulous faux cheetah fur hat and boots.

"No. My dad dropped her." My throat tightens. "It was a few years after the Olympics, and my parents were out on tour. They'd had a fight about something right before the show. It threw them off-balance, and Mom hit the ice. Her back has never been the same since."

I don't remember seeing Mom hit the ice. Whether I've blocked it out of my memory or was too distracted by the sparkles on my skirt that night, I don't know. I do remember the collective gasp of the crowd, though, and the music coming to an abrupt halt. I remember the lights coming up and my nanny saying, "Oh my God," over and over as she shuffled me away somewhere.

"One moment of lost trust is all it takes." Egg's arm around my shoulders brings me back from the dark place I haven't been to in a long time. "One moment and everything can go horribly wrong. Coach Michael Kennedy's Rule Number One—always look out for your partner. It took me two years as Olivia's partner before her dad would even teach me the easiest of lifts." Egg looks down his nose at Jonah. "So it ain't gonna happen with you, dude. Sorry."

I duck out from under Egg's arm and lace my fingers through Jonah's.

"I can do lifts with Jonah if I want to. I trust him. He won't hurt me." I look up at Jonah and smile. "Plus, I'm a free agent now, since you ditched me for the Trout Triplets Freak Show at Tech."

"And how's that going for you?"

"Great."

"Are you sure about that? The tea is that you've quit skating for good."

I stumble over my words. "I'm still looking for a partner."

Egg gives Jonah a hard stare. "So, are you going all *Cutting Edge* now and auditioning for Olivia's new partner?"

Jonah scoffs. "What? No. I just like skating with Olivia."

"Me too. Therefore," Egg says, sticking out his hand for me to shake, "I'm ready to restart our partnership."

I grab Egg's hand with my other hand and shake it. "Me too."

"Are you two dating or skating?" Mack waves the scraper at us. "Shut up and get on the ice."

"I still have twenty minutes of ice time left," Jonah says.

"Yes, you do, mister." Mack yanks Jonah away from me. "I promised your dad I wouldn't let you screw around this afternoon while he was at his job interview. He said he'd be back as close to five as he could."

"I don't need a babysitter." Jonah pulls away from Mack's grasp.

"Honey, I saw what you and Olivia did to my supply closet the other day. You most certainly do."

"You have twenty minutes, and then the ice is mine," Egg calls after Jonah, who ignores him. "Go warm up, Livy. I need you in fifteen."

I watch Jonah from the mirrors in the barre area. He laces his skates back up and steps out onto the ice. As he nears the barre area, he breaks off his normal path.

"And plié . . . 2 . . . 3 . . . 4." I take Egg through the first section of our barre routine.

Jonah stops at the boards and reaches his hand over the side.

"Come warm up with me, Livy."

My heart melts. Egg clears his throat.

"We have barre warm-up to do, Livy."

"*You* have barre warm-up to do. I'm going to warm up on the ice."

"Suit yourself." Egg shrugs, but I know he's annoyed with me.

I get my skates on in record time and intersect Jonah on the ice. "Don't call me Livy. I am not twelve."

Jonah looks me up and down. I forget that he's used to seeing me in street clothes, not skating attire. "No, you most certainly are not."

I lace my fingers through Jonah's and push off the ice. On the straightaway, I flip around in front of him and take both of Jonah's gloved hands in mine. The in-sync slicing of our blades on the ice sounds like a metronome.

"I can't wait to see you all dressed up on Saturday." I stare into Jonah's deep brown eyes. "I've never seen you in anything but a skinsuit or jeans and a long-sleeved T-shirt."

"Oh! That reminds me. According to my mother, I am supposed to ask what color your dress is so that I can purchase the appropriate flower to match."

"Fuchsia. Mack found the perfect dress for me."

"Fuchsia. Do fuchsia flowers exist?" Jonah says, and I shrug. "I'll ask Mom."

"Hey, wanna show Egg our tricks?"

"Will it make him want to kick my ass even more?"

"Why is everything a competition with guys?"

"So, you're saying that if Stuart was laughing and goofing off around the rink with whoever this Britney person is Stuart and Mack were gossiping about before you came out of the locker room, that wouldn't bother you at all?"

Hell, yes! "No. Not at all."

"Tick-tock, tick-tock," Egg says as we pass the barre area. Jonah scratches his temple with his middle finger in response.

"C'mon, Ice Prince." I shake Jonah's gloved hands to refocus him. "Let's kick it up a notch. Let's make our two moves into a combination."

When Jonah releases my hands and unzips the top of his skinsuit, I contemplate concocting a sudden need for toilet paper in the women's locker room, so we can visit the supply closet together instead of skating. Jonah tucks the gloves inside his skinsuit and then shakes my bare hands to refocus me.

A large smile cuts across Jonah's face as we build up speed. We go through what has become our signature move. *Our* move. Every time it gets a little better. As we come back out of the hydroblade counterbalance, Jonah seamlessly passes my hand from his right to his left until we are skating facing each other. I flip around, and with a nod, Jonah and I stretch out our limbs into a low but solid arabesque spiral.

Egg claps slowly when Jonah and I finally come to a stop. "Okay, that wasn't a complete disaster. Your form sucks, and Olivia's arabesque was ridiculously low, but the hydroblade was interesting."

"What?!" I say.

Jonah wraps his arms around me and pulls me in between his feet. His head dips down to my ear. "Well, I think it was perfect."

I want to reward Jonah for his perfect answer, but the front door of Ice Dreams flies open, and Mr. Choi sprints in.

"Jonah! Son! Great news!" Mr. Choi runs up to the cut in the boards. "Zack Song pulled out of competition with a hamstring injury. We're clear for Utah! Come on. We gotta get home. Our flight leaves at nine."

Jonah whoops and then catches himself. "Olivia, I—"

"It's okay." I unwrap my arms from around Jonah's waist.

"Oh, the dance thing," Mr. Choi says.

The Winter Dance is the latest in a long line of missed events in my life. I've missed sleepovers, class trips, birthday parties, and multiple holidays with my extended family. People are used to me being a no-show.

"It's just a dance." I shrug, but my eyes are suddenly stinging. "Good luck this weekend."

"Thanks." Jonah pushes a wayward piece of hair behind my ear. "If I could clone myself, you know I would."

"I know." I force a smile across my face, even as I feel my heart being ripped out of my chest. "Bring home the gold, okay?"

"Is there any other option?"

I put out my fist for Jonah to bump. After we make our dorky hand sign, Jonah grabs me in a tight hug. Mr. Choi clears his throat.

"Sorry, son. We need to go. We can't miss our flight."

Jonah gives me another tight hug and kisses the top of my head before skating off.

"It sucks, doesn't it?" Egg skates up next to me. "But we can't change it. So channel it into your art. Now, let's see how much of the phoenix number you remember."

"I thought we were trying to get people to *forget* that was us."

"I don't know. We're short on time. Maybe we could Frankenstein something together from the parts of our previous routines that *didn't* suck. Or start like our old routine and then—*bam*—hit 'em with something new. Let's start with the phoenix number."

Egg grabs my hand, and we skate out to the middle of the rink for our opening pose. He lunges and throws a jazz hand to the ceiling. I drape my left arm over Egg's shoulders and weave my legs around his back leg. Egg reaches his lower hand down to make a perfect diagonal, like Alexei told us to do: "Make the heat. Make the passion." Except Egg's hand doesn't cup my hipbone anymore. Now that I'm curvier, Egg's hand cups my butt cheek instead.

Well, this is awkward. I bite my lip to keep my mouth shut because I am a professional.

"Ready?" Mack's voice booms over the sound system.

Egg gives Mack a nod. The Chois pass Table #1 just as the opening strains echo around the rink. Mr. Choi herds a conflicted-looking Jonah out the door. As we step out into our opening pattern, which I've done a million times, everything feels wrong. The ice. My boots. My body. Even Egg. It's like I'm ten years old again. Back when my parents suddenly decided that I was going to be a pairs skater like them and not a single skater like I wanted to be. Granted, part of my reason was because I thought boys were stupid. For the first six months of our partnership, Egg proved me right pretty much every day.

"Loosen up, Livy." Egg shakes my arms that are currently caressing his chest in Alexei's awkward choreography. "Find the girl I've been skating with for forever. The one who can nail triple-doubles like there's no tomorrow."

Unfortunately, that girl is currently missing, and she took all her jumping skills with her. I hit the ice hard during our throw triple lutz. I jump back up, and we stumble through the rest of the routine.

"Wow, that sucked," I say when we freeze in our final pose.

"It's okay. At least you attempted the triple-double-double." Egg releases me. "So, we're a little rusty, but we'll get it. Team Kennedy/Trout always does."

Old demons come back to haunt me. *You two have so much potential, but you can't seem to get your footing at the senior level. The USFSA regrets that we will not be able to fund your training this season. I'm sorry.*

But I smile and nod at Egg.

Chapter 17

The news doesn't go over well on Friday. Jonah and I have thrown yet another wrench into Naomi's master plan.

"I'm sorry," I apologize for the hundredth time. I sneak contraband ibuprofen out of my purse and throw it down my throat. My back hurts. My calves hurt. My hip hurts from the four hundred or so times I *didn't* land the triple-double-double last night. Brandon already greeted me in chemistry this morning with, "Why do you smell like a giant cough drop?"

"You and Choi. Dead to me. Dead, I say," Brandon jokes.

Naomi and Erika shrug. The climate around our lunch table hits subzero.

"It's one dance. There'll be others." I had to practice those words a dozen times in the mirror last night before my stupid eyes would stop watering. Cramming the perfect fuchsia dress Mack found into the back of my closet first helped.

"You can come without Jonah, you know," Brandon says.

Naomi's face lights up. "Ask Stuart to be your date."

"What? No. That would be weird." Though we still have a good twenty minutes of our lunch period left, I pack up my bag and grab my half-eaten lunch. "I'll see you guys in English."

"Don't you regret having all your eggs in one basket sometimes?" Erika's voice trails behind me.

"No," I say. Then again, I'm the person who thinks she can land a triple-double-double without solidly training for four months. What do I know?

Egg is waiting for me at Ice Dreams after school. The pink rubber gloves he's sporting with his black warm-up suit makes me chuckle.

"Where's Mack?" I miss my usual derby girl intro. I pull my Ice Dreams jacket off its peg out of habit and then hang it back up. I'm not cleaning skates or filling Barbie's empty head with Tootsie Rolls today. I'm working.

"Fiona had a fever this morning, so I told Mack to stay home with her." Egg digs into the bucket of sudsy water in front of him and pulls out a part for some machine in the snack area. "God knows I didn't have anything else better to do while I was waiting on you."

"Sorry my education is so inconvenient for you."

"A necessary evil."

"Where's Mom?"

"She went home after her last private lesson this morning. I told Midori I'd give you a ride home since I have Mack's car." Egg dries off the piece and holds it up to the light to make sure that it's clean. "Go change while I put the soda machine back together. What? In between classes, I work at the campus pizza shop. Got my food handlers' card and everything. Gotta have a plan B if I don't get this skating job, because I'm not going back to college in the spring."

I give him a look. "Whoa."

"Which is why I am staying with Mack and not at my parents' house. They will not be on board with this. I might as well pull the plug on this failed experiment before Tech kicks me out. I don't have the grades to keep my pity scholarship anyway." Egg screws the machine back together with unnecessary force. "Don't get me wrong. I want to go to college and get a degree. Eventually. But I want to do it on my terms. Not somebody else's. I need to start looking out for number one for a change."

Erika's question from lunch haunts me.

"Do you ever regret having all of your eggs in one basket?"

Egg scrubs another piece of the soda machine for so long, I start to think that he didn't hear me.

Finally, he looks up at me and says in all seriousness, "I don't know yet. It depends on how this audition goes. Working at a pizza shop in Phoenix for minimum wage isn't exactly a sexy plan B."

"No pressure or anything."

"Sorry. This is my problem, not yours." Egg strips off his gloves. He pulls a computer bag out from underneath the counter. Egg digs around and then places a large pile of twenties on the counter.

"Motivation, not pressure." Egg slides the bills toward me. "Now you can take *Jonah* to the movies next weekend and buy him some popcorn. Maybe even candy. Be a normal teenager, since I never got to be one."

I laugh. It's the three-quarters mark of the short track season. The likelihood of Jonah being able to go to the movies next weekend with me is about as likely as him eating candy.

"Take it," Egg insists, and I slide the pile of bills into my backpack. "I need you on the ice and warmed up in thirty minutes. Twenty would be even better. And we need to talk about that triple-double-double."

"It's fine, Egg." I'm glad he can't see the bruise on my hip.

"You haven't landed one yet, Livy. And you haven't landed the throw triple lutz cleanly yet either. Let's take it out of the choreography? It's not really showcasing me anyway. I'll pull one from past footage and put it in."

He's right, but pride won't let me take it out. "I'll land it to-night. Every element that we didn't nail last season needs to be in the new piece. We have to prove the haters wrong."

"Are you sure your hip is up for that?"

"It's fine, Stuart," I say, though I catch myself rubbing my hip.

"I hope so, because we're skating until Ernie and Crystal come in at five thirty to prep for Open Skate. Then we'll take a dinner break and strategize until the rink closes. Your mom said as long as you are home by one, she's cool with you skating really late."

"No problem." My feet beg to differ, though. I hope I have enough moleskin to make it through the night.

Once upon a time, there was a figure skater who didn't blink an eye at six hours of practice. I'm not sure where she went.

"Please take it down to a double-double-single instead," Egg says when I crash into the ice yet again.

"No," I growl and pull myself back to my feet. My hip feels like it's on fire. "I'm fine. Cue the music again."

"Seriously, Livy, you're going to hurt yourself if you keep this up. Let's face it. You hit the Puberty Wall last season. Hard. You're going to have to relearn everything with your new body and new center of gravity. Nobody expects you to land a triple-double-double tonight. It doesn't matter anyway. It's *my* audition."

"*I* expect me to land a triple-double-double tonight. And I will land one tonight if it kills me."

"That's what I'm afraid of." Egg grabs my arm as I start to skate away. "Okay, we're done for tonight."

"I'm fine, Stuart." I jerk my arm out of his hand.

"No, you're not. And you are so stubborn that you are going to permanently injure yourself. You're tired. I'm taking you home.

Take a hot bath. Ice your hip. Sleep. I'll pick you up at nine to-morrow, and we'll get in a couple of hours of practice before the rink opens to the public."

I want to protest. I want to cuss Egg out. But I don't have the energy. I want to take my cramping back, blistered feet, and bruised hip home and curl up in the fetal position for the next three days. I bite my lip to keep the sob of desperation inside me.

How did I do this day after day? How was *this* my normal?

Once upon a time, I did occasionally have one of these types of practices where nothing seemed to go right. Dad would pull me aside, dry my tears of frustration, and give me a hug.

"One time, Livy. One time clean and I'll call a Code Peach," Dad would whisper in my ear. "Can you do it?"

I'd nod and use Dad's Ice Dreams jacket to dry my eyes.

"Then grab it and growl, tiger." Dad would give me a final hug to balance me and then send me back out on the ice.

"Livy? Olivia? Hey." Egg waves his hand in front of my face. "You went blank there for a minute. I thought you were about to pass out."

"Can you give me a minute to figure things out and then we'll call it a night?"

Egg yawns. "Figure quickly, please."

Egg enters the men's locker room as I loop around the rink one last time. I pull up all the memories I have about Dad coaching me on a triple salchow–double toe loop–double toe loop. I walk through it over and over in my brain. Why isn't it working? I keep popping out too early on the triple, which doesn't give me enough momentum to make the first double clean much less the second one. I either make a sloppy, two-footed landing or under-rotate and hit the ice.

What are you afraid of? Grab it and growl, tiger. One last time. Then we'll call a Code Peach.

I push off the ice and dig deep, trying to find the last bit of energy stored in my aching muscles. I align myself for the triple-double-double. I don't have the strength left to control it, so I let it go instead. I throw all of my energy into the combination I know my muscles still remember how to do.

And. I. Land. It. I whoop.

"What, what, what!" Egg sprints out of the locker room clad only in his sock feet and skate pants.

Part of me is mad that Egg missed it. Another part of me wants to keep this small triumph to myself, at least for tonight.

"Sorry. Nothing." I skate to the edge of the ice and grab my blade covers. "Hey, Egg, can we stop at the twenty-four-hour Walmart on the way home?"

"Sure. Why?" Egg slides his sweatshirt over his head.

'Cause I'm calling a Code Peach.

"Tampons. I need tampons," I say instead.

"Oh, okay. Do I have to go in with you?"

"No. I'm going to skate this one solo."

"Good."

An hour later, I'm home, showered, and reeking of Tiger Balm. I wanted to use one of the four TENS units we own but Mom has them all attached to her back. I adjust the bag of frozen peas on my hip and tuck the blankets around my loosely bandaged feet. I grab my phone and text Dad.

> Finally landed a 3S-2T-2T again. Called a Code Peach on myself. Wish you were here to share these with me. Not quite the same thing but it'll do for now. Love you. Night.

I dig out a small cloud of cotton candy and take a selfie with it for him.

The cotton candy is halfway gone by the time my ancient Nintendo DS boots up. I hum along to the familiar music and choose my favorite character, Princess Peach. Dad is always Luigi.

"Not a word to your mother," Dad says as we enter Chuck E. Cheese. "If she asks, we went to see Sandy for massages."

"Got it. This is so much better than massages."

"Agreed." Dad pulls a couple of twenties out of his wallet. He hands me one. "I'll order the pizza. You get the tokens. You owe me a rematch from last time."

"You got it, Luigi." I give Dad a quick hug. We have the whole place to ourselves, because who else over the age of four goes to Chuck E. Cheese at eleven o'clock on a Tuesday morning during the school year? "Can we get cotton candy?"

"Pfft. Duh," Dad says. "If you're not gonna do it at a hundred percent, then why bother?"

I race off into the blur of lights and loud music. I hear my name. I look back over my shoulder. It isn't Dad who follows after me with a piping hot cheese pizza. It's Jonah, and he's holding a plate of piping hot hotteok. I step into Jonah, and he wraps his free arm around my waist. And though it's probably not appropriate for eleven o'clock on a Tuesday morning in the middle of a Chuck E. Cheese with your dad in the building somewhere, I pull Jonah into me until our bodies are pressed up against the video game machine. Jonah drops the plate of hotteok as we engage in PDA that would definitely get us kicked out of any Chuck E. Cheese.

A loud thunk interrupts my make-out session with Jonah. My eyelids flutter open. I wipe the drool from the side of my mouth and find my DS on the floor. Worst of all, the tingling all over my body disappears as the pain creeps back in. I turn off the game and chuck the empty container of cotton candy toward the trash

can. It misses. Just like everything else today. I flop back onto my
pillows with a groan and put the half-melted bag of peas back on
my hip. Even my normal isn't normal anymore.

I remember our last Code Peach now. It was near the middle
of last season. Nothing was going right. The gossip had already
started. Why was the USFSA wasting training money on a team
that clearly was not ready for Olympic-level competition? When
we got home, Mom informed me that Alexei was going to be our
new coach and that he wanted to scrap everything and start over.
My heart cracks open. It's probably too late to talk to Jonah, but I
wipe my eyes on my pajama sleeve and text him anyway.

> I miss you.

I miss you too. And again I'm sorry.

Shrugs Spending some quality time tonight with someone special. I send Jonah a picture of the frozen peas.

Me too. A second later, he sends me back a picture of his version
of frozen peas, the non-broke-ass version. The kind that doesn't
actually use . . . peas.

> How was your practice today?

Brutal. Yours?

> Same. I finally landed the triple-double-
> double, but the ice gods took their
> payment for it out of my hip. Owwww.

Awww, I'm sorry. Also, pretending I know
what a triple-double-double is. Sounds impressive tho.

Triple salchow–double toe loop–double toe loop.

Crickets Will Google that later. Got to get some sleep.

Night, Ice Prince.

Gives you hotteok-flavored kiss Night

Chapter 18

I skate better after eight hours of sleep, but I lose the triple-double-double again. I'm back to hitting the ice every time.

"Damn it, damn it, damn iiiiiiit!" I bang on the ice with my fists.

"Let it go, Livy." Egg reaches his hand down to me. "We need to move on. Jumps are fine, but Olympians on Ice is looking for artistry—the one thing that cost us big at Nationals."

Like I needed that reminder. "No, I'm pretty sure it was the jacked-up throw triple lutz."

"It wasn't the jacked-up throw triple lutz."

"It was."

"It wasn't. And you're lucky it was only your pride that was hurt. Even if we had nailed the jump, we still wouldn't have had enough points to make the podium."

"We had a shot."

"No, Olivia, we didn't. Sorry to burst your bubble about that, but we didn't. We were nowhere close." When I open my mouth to argue, Egg cuts me off. "Look, I'm not paying you the big bucks to rehash past skates. I'm paying you to make me look good right now. So, as your boss, the triple-double-double is now officially a double salchow–double toe loop. And if you don't land your next throw triple lutz, I'm taking it out and using old footage instead. Understood? If you can't follow directions, I want a refund so I can hire Crystal. I know she hasn't skated as a pair for a while, but I'm getting desperate. Sorry to be such a hard-ass about this, but I'm on the clock, and I need a professional skater for this job."

"Any other changes in the choreography you would like me to make, Mr. Trout?"

"No." Egg wipes his sweaty bangs out of his eyes. "Thank you for being an adult about it."

I chug from my water bottle, trying to put out the indignant fire raging in my empty stomach. Egg has the good sense not to talk to me right now.

If you're not gonna do it at 100 percent, then why bother?

You might be corps material, Stuart Trout, but I plan to go all the way to the top. And that means I will start looking for a new partner for real, come Monday. Stuart Trout is not gold medal material. It's time to cut him loose.

"Okay, once more from the top." Egg pushes Record on his phone and skates out to the center of the rink.

We go over the Frankensteined phoenix number to the boss's specifications until Ernie—who has already hand-filled all the holes in the ice created by our toe picks this morning—threatens to run us over with the Zamboni if we don't get off the ice.

"You have the choreography down, but it still lacks something." Egg looks at some of the rough footage on his phone.

"What are you talking about?" I fall into Table #1 across from Egg. "I finally got the throw triple lutz. Okay, that last one was a little sloppy, but I'll have it consistently tomorrow. I promise."

"You still don't get it. It's *not* about the jumps." Egg collapses over the table. He bangs his head several times before looking up again. "It's that you still skate like a little girl. Why can't you skate like a woman?"

The idea knocks the wind out of me. He thinks I'm the weakest link.

Egg runs a hand through his sweat-flattened hair and blows air out of his cheeks. "Sorry. I forget that you're only sixteen. Your whole frame of reference is like, reality TV and five months of high school. What do you know about real life?"

He's been at college for five months, and suddenly he's an expert on real life.

"Have you ever even been on a date, Stuart?" I say, and Egg mumbles a nonanswer. "Have you ever kissed a girl? Or a guy?"

"I don't see what this has to do with anything."

"Then don't lecture me about real life when you obviously don't know what the hell you are talking about."

"Hey, Miss Low Blood Sugar, go take a break. Eat. Nap. Whatever helps you get your panties out of a bunch." Egg snatches his phone and empty water bottle off the table and stomps into the snack bar area. "I'm going to call Midori and see if she'll let me rent out the rink tonight. Time is flying by. I've got to get this project done. No matter what it takes."

I snatch my water bottle off the table and head toward the locker room. Except I forget my phone. When I double back to Table #1, Egg is on his phone, his back to me. The Zamboni is so loud that Egg has one hand over his ear.

"C'mon, Crystal, I need a woman for the job," Egg yells into the phone. "You don't even have to get all the choreography. I'll splice the footage together with some of my solo stuff and some of the stuff with Olivia. I need someone more mature than Olivia. I know she has a throw triple lutz, but she doesn't have the artistry that you do. She will one day when she's older. Yeah. Maybe not. Being washed-up at sixteen is a hard pill to swallow. No, Britney is in London right now. She wouldn't be able to get back in time. Please, Crystal. I'm desperate here. How about Sunday, then? I can switch my flight and leave early Monday instead. Awesome! Thank you. I owe you so big."

I snatch my phone off the table without Egg seeing me and storm back to the locker room. I only need five minutes to change, but it takes another fifteen to get the knife out of my back.

"Hey, good news," Egg says like we're totally cool again.

Before I can reply, "You've replaced me with Crystal?" Egg holds up a piece of paper.

Closed for a private function. 7—10 p.m. We apologize for any inconvenience. Ice Dreams.

"Your mom said I could buy the rink tonight so we can have more practice time. Crystal has privates this afternoon, but then it's all ours."

"Must be nice to have a never-ending cash flow to buy whatever and *whoever* you want."

"I know you're frustrated, but don't take it out on me."

"You're one to talk."

"I gave you five hundred bucks. What else do you want from me?"

"How about some honesty?"

"What?"

"If you don't think I'm good enough for this job, then say so. Don't go behind my back and outsource it," I say, and Egg recoils. "Because I am the best. Yes, I'm having some consistency issues, but Crystal doesn't even *have* a throw triple lutz. And Britney Freakin' Xiao? Are you kidding me?"

Egg slumps down at Table #1.

"You can switch partners all you want, but maybe you need to face the fact that *you* are the weakest link here." I give Egg a matching third-degree burn like the one I've been carrying around inside me since Skate Detroit.

Instead of arguing with me, Egg says, "I know."

Egg's eyes turn watery. He grabs his workout bag and stomps out the front door. I limp into Mom's office and slam the door. My skate bag slides off my aching shoulder and thunks on the floor. A sob hitches in my chest. If I can't be a normal teen and I can't be a normal skater, who am I? I rest my forehead against the door and listen to Ernie driving around on the ice. My ice.

Family legend is that I was the most colicky baby on the face of the planet. Some desperate new parents drive their cranky kid around in a car. My parents used to drive me around on a Zamboni. The loud, hypnotic buzz has always had an effect on me. Even now. I close my eyes and listen. The storm raging inside me begins to calm.

"You know what, Midori?" Dad gives Mom a pointed look as I fall down on the ice and kick my booted feet like frustrated five-year-olds tend to do when they are so done with today. "The ice is looking a little ragged."

Mom, who looks so done with me, says, "Agreed. Livy? Olivia? Olivia Midori Kennedy! Never mind, Daddy, I guess Olivia is too tired to drive the Zamboni with you today."

"No, I'm not!" I can see five-year-old Olivia clearly. Her hair is in a sloppy bun because she refuses to let her mom brush it. And she has on her favorite red, sparkly skate outfit that she's worn every day for two weeks straight. "I wanna drive the 'boni."

"You can ride the Zamboni with me if you can be calm." Dad gives me a hand off the ice. "I'll let you drive the Zamboni if you can show me a solid toe loop."

And I do, plus a salchow—because even at five, I'm extra.

"Now, that's my girl." Dad scoops me up, plants a cold kiss on my cheek, and lifts me up to his shoulder.

"Careful, Mike." Mom puts her hands out to break my fall.

"I'm not going to drop her, Midori." Dad's voice is unusually hard.

I squeal as he skates off with me perched on his left shoulder. "Come on. Let's get our skates off and the 'boni out. Afterward, we'll show Mommy how you do your sit spins like the big girls do."

The buzz of the Zamboni fades. My eyes flutter open. I turn and catch my reflection in the small mirror that hangs on Mom's wall.

The ice is looking a little ragged.

I'm still pissed at Egg, but at least my tantrum is over. I wonder if Ernie would let me drive the 'boni a few laps. I promise not to run over Egg with it, even if he deserves it. I open the door to ask Ernie, but he's already putting the Zamboni in the shed. My heart sinks. Crystal's melodic laugh echoes through the now-quiet rink as she helps her student get into a jumping harness. I can't even with her right now. I close the door, hobble over to Mom's thread-bare couch, and flop onto it. I dig my phone out, hoping for a text from Jonah. I need something to help me pull all the pieces back together. But there's nothing. That's because Jonah is a gold medal–level skater. He doesn't let anything distract him. Not even me.

I tuck my legs up and bury my face in my kneecaps. I don't have to do this. Egg doesn't even want me here, anyway. I could go to the dance tonight instead. I could call Naomi right now. I'm sure she'd welcome me back. I fantasize about pushing the stack of bills back into Egg's hands and telling him that he can't buy me. That I'm sure Crystal would be happy to take his money. But there is so much I could buy. Tickets to the next roller derby bout. A new mini laptop. A few new pieces for my tiny school wardrobe. Not to mention I already spent part of the money last night. I can't pay it back.

Why couldn't I have been born into the Trout family, where money is never an issue?

My stomach growls so loudly that it practically launches me off the couch. I drag myself over to Mom's mini refrigerator with the hope that it doesn't look like our one at home. Nope. The refrigerator is so empty, it almost falls over, especially with the small TV and DVD player perched precariously on top of it. I grab a water bottle and two bites' worth of a granola bar that's been in the fridge since who-knows-when and collapse back on the couch. I gnaw at the stale granola bar.

Forget clothes. I would buy groceries. Steak. Broccoli. Strawberries. Bread. Peanut butter. Milk.

I push the clutter piled on the coffee table to the side so I can prop up my swollen feet. A pile of DVDs landslides into the floor. I slap them back onto the table one by one. Several are autographed Olympians on Ice highlight DVDs to be sold online for a little extra cash. One says *Olympics* on it. My heart clenches. While I've been out being a normal teen, Mom has been reliving her teen years. One last DVD peeks out from underneath the table. I place it on top of the others.

Olivia.

Not Olivia and Stuart. Just Olivia. I smile. I wouldn't mind a trip down memory lane with Baby Olivia, even if she was kind of a pain in the ass. I take the DVD out and spin it around my finger. Is this footage of the little firecracker whose first years as a solo skater could be charitably described as "promising but inconsistent"? At ten years old, the "ice was so ragged" most days that it was Mom who begged Shirley Trout to let Egg skate with me. While the Trouts were traveling most weekends with Scott and Steven's club football teams, the oldest brother, Patrick, got stuck babysitting thirteen-year-old Egg. No college student wants to be saddled with their mouthy little brother most weekends, so Patrick dropped Egg off every Saturday and Sunday for Open Skate whether he wanted to come or not. At first, Egg straight up mocked me. He and his buddy would skate by me, imitating badly whatever jump I was working on. The only difference: Egg started landing the jumps even as his obnoxious friend continued to hit the ice and then howl with laughter at his stupid joke. Mom noticed. Stupid Friend moved on to tormenting someone else, but Egg started training with two Olympic medalists for free in return for partnering their headstrong daughter. And it worked. I became consistent. Not because I was so awesome, but because I wasn't about to let some boy show me up.

I clearly have underestimated my parents. I plan to call Dad out on his part of the subterfuge the next time I see him.

I put the DVD in the player and fall back onto the couch with the grace of a ninety-year-old. I hear the crowd first even though the screen is still black. I settle in to watch Baby Olivia do her thing. My breath hitches when it's my teenage face—not Baby Olivia's—that suddenly fills the screen. The shot is wobbly, as usual, and vertical. Mom has never been the greatest camerawoman.

"Skate Detroit! Number one!" I squeal and do cheerleader-worthy spirit fingers. I'm still wearing my warm-up outfit, but my hair is up, and I have about four inches of makeup on. Because Alexei's motto is "Why do, when you can overdo?"

Mom pans around to Dad, who adds his own pep talk. "You and Stuart go out there and show 'em how it's done. Grab it and growl, tiger."

I give the camera one last goofy wave before skating off to the prep area. The footage cuts off abruptly and then comes back on. Now Egg and I are in full phoenix mode. Our choreography and music are new, but our costumes are the same. Alexei was pissed—though surprisingly, Mom wasn't—when the seamstress said she couldn't get our new costumes made in time for this beginning-of-the-season competition.

Turn it off, my inner voice commands. *Turn it off before it's too late.*

It's like a car wreck. I can't turn my head even though I know there is carnage waiting on the other side.

"I hate that costume," Dad mumbles in the background. "It's too sexy for a sixteen-year-old. Oompf."

Mom must have elbowed him.

"I hope she can land that triple-double-double," Dad says like he's concerned that I can't.

"Hush, Mike," Mom says in the background, and I have to agree with her.

Mom pans over to Alexei, who is giving us last-minute instructions before our names are announced.

"We should be over there," Dad says.

"I know, but Alexei thinks we're part of the problem. They're senior level now. We have to completely step away this season and trust Alexei's coaching."

Our names echo across the Detroit Skating Club's rink and the small crowd gives us some polite applause. Egg and I skate out to the middle and take our opening pose. I put on the "sexy face" that Alexei told me I needed for our opening pose. Granola bar almost comes out my nose. It's one step up from a duck face. It's not sexy. It's ridiculous. The music starts mercifully soon after *the face.* The knot in my stomach releases as the routine progresses on. It's not great, but it doesn't completely suck.

"Oooooo, here comes the throw triple lutz. Land it. Land it. Land it. OH! So close," Dad says from off-screen.

Dad adds color commentary throughout my performance. Our perfectly matched spin combo elicits a squeal from Mom. And then comes the platter lift. We set up for the lift. I grab Egg's forearms right above his wrists, and he grabs my hip bones. We push off the ice until I am above Egg's head in a plank, my legs crossed at the ankles. As Egg starts to rotate on the ice, I release his forearms and reach back into a swan dive shape. My heart jumps to my throat as I watch Egg's back foot hit a rough patch of ice. Thank God, Egg stumbled forward and not backward. Otherwise, I would've taken a header into the ice like Mom did. Off-camera, I hear Mom's scream and the crowd's gasp as Egg pitches forward. You can see the fear on my face. My ankles flame remembering how hard my blades struck the ice coming down. Egg honors Rule #1. Instead of letting me go and saving himself, he holds me even tighter. I remember the sound of Egg's shirt ripping under the armpits as his shoulders hyperflexed and nearly dislocated because of me. We wobble and bobble, but Egg holds on to me until we get our blades under us again and finish the routine. Finally, we dip into our final pose, and I make *the face* again. It looks even worse this time because the pain is shining through.

"She's okay," Dad says off-camera, and I hear Mom sniffle.

Mom cheers loudly, the footage bouncing around with her clapping. I wave to the small crowd with a huge fake smile on my face, like my ankles don't feel like someone has a blowtorch on them. For the first time, I notice Egg's face. Egg is always pale, but former Junior US Pairs Champion Stuart Trout looks positively green. He waves to the crowd, but he's not smiling. Egg is not that good of an actor. Finally, the screen goes black even though I can still hear the crowd. I shake my head. This isn't the first time Mom has shot fascinating footage of the inside of her purse. Before I can peel myself off the couch to pop the DVD out, I hear Mom's voice again.

"That was scary, Mike. Really scary."

"Livy looks okay. Stuart, however, I'm not so sure about. Be sure that Mr. Trout and I will be having a word about that drop. And I'll make damn sure Alexei gives Stuart extra laps for breaking Rule Number One."

"Honey, he's rubbing his right shoulder."

"Okay, he'll get penalty laps *after* he checks out clean with Sandy."

"I hope the judges are merciful this time."

"That performance . . . hmmm. In fact, the whole last season . . . hmmm. Maybe they should have stayed at the junior level another year?"

"You were right, honey. I should've never listened to Alexei. They aren't ready for senior level competition," Mom says, her voice tight with emotion.

"We better get over there. Reality is about to crash down on Livy in about thirty seconds."

"Mike, maybe it's time to stop."

"Unfortunately, I think so."

My parents' voices silence as Egg's and my dismal score echoes around the rink.

The crowd hisses and Dad drops an f-bomb.

"Oh God, it's worse than we thought," Dad says. "The USFSA rep is headed their way and it *won't* be good news after that performance."

I hear scrambling and shuffling before the footage cuts off. Mom didn't need to film what happened next. I remember it clearly.

The world as I knew it ended.

Chapter 19

I ugly cry until I'm sure there is more moisture in the couch than in my body. I knew my parents were disappointed with our Skate Detroit performance, but they let the USFSA rep be the bad guy. The truth is, they gave up on us—really, me—long before the USFSA did. Dad and Alexei had argued all through the last half of our senior debut year. Sometimes about Egg, but mostly about me. Especially how I wasn't getting any better despite all the changes.

I grab my knees close to my chest to keep from exploding. Egg isn't the weakest link. I am. I bury my head in a paisley throw pillow and scream until my throat hurts as bad as the rest of my body.

Not only does the USFSA think I'm not good enough to be a competitive skater, neither do my parents. Or Alexei. Or Crystal. Or Egg. If I'm completely honest with myself, neither do I. I didn't inherit that X factor that Mom and Dad had. That one magical element that takes a great skater and makes them an Olympic skater.

That thing Jonah has. I both love him and hate him for it.

Screw this. I'm going home.

My abductors and adductors are so tight that I can't get off the couch, though. I'll wait ten minutes. Maybe by then, my face won't be so blotchy for my one-mile walk of shame back home. My left calf cramps thinking about it. Even worse, I can hear Crystal's voice echoing around the rink, encouraging her student. The knife in my back twists a little more.

I grab my phone and pull up Mack's number. At least there is one person in my life who thinks I'm good enough. Yeah, what a great pair we are. Losers. Complete losers. At least Mack has the derby girls. I'm not even 100 percent sure I have Jonah in my corner. Yeah, he likes my outer package, but does he think I'm good enough on the inside too?

Instead of calling her, I pull up the video Mack made of Jonah and me doing our signature move. I watch it a good hundred times. It soothes my heart even though my body still aches. I'm on the 101st repeat when my eyelids get heavy. My phone slips out of my hand onto the floor, but I don't care. Jonah has chased the demons away.

I'm not sure what time it is when I finally wake up again. A puddle of slobber has escaped the corner of my mouth while I was comatose on the couch. Mom's office is pitch-black except for the tiny red light on the DVD player. It's not enough light to guide me to the light switch, and the new bruise on my shin proves that.

Crap, what time is it?

I slap around the doorframe until the lights come on, burning my retinas. I retrieve my phone to find that I have four texts and two voice messages from Egg, but I ignore them. It's a little after eight. I could still go to the dance. I could go home right now, shower, change, and enjoy the rest of the dance like a normal teen.

I slump back down on the couch. There's only one person I want to be a normal teen with, and he's currently in Utah trying to become the next Apolo Ohno.

Using my cell phone as a flashlight, I weave through the pitch-black rink over to the snack bar and flip on the lights. The snack bar is immaculate, as always. Mack doesn't do anything half-assed. The drink cups are stacked in equal piles. The napkins, straws, and condiment packets have been filled to the rims. I can even see my reflection in the highly polished glass of the pretzel display.

Wow, I look like crap. I press down the pieces of hair that are sticking out the side of my head at a ninety-degree angle. The small amount of eyeliner I had on this morning has run down under my right eye and completely disappeared from my left.

The pretzels sing their salty siren song from their hangers. I'm not supposed to eat the merchandise. I shouldn't eat the merchandise. My stomach growls. I eat three of the merchandise anyway. My stomach balloons out, and I don't care. I add a large Pepsi to the damage. And when I'm sure my stomach might burst, I add a Pixy Stix on top of it all because I haven't had Pixy Stix since I was eight.

Damn it. I deserve a Pixy Stix.

I waddle over to Table #1 and collapse in a gluttonous stupor. I'm seriously going to puke. In an attempt not to fall into a carb coma, I pull my phone back out and watch Jonah's and my footage again. This time, I don't focus on Jonah. Instead, I focus on me. I push pause when Jonah and I look over at each other in our hydroblade counterbalance. My eyes are closed, but a huge smile lights up my face. I look like one of those busty women on the front of the Walmart romance novels that Crystal is always reading.

I restart the short video and watch me again. I watch my face, my arms, my legs, my upper back. This girl looks nothing like the one skating on Mom's DVD. Who is this girl?

I scramble out of the snack bar and head back to Mom's office for my skate bag.

I watch Jonah's and my video one last time as I lace up my skates. It's time to find that new girl and bring her forward. I click on my skating music playlist and pop in my Bluetooth earbuds. "Stay with Me" by Epic Danger comes on. The haunting melody tugs at my heart.

I've always liked this song, but now the lyrics have a completely new meaning. I put my phone on top of the rink's tissue box and step out onto the mostly clean ice. My heart feels lighter than it has in years. I apply the phoenix choreography, minus the jumps, to the music. I remember the artistry of the ice dancers from Australia and the passion of the British couple. His strong arms wrapped around her sequined waist. The look on her face—which was not *the face*. I close my eyes and imagine that Jonah is here with me. I feel his hands in mine. The pull in my arm as we come into a perfect counterbalance. The heat flowing between us even though the air is cool. Strong. Rooted. Balanced. Happy.

A stupid tear sneaks down my cheek. I reach my hands out and shadow skate the routine like Jonah is here. Halfway through, I throw out Egg's Frankensteined choreography all together. I restart the song and create a new piece for Jonah and me. And somehow, my dream Jonah miraculously knows this choreography. Our chemistry shines through, and the judges can see it. I let that fantasy play through my mind for three more repeats of "Stay with Me" before I have a reality check. Even if he weren't on the Olympic gold path for short track speed skating, there's no way that Jonah could be at my level anytime soon. We can never be partners.

As the song comes to an end, I do a variation on the final phoenix pose—minus *the face*—and let my mind wander. I still want to be a skater, but I want to do it on my terms. Not somebody else's. Just like Egg, I need to start looking out for #1 for a change. Maybe it's time for me to return to being a solo skater.

Slow clapping interrupts my thoughts. I whip around to see Egg standing at Table #1. When I get to the wall, Egg drops his gaze. I drop mine too. Always in tandem, we look up at the same time and say, "I'm sorry."

I come off the ice and stand in front of Egg. "Can we pretend like today never happened?"

"Yes, but I'm still mad at you for not answering your damn phone."

"I know. I promise I'll be a professional for the rest of the weekend. I'll even give you a refund for wasting your time."

Egg gives me a confused look and then a dismayed chuckle. "What? No. I thought you'd been abducted or hit by a car or something on your way home. And it would be all my fault for being a first class a-hole about some stupid audition. I forgot Coach Kennedy's Rule Number One today. I'm sorry."

I throw my arms around Egg and bury my face in his chest, so he won't see the tears beading up in my eyes. Mom is probably passed out on the couch at home. Dad is soaking up the limelight out on the road somewhere. When would they notice I was missing? The waterworks completely open up.

"What? What? What?" Egg wraps his arms around me tighter, and I blubber into his shoulder. Egg lets me emotionally vomit all over him for several more minutes before I can finally get it all back together. "Talk to me, Olivia. We've been partners for a long time. Sometimes I feel like you're closer to me than even my brothers. In fact, on most days, I would happily give your parents a two-for-one trade so you could be my little sister. Despite this afternoon, we really do work better together than anybody else I've ever met."

"I'm sorry. I know I'm the weakest link. Not you. Me." I sniff and wipe my eyes on my shoulder. "The USFSA cut our funding because of me."

"Don't." Egg gently pushes me away.

But I do anyway. "Why didn't you cut me loose well before the phoenix fiasco? You could be so much further along in your career by now if you didn't have me weighing you down."

"What are you talking about? You didn't weigh me down. You lifted me up. You're the one with the real talent here. Somebody should have put me out of my misery a long time ago. You're right. I'm not gold medal material. I wish I were, but I'm not."

"No, that was me being a jerk. I take it all back."

"Well, yes, it was a jerk thing to say, but it was the truth. And sometimes the truth hurts. That's why this audition is so important to me, Livy. I may not be good enough for the Olympics, but I still love to skate. I don't want to be a rent-a-skater-boy anymore. I don't want to be bought by Britney Xiao or any other ice princess. I want to skate on my own terms. I want to be Stuart. I want to travel the world. I want to fall in love. Multiple times. I want to cram as many memories into my head as I can before settling down and being an adult."

"Me too." I should tell him the whole truth, but I can't. Not yet. I'm afraid to say the dream out loud. It's too new. But I do admit to Egg, "I don't know how to be a normal teen. I've been trying for the last five months, but I totally suck at it."

Egg laughs and throws his arm around my shoulders. "Me too. So let's stop trying to be someone we aren't and do what we're best at. Whatever happens, happens."

"I don't want to do Alexei's choreography. I have a new idea."

I grab my phone and a tissue. Egg looks over my shoulder at my song choice.

"Man, this song? Are you trying to make me cry?" Egg fakes melodramatic sobs until we're both laughing. "C'mon, Short Stuff, let's channel some of our angst into art."

"Got it. And Egg, why didn't you stop me from making *the face*? I looked like a complete idiot."

"Yeah, there are quite a few things I wish I could go back and change." Egg stops, takes a dramatic pose, and makes *the face*. I laugh. "But having you as my partner wouldn't be one of them."

My heart warms. I'm going to stop pretending like I'm a mature adult skater and be the passionate, mature teen skater that I am.

It's midnight before we finally call it quits for the day. My feet sting, my back aches, and my hands are frozen, but my heart is content. The new choreography is set. *My* choreography. My art. My expression. My love song for Jonah. I can't wait for him to see it.

Chapter 20

We get a late start on Sunday. Egg insists on taking Mom and me out for an early dinner at the Wisteria Village Cafe to thank her for the extra rink time. Closing time at Ice Dreams can't come fast enough for me.

"I can't wait to show you our new choreography," I tell Mom as we enter her favorite restaurant.

"*Irasshaimase!*" the chef standing in the back yells without looking up.

"*Sato-san, ohisashiburi desu,*" Mom yells back across the empty restaurant.

"Midori-san!" The middle-aged man puts down whatever he was working on, wipes his hands on his apron, and jogs to the front of the store. Though Mr. Sato bows, Mom offers her hand to shake instead. "It's good to see you again. And your lovely daughter. Where is your husband tonight?"

"Houston, I believe."

"That's too bad. Come in." Mr. Sato grabs a couple of menus and leads us to a booth near the back. "Your usual table. Skyler will be over in a minute to take your order. If you want something not listed on the menu, Midori-san, let me know."

"You are too kind." Mom looks better than she has in months. But as soon as Mr. Sato leaves, the facade falls away. She blows a pained breath out between her teeth and kneads her lower back.

Out in the real world—the supersized world—I realize how much weight my mom has lost in the last couple of months. Mom's never been big, but now she's looking skeletal.

"I wish Mack could have come with us. She would have loved this." Egg pulls out his phone and takes a picture of the framed picture on the wall, which is surrounded by fake wisteria.

I groan. I'm used to seeing autographed pictures of my parents hanging in some of the smaller restaurants and businesses in town. This one is different, though. Five-year-old Olivia had insisted on inserting herself into their Olympic medal picture, and Mr. Sato gladly provided the Sharpie for me to do it. I even wrote *Olivia* in big, messy letters above my stick-figure self-portrait. Like I said, even at five, I was extra.

"No phones at the dinner table, Stuart," Mom says as a tall, white teen girl with long brown hair arrives at our table.

"*Irasshaimase,*" she says, sounding just like Mr. Sato. She pulls a pad of paper from her lavender-colored apron. "I'm Skyler, and I will be your server tonight. Mr. Sato insists that your meal is on the house and for you to order whatever you'd like."

Though my tongue wants tonkatsu, my brain knows a fried pork cutlet is going to sit like a rock in my stomach when I'm skating later. I order zaru soba—cold buckwheat noodles—and a side of teriyaki salmon instead. Egg orders a whole bento set with tempura shrimp and vegetables. He's going to regret that later.

"I'm feeling a little under the weather today," Mom reads the girl's name tag, "Skyler. Would you ask Sato-san if he could make me ochazuke? I know that is insulting to ask of such an accomplished chef, but that's the comfort food I've been craving lately."

Skyler reads our orders back to us in reverse, looking at each of us as she does. She gives me a second look.

"Are you Olivia?" Skyler says, and I blink.

I nod my head at the picture on the wall. "Yeah, I was kinda extra when I was five."

"You're my little sister's ice skating teacher," Skyler says. When I give her a blank look because neither of my remaining two pupils is white, she adds, "Lina Kitagawa. She's my half sister. She talks about you all the time. 'Miss Olivia said this. Miss Olivia said that.' You are like her idol. And the fact that you are biracial like Lina makes you even cooler in her book."

"Aw, everybody appreciates having their own personal fan club of one," I joke.

Skyler looks over her shoulder and then slides out her phone. "Could I possibly take a selfie with you? It would make Lina's day."

As this hasn't happened in a long, long, looooong time, I'm happy to oblige. I slide out of the booth. Skyler is so much taller than I am that I could practically fit under her armpit. We do a couple of different shots before she races off.

"Aaand this is pretty much what my life looks like at Tech when I'm with my brothers. Stuart who?" Egg laughs, but I know it hurts him.

"Believe me, sometimes I wish everybody would forget who I am." Mom fingers a piece of faux wisteria decorating the candle on our table. "And what happened to me."

"We decided to chuck Alexei's choreography," Egg says, bringing Mom back to the present. "It just wasn't us."

"It was a little too adult for you."

"It's not that," I say. "This new choreography reflects more of who I am. Who Egg is. It's about our experience versus Alexei's experience."

"And the dude's had a lot of 'experiences' with multiple members of your generation of skaters, Midori," Egg says, and Mom colors. "Or so I hear."

Mom clears her throat. "I can't wait to see it tomorrow. I'm sure it will be special."

Egg smiles, but I know my mom. That wasn't a compliment. She doesn't think I can pull it off. Then again, she's not my #1 fan.

"Mack's going to meet us at the rink to film tonight," I say, and add my own dig, "That way we know we will get footage we can actually use."

The crease between Mom's eyebrows deepens.

"But we want your feedback, of course, when we're completely done," Egg backpedals. "You *are* the expert here."

"Of course. We aren't going to send out anything that isn't the best . . . that you can do."

The only thing that keeps me from completely going off is Skyler returning with our dinner. Mom and I both put on our best kiss-and-cry smiles.

Skyler places Mom's small bowl of rice and shredded seaweed swimming in green tea in front of her. My box with gray noodles is next.

"Is it okay if I put the picture on my social media?" Skyler says.

"Sure. I'd love that." I can't admit that Mom deactivated my account, so I add, "Will you tag Ice Dreams?"

"Sure thing." Skyler fangirls a bit before racing back to the kitchen to retrieve Egg's bento.

To make my Japanese teacher proud, I say, "*Itadakimasu*" before grabbing a pair of chopsticks and digging into the best meal I've had since Jonah's birthday party.

"So what's the gossip on Alexei?" Mom says to Egg. "Did he go back to the Ukraine after we . . . parted company after Skate Detroit?"

"Yes, but not without a stint with Britney Xiao first." Egg digs into his bento. "I heard he lasted two weeks. A new personal best for Britney, I'm sure."

Mom and I both roll our eyes. Mom was definitely your stereo-typical overly involved skater mom, but Mrs. Xiao takes the gold in the Obnoxious Skater Mom category.

"It's a shame. Britney has so much potential." Mom shakes her head in mock pity.

"Too bad you can't buy class." Egg says what everybody is thinking.

Egg fills Mom in on all the hot skating gossip while we eat. The senior level is one big dysfunctional—and occasionally back-stabbing—family. The stories are endless. Whether they are true or not doesn't matter.

"Are they still talking about us?" I have to know. When Egg makes a noncommittal noise, I know the answer is yes.

"Skate Detroit was months ago," Egg says through a mouthful of rice. "Move on, people. Nothing to see here."

"Give it time. The whole thing will burn out soon enough." Mom sips her tea.

But I *want* people to talk about us again. Only, in a good way.

"Here, Livy, finish this off for me." Mom pushes her half-eaten bowl of ochazuke at me. "I'm full."

Egg checks the time on his phone. "We've got to get going. Ice Dreams will be closing soon."

Mom tells Egg to put his wallet away and then pretends like she's going to pay. Mr. Sato insists on comping our meal. Mom finally puts her empty wallet back in her purse and over-thanks him.

"Wait!" Skyler runs from the back of the now-bustling restau-rant with a small paper gift bag. "I made these today."

She bows and presents the bag to my mom with two hands. Mom nods her head and accepts them with two hands. When Mom opens the bag to peek inside, a familiar scent wafts out.

"Melon pan!" I recognize the little domes of sugary goodness immediately. "My Japanese grandparents buy these for me every time I visit them in California."

Granted, that's been a while, but it's still a positive memory for me.

"Thank you. Both of you. Your kindness and support mean so much to me." Mom's eyes glisten. "To all of us at Ice Dreams."

As we walk out into the parking lot, Mom hands her keys to Egg to drive her back home. Ice Dreams' reigning queen has morphed back into her unfortunate normal.

"Thank you for insisting we go out, Stuart." Mom puts her hand on Egg's arm. "My body might be hurting, but my spirit is lifted."

Egg puts his hand over Mom's and squeezes it. "I'm glad. You deserve it after all you've done for me. I wouldn't be here if you hadn't taken a chance on that brat who was dumped at your rink every weekend by his slacker older brother."

"Believe me, you were an answer to our prayers."

Mom's words burn in the pit of my stomach. She still sees me as ragged ice. I can't wait to prove her wrong. I slide into the back seat with the melon pan. I'm going to save mine until Jonah gets back. He might have hotteok, but I have something even sweeter to share with him.

Chapter 21

The always-punctual Mack is already at the rink and set up to record by the time Egg and I get there. I double-check the glittery eyeliner and bloodred lipstick Mack talked me into. Mack also insisted that I slick the sides of my hair back to "look fierce." I wasn't sure at first, but it's growing on me. Naomi's Auntie Jennifer ain't got nothin' on Mack's aesthetic skills. And I definitely don't look like a little kid now.

"Are you ready for Kennedy and Trout 2.0?" Egg says when I lap him during our warm-up. I set up and land a perfect triple salchow. "I will take that as a yes."

"Wooooo, you go girl!" Mack hoots from the side. "No wait, don't. I don't have the camera turned on yet. Okay. Now let's do this thing."

I go to the boards and shed my Ice Dreams jacket. I smooth the wrinkles out of my phoenix costume. I hope the seams can take the strain.

"Yeah, I'm thinking these costumes are a bad idea," Egg says as we set up for our opening pose. "Wait. Hold on a sec. This thing is riding up on me."

Egg digs at his costume. Both of us have filled out since we last skated together. We finally look like adults even if technically only one of us is.

"Are you sure I can't change?" Egg says.

"No," Mack yells across the ice. "Honey, if you got it, flaunt it."

Egg stands a little taller and hits his pose. Mack whoops. I weave myself around Egg while shaking my head.

Mack could make an hour-long special with all the footage she's taken of us tonight. Egg sends her home at nine to start the editing process while we fine-tune. We send our costumes with her too, so Granny MacIntosh can reinforce a couple of the seams that have already started to fray. As it is, I'm about one sneeze away from a wardrobe malfunction.

"I should call in sick to school tomorrow so we can keep filming." I pull my Ice Dreams jacket over my plain black skate top and yoga pants. I'm glad to be rid of the eyeliner and lipstick for the night, though my hair may never go back to normal, thanks to the amount of hair product Mack used on me.

Egg sits down at Table #1 and unlaces his boots with a sigh of relief. "Or we could splice something over that last throw triple lutz and call it done." Egg places his tiger-striped soakers over his blades and throws his blade towel in his bag.

"No, we should fix it. Mom can film for us. Though we should probably buy her a tripod on our way home." I pull at Egg's arm. "C'mon, put your skates back on. We'll run the throw triple lutz a couple more times, and then we'll call it a day. I know we can get this perfect by tomorrow."

Egg flops over on the table, groaning. "Kill me now."

"Stop being such a baby." I slide my guards off and step back out on the ice.

Instead of joining me, though, Egg fiddles with his phone. A moment later he suddenly takes off toward the front door.

"C'mon, Egg, fifteen more minutes," I yell after him. "I want to fix that one part in the middle. Let's change the butterfly-into-a-back-sit part. How about we do a butterfly into a back camel instead? It will make the whole sequence look smoother."

Instead, Egg flips off half the lights.

"Egg! Stuart Trout!" I come into a pool of light so I can practice my sit spins. "Your work ethic sucks."

I wind up and pull my arms in tight. The rink blurs as I rotate faster. I drop down into a sit spin. When I come back up, I spin even faster. Like I haven't since competition. Like I'm using centrifugal force to throw off the rest of Old Olivia. Finally, I push out and dig my toe pick into the ice.

"Woo, Egg, did you see the speed on that one? Egg?" I look out into the dim light of the rink for my partner, but he's not there.

Instead, in a shaft of light at the edge of the ice stands a cutting figure with a large bouquet of roses in one hand and my skate guards in the other. Jonah doesn't even flinch when my sharp stop flings snow all over the top of his shiny black dress shoes. I look him up and down. In a royal-blue button-down shirt and charcoal dress pants, Jonah looks even better in real life than in my fantasy. I throw my arms around him, and the spark from Jonah's lips reignites my weary body back to full burn.

"I'm sorry about this weekend." Jonah holds out the flowers to me when we finally break back apart. "Please don't be mad at me."

I slip my skate guards on and take the fuchsia roses from him. These could possibly be the most beautiful flowers in existence, even if the tag left on them says they were $12.99 and came from Target.

"Thank you. I'm so glad you're home. Well, back in Phoenix." I lace my fingers through Jonah's and lead him to Table #1.

Jonah sits first and pulls me onto his lap, wrapping his arms around me and the flowers protectively. "I am home."

"Wait. Where's Egg?" Jonah and I may need to take our welcome home to a more secluded area, like the supply closet.

"He's in the parking lot running interference with my dad."

"Nice. Speaking of nice, you clean up nice." I put my flowers on the table next to a gift bag so I can wrap both arms around Jonah. His outfit is perfect. His hair is perfect. His smile is perfect. "Seriously, like K-pop-idol nice."

"Thanks." Jonah pulls me in closer to him. "Gotta have a plan B in case this whole Olympic speed skater thing doesn't work out."

I nuzzle Jonah's neck, letting my lips trail down toward the collar of his shirt. My eyes pop open when I hit a piece of thick fabric unlike the softness of Jonah's shirt. A red, white, and blue ribbon peeks out from under his collar. I loop my fingers under the ribbon and follow it down Jonah's chest. I have to unbutton three of the buttons on his shirt to see, but there it is. A gold medal glows against his skin.

"It has a twin for the one-thousand-meter race, but I thought it would be too pretentious to wear both of them. I guess K-pop will have to wait for a while longer."

I throw my arms around Jonah's neck and hug him tight. "Congratulations."

"Does this mean you've forgiven me?"

"Yes. I get it. When you're in the zone, everything else melts away. It has to. We can't be distracted when we're competing."

"Oh, I was distracted." Jonah digs his phone out of his back pocket. "How am I supposed to concentrate after seeing this?"

My heart hiccups. It's the phoenix costume. Oh Lord, I'm making *the face*. Somebody shoot me now.

"Where did you get this?"

"The internet. Apparently this costume caused quite a stir on the skating circuit." One eyebrow pops up as Jonah enlarges the picture. "I can see why. It does make the perfect screen saver, though."

"Do not show that picture to anybody. Ever. I'm not kidding."

"Why? It's on the internet. It wasn't hard to find." Jonah and I wrestle over the phone. "So, do I ever get to see the costume in person?"

"We'll see." I pull the phone out of his hand and slap it on the table. "What's in the bag?"

"A gift. For you." Jonah plops the large, shiny black bag on my lap.

I dig through the tissue paper to find a heavy shoebox. I pull a black skate boot from the box.

"Um, these are men's skates."

"I know. They're actually for me." Jonah puts both skates on the table. "Dad and I made a deal. One gold in Utah and I get to add an hour of cross-training with you each week. I got two golds. He bought me ice skates as soon as the store opened this morning."

"Skate with me."

"Right now?"

"Yes, for a little bit."

A few minutes later, Jonah steps out onto the ice and enters my world. My new normal.

"Wow, this feels awkward." Jonah trips on his toe pick and collides with me. "I know how to skate. I swear, I do."

I wrap my arms around Jonah until he can find his balance again. "It's okay. You have to get used to them. Keep going. Find your balance."

It takes a few minutes, but soon Jonah is balanced enough that he can lace his fingers through mine. We glide around the rink between the patches of light and shadow. On our second loop, Jonah suddenly cuts to the left, pulling me into the darkest part of the rink. His arms wrap around me, pushing me backward. Soon I'm sandwiched between the padded wall and Jonah. Our blades tangle as I pull Jonah even closer to me. The gold medal presses into my skin.

We are busy perfecting our performance when the lights suddenly come on, blinding us.

"Well, this is awkward." Egg flips the lights back down to half. "I hate to interrupt your hero's welcome, but I'm beat. Can we wrap things up here? Your dad is waiting, Jonah."

My cheeks burn, but Jonah laughs. He laces his fingers through mine and pulls me back to the cut in the boards next to Table #1.

"Lock up and meet me in the car in five, Livy," Egg says.

It's ten minutes before we get our skates off and finish our goodnight kiss. Egg gives me a weird look when I finally slide into the passenger seat of Mom's car.

"What?" I say.

"Feel free to channel some of *that* into our performance tomorrow. Also, can you call in sick to school tomorrow after all? While I was sitting here for-freakin'-ever, I realized you're right. A butterfly into a back camel would work better." Egg continues to talk, but I'm distracted by thoughts of Jonah. Egg taps my thigh to bring me back down to earth. "Ahem. As your surrogate big brother, I'm going to have a little man-to-man chat tomorrow with Skater Boy titled: 'You hurt her, and I kick your ass.'"

"I'm not going to do lifts with Jonah. Stop worrying."

"Thanks, but Rule Number One applies *off* the ice too."

Chapter 22

You're not coming to school today? Jonah texts me during his lunch period.

I've been at the rink since sunup. It was no biggie talking Mom into letting me skip school today to help Egg. In fact, after seeing some of yesterday's rough footage on my phone, Mom insisted on having Egg pick up both of us this morning. Even Mack came in early with her laptop to tweak yesterday's footage before her shift. It's like a freakin' family reunion. All we need is Dad. And a certain gold-medal-winning skater boy.

I text Jonah back. I'll be back tomorrow. We have to finish the audition tape today.

I miss you.

I miss you too.

Also, I just sat through 300 pictures from the dance. Normal is so overrated. My weekend was way better.

I feel a little stab.

Jonah immediately texts back: The very last part was totally better. At least until Stuart interrupted. Redo? Sometime soon?

YES! You tell me when and where.

Casa de la Choi . . . hmmm. Maybe next
weekend? Need to look at skate calendar
and get back to you.

My phone suddenly flies out of my hand.

"Are we gonna skate or what?" Egg holds my phone over his head. "Put your personal life on hold and be a professional skater."

"I *am* a professional skater." And for the first time in a long time, I mean that.

Egg puts my phone in his gym bag. "You get it back when you land a throw triple lutz. No wobbles."

"Fine."

"Okay, Stuart, Livy, I'm ready." Mom perches on the edge of a stool behind the tripod.

I head for the ice. I stop to pop the lens cap off and hand it to Mom.

"I knew that," Mom says.

"It's the second button."

"I know."

"And don't zoom in and out. Leave it where it is."

"I know how to use a video camera, Olivia Midori Kennedy."

And even though that's debatable, Mom's crappy videography skills have changed my life this weekend. So I cut her some slack.

"I know you do." I give her a gentle hug.

She still winces, but smiles. "Now get out there and show 'em how it's done. No wobble on that throw triple lutz. Hold that landing and don't release it until all the energy flows out."

"Yes, Coach."

"That's my girl."

The afternoon flies by as we tweak this and that. I earned my phone back a while ago, but I don't stop to take it. I'm in the zone. I am finally home again.

"Awesome." Egg gives me a bear hug after our last pass. "I knew we still had it, and the platter lift was textbook."

"We should do it one more time from a different angle," Mack says.

"It's good enough, Mack." Mom puts the lens cap back on the video camera. "We don't want to overwork it."

"Just one last time, I swear. Then I'll leave it alone."

"I need a break." Egg comes off the ice and flops down next to Mack.

"I'll make us a round of hot tea." Mom slides off the stool and hobbles toward the snack bar.

I lie down on the ice. That way I can ice my sore back and nap at the same time, because I'm all about multitasking. I listen to Mack and Egg discuss camera shots for about ten seconds before their words begin to melt in my ears. Thankfully, they don't ask for my opinion, because my catnap turns into me being comatose.

"Olivia? Are you okay?" A warm hand on my shoulder lures me back to the surface.

I force my heavy eyelids open. A beautiful face comes into focus above me. When I smile at him, the wrinkle between his eyebrows relaxes.

"You scared me." Jonah pushes a lock of hair behind his ear. "I thought you were hurt."

"Would I have left her on the ice if she were injured?" Egg's voice cascades over the wall from Table #1. "Rule Number One, buddy. Rule Number One."

I push up on my elbows. My heart is warm, but my body is not. Jonah puts out his hands and pulls me to my feet.

"I'm freezing," I say, in case my teeth chattering didn't give that away.

Jonah unzips his hoodie. He steps into me so he can wrap it around both of us. I skate in between Jonah's feet and tuck my icy hands into the back pockets of his jeans.

Jonah's warm breath washes across my neck, and he whispers into my ear, "Your mom is looking at us, isn't she?"

I peek over Jonah's shoulder. Mom is looking at us, a wistful smile on her face.

"Not at all," I say.

"Good."

The gentle press of Jonah's lips on mine still ignites the fire in my veins. My teeth stop chattering immediately. When I come back down to earth, I look over at Mom again. She gives me a thumbs-up.

"Livy, your tea is ready," Mom calls from the snack bar.

After a brief pit stop to retrieve my Ice Dreams jacket and skate guards, I walk proudly hand in hand with Jonah to the snack bar. Mom slides my special "Go for the Gold!" insulated mug filled with honey-lemon tea across the counter to me.

"Jonah, are you skipping school?" Mom chastises him.

"No." Jonah refuses to look Mom in the eye. "Okay, yes. But only seventh period. I wanted to see Olivia skate before it was my turn on the ice."

Mom tuts, but immediately gives in because she's a giant marshmallow. "Okay, but no talking during filming."

"You're one to talk, Mom. You've ruined several takes today with your enthusiastic squealing."

"Oh, hush. You know I love watching my babies skate. Even if you aren't babies anymore." Mom's eyes glisten. She clears her throat. "Annabelle's right. We should film one last time from a different angle to showcase the platter lift. Drink your tea first, though."

I take my tea back to Table #1. Since we are officially out as a couple now, when Jonah sits down across from Mack, I sit on his lap. Jonah wraps his arms around me.

"I had to escape," Jonah says as I sip my tea. "Had to get back to my normal. If Dad asks, though, we rollerbladed here together."

"Got it. So you wanna see my normal?"

"You know it."

I lean in and give Jonah a quick kiss even though everybody is looking at us. "This is what you inspired in me. Ignited in me."

"I'm gonna hurl." Egg puts his skate guards on the wall and takes the ice.

"You drop her, and I kill you. Got it, tough guy?" Jonah says. Egg skates away while making a rude hand gesture. "Seriously, Liv, be careful. You want to borrow my helmet?"

"I'm fine, Jonah."

"Are you sure?" Jonah follows behind me.

"Yes, I've been doing this since I was two years old." I put my fist out, and we do our hand sign. "Enjoy."

"Outta the way, Choi." Mack, video camera in hand, steps out on the ice. She shuffles gingerly toward the middle of the rink.

I skate out to the middle of the ice with Egg to take our original opening position, the only thing we kept from Alexei's choreography. It's still ridiculous, but it's part of our history. Part of our new story. Egg lunges and throws a jazz hand to the ceiling. I hear a snort, undoubtedly from Jonah. I drape my left arm over Egg's shoulders and weave my legs around his back leg. Egg reaches his lower hand down to make a perfect diagonal, which still, unfortunately, requires him to clasp my butt cheek.

"Make za heat. Make za passion," Egg says in the worst Russian accent ever, mimicking Alexei.

I close my eyes and remember back to the shadows last night. Jonah's warm fingers traveling over my skin. His mouth on mine.

The tingling in the pit of my belly. I don't need to fake a passionate expression. I call up an authentic one instead.

"And . . . cue music," Mack says from where she's reclined on the ice. "Cue music. Music. Midori!"

"Sorry!" Mom says.

"And . . . action."

We skate my new choreography, pulled out of the ashes of the old phoenix one. I turn off my brain and let my body craft this moving, twirling, jumping piece of art. Everything clicks. I've skated cleanly all morning, but having Jonah in the audience takes the performance to the next level. I link my hands with Egg's, and he pushes me above his head into a platter lift. I catch Jonah's eyes as I rotate effortlessly in the air. His jaw rests on the wall, and I don't think it's because of my costume. This is gold-medal-level Olivia Kennedy, the phoenix coming out of the ashes of her previous skating life. The music swells. I close my eyes and envision Jonah's face on Egg's body. Egg and I circle each other, spiraling closer and closer together for our climax. Jonah's gasp echoes around the rink when Egg dips me down into a death spiral so low that I can hear the spikes of my hair scrape the ice. When I come back up, Egg and I press together for our final spin combo. I remember the heat flowing from Jonah's skin. The way his body pressed into mine. The sparks shooting up my spine as his lips traveled over my skin. Egg and I pull in tighter together so we can spin even faster. The music crescendos. Blood pulses through my veins and the tingling in my belly travels to every nerve fiber in my body.

Three . . . two . . . one.

Egg jams his toe pick into the ice to slow our rotation. We unravel and Egg dips me back for our final pose. I reach up and caress Egg's face. We stare into each other's eyes knowing that something has changed between us. *This* is what we never had. *This* was the missing element. *This* is chemistry. Egg's warm breath washes across my face as the music fades. Egg leans in for our non-kiss. Except this time, our lips connect.

Egg rights us with a jerk.

"And . . . cut!" Mack yells from the side. "Now that's what I'm talkin' about! Except for the herky-jerky ending. I can edit that out, though."

"What the hell, Egg?" I whisper.

"What?" Egg says under his breath. "You kissed me."

"I did not."

"Do you want to watch the footage?"

"No." Because a tiny part of me is afraid that I did kiss Egg. On purpose even. Just to see what it was like. Chemistry is dangerous like that. It only takes one careless spark to burn down an entire forest.

I'm burning now, and it's not from exertion. Egg takes off to do a couple of cooldown laps. Jonah's jaw is still on the wall when I come off the ice and unlace my skates.

"Wow . . . that was . . . wow. Just . . . wow."

"I told you I could skate." I beam because sometimes you need to put up or shut up. "I'm glad you finally believe me."

"That was some ending," Jonah says as Egg skates by.

My stomach clenches.

"Acting. It's all about the acting." Egg's laugh is unnatural. "Gotta sell it to the cheap seats, right, Livy?"

"Yeah. Acting."

"So are you guys done now?" Jonah says.

Right as Egg and I say "yes," Mack says, "Weeeelll, we could go one more time."

"No!" Egg and I say.

"In that case." Jonah unzips his backpack. He pulls out an eight-by-ten framed photograph of himself with two gold medals around his neck. He shows it to everybody.

"Wow, Jonah! Congratulations! I get to put this up on the Wall of Fame, right?" Mom inches toward Jonah.

Now it's Jonah's turn to beam. "I'd like that."

"I'll hang it up, Mom. You rest a bit."

I wipe down my blades and put my soakers on before slipping my Chucks back on.

"That costume is something," Jonah says, following me to the skate counter.

I hold his picture over my butt to block his view. "Let me go change first."

"Do you have to?"

I remove the picture. I am a phoenix. This is the new Olivia. I earned these new sparkly feathers and the stronger, womanly body that comes with it. Jonah comes behind the counter with me. I squat down to look for a hammer, but it's not in its usual spot. When I stand again, Jonah steps into me, wrapping his arms around my waist. Since I can hear Mom giving Egg and Mack unsolicited video editing advice, I step into Jonah's embrace.

"I can't find the hammer," I say as Jonah kisses the skin below my ear. "I don't think we have any more nails anyway."

Without stopping the trail of kisses from my ear to my throat, Jonah reaches behind my head and pulls a picture off the Wall of Fame. He slaps his new picture around until it hooks on the wall.

"Problem solved." Jonah tilts my face toward his and gives me a kiss that is neither gentle nor soft.

I pull Jonah down until we are both kneeling on the well-worn carpet behind the skate counter. Nobody else in the rink notices we are missing, or maybe they leave us alone on purpose. I don't question. I just give thanks and try my best to make Jonah forget all about the kiss he witnessed earlier.

"Is my son here?" Mr. Choi's voice echoes around the rink.

Jonah pops to his feet, but mine have fallen asleep. The

thousand pins and needles in my calves compete with the buzzing in my belly.

"Nope, I can't find the hammer either," Jonah says loudly. "Guess we'll have to leave it as it is."

Jonah leans over and straightens his new picture on the Wall of Fame. I hang on to the counter for balance as the blood rushes back to my feet. I flip over the old picture frame lying facedown on the counter. It's mine and Egg's. Our last gold medal performance. Until I can replace it with a new one, that picture needs to stay on the wall to remind me every day to get off my ass and take that life back.

"Hey, not this one." I take down Jonah's first gold medal picture and put mine back up.

"But that one's old. These two are new."

When Jonah reaches for his picture, I move it over to the other side.

"I'll ask Ernie about the hammer the next time I see him. Until then . . ." I lean the picture up against the other wall.

I give Jonah a peck on the cheek before exiting. He stands there slack-jawed. I touch the back of my costume to make sure I haven't had a wardrobe malfunction or something.

Mr. Choi does a double take when he sees me. A crease forms between his eyebrows, especially when Jonah comes out of the skate booth wiping bloodred lipstick off his mouth with the back of his hand.

Jonah is already on the ice doing warm-up laps by the time the normal teen version of Olivia emerges from the women's locker room.

"C'mon, Mack, it's good enough. Just fix it right there, and save it." Egg points to the computer screen. "I gotta get this uploaded before 11:59 p.m. And my flight leaves at nine thirty."

"You don't have to leave, you know," Mack says, not realizing

I'm behind them. Egg makes a noncommittal noise like he's actually considering the suggestion.

"It's too hard making minute changes on my laptop." Mack closes her computer. "I'm off at seven. I'll grab some takeout on the way home. We'll do a quick final polish, and have this up by eight."

Egg gives Mack's shoulder a squeeze. "Fine, but at least let me make you dinner."

"You're on. And, seriously, Stu, Granny said you were welcome to stay for as long as you want. Especially if you keep cooking for her." Mack packs up her laptop.

"Really? Well, in that case, I guess I *could* stick around for a few more days. I've already maxed out my absences in most of my classes, so what's the point of going anymore?"

I clear my throat. "So, do you need me, Egg, or can I take Mom home now?"

"Nah, I'm fine. I don't need any more help. Thanks, though." Egg goes to hug me but drops his arm before contact. "Er, I'll call you if I need anything."

"Okay, guess I'll go do homework or something." I shift my workout bag over my shoulder. "Call me as soon as you know something."

"Sure thing, Short Stuff." Egg puts out his hand for a high five.

Egg has never high-fived me in his life. I leave him hanging. The kiss was a mistake. One small mistake.

"Hey, Olivia! Wait!" Jonah powers over to the wall. "Want to hang out after my private coaching session on Saturday afternoon?"

Half of me wants to yell, "Hell, yeah!" The other half is still pissy about the picture situation. "Let me check my schedule and get back to you."

"Oh." Jonah tilts his head to the side, obviously not expecting that response. "Okay. You know where I'll be."

Chapter 23

We now return you to your regularly scheduled Normal Teen Life.

Tuesday, Jonah insists I show everybody the final cut of Egg's audition reel. Though I've already watched the five-minute audition piece a good hundred times on my laptop since Mack emailed it to me last night, it looks completely different on Jonah's phone in the middle of our lunch table. Who knew that Mack was such a talented videographer? The shots connect seamlessly, even the final kiss. The herky-jerky ending is gone. Instead, the kiss melts into a final headshot of Egg alone with his email address, cell number, and social media information.

"Wow, that was awesome," Naomi gushes.

"I would pay money to see him perform," Erika says.

All the air deflates out of my giant head. Yes, it's Egg's audition piece, so most of the footage is of him, or has him in the foreground and me in the background. But they only see Egg's transformation, not mine.

Brandon takes Jonah's phone and backs up the video. He freezes on the only frame of the entire piece where I am front and center. Finally. A little recognition.

"Are you wearing a bikini?" Brandon pulls the phone closer to his face.

Jonah rips the phone out of Brandon's hand. "No, she's not."

"Hey, did you guys remember to pick up your National Honor Society application this morning?" Naomi digs in her backpack and pulls out a paper.

Erika pulls out a matching piece of paper. "Got it."

"Don't have it," Brandon says, and Erika lets out a sigh of disappointment. "Will have it by the end of the day, though."

"Good. Which teacher are you going to get to write your recommendation?" Erika says.

"Probably Dr. Woods," Brandon says. "He laughs at my jokes in history class."

"You guys didn't get one?" Naomi looks at Jonah and me. "They're due on Friday. No exceptions."

"Nah." Jonah pulls his headphones out of his backpack and connects them to his phone. "I got a deficiency notice in English last night."

Erika and Naomi look at Jonah like he said, "I knocked over a bank last night."

"It's no big deal," Jonah assures them. "My grades always take a hit this time of year. Once the skating season is over, I'll have more time for school."

"And volunteer work," Erika—who is currently manifesting *being valedictorian senior year*—adds. "I hope you both will come volunteer with me over spring break at the Child Crisis Home. It's only six hours each day."

Jonah cringes. "I don't really like little kids."

"Me neither, but it's an easy thirty volunteer hours. All you have to do is show up, wipe noses, read to them, keep them from whacking one another on the head with toys, and then you go home." Erika turns to me. "You'll come, right, Olivia? You're good with little kids. Plus, I'm sure you need to diversify more for your college applications."

"Diversify?" Jonah says.

"Yeah, 'cause not all of us get to play the top athlete card, bro," Brandon says. "I mean, I've played on the school's golf team since freshman year, but it's not like I'm winning gold medals at it."

I forget that other people do stuff besides study. "I didn't even know you liked golf."

Brandon shrugs. "Ehhh. My dad says it's a good skill for future CEOs."

"Even I need to diversify and be more well-rounded. Therefore—" Erika looks at Naomi, who gives her a nod of encouragement. Then, she blurts out, "I'm going to audition for the school musical. There. I said it. I know I'm not going to get a lead role. I can't compete against the theatre kids who have been doing shows since, like, birth, but I'm not too proud. I'll be a tree or build sets or pass out programs or whatever. You guys will still come, though, right?"

Though Naomi and Brandon pledge their immediate loyalty to this high school phenomenon called the spring musical, I notice Jonah is as noncommittal as I am. Is it because he knows his skating will always come first? Or is he feeling as conflicted as I am? I look around the table. Though I genuinely enjoy Brandon's quirky, unfiltered take on life, sometimes I don't feel like I belong at this table at all. Yeah, I'm half Asian and sometimes like attracts like, but I don't know if you can build a true friendship on just that. What would happen if Jonah and I stopped sitting here each day?

"The rest of us are going to have to step up our game if we want scholarships," Naomi says. "Good scholarships. Not some dinky $1,000 one that will barely cover books for one semester. What are you going to do to stand out with colleges, Olivia?"

Oh, I don't know. Maybe land a few triple-double-doubles? Or I could just set myself on fire.

"She skates," Jonah answers for me. "You all saw it. Olivia is a talented pairs figure skater. Gold medal quality."

"Egg and I were the US Junior Pairs champs," I brag shamelessly.

"I don't think colleges count the work you did in junior high school." Erika is deadly serious, though the two are not the same at all. "What do you have that is a little more recent?"

Are you freaking kidding me?!

"Seriously, Olivia, join the National Honor Society with us." Naomi puts away her paper. "It'll improve your chances of getting into a good college. I'll help you do the paperwork. I'm good at making stuff sound bigger and more important than it is without actually lying about it."

"I have a C-minus in geometry. I think that disqualifies me." I push my tray of mostly uneaten food away. I'm so tired after this long weekend that I don't have the energy to pretend like I care.

"Maybe the committee will make an exception since it's your first semester of real school."

"Wow. Just . . . wow." Jonah shakes his head.

"You know what we need?" Brandon pulls at the neck of his T-shirt. "Pastries. A good bake always makes things better. I'm thinking apple pie? No, lemon meringue. Key lime?"

When the bell rings, Jonah walks with me to the trash can while everybody else moves on to English class.

"Are you really going to do it?" Jonah says.

"Apply for the National Honor Society?"

"No, start skating with Stuart again as a pair if he doesn't get this gig."

"Why? Are you jealous?" I give Jonah a flirty smile.

He shrugs. He *is* jealous. Bad.

"Jonah, Egg is like my big brother, okay?"

"I know I'm an only child, but I still don't think I would be able to kiss my sibling like that."

"It's called acting. Egg and I were never a couple off the ice. We are never going to be a couple off the ice. And if Egg gets this gig, we won't be a couple on the ice either."

"Okay." Jonah takes my backpack and slides it over his other shoulder. "Thanks."

"You're welcome. And you don't have to carry that for me."

"I know. It's weight training." Jonah does a series of lunge walks out of the cafeteria. "Seriously, what are you carrying in here, bowling balls?"

"Stooooop." I pull Jonah to a stand. "People think we're weird enough as it is."

"We're not weird. Maybe a little extra."

"Definitely extra. And I wouldn't have it any other way."

Jonah puts out his fist, and we do our still incredibly dorky hand sign.

"C'mon, we're going to be late to English."

I squeeze Jonah's hand, but let it go. Principal Green is always in the hallway outside of the cafeteria, busting up post-lunch PDA. I don't want to get detention for something so stupid. I've got skating to do.

"So, did you check your schedule? Are you free on Saturday night?" Jonah says as we drag ourselves to English.

I look around the hall. Principal Green isn't in his usual perch. In fact, there aren't any teachers or staff in the hall at all. Weird. I'm not going to complain, though. I flip around in front of Jonah and lace my fingers through his.

"Yeah, I am. Think we could hang out at your house?" I walk backward down the hallway in perfect synchronization with Jonah, just like we're on the ice. "I'm dying to see what your room looks like."

Since the coast is clear, I stop and raise up on my toes. My lips are millimeters away from Jonah's when a warning blare erupts from the school intercom.

"Attention, everyone. We are in a lockdown situation," Ms. Walters—whose voice is usually annoyingly perky even during disaster drills—says, her voice tight and flat. "We are in lockdown with an intruder. I repeat. We are in lockdown with an intruder."

You want to motivate 2,500-plus kids in two seconds flat? This is how you do it. A burst of sound—scraping chairs and pounding feet—follows, as everyone flies into action.

"What the hell are you two doing? Get in here." Mrs. Diaz yanks Jonah by a backpack strap into her Spanish class. Still connected to Jonah, I stumble in the door behind him. Mrs. Diaz slams the door and locks it. "Get over there with the rest of my class. Right now."

Mrs. Diaz flips off the lights. I walk blindly down the side of the dark, unfamiliar classroom. My foot tangles in the strap of someone's hastily discarded backpack. Jonah's strong hands on my waist keep me from taking a header into the floor.

"Thanks," I whisper.

The emergency blare goes off again, and several people shriek.

"Silence," Mrs. Diaz barks.

Ms. Walters repeats her plea, but her voice cracks: "Attention. We are in lockdown with an intruder. I repeat. We are in lockdown with an intruder."

Muffled whimpering erupts from several areas of the room. Jonah slides down the wall and throws his backpack between him and some girl I don't know wearing a soccer jersey. I kneel next to him, putting my backpack on the other side of us like a buffer. I lace my fingers through Jonah's and squeeze his hand tight. Footsteps echo down the hall. Someone is running. The whimpering gets louder as the footsteps get closer.

Please don't stop. Please keep running.

As the footsteps get close to our door, Jonah's free hand comes up to his throat. In the dim light, I can see him pulling the thin-chained necklace out from under his T-shirt. His hand wraps around the cross pendant his halmeoni gave him—the one he wears because he's convinced it brings him good luck. Maybe it does, because the feet pass our door and continue down the long hall.

An audible sigh escapes from several students. Mrs. Diaz shushes us. Everybody's phone goes off. Well, everyone who doesn't follow the school rule to turn off your phone during class, which is everybody. The emergency message from the school system overrides everyone's mute setting to warn us that our school is currently in lockdown. Less than five seconds later, everybody's phone goes off again. Probably panicked parents responding to the school system's message.

"Turn them off!" Mrs. Diaz snaps.

I dig in my backpack as Jonah texts furiously. Besides the school system notification, I don't have any other messages. I look over Jonah's shoulder at his phone. His mom has sent him five texts in less than thirty seconds.

I'm okay. I love you, Jonah texts his mom back.

I look at my phone. Nothing.

I'm okay. I love you. I text Mom and Dad at the same time.

Nothing.

There are footsteps in the hallway again. They run a few steps and then stop. Run a few steps more and stop. As the sound gets closer, I know why. Someone is checking all the doors. My heart pounds, even though I saw Mrs. Diaz lock our door. The door-knob on the classroom across the hall from us rattles. The soccer player next to Jonah completely loses it.

"Get down!" Mrs. Diaz says when two girls wearing matching jerseys fling themselves across the room and wrap their arms around their teammate. They huddle together, muffling her sobs.

My phone vibrates. It's not from Mom. It's from Mack. Of course it's from Mack.

HOLY SHIT! ARE YOU OK? IT'S ALL OVER
TV. DAMN IT OLIVIA YOU BETTER BE OK
TEXT ME NOW TELL ME YOU ARE OK

I drop my phone when Jonah pulls me in front of him. His long arms and legs wrap around me. Encase me. Shield me. He rests his chin on my shoulder. As he rocks us gently back and forth, his long hair tickles my cheek, but I don't brush it away. Instead, I fold my hands around Jonah's and pull myself as tightly into him as I can. Our classroom's doorknob rattles and both of us stop breathing. Jonah's pounding heart behind me is in perfect sync with the one threatening to explode out of my chest. When the footsteps move on, we breathe out as one. We stay connected even as I slap around on the floor to find my phone.

My hands are shaking so badly that I can barely text Mack back. Im ok jonah is w me.

My phone buzzes. THANK GOD!!!!!!!!!!

I hold the phone up so Jonah can see what I am texting. What's happening? We don't know.

Stu says the news isn't sure. Some think
gang violence. Some think it's a bullied kid
with dad's gun. One said a heartbroken boy
killed his former girlfriend. Nobody really
knows. Police are on the scene. The whole
block around the school is barricaded.

The warning system blares, and Jonah pulls me in tight.

"Attention, students, teachers, and staff." It's Principal Green this time. I can tell by the Boston accent he usually tries to hide.

"We are all clear. I repeat. We are now all clear. Please report back to your first-period class for attendance and dismissal."

Mrs. Diaz flips on the lights. Many people wipe at their eyes. Jonah texts madly.

"Students," Mrs. Diaz's voice wavers. "Go to your first-period class directly. Do not stop at the bathroom. Do not stop to talk with friends. Go. Now."

"Ma'am." Jonah rolls to his feet and shows her his phone. "My dad wants me to come outside right now."

"No, you will report to first period. Then you will wait to be dismissed by Principal Green."

"But, I—"

"Do as you are told, young man." Mrs. Diaz's hands are shaking so much that she grabs a chair to steady them. "Let's go, students. *Vámonos.*"

"Come on, Jonah." I take Jonah by the hand and lead him out of the class.

"Olivia! Jonah!" Erika sprints down the hall the wrong way, with Naomi and Brandon hot on her heels. The trio practically tackles us into the floor.

"Oh my God, we were so worried." Erika's eye makeup is smeared.

"Nobody knew where you two were." Naomi puts a hand on each of us.

"Seriously, bro." Brandon takes a deep breath and runs his hand through his hair. "I see some stress-baking in my immediate future. Macarons. Eclairs. A Victoria sponge. Prepare for the sugar avalanche coming tomorrow."

"Stop talking and move it along." Mrs. Diaz shoos us down the hall.

I go to my first period solo. Everybody is on their phones—including the teacher—so I take mine out too. I still haven't re-

ceived a text or call from either of my parents but I have a text
from Jonah.

> I love you. I should have told you that in per-
> son sooner. I *will* tell you that in person the
> next time I see you.

It's amazing how you can have both the worst day and the best
day of your life all in the same thirty minutes.

A warmth flows from the center of my chest. I love you too.

> Dad says we're going straight home after
> school today on Mom's orders. Will try to
> come to the rink later though.

After an eternity, we are officially dismissed with a warning not
to indulge in gossip about what went on today and are told that
everyone will receive an accurate account of today's event at a later
time. No one follows that rule either, including the teacher.

Can you come pick me up? I need to talk, I text Mom.

I stand in the parking lot for forty-five minutes. Mom never
comes or answers any of my texts.

Chapter 24

"What the hell are you doing here?" Mack abandons our normal derby girl intro when I roll into Ice Dreams after giving up on Mom.

"I work here." I slide my Ice Dreams jacket off its peg and throw my backpack onto Table #1.

"You could have died today, and the first thing you think of is coming to work?"

"This is my home, Mack. All the people who care about me the most practically live here too. Where's Mom? She hasn't answered my texts all day."

"She's not here. She hasn't answered my calls or texts either. Stu said he was going to Uber over to your house to check on Midori. And Jonah texted that his mom won't let him come to the rink today."

"Like I said, all the people who care about me the most are here." I jog toward the skate booth before Mack can see the tears flowing down my cheeks.

"Hey. Hey! Olivia!" Mack races up from behind me and grabs my elbow.

I can't look her in the eye. I am so embarrassed by my blubbering. My ice princess exterior completely melts away. Mack pulls me into her and wraps her arms around me as I continue to bawl. She's soft and soothing, like the down comforter on my parents' bed.

"Shhh. Shhh. You're okay now. Everything is going to be okay." Mack's voice wavers as she holds me even tighter. "You're safe. Nothing can hurt you here."

I sob even harder because that's not true either.

"I'm so sorry, Olivia. Sometimes parents really suck. Ask me how I know this."

When I finally can control my breathing again, I say, "How do you know this?"

"Olivia, I live with my grandmother. What do you think?" Mack leads me to Table #1, and we plop down side by side on the bench seat. "Our downward spiral started the day I finally had the guts to say no to them."

"Huh?" I sniff and wipe my eyes.

"From the day I was born, my parents informed me I was going to go to Stanford University, my father's alma mater. I was going to go to Stanford to be either a doctor, a lawyer, or an engineer, my choice. And I toed the party line from preschool until senior year. Well, guess what? Just because you're valedictorian of your class and student council president. Just because you stand in the outfield for four seasons of softball and pray that nobody hits the ball your way. Just because you give up any free time you might have to volunteer at places you don't even care about. Just because you dot every *i* and cross every *t*, you STILL might not get into Stanford University. You know why? Because all the other applicants were valedictorians and student council presidents and played sports and were the lead in the school musical and volunteered for their local congressperson and cured cancer in their free time and never slept and lived off coffee and occasionally snuck into their parents' medicine cabinet to take a Xanax or two because their anxiety was off the charts. And then the day comes when you get your rejection letter from Stanford, when life tells you that you aren't the little sparkle pony your parents have always told you that you are. You're not special. In fact, you're not even average. You're just . . . extra. But the time is already gone, and you can never get it back."

Mack finally stops to take a long, ragged breath. She looks at me with a raw, deep hurt like I've never seen in her before.

"They lied." Mack's voice is tight. "They said Stanford was the gold medal. I spent my entire high school career completely miserable, and what do I have to show for it now? But it gets even better. Not only was I rejected by Stanford, I also got rejected by MIT and UC Berkeley and wait-listed at a bunch more top-notch schools. And my parents couldn't just buy my way in like the one percent do. 'But you got into ASU,' my guidance counselor said after I cried in her office after my last rejection letter. That's like . . ." Mack waves her hands around, trying to find a comparison.

"Skating in the corps for Olympians on Ice after being US Junior Pairs champions?"

"Yes! No. Okay, yes, but don't tell Stuart that. So, I said I'd rather take a gap year than go to ASU. That I would work for my dad's friend's engineering firm and become fluent in Mandarin Chinese and work at a homeless shelter every weekend and prove to Stanford that I was good enough. That they were wrong."

"And then you got pregnant?"

"Yes, but my heart wasn't in any of the other stuff anyway. I had already quit my job and not made any forward movement on the other goals when my parents kicked me out. I'd only planned on staying with Granny for a few weeks until I could get another job. This job. Then I realized I was pregnant, and here we are."

"Oh, wow." I tip my head until it rests on Mack's shoulder. "I'm glad you took this job."

"Me too. It's not—as my father would say—a career move, but I like it here. Scraping gum off the bottom of tables and cleaning toilets is a pain in my ass, but the rest of it isn't so bad. I know eventually I'll have to move on, but for right now, this is my home. And there's no other place I'd rather be."

Mack and I sit in silence, waiting for our worlds to stop spinning out of control and find balance again. For all of thirty seconds, that is.

"Okay, enough with the drama llamas." Mack pushes me away from her. "Go change. We need to skate."

Forty-five minutes later, Mack and I come off the ice, sweaty and groaning.

"Thanks. I needed that," Mack says as I fall onto the bench at Table #1, panting. "Want some water?"

"Yeah. Thanks." I slide off my skates and lie back on the bench. Sweat drips down the sides of my face, pooling in my ears. I'm about two seconds from dozing off when Mack lets out an impressive stream of profanity.

"Do I need to call nine-one-one?" I yell from the bench.

"Stu says to turn the TV to channel twelve."

Thankfully, the rarely used TV monitor in the snack bar decides to cooperate with us. Mostly. Mack changes channels until we get a grainy, but audible, reception. The reporter is mid-story already, but I recognize my high school on the screen. My stomach clenches.

"The school was in lockdown for about thirty minutes earlier today while law enforcement agents contained the situation," the woman on the screen says without any emotion. "Principal Warren Green insists the students were never in any danger, but that in light of other recent school shootings, going into lockdown is now the standard procedure. Principal Green declined our request for an on-camera interview, but sources say this man was involved in the verbal altercation which sent the school into lockdown."

On the screen appears the mug shot of a white, middle-aged man in a polo shirt. He looks like the kind of dad you see at band concerts and National Honor Society inductions. Or the guy standing in front of you at Starbucks ordering a two-pump soy latte. Or the guy who waves at you when you rollerblade in front of his house at 8:30 a.m. on a Sunday morning.

"Randall Collins, age forty-four, was arrested shortly after police responded to the school's intruder call," the newscaster's voice continues. "Sources tell us the lockdown was in response to an angry exchange by phone between Collins and administrators at the school."

Collins. Collins. Collins. Jeremiah Collins? The kid who sits in front of me in English class? The only one who might—according to Erika—beat her for the valedictorian spot?

"Hey, I know that guy's son," I say, but Mack shushes me.

The newscaster appears back on the screen. "Collins, upset at a test score, was reportedly on his way to the school to disenroll his child. Official police reports say that Collins was arrested on school property for disorderly conduct after a confrontation with Principal Green and one of the school's resource officers. Despite rumors, police report there was no weapon at the scene. That news wasn't of much comfort to parents. . . ."

My throat closes up again as the scene changes to a mom running toward her basketball jersey–wearing son and grabbing him in a rib-crushing embrace.

"Hey, that's Mr. Choi in the background," Mack says.

He's a little obscured, but you can see Mr. Choi grab Jonah's arm, drag him across the parking lot, and push him into the passenger side of the BMW like they are avoiding the paparazzi. The on-scene newscaster interviews the basketball mom, but I watch the background scene instead. Inside the car, Mr. Choi cups his hand around the back of Jonah's neck and pulls him in tight.

Though Jonah's forehead rests on his dad's shoulder, I can see his back moving. Heaving. Sobbing.

Are you okay? I text Jonah as the newscasters move on to the next horror of the day.

Yeah, Jonah texts back.

Are you sure? The image of Jonah sobbing against his dad haunts me.

I wish I could skate today.

I wish you could too. I miss you.

We're having a *family discussion* about whether or not I will be returning to school. Mom wants Dad to homeschool me since he turned down the job he interviewed for last week.

My heart clenches. I like having Jonah at school. Noooooo! I need you. You make HS bearable. I love you.

THAT'S VERY SWEET, OLIVIA. MY SON WILL HAVE HIS PHONE RETURNED TO HIM TOMORROW MORNING *IF* HE LOSES THE ATTITUDE AND TALKS TO ME IN A RESPECTFUL TONE. THANK YOU FOR YOUR UNDERSTANDING, JOCELYN CHOI

My face flames, and then I panic. I hope Jonah routinely deletes our texts, especially some of the late-night ones. Oh, God. I will never be able to look Mrs. Choi in the eye again.

"Since the Chois aren't coming in today, and we don't have any birthday parties or privates this evening, I say we knock off early." Mack slides my bedazzled *O* cup full of water in front of me, and

I chug it down. "Granny has community choir practice tonight, so Stu and I are getting Chinese takeout and binge-watching *My Ice Life* after we get Fi down."

"Who are you?"

"Shut up." Mack snaps her cleaning rag at me. "Get your stuff, and I'll drop you off on my way home. Unless, of course, you want to hang out with Stu and me."

"Nah, that's okay. Besides, I've got homework."

"Really? After what happened today?"

"Screw homework, I'll . . . I'll . . ." I'll what? All I do is go to school, skate, and hang out with either Mack or Jonah. I don't have any other hobbies. I don't have time for other interests. I don't even stress-bake like Brandon. "I'll take a long bath and go to bed. Tomorrow has got to be better than today."

"Hey, honey. You're home early," Mom says from her usual spot on the couch. Wires protrude from underneath her body. The four TENS units we own are attached to her back and hips, sending electrical impulses into her muscles in an attempt to override the pain signals coming from her spine. "How was your day?"

Are you kidding me?!

"Fine," I say, throwing today's mail into the huge pile next to the door. A letter with the words *Final Notice* in bloodred letters falls onto the floor. I snatch it off the ground and add it to the pile that I know already contains warning letters from the electric company and probably the water company too.

"Good. Want some dinner? Karrie put on some rice for us when she dropped me off after my MRI appointment today."

I hold up the carton of beef and broccoli Mack insisted on buying for me because she thinks I'm getting too bony. I'm getting back into shape. There's a difference. I'm not too proud to turn down a hot dinner, though.

"Oh, okay. Enjoy it while it's still hot, then." Pain crosses Mom's face as she shifts to be able to see me. "I'll eat some ochazuke later. The meds they gave me before the MRI today are making me nauseous."

"So, you didn't get my texts?" My throat starts closing up again.

"Uh-uh. I left my phone upstairs this morning, and I haven't been able to go back up and get it. Was it something important? Stuart left a message on our door earlier. It just said to call him. Was there a problem with yesterday's shooting? Can you call him for me?"

Shooting. If I open my mouth, a sob will come out. And venom. And possibly a long list of four-letter words. I shake my head. I walk upstairs with my beef and broccoli and a gaping hole in my chest.

"Wake me up in an hour or so, and we'll talk," Mom calls up the stairs after me.

I don't answer her.

When I come out of a long, hot bath an hour later, someone is blowing up my phone. My heart leaps, but then crashes when I realize it isn't Jonah's number. It's Dad's.

"Oh my God, Olivia," Dad says. "I just got your text and saw the news report. Are you okay?"

"Yeah."

"Honey, I am so sorry. I wish I could teleport home right now."

"I wish you could too."

"Did you at least talk to your mom about it?"

I talked to *a* mom today. Does that count?

"Yes," I decide because Dad has his own stressors with work, all the problems with our rink, Mom's health issues, and the growing collection-letter pile.

"Okay. Now I feel at least slightly less like a failure." Dad sounds so defeated and tired.

"You're not a failure. You're Olympic Gold Medalist Michael Kennedy." I make a fake crowd-cheering sound.

Dad chuckles. "I'm calling a Code Peach as soon as I come off the road. You deserve it, and so much more."

"Yes, I do."

"So, I hear Stuart finally got off his butt and auditioned for Olympians on Ice."

I collapse onto my bed and snuggle under the flannel sheets. "Yeah. I think it turned out really well. You'll have to watch it sometime."

"I already did. Annabelle emailed it to me early this morning."

"Aaaaaand?"

"Stuart did a great job."

"Aaaaaand?"

"I have no idea who that attractive young woman is skating with Stuart."

"C'mon, Dad, you know it's me."

"No, my daughter is five and has curly pigtails."

"Daaaaad."

"I know. I'm having a hard time getting my head wrapped around how fast you're growing up." I can picture Dad raking his fingers through his receding blond hairline. "And I still hate that costume. Also, Stuart needs to find a new opening pose that does not require his hand to be on your posterior."

This time I laugh. "Dad, I want to start skating again."

"Good for you. Go to Ice Dreams and knock yourself out," Dad says and then corrects himself. "Figuratively speaking, of course."

"No, like *skating* skating."

"Oh." Dad is quiet for so long that I look at my phone to make sure we haven't been cut off. "I'm not saying no, but please understand that we—none of us—are where we used to be, physically or financially. I wish we could go back in time and do things differently, but we can't."

Tears well up in my eyes as my parents' harsh criticism comes racing back to me. "I know you don't think I'm good enough, but I want to try again."

"What?"

"I've changed. I found the missing element. I have passion in my skating now to go with my technique. I'm learning how to work with my new body."

"Please, Olivia. It's late. Let's discuss this when I get home."

"When will that be?" I say.

"I don't know."

"Dad, I really want this."

"Olivia, honey, be reasonable. It's too late."

"For this Olympic cycle, yes. But I'm only sixteen. I can't be washed-up yet."

"Baby, skating is a very expensive sport—"

"You know what? Never mind. I gotta go." I hang up on him.

I wait for Dad to call me back and beg me to talk to him about all the plans that have been circulating in my brain. He never does. Mack's right. Parents suck sometimes. Or maybe all the time.

Chapter 25

I text Jonah multiple times the next morning, but he never responds. My heart sinks. After attendance, everyone who actually came to school today—Jonah isn't the only one who is a no-show—plods into the auditorium for a mandatory assembly. Though we've been ordered to put away our phones, everyone stares intensely into their crotches as Principal Green attempts to diffuse yesterday's drama.

"Please know that your safety is always our biggest concern," Principal Green, who sports an impressive black eye, says while pacing the stage. "If you need to talk to someone, we have brought in some extra social workers to assist our regular counselors with seeing students. Our doors are always open. Please come by any time. For any reason. We are here to help."

Principal Green invites one of our counselors—a momly looking woman with hipster glasses—to talk about stress management, especially after disturbing events. My phone vibrates repeatedly until the guy sitting beside me gives me a dirty look. I silence my phone's ringer and glance at the group text.

BRANDON PARK

You know what would ease my stress? The midnight showing of Street Fight Race 6 next Thursday. You guys in?

NAOMI ITO

YES!

ERIKA ITO

Maybe? Let me see how I'm feeling.

NAOMI ITO

Did you have another panic attack yesterday?

ERIKA ITO

Yeah but not as bad as some of the others. The new medication helps. I still spent the rest of the day in bed surrounded by all my dogs and watching sea otter videos though.

BRANDON PARK

What about you guys, Olivia and Jonah?

NAOMI ITO

I hope you did some self-care last night. <3

ME

Yeah. Some. Jonah's mom took his phone. They're thinking about home-schooling him.

BRANDON PARK

WTF?!?!

NAOMI ITO

Nooooo! I like having Jonah around.

ERIKA ITO

Me too, even if we don't always agree. He challenges me. Makes me think.

BRANDON PARK

Yeah, you two are extra, but that's what makes you fun. Chemistry wouldn't be the same without you, Olivia.

NAOMI ITO

And lunch!

ERIKA ITO
Screw it. Let's all go to the midnight show of
SFR6. You only live once.

The gaping hole in my chest begins to close, especially when I
see Brandon lean forward a few seats away from mine and dig a
plastic box out of his backpack. A minute later, a box of perfectly
crafted pastel macarons with vanilla buttercream centers floats
down our row as the lady drones on. Everybody takes one, including me. *And* Principal Green, who suddenly appears at the end of
our row. He takes the box back to his seat but allows us to enjoy
our moment of sweetness.

Finally, we are excused with one last admonishment to drink
more water. Like good hydration is going to help; and yet I catch
myself taking a swig of water anyway. Hipster Mom Counselor
stands at the door, patting students on their arms and offering
words of encouragement. I try not to make eye contact with her,
but she puts a hand on my arm anyway.

"I know you're new to all of this, Olivia," Hipster Mom Counselor says in a hushed tone. "But I'm here to help."

I'm not sure if I should be flattered or horrified that out of
2,500 students at our school, she somehow knows who I am. I
nod and plan never to talk to her again. I'm halfway to Japanese
when Naomi and Erika run up beside me.

"Hey. How ya doing?" Naomi puts her hand on my arm to
make me stop.

I shrug. "I couldn't sleep last night."

"Me neither." Erika points at her puffy eyes. "I have, like, two
inches of concealer on this morning."

"Let's go to the midnight movie with Brandon," Naomi pleads.
"Life is too short."

"You've finally forgiven him for the great Flower Day Debacle?" I say.

Naomi shrugs. "It's okay. He's going to be my boyfriend by junior year. I've already decided."

Granted, I'm no expert on love, but I'm pretty sure you can't manifest something like that into existence, no matter how good you are at meeting all of your goals. But I keep that to myself because maybe I need to try a little harder too.

"Sure. Let's go. Can somebody give me a ride?" I say.

"I'm sure my mom will drive us," Erika says.

Naomi throws an arm around both of our shoulders. "You two can even spend the night at my house after if you want."

I've never been to a sleepover. Part of me wants to create an excuse not to go.

"I'd love to," I say instead, even though it isn't 100 percent true. Yet.

The closer we get to the door, the less I want to go in. I like Japanese class. Morinaka-sensei is strict but kind. But I don't want to be here today. I need to go home.

"Can you tell Morinaka-sensei I'm not feeling well?" I say, blocking the door.

"Do you need to go see Mrs. Dean? She's the best," Erika says. "I saw her pull you aside this morning. She said we could skip class to talk to a counselor if we needed to."

"Yeah" is the easiest answer right now.

While Erika and Naomi smother me in an overly supportive hug, Brandon passes us on his way to culinary arts class.

"Heeeeeey, don't forget about me." Brandon throws his arms around our huddle and squeezes so hard that we all almost end up on the floor.

The bell rings, and Brandon sprints down the hallway.

Meanwhile, Naomi stands there with a big goofy smile on her face.

"*Daijōbu desu ka*," Morinaka-sensei asks from the doorway.

"*Daijōbu desu.*" Naomi answers that we are okay, before switching back to English. "But Olivia wants to see a counselor about yesterday."

Sort of, but I don't correct her.

Morinaka-sensei whips a counselor pass—the teachers must have all received a fresh stack of them this morning—out of her pocket and hands it to me. "I'm here anytime too, Olivia. Come in during lunch if you want to. My class is open then."

Now I feel bad for not being 100 percent honest with them, but they wouldn't understand.

"*Dōmo arigatō gozaimasu*, Morinaka-sensei." I thank her and take the pass.

I tuck the pass in my pocket as I pass the counselors' office and keep on walking straight out the front door. If Naomi can manifest a boyfriend, then surely I can manifest my dream.

Meet me at Ice Dreams whenever you get this. I text Jonah. I want you to teach me how to lift weights to build my upper-body strength without muscle bulk. To be able to do triple-triple combos with my new shape, I need to increase my propulsion into the jumps. Maybe you and Miss I'm-just-freakishly-good-at-physics can help me figure this out.

Chapter 26

My training begins today for real. Even if I have to train myself. Tomorrow, I'll start getting up at four thirty so I can get a workout in before school starts. If his parents are going to homeschool him anyway, maybe they'll let Jonah run with me in the mornings for safety. Or we could just do it anyway. Maybe I should start doing online school again too? That way I can skate during the school day, see if I can pick up some more baby skaters in the afternoon, and work a fast-food job on the weekends. As much as I hate to admit it, Dad is right. Skating is a very expensive sport. If Jonah can get a car dealership to sponsor him without an Olympic medal, surely I can too. Maybe some of the local businesses that have Mom and Dad's picture on their walls would pitch in. Maybe Mr. Sato's Wisteria Village Cafe would sponsor me? I'm sure Mack could come up with some kind of fun promotion or fundraiser with them. If I can work my ass off this year, then maybe I'll be able to save up enough money to cover next season's expenses.

I'm out on the ice working on deepening my edges when a sudden high-pitched screech punctures the silence of the rink.

"Shh, shh, you're okay." Mack pushes Fiona's stroller into the snack bar. "You just dropped your binkie."

Fiona's screams turn into muffled sniffs as Mack pushes the stroller over to Table #1. She falls onto the bench seat and puts her head down on her arms. I skate over to the boards.

"Hey," I say, and Mack looks up at me. "You look like crap."

"Yeah, that happens when *somebody* decides to sprout teeth. I think I've gotten maybe two hours of quality sleep in the last three days. Gran, Stuart, and I have tried every trick in the book."

With that, Fiona spits out her binkie and howls. Mack bends over the table and bangs her head a few times.

"Here, give her to me." I hold out my hands.

"No way. You're not going to drop my baby on the ice."

"I'm going to do a lap with her, not a triple axel. C'mon, trust me."

Mack unhooks Fiona from her stroller and wraps her tightly in a blanket. "You drop her, and I kill you."

"As Egg would say, 'Rule Number One.'"

I tuck Fiona into my chest and take off around the rink in a slow loop. Her wails die down into hiccups. I pick up speed on the second loop and watch her little brown tuft of hair wave in the air current. I rotate her out a little more and the cold air hits her face. Fiona looks up at me and blinks her big blue eyes.

"See, it's fun, isn't it?" I say, and Mack snorts at my high-pitched voice. "Look at this big girl skating with her auntie Olivia."

"Do you have any ibuprofen or something, *Auntie*?" Mack mocks me. "My head feels ready to explode."

"Mom has over-the-counter stuff in her office. I know I saw them somewhere in that mess."

"Be back in a second."

As soon as Mack's back is turned, I do a quick spin with Fiona. Her eyes open up wide and her little pink lips pucker into a surprised *O*. When I do it a second time, she makes the same face. The third time, she squeals with joy.

"We're going to make you into a figure skater yet," I whisper as we do another loop with random spins popped in at varying intervals so I can hear Fiona's laugh echo around the rink. Suddenly, my ice doesn't feel quite so ragged either.

"Excuse me." A middle-aged African American man with a clipboard suddenly appears at Table #1. "I'm looking for an Annabelle MacIntosh. I was told she would be meeting me here."

I skate over to the wall. Before I can say anything, Mack jogs over with an industrial-size bottle of medicine in her hand.

"Are you Mr. Russell?" Mack plops down the bottle and reaches out her hand. I realize that Mack is wearing a dark blue button-down shirt and khaki pants instead of her usual uniform of a GNR T-shirt and jeans, and her hair is pulled up in a bun.

"I am. Do you mind if I take a look around?" Mr. Russell waves his clipboard around a bit. "Take some notes?"

"Sure, go right ahead. If you have any questions, feel free to ask," Mack says in her best adulting voice.

"Thank you."

After Mr. Russell is out of earshot, I raise my eyebrow and imitate Mack's voice. "*If you have any questions, feel free to ask.* Yeah, I have questions. Who the hell is that? Why is your hair in a bun? And is that . . . gasp . . . khaki?"

"Language, Olivia." Mack nods at Fiona. "He's some kind of real estate appraiser or something. I don't know. You're dad asked me to let him in this morning." Mack puts her hand on her hip. "Since you are supposed to be at school. And *this* is my professional look. Sorta."

"Hey, there are a lot of worse things I could be doing."

"Very true. Doesn't ditch day usually require an accomplice, though?"

"You tell me. I've given up on trying to be a normal teen."

"I think so, but I don't know that from firsthand experience."

"Really?"

Mack pretends to buff her imaginary halo. "Valedictorian, remember?"

Feeling ignored, Fiona screeches. Mack sighs and stretches her hands out toward me.

"Wait. Watch this." I skate and spin with Fiona until all three of us are laughing.

"Who knew?"

Mack clears her throat and stands up straight as Mr. Russell walks by on his way to the snack bar. I try a slow sit spin with Fiona. She laughs at first, but when I come back up, her laugh turns into a burp followed by projectile spit-up all over my chest. Mack laughs harder.

"Ms. MacIntosh, could you come over here and answer some questions about this equipment?"

"Yes, sir." Mack jogs over to the snack bar as Fiona and I come off the ice.

Just as I get the top end cleaned up, Fiona's bottom end needs a cleaning. Nope. I am not here for that. I take a step back to avoid the stench.

"Thank you." Mr. Russell shakes Mack's hand. "I'll send Mr. Kennedy the results in a day or so. Good luck with selling the rink."

My stomach drops. I bite my lip to keep from yelling, "*What?!?!*"

Mack adults Mr. Russell out of the rink with some last-minute pleasantries, but when she comes back to Table #1, she's gnawing on her lip ring.

"Why didn't you tell me you were selling the rink?" Mack says, hurt flashing across her blue eyes before she hits the Wall of Stink coming off her daughter. "Oh, wow. Hold that thought."

"Because up until about one minute ago, I didn't know we were either." I slap my skate guards on and dig my phone out of my backpack. "But I'm going to find out."

While Mack takes care of the diaper situation, I text Dad about the morning. My phone pings a minute later.

Don't worry about it, Livy. I am just gathering information so we can make an informed decision.

About selling the rink?!?!?!

No, about what our current assets are to offset some of the upcoming debt of Mom's surgery. You let me worry about it. Also, DON'T mention it to your mother. She has enough on her mind. You and Annabelle keep this info to yourself.

No more surprises!

Dad sends me a GIF of an otter hugging her pup, but that doesn't make me feel any better. I relay the message to Mack.

"I wish we could skate." I nod at Mack, who has a clean and dozing Fiona in her arms.

"Me too." Mack pulls the corner of the blanket over Fiona's exposed head. "I'm gonna go. It's too cold in here for Fiona. And I'm ready to burn these pants. I swore I'd never wear khaki or green plaid ever again after graduation, and yet, here I am. Kill me now." Mack pulls her hair out of the bun and fluffs her magenta-streaked blond locks out. "I'll be back this afternoon. You should go home too. You shouldn't skate without a buddy."

I wave my phone at Mack. "I'll see if Jonah will come."

"Yeah, that's not going to happen."

"I promise we'll stay out of your supply closet." Or at least, we'll clean it up afterward.

"No. Well, yes, that too. No, he's in trouble right now."

"I know. He was salty with his mom and she took his phone last night."

"Yeah, that was *before* she busted him."

"For what?"

"Doing dry land training with the Surly Gurlz at Orange Blossom Park."

"So what? He does dry land training at that park all the time."

"Yeah, we were going down the whole wink-wink-nod-nod 'I ran into Mack and she asked me to stay' path, but then Barnacle Barb completely outed how fun it is to have you and Jonah come with me to bouts."

I suck air through my teeth.

"Yeah, he's not getting his phone back anytime soon." Mack slides off the bench and tucks Fiona back in her stroller. "Aaaand, he's probably not going to any bouts with us anytime soon either."

"Well, this all sucks."

"Welcome to life as a normal teen." Mack slides her diaper bag–purse over her shoulder. "The constant push and pull with your parents. *Grow up and act more like an adult* but also, *When you live under our roof, you will follow our rules.* And let's not forget, *I pay for that phone, so I can put a tracker on it if I want to.*"

"Parents . . ."

"Parents, what?" Mom hobbles past the snack bar.

Mack and I share a look.

"Parents work hard and make sacrifices to take care of their children." Mack gestures at Fiona. "Presenting exhibit A."

Mom pliés beside Fiona's stroller and strokes Fiona's cheek with her thumb. A genuine smile crosses her face.

"That they do." Mom grimaces as she stands back up. "You're both early. Why?"

"Teething." Mack points at Fiona and then at herself. "Not sleeping."

"I remember those days. And not fondly." Mom chuckles and puts a comforting hand on Mack's arm. "There are days when you do whatever it takes just to keep going. Even if all the *experts* disagree."

"Yeah, a change of scenery did us both some good. Thankfully, it worked. Two more minutes of crying and I would have pulled out the Zamboni like you used to do with Olivia when she was cranky."

"And, boy, was she cranky." Mom and Mack share a laugh, oblivious to me standing there. "A lot."

"She still is," I say, pretty much proving their point, but whatever.

Mom slides onto the bench at Table #1. She kneads her lower back with her fists.

"Livy, could you get me a cup of water?" Mom grabs the industrial-size bottle and pours some of its blue tablets into her hand. "Annabelle, remember tonight is Youth Group Night. And this time, stick to their playlist."

"It was one swear word, Midori, and it wasn't my idea. A kid requested it."

"Doesn't matter. Stick to the list."

"I'm just sayin' a little GNR might spice things up," Mack says, and Mom gives her a hard look. "Okay, boss lady. See you later."

Mack and Fiona follow me over to the snack bar.

"Let me know if you hear anything about . . . you know," Mack whispers.

"I will, and you too," I whisper back, and Mack nods.

I deliver Mom's water cup, and she throws back a half dozen low-level painkillers.

"Thanks, baby."

"I'm not a baby."

"I know." Mom puts her hand over mine. "I also know what

happened yesterday. Your dad called me this morning. I'm guessing that's why you are here instead of school right now. I'm sorry. Sometimes I get so caught up with all my health issues that I forget you might need a piece of me too. I'll try harder, I promise. But first . . . my three back-to-back privates and the third one is a new student."

Mom only gets halfway to a stand before the pain makes her sit back down. She closes her eyes and takes a few deep breaths.

"I'm going to have to call Crystal," Mom says, her eyes teary.

"Why? I'm here. Let me teach," I say.

"Honey, I don't know . . ."

"Let me prove the Yelp reviews wrong. I'm a better skater now. You saw our audition tape."

Mom pats my hand. I know she's still not convinced, but we're also desperate. "Okay, but just for today. And if they ask, it's because we are working on your coaching skills and that I'll be right here supervising the whole time."

I bite my tongue because a bad day at the rink will always be better than a good day at school.

"Go get changed into something more professional. Your shirt has a big stain on the front. Look in my office. You might still be able to fit in one of my outfits," Mom says. I am about to lose it when Mom adds, "Dad said that Lina Kitagawa's parents left us a five-star review on Yelp recently. Lina's mom wrote a whole gushing paragraph about how wonderful you are and what a 'transformative experience' her daughter has had at Ice Dreams these last few months, because you made skating fun again. And they left a certain other ice rink because the coaches and other parents were so hyper-competitive that her daughter often left the rink in tears. But now, Lina leaves her private lesson each week with a huge smile on her face. Their only complaint was that Miss Olivia doesn't teach group classes, because private lessons are expensive."

A warmth expands in my chest. "So what if we do some simple group 'Learn to Skate' classes? It would be a great way to make some extra money."

"Honey, I'm having a hard time with the privates as it is."

"No, for me to teach. For me to make some more money for the rink." Dad's secret sits on the tip of my tongue. "I want to be more of an asset to the rink."

My heart soars as Mom tips her head from side to side, genuinely considering my idea. "Let's wait until Dad comes off the road and see what he thinks. Maybe we can skim off some of my less-than-stellar students and switch them over to your class."

My heart crashes back to earth in a fireball. Parents. Completely exasperating. Even the not-so-normal ones.

Chapter 27

This could be my new normal. Even if Egg totally stole my spot-light today.

"Did you enjoy trying partner skating, Ella?" Mom says to our third private lesson of the day, a new thirteen-year-old girl who has potential.

She nods emphatically. Of course she does. Who wouldn't enjoy Ice Dreams' resident unicorn's undivided attention for thirty minutes? Stuart Trout is an asset. He may have earned us a new student. He also brought homemade lasagna with him, and I haven't had anything to eat since Brandon's macaron. So as much as I want to be mad at him for suddenly appearing at Ice Dreams and squeezing me out of this private lesson, I'll let it slide this time.

"So, are you the partnering teacher?" Mrs. Booker looks at Egg and he gives her a boy-next-door smile. She pulls out her wallet.

"Not full-time," Mom says and the woman puts her wallet away. "But we love having Stuart teach a few privates every time he comes home to Phoenix."

Mom gives Egg a pleading look.

"That's right." Egg is selling it to the cheap seats. "I'm here in Phoenix . . . a lot. And I love helping out at Ice Dreams."

I roll my eyes.

"We can help you look for a partner for Ella," Mom says.

"Though it may take a little while. In the meantime, we'd be happy to keep training your daughter as a single skater. And if you want to book some extra pairs sessions with Stuart when he's in town, our private lesson skaters have priority."

Mack waves from the snack bar to get my attention.

"What?" I mouth at her.

"Choi," she mouths back and points at the door.

Mom puts her hand on my arm. "Olivia, could you get the new student packet from my office for the Bookers?"

"Sure. Give me a second." I swap my skates for Chucks as Mom asks the Bookers what kind of partner they would like for their little sparkle pony. Like Ella's suddenly going to have boys lined up at her door. Nope. Not how this works.

I jog over to Mom's office and blow the dust off the packet before heading back.

"Hey, Olivia, could you come take the garbage out for me after you're done?" Mack says on my way back.

"I thought you already did."

"Well, there's more. Come. Get. It."

"Oh, ohhhh. Sure thing." Our wingwoman skills are severely lacking.

Since the Bookers don't seem to remember I exist, thanks to Egg, I hand Mom the packet and then collect a quarter-full bag of trash from Mack. As soon as I walk out the front door, Jonah grabs the trash with one hand and my hand with the other and pulls me behind the building to the dumpster. His lips meet mine before the bag of trash even hits the bottom of the dumpster.

"I love you," Jonah says when we finally break away.

We both take a deep breath and gag. The stench is unbearable.

"I love you too." I push Jonah back a few steps away from the dumpster. "But you win the gold medal for the *least* romantic declaration of love ever."

He pulls me back a few more steps. "Can I have a redo somewhere more romantic when I get back?"

"Get back? From where?"

"Salt Lake City, well, Kearns to be exact. The Utah Olympic Oval. They're considering me for the FAST program. It's a training team."

"That's . . . great." All the bubbles in my belly from thirty seconds ago suddenly feel like porcupines.

"Yeah, it is. Except the part where I'd have to live in Utah."

"But that's what you've always wanted. It's one step closer to the Olympics."

"Yeah. I did. I do." Jonah runs a hand through his hair. "Who knows? They might not even want me, and then all of this drama will have been unnecessary."

I step into Jonah and wrap my arms around him. "Of course they're going to want you. Sharing you with them for a little while will be hard, but it will also make your return even sweeter."

"Ten months." Jonah's arms tighten around me. "Dad and I would be gone for ten months."

The porcupines turn into cinderblocks. I have no words.

Jonah's fingers tip up my chin until I can look him in the eyes again. "You know, a few months ago, I wouldn't have given this a second thought. I would already be sitting in the car with my suitcase packed ready to move to Utah. Anything to get the hell out of Phoenix. But then I met you, and I don't want to be inside the Skater Bubble twenty-four-seven anymore. I want to be out here with you. Okay, not by a dumpster, but you know what I mean."

We shuffle backward together a few more feet.

"'A' Mountain," I say and Jonah looks confused. "When you return from Utah, I want to hike to the top of 'A' Mountain in Tempe with you, and then you can tell me loudly, profusely, and repeatedly that you love me. Chocolate optional. Flowers mandatory. That would be a gold-medal-worthy declaration of love. Deal?"

"Deal." Jonah puts out his fist for me to bump.

When we flick out our #1s, I feel a stab in my heart. That's the price you have to pay to be #1.

"I better head inside. I promised my parents I would skate directly here if they'd release me from house arrest. Dad is meeting me here." Jonah kisses me one last time before lacing his fingers through mine.

We head back to the front of the building to retrieve his gear. Jonah slides the strap of his bag across his chest and retakes my hand. My heart fissures. I don't know how the light is going to stay on at Ice Dreams—not to mention the literal lights—without Jonah here.

"Don't say anything to your mom or Stuart, okay? Not even Mack yet."

I nod. I am not okay with this. Any of this.

"I'm still working on the phone situation." Jonah opens the door for me. "Note to self: Reminding your mother when she catches you in the middle of a half-truth that she's the one who told you to act more like a normal teen . . . not a good idea. Especially when other moms are standing around. I mom-shamed her in front of the Surly Gurlz, and now I'm paying for it big-time."

Parents. I purposely don't slap a kiss on my parents' poster as we enter Ice Dreams.

When we pass the Bookers on their way out, Ella's eyes follow Jonah. Yep, Gold Medal Ice ain't got nothin' on us.

"Put your hands together for JONAHHHH 'QUICK SILVER' CHOOOOOOI," Mack yells across the rink.

"Hey, I don't get a derby intro today?" I say.

"No, because you've pooh-poohed every one I've come up with so far." Mack retrieves our water cups out of habit. "Also, I have exactly six brain cells firing at the moment, thanks to Fiona, so all you're gonna get is a 'welcome back, Liv.' How was the dumpster?"

Jonah and I look at each other. Parentheses appear at the corners of his mouth.

"Never mind, I don't wanna know." Mack pushes our filled water cups across the counter.

"Thanks, Mack." Jonah chugs down his water. "I better go change. Skate with me during my break, Olivia?"

"Of course." I'm on borrowed time as it is.

After Jonah enters the locker room, Egg and Mom meet us in the snack bar. Mack slides a cup of water to Egg and some hot tea with honey to Mom before they even ask.

"So what do you think, Stuart?" Mom waves her phone at Egg. "Since Mr. Choi says they'll be gone for the next few days for the coaching or whatever up in Utah. It'll be a win-win situation."

"Yeah, I need to do something. I can't go back to Tech, but I also can't hide out at Mack's house for too much longer either."

"And you need to be an adult and tell your parents." Mom sips her tea. "I would want to know, even if I was upset at first."

"I will. Did Mack tell you I had to hide in the freezer section of Costco yesterday to avoid my mom? Yeah, I know I need to come clean to them, but I want to hear back from Olympians on Ice first."

"Then let's give you a temporary job. We'll split the coaching fee fifty-fifty. I'll send the email out to all our old students too."

"Mom, do *not* pimp Egg out like that."

"She's not pimping me out," Egg says. "I would rather partner little ice princesses all day long than make pizzas for minimum wage. Besides, those are the only two marketable skills I currently possess."

I think about Mr. Russell and what might be coming down the road for us, especially if we lose Jonah to Utah.

"I really think we should add 'Learn to Skate' classes too," I say.

"One thing at a time, Olivia." Mom sips her tea. "Let's start with Stuart. I know this one is a sure bet."

I slam my empty water cup down. "Because, as usual, I'm not."

"That's not what I'm saying, Olivia."

The front door of Ice Dreams opens and Mr. Choi walks in.

"I'm going to go clean the women's locker room. I think I forgot to do that earlier." Mack ducks her head and sprints toward the locker rooms.

No, she didn't. Mack never forgets anything.

"I'll do the men's." Egg follows two steps behind her.

"We'll talk more about your idea *later*, Olivia." Mom's scowl melts into a perfect "kiss and cry" smile. "Mr. Choi! Good afternoon. I got your email."

"Fine. Whatever." I head toward the skate booth.

"Teens," Mr. Choi says. He and Mom shake their heads. "They didn't mention this part in the training manual, did they?"

They share a parental chuckle. Ugh.

"I hear you. And I want to apologize again about the roller derby nonsense. I didn't realize that Annabelle hadn't cleared it with you."

"I appreciate you saying that. My wife . . . will come around eventually. These kids. You give them an inch, and they take a mile." Mr. Choi's voice echoes through the empty rink. "That stops today. At least for Jonah."

I intersect Jonah in front of the skate booth. He grimaces, having obviously overheard the whole conversation.

"It's okay, Jonah. We're going to be okay," I say, and Jonah nods.

"I'm going to be okay," I whisper as Jonah steps out onto the ice.

Chapter 28

I was perfectly fine with taking another mental health day—or ten—and teaching private lessons with Mom again. Unfortunately, Mom must be suffering mom-shame thanks to Mr. Choi, and decides not to give me an inch today either.

School is a dumpster fire. I doze off during geometry. I flunk the Japanese test I forgot all about. And I nearly set Brandon on fire with the Bunsen burner during chem lab.

"Hey hey hey!" Brandon jumps back as the flame shoots up in the air, singeing a few strands of his hair. "Olivia, what is up with you today?"

"Nothing." I turn the gas back down to a non-flamethrower level, but the air still smells of charred hair.

"BS." Brandon arranges our beaker over top of the flame. "You and Choi have a fight or something? And is he ever coming back?"

"No, we . . . it's complicated."

Mr. Verne stops at our lab bench and barks from underneath his silver-flecked mustache, "Kennedy and Park, a ten-point deduction for breaking the safety rule."

"Wha wha wha . . . ?" Brandon says.

"Five points for Kennedy not wearing her safety goggles. Five points for Park for not reminding Kennedy to wear her safety goggles." Mr. Verne points his stick-like finger at my goggles.

I immediately put them on, but the damage is done. I let my partner down. I broke Rule Number One. Mr. Verne sniffs the air. Brandon purposely drops his pencil on the floor before we lose more points for his singed hair. When Mr. Verne moves on, Brandon pops back up.

"Sorry," I say. "I'm a little distracted today."

"Ya think?" Brandon grabs my hand before I add the wrong solution to our beaker and completely ruin the experiment. And our grade.

Mr. Verne passes by again and barks at us for having the temperature too high. When he disappears into the lab's supply closet to get more equipment or take a personal moment or do a shot of ethanol or whatever he does to get through the day when a hundred-plus teenagers pluck his last nerve, Brandon leans in toward me.

"You wanna come over to my house on Saturday? Have some pizza. Play a little *Call of Duty*." Brandon looks at me, his goggles distorting his face. "Not like a date or anything. Naomi and Erika too. Let's hang. You never have time to hang. It's not normal."

With Jonah possibly spending at least the next week in Utah, I'm going to need something to distract me from the giant hole in my chest, and I can't hide at the rink twenty-four-seven.

"I think so, but I usually work Saturday afternoons."

"Then let's say five. Still plenty of time before curfew." Just as the whole scene starts to get awkward, Brandon adds, "Can I see your English packet while the solution is coming to a boil? I didn't get number one. Or two. Or really any of them. But I did get thirty waves on Shi No Numa yesterday with the Wunderwaffe."

"Wow. That's . . . um . . . great. I almost landed a triple lutz–triple toe loop, and my one-handed Biellmann was epic."

Though it is obvious Brandon has no clue what I'm talking about either, he still says, "Cool."

As we stand in the lunch line, Brandon attempts to explain this normal teen guy obsession to me.

"It's not *wonder-waffle*. It's Wunderwaffe," he says, like that clears everything up. "Just come over on Saturday, and I'll show you."

Erika and Naomi are already at the table by the time we arrive with our corndogs, fat fries, iceberg lettuce salad with flecks of carrot, and a whole apple. I look at Naomi's bento—mini sausages cut to look like octopi, bite-size broccoli pieces, and a corn on the cob disk turned on its side until it looks like a sun. A second smaller box is filled with apple slices fanned out with a decorative pick in the center.

"Can your family adopt me?" I nod at Naomi's lunch.

"Can your mom make my lunch too?" Brandon slides in next to me.

"I can make you a bento sometime." Naomi drops her eyes. "It's not that hard."

"Really?" Brandon drops the corndog and it thuds against his tray. "I'd love that."

Naomi beams. I make a mental note to remind Brandon to make something—just for Naomi—to reciprocate. I can practically see Matchmaker Mack high-fiving me.

"So what happened to Jonah?" Erika nibbles her chicken salad sandwich. "Is he ever coming back to school?"

"Bro is probably training in Iceland or having brunch with the Olympic team or something us mere mortals wouldn't understand," Brandon says. "Okay, maybe you would understand, Olivia, but the rest of us are too ordinary to get it."

"Jonah is skating in Utah. And you're not ordinary," I say to be kind, though he's right.

"Yeah, I am. Nobody's going to give me a gold medal for anything. That's for sure."

"Can you medal in *Call of Duty*?" Part of me feels bad that Brandon will never know the rush of standing on a podium with a medal around your neck, even if it isn't an Olympic one.

Brandon laughs. "You know, I should train harder. So, Saturday night. Five o'clock. My house. Pizza and video games. Yes?"

"I'm in," Naomi says.

"Maybe," Erika says. "Don't forget, midterms are next week."

"We can take a study break, Erika," Naomi says pointedly.

Though I would rather spend my Saturday night with Jonah or at least Mack, I decide to try a little harder.

"I'm in, but can somebody pick me up? At the rink." There's a reason why we don't have people over to our house. "Any time after four is fine."

"Yeah, we'll work something out." Brandon pulls out his English packet. "But first. Mr. Balducci's latest torture device. If I get a B again this quarter, my parents are going to confiscate my games. We can't have that. My life would be over."

"They can take my games, but not my phone." Naomi snatches her phone to her chest in mock horror.

"They can take my games and my phone, but if you touch my dogs, it's on." Erika wields her fork in mock battle, and we laugh. "What about you, Olivia?"

I want to lie. I want to put on my "kiss and cry" smile and say my phone too. It's easier. It doesn't invite any more questions. It's normal. The truth sits on the tip of my tongue. I look at Brandon, who has no trouble speaking his truth, even when he really shouldn't. And Erika, who stands by her truth even when nobody agrees with her. Naomi is the peacekeeper of the group, but she'll push back if you cross the line.

"They can take my games and my phone. I've never had a pet, and they can take my house." I take a deep breath and blink back the tears in my eyes. My words waver. "But they can't—they won't—take Ice Dreams away from me without a fight."

An awkward silence falls over our lunch table. Naomi and Erika look at each other. Brandon puts his hand on my arm. I look at him.

"Hey, whatever is going on with you, Choi, the rink. You can tell us." Brandon's voice is serious for the first time ever. "Not sure what we can actually *do* about any of your problems, but if you need to unload, I'm all ears."

If I tell them what's on my mind—what's breaking my heart— I'm going to start crying, and I'm not sure they are quite ready for that level of honesty.

"Thanks. I appreciate it." I sniff. "Could you teach me how to bake something on Saturday? The last thing I remember baking was brownies from a box for my dad's birthday about ten years ago."

"Brownies. From a box?" Brandon squeaks before grabbing his chest and collapsing over his lunch tray. He pops open one eye. "Milk chocolate, dark chocolate, German chocolate, or white chocolate?"

"You tell me. You're the expert."

"Hmmm, milk chocolate with a salted caramel ribbon."

"How about dark chocolate with peanut butter?" Erika says.

"Nope," Naomi says. "German chocolate with coconut on top."

My mouth waters and I shrug. "Any of the above."

"All of the above. Bring an apron." A giant smile cuts across Brandon's face, and he affects a British announcer's voice.

"Because it's Chocolate Week in the tent. Saturday, our contestants go cocoa-loco as they create their own versions of the perfect homemade—cuz ain't nobody got time for box mixes—brownie. On your marks. Get set. Baaaake!"

We laugh so hard that other people stare at us as they pass by our table.

"And you guys think I'm extra." I wipe the corners of my eyes. "And thanks."

Brandon takes a mock bow. "Hey, that's what friends are for."

I like my Skater Bubble, but sometimes I like it out here too.

"Now seriously," Brandon says. "Somebody help me with this stupid English packet."

Chapter 29

"Are you tired of being Ice Dreams' poster boy yet?" I ask Egg on Saturday afternoon after his fifth private lesson of the day. Mack created the "One-on-one partnering session with US Junior Pairs Champion Stuart Trout, limited spaces available" promo for our website and social media, complete with some of the footage from Egg's Olympians on Ice demo. By Friday morning, every slot for the weekend was filled. We even picked up skaters from Gold Medal Ice. Mom gave Mack a hundred-dollar bonus.

"Your boy is makin' bank." Egg rotates his shoulders and cracks his neck. He pulls a piece of paper out of his pocket. "And collecting digits. Moms want me."

The horror of that statement must show on my face, because Egg laughs so loud, Mack looks over from the snack bar at us.

"To be their daughter's skating partner," Egg clarifies. "Though there was that one cougarific Gold Medal Ice mom from earlier today . . ."

"Gross gross gross. Stop talking." I put my hands over my ears.

"You're just jelly because, for once, *I'm* getting all the attention."

"What? No." Yes. Horribly.

"Yeah, you are."

"I'm used to other people trying to steal you from me. Ahem, Britney Freakin' Xiao."

"All this got me thinking, though." Egg steps in closer to me and lowers his voice. "If I don't get a callback with Olympians on Ice, what if I started doing this, instead? I can't compete with the big boys for Olympic gigs, but I could be the king of mediocrity at local rinks all over America. As you can see by my full schedule this weekend, I'm a hot commodity."

My stomach falls. "I thought plan B was making an Olympic run with me."

"I don't know if I've got it in me to invest another four years of my life on that pipe dream. What if this is enough? At least for now."

"Yes, I think you should keep doing *this*, but don't give up on us."

"You mean don't give up on *you*." Egg pulls me into a hug. "I swear on my life that if I ever decide to give the Olympics a shot, the only person I will do it with is you."

"What if I can't do it without you though?" I squeeze my eyes tight to keep the tears inside. "What if I'm not good enough to be a single skater?"

Egg pushes away and shakes me gently until I open my eyes. "How about you at least try before you make up your mind on that?" Egg looks over the top of my head. "Sorry, we're not open for public skating yet."

"Oh, okay, sorry," a familiar female voice says. "We'll come back."

"Hey, look, it's Choi."

My heart leaps. When I whip around, though, I find Brandon holding Jonah's last picture frame. The one we were fighting over.

"What are you guys doing here?" I'd planned on meeting them outside. I didn't expect them to invade my Skater Bubble.

"You told us to pick you up here." Brandon leans Jonah's picture back against the wall. "You know we roll on Erika Standard Time, which means we have to be twenty minutes early to everything."

"What? I hate being late," Erika says.

"It was my idea. I've been thinking about what you said earlier." Naomi looks around the rink. "I wanted to see what you said you were willing to fight for."

Erika steps up next to Egg. "Hey, Stuart."

"What are you wearing in this picture?" Brandon points at my last gold medal picture.

Naomi links her arm through mine. "Show me around, Olivia. I want to step into your world for a little while."

"Me too." Brandon links his arm through Naomi's. "What's it like here in Skatelandia?"

"Cold," I say.

"Yeah, wishing I had brought a jacket," Naomi says.

"Here." Brandon slides off his jacket and hands it to her.

I wish we could tap Naomi's megawatt smile. We could power the whole rink with it.

"So, give us the tour. Show us everything." Brandon relinks his arm with Naomi's. "Let us into this secret club you and Choi seem to have. Erika! Stop flirting and get over here."

A red-faced Erika runs up to us and grabs my other arm. "Hey, is that a ballet barre over there?"

They weren't kidding about me showing them everything. We start at the barre area. While Erika and Naomi try to remember some basic ballet from when they were eight, Brandon has me record him doing goofy walks and dance moves on Jonah's state-of-the-art treadmill.

"You better not show that to Jonah." I laugh at the playback. "He takes his skating and his equipment very seriously."

Brandon hops off the treadmill. "Show us the rest."

"This is the skate booth where I frequently have the glamorous job of disinfecting skates," I say in my best tour-guide voice. "And to your left is Olympic Gold Medalist Midori Nakashima's office."

Mom pops her head out of her office as we pass. "Aren't you going to introduce me to your new friends, Olivia?"

"New?" Brandon says.

"Not new?" Mom hobbles out of her office.

"You've never told your mom about our lunch crew?"

Mom puts on her "kiss and cry" smile. "Of course she has. She talks about you all the time. I'm sorry. It's been a long day. I'm completely blanking on your names."

"Brandon. Erika. Naomi." I point at each of them in turn.

"That's right," Mom lies.

"Ms. Nakashima, would you mind if we took a picture with you?" Naomi says after Erika nudges her. "My mom is a huge fan. She even had her hair cut like yours in high school."

Mom laughs. "My apologies. We thought it looked cool at the time, but now . . . yikes. Let me make it up to her. Livy, can you take our picture?"

This isn't the first time this has happened. Everyone in Skatelandia knows who my parents are. Midori Nakashima and Michael Kennedy have signed autographs and taken selfies with skaters who—ten minutes later—skated against me. But today it feels weird, like my two worlds are colliding and jumbling into something new. I wish Jonah were here. He keeps me balanced.

Mom insists on sending Naomi home with one of their previously autographed pictures from the Olympics. She adds, *Sorry about the hair, Yukiko!* above her signature.

"You're all going to stay for the Open Skate tonight, right? As our guests, of course," Mom says.

"Not tonight." I need more time to find my balance first. "Maybe next weekend, when Jonah is back and can skate with us?"

"Yeah, we'll be on winter break then," Erika says.

Brandon waves his phone. "Plus my dad is in the parking lot. He's back from Fry's with the brownie-making supplies."

"You're making brownies tonight? At our house?" A panicked look crosses Mom's face.

"At Brandon's."

"Oh, okay. You have fun. I'm going home as soon as Ernie and Crystal get here." Mom kneads her back.

"We should ask Stuart to join us," Erika says.

"He's . . . busy," I say. "He already has plans with Mack."

"Mack can come too," Brandon says. "Any friend of yours is a friend of mine."

"Maybe another time." My Skater Bubble already feels cramped.

As we walk toward the front door, Mom calls me back. "What time should I pick you up?"

"I'll get a ride, don't worry."

"Okay." Mom looks relieved, but then she straightens up. "No, I should come get you. Or at least let Stuart borrow my car and have him pick you up."

"I said I got it, Mom. See you tomorrow morning." I jog away as Mom calls after me.

"You're so lucky," Erika says as we walk across the parking lot toward Mr. Park's SUV. "Your mom is so chill. Meanwhile, I get the third degree if I want to take the dogs over two streets to visit Naomi. I'm like, let me live, Jennifer!"

"I'm going to wrap this up and give it to my mom for Christmas. Best. Present. Ever." Naomi, still wearing Brandon's oversize jacket, squeezes the autographed picture to her chest. "Also, I'm totally broke."

Brandon's dad waves his fingers out of the moonroof to get our attention. Whatever song he's listening to has a bumping bass to it. It floods out of the car. Brandon groans.

"If my dad asks what we want to listen to in the car, the answer is always nothing. Complete silence. Trust me on this. Otherwise, he will attempt to sing along to any song whether he actually knows the words or not."

At 10:58 p.m.—because everybody is way more concerned about curfew than I am—I arrive back home. To her credit, Mom is sitting up on the couch, still in her street clothes, waiting for me. Since her head is tipped back and her eyes are closed, I don't bother waking her. I balance the paper plate of brownies—that Brandon insisted I take home and that Naomi wouldn't let me "accidentally" leave in her mom's car—on my palm as I slip off my Chucks at the front door. The basket of overdue bills and mail is gone. Even the coffee table, which is usually filled with medicine bottles and other medical clutter, is clear. Mom must be afraid of being mom-shamed if somebody else's overly involved parent insists on invading our normal here too tonight. I tiptoe through to the kitchen and hang up my keys. As much as it pains me, the brownies go straight into the trash.

I open the refrigerator to grab some water and discover a bowl of cooked vegetables inside. And a dozen apples. There's even a gallon of skim milk with a note on it.

Your favorite oatmeal is in the pantry.

A second note sits in front of the rice cooker which, when I pop it open, is filled with freshly cooked rice.

Since the Chois are gone, do you want to train
together tomorrow morning? Love, Mom

A warmth spreads in my chest. I pull the still carefully cov-ered plate of brownies out of the trash. With clean hands, I pick the best one out from underneath the plastic wrap and arrange it artfully on possibly the ugliest plate in existence. I should know. I painted it. I'm not sure what five-year-old Olivia was thinking when she picked this color scheme, but Mom refuses to get rid of it. Going to the paint-your-own-pottery place to make this plate is one of the few non-skating memories I have of my mom. Back before she and Dad decided to mold me into a single skater and then a pairs skater with Egg. Back when we were more parent and child, and less coach and skater.

The rest of the brownies go back in the trash because I already had too many tonight and licked the batter off the beaters on top of it. And that was after the pizza we ate for dinner. Brandon insisted that nobody won our impromptu brownie-baking contest because he couldn't pick a favorite. Nobody was #1. That's an odd experience.

As I pass back through the living room on my way upstairs, I lean over the back of the couch and balance the ugly-ass plate with the brownie on top of the armrest. I place a note beside it.

> *Let's train at 9. I made this for you at Brandon's*
> *tonight. <3, Livy*

Chapter 30

My waterlogged Chucks squish and squeak into Ice Dreams on Wednesday, my mood as dark as the nonstop rain since Monday morning.

"Hey, hey, hey, you're dripping all over the entryway," Mom scolds from her barstool in front of the snack bar.

I toss my next-to-useless umbrella into the makeshift umbrella stand Mom created at the front door and roll my pant legs back down. Even with my Ice Dreams jacket on, I can't stop shivering.

"No Mack again today?" My teeth chatter.

Mom looks up from the spreadsheet on her laptop. "She's coming in as soon as she and Fiona check out okay."

My heart squeezes. "I thought it was a small fender bender?"

"The insurance company said Mack's car was totaled, so she must have hit the other vehicle harder than she thought."

"Oh, Mack." I feel as sorry for me as I do Mack. We have so many fun memories in that car.

"One piece of good news." Without turning, Mom points toward the barre area.

My heart leaps, but when I turn, there's nobody there.

"What time is the party tonight?" I say, figuring it is Mom's attempt at a joke. "I'll put Skater Barbie together after I find some dry socks."

"What?" Mom rotates her whole body on the barstool to face me. "Where'd he go?"

At that, Jonah with his headphones on pops up from the floor of the barre area where he must have been doing push-ups, based on the amount of flexing of his biceps he's doing in the barre mirror. At least until he catches my eye.

"Five minutes to welcome him back, and then leave him to his training. I thought Mr. Choi would have been here by now." Mom checks the time on her phone. "Leave those shoes here. You're getting water everywhere. I have extra socks and slides you can borrow in my office. They're in the basket next to the door."

Though it is probably a health code violation, I ditch my sopping socks and shoes next to the snack bar and hightail it toward Mom's office. Though the cold floor stings the bottoms of my feet, I bypass Mom's office and head straight to the barre area. Jonah intersects me at its edge, grabbing me in a bear hug, and swinging me around. His kiss welcomes me home.

"Keeping it G-rated since your mom is right there," Jonah whispers in my ear when my feet touch the ground again. "When we have some personal space, though . . ."

"Yeah, I can . . . *we* can definitely do better." I adjust the folded blue bandana keeping Jonah's hair off his beautiful face. "Welcome home."

Jonah tips his head until his fabric-covered forehead presses into mine. "I missed you."

We stand there, rebalancing, for several minutes.

"Soooo?" I can't ask the question, but Jonah reads my mind.

"They offered me a spot."

My heart drops, but I say, "They would be stupid not to."

"Oh, believe me, I was shocked. They had me skate with some of the regulars. I lost. Every race. Every day. And I wasn't even close. I was the last to finish the training runs. I was the last to finish the ten-mile daily bike ride. I was the last to finish the stair runs. I was even last to breakfast every morning because my body was so tired. So. Much. Losing." A smile pulls across Jonah's face. "Yet, part of me loved it. I finally felt like I—"

My heart fissures. "Was home?"

"No, this is home. This will always be home." Jonah's cold fingers brush my cheek. "I finally felt like I belonged somewhere."

The fissures deepen into cracks. Mom's mood has been better than it has in months, but her back will never be healed. She's still going to have to have surgery. I step into Jonah and hold him tight. I need to rebalance.

"I don't want to move to Utah," Jonah whispers.

"You have to."

"We still have two and a half years before the next Winter Games."

"But we have to start training now if we are going to even have a shot at the medal podium."

"And I will, but maybe I should stay in Phoenix a little longer."

"Why? I thought the fine-tuned machine is chronically dehydrated here."

"It is. But that's not why." Jonah leads me over to the box he routinely hops on and off. He tosses his headphones attached to an old-school iPod into his workout bag and sits next to me. "Because the cost to go to Utah is too high, literally and figuratively. Housing is in such short supply that I would have to live in the athletes' apartments, probably with a couple of roommates. Alone. And though part of me would love that, especially as Mom still won't give me back my phone, I'm not sure I can do it. Be *that* alone for ten months. Be *that* focused on being number one for ten months. Wow, I sound like such a baby. I need to man up. I need to go to Utah. I need to at least attempt to be number one there."

"What in the world?" Mom's voice echoes across the rink as a muffled car horn honks outside.

My phone buzzes. It's a text from Mack.

Come outside.

"Mack is hailing us." I can see someone in the parking lot flashing their headlights. "But first, footwear."

Thankfully, the rain has turned to a light drizzle. We leap across the puddle creating a moat around Ice Dreams until we are next to a shiny compact SUV. Egg opens the passenger side door and slides out.

"They did? Why would you do that?" Whoever Egg is talking to on the phone has pissed him off. A deep scowl crosses his usually happy face. He gives us a short wave but jumps the moat and heads into Ice Dreams.

"Shotgun." Jonah nods at the still-open car door.

I groan but climb in the back next to a new, high-end baby car seat. Mack looks over her shoulder at me and beams. I don't know how the queen of bargain shopping has pulled this off.

"Niiiiiice," Jonah says, looking around the pristine car.

"I thought the accident on Monday was your fault?" I say.

Mack's smile dampens. "It was. Fiona was screaming. I looked away from the road for a few seconds, and when I turned back, I ran up on this tank of a pickup's trailer hitch. I owe him $2,000 to buff out a quarter-size dent in his bumper. Meanwhile, my beloved Toyota lost its life during my brief moment of stupidity."

"Better the Toyota than you. Or Fiona," Jonah says.

"True. It could have been much worse."

"So where did this sweet ride come from?" Jonah pushes a button that makes his seat dip back until his head is practically in my lap. "It's got power everything."

"I know, right? I'm not even sure what some of these buttons are for." Mack stabs at a few as Jonah rises back up. "The car is on permanent loan from my father. He insists that he was planning to buy a 'midlife-crisis car' anyway and Monday's disaster sped up his timeline. The new car seat was a belated baby shower gift from my mother. Oh, make no mistake. There are strings attached. There always are, but we gotta start somewhere."

"I'm glad you reached out to them," I say.

"I didn't have much of a choice. Gran's on a road trip to Las Vegas with her Bunco friends. This was my week to be the adult of the house while she was gone. I wanted to give Gran a break from having to take care of Fiona and me and to just enjoy her retirement for a change. And, as usual, I . . ." Mack's breath hitches and she looks away. "Why do I always mess everything up?"

I tap Mack on the shoulder with Fiona's obviously new Santa-themed rattle until she looks at me.

"It's okay to ask for help." I think about what Brandon said to me the other day. "I'm not sure what we can actually *do* about any of your problems, but if you need to unload, I'm all ears."

"That goes for me too," Jonah says. "You know I always got your back."

"Thanks, guys. Really. That means a lot. I hate that I'm such an emotional and financial burden on Gran." Mack grinds the heels of her hands in her eyes and lets out a frustrated sigh. "I feel like I'm stuck in limbo. One part of me still in high school and the other part in adulthood. There are days when I wish I could rewind the clock and tell past perfectionist Mack to get over herself and just go to freakin' ASU. To enjoy being a college student. Go to parties. Join a ridiculous club. Stay up all night studying. Watch the sun rise from 'A' Mountain. Make pancakes at 4:00 a.m. on a Tuesday just because I can. Go to Mexico for spring break. My life isn't going quite the way I planned. And now with this accident on top of it, *nothing* is going right."

"I don't know about that. You got us. And Stuart and Midori. And the derby girls." Jonah points at Mack's expensive sound system. "And this new car stereo system is sick."

Mack sniffs. "Yeah, it even has satellite radio and Bluetooth capabilities. I mean, what kind of sorcery is this? How am I supposed to play my GNR cassettes now?"

Jonah strokes the sound system. "Shh. You're going to offend it with your choice of archaic technology. Besides . . ." Jonah pushes a series of buttons until a specific channel comes up on the satellite radio. He sits back in his seat with a smug look on his face. "You're welcome."

I'm not sure what song it is, but it's obviously something by Guns N' Roses based on Mack's off-key singing. It starts off innocently enough. A little head bobbing. A little air guitar. A little car dancing. Then Jonah cranks up the volume until the bass buzzes the glass windows and all hell breaks loose. By the end of the song, my neck hurts, but my soul feels better.

A polite knocking on Mack's window interrupts our gut-busting laughter. I hand Jonah back his bandana, which flew off his head some time during the second chorus.

Mack rolls down the window. "Oh, hey, Midori. Just checkin' out my new sound system with the kids."

"So I heard. Along with everybody else in a five-mile radius," Mom says, massaging her lower back with her fists. "Jonah is supposed to be training. I don't know what's happened to Mr. Choi. He's usually here by now."

Jonah's eyes widen. "I'll text him. He's probably running late."

I'm not sure how Jonah is supposed to do that exactly since his mom still has his phone, but I keep my mouth closed.

"Midori, go home. You've been here all day. Give your back a break. Stuart and I'll keep an eye on these two. My parents have Fiona, and they aren't in a hurry to give her back, so I can lock up."

Mom puts her hand on Mack's arm and gives it a squeeze. "I'm glad to hear that, Annabelle. Okay, then, see you at home, Livy. And don't stay out late. You have school tomorrow."

I groan. Now she's interested in my education. "Okay."

Our odd trio enters Ice Dreams to find Egg jumping up and down like the time he found a scorpion curled up in his skate pants in his locker.

"Yes, yes, yeeeeeeeessss!" Egg says.

"What, what, whaaaaat?" I say.

"I got a callback!" Egg's voice crescendos with every word. "And they want you to come with me! They said, and I quote, 'Is your partner under contract right now? If not, we'd like to extend the invitation to her too, to audition for the next leg of our tour.'"

"We did it! We did it! We did it!" Egg and I grab hands and jump up and down in a circle.

"When's the audition?"

"Friday. If we make it through the cattle call, then we skate our choreography in the afternoon. If we make it through that hoop, then they give us new choreography together or make us switch partners or skate solo or maybe all of the above. If they love us, then we stay through the weekend and learn a few of the easier numbers. We'll fly out tomorrow morning."

"Oh." After the brownie bakeoff and the crash course in *Call of Duty*, part of me actually is looking forward to experiencing the normal teen event called a midnight movie and a sleepover. And then there's my midterms.

"Don't tell me that's a problem."

If you aren't going to do it at 100 percent then why bother?

"No problem at all."

Jonah puts his hand on my lower back. "Congratulations, man. I guess Olivia is your lucky charm too."

Egg drops my hands and takes a step back. "There's one bad thing, though. We'll miss Mack's debut with the Surly Gurlz on Saturday."

"Wait, I thought you *didn't* make the team?" I say.

"I didn't." Mack plunks her diaper bag–purse on the snack bar's counter. "Barnacle Barb is organizing a charity bout for Toys for Tots this Saturday and their roster is a little light. There's no guarantee I'll get to skate, but I'm happy to be a benchwarmer if it takes me one step closer to my goal. I was hoping at least one of you would be able to come, though."

Egg holds up an imaginary glass to Mack. "Here's to Mack Truck. Go out there and kick some ass on Saturday."

"You too. Here's to kicking ass." Mack and Egg clink their imaginary glasses together.

"You guys are so extra," I say. "And yet, I wouldn't want it any other way."

"Me neither." Jonah rocks back and forth on his Chucks. "By the way, I should warn you guys that my parents don't know I'm here."

"Choooi!" Mack gives Jonah an exasperated look.

"Dad is doing a follow-up job interview, and Mom is still at work. I would text them and let them know where I am but, hey, they still have my phone."

Mack's scowl melts into a smile. "That is possibly the most normal teen thing you've ever said."

"Can you talk them into letting me come to the bout? I want to support *you* for a change."

"Maybe this will help." Mack rummages around in her bag and chucks a mess of black fabric at Jonah.

Jonah smiles at his new Surly Gurlz–themed T-shirt. "Cool. Thanks, Mack. I'll wear it on Saturday. I hope."

"Turn it over. The Gurlz said you deserve it after all your dry land training help. Even if you insist on making us do squats until we cry." Mack smiles so big, her lip ring clinks against her bottom teeth. Big silver foil letters spell out QUICK SILVER. "Welcome to the team, Jonah."

Jonah is speechless. He gives Mack an awkward side hug.

"You better cheer loudly for me on Saturday night even if I get my ass handed to me or never make it off the bench," Mack says.

"I'll definitely be there. Even if I have to sneak out my second-story window to do it."

Something pings in my chest. He doesn't have to sound so okay with me being gone.

"I heard you were looking for nails and a hammer earlier." Mack rummages in her bag again. She hands Jonah a little brown paper bag that jingles. "Ernie had the hammer. It's back in its correct spot now underneath the skate counter."

"Thanks! Now I can finally fix that wall."

I follow Jonah to the skate counter. Without consulting me, Jonah puts a nail above my old gold medal picture and hangs his instead. Jonah takes a step back and admires his handiwork.

"There ya go." Jonah pushes the picture up a millimeter on the left. "Perfect. Situation solved."

"Wait. While you have the tools out, put another nail above that one."

"Aw, thank you." Jonah brushes my lips with his before putting the nail in. "You're my number-one fan."

"It's for me."

Jonah gives me a confused look, then he nods. "Oh, the audition."

"As Erika would say, I'm *manifesting* my new Olympians on Ice headshot going in that spot."

Jonah chuckles. I don't.

"I mean, of course, manifest away," Jonah backpedals. "I'm sure you are going to do great."

A knot forms in my stomach. "So glad you're my number-one fan."

"I am! Of course I am." Jonah wraps his arms around me. "But do they even let minors skate on tour?"

"Yes. I know my dad is, like, the old man of the show, but they also have some newer Olympians. And not all of them are adults."

"But they have medals, and you—" Jonah's mouth snaps closed.

"Don't," I finish for him and he winces.

"I'm sorry." Jonah's arms tighten around me. "That didn't come out right."

"Olivia! We have a problem. A *big* problem." Egg kicks one of the stools in the snack bar. "I hate my brothers so much right now."

I jog over to find Egg banging his head on the counter. Beside him is his wallet with his debit and credit cards pulled out.

"What's wrong?"

When Egg looks up at me, his face is scarlet with rage. "Steven and Scott ratted me out to Mom and Dad. Steven told them I hadn't been to our English class in the last month and am currently blowing off finals. They are so pissed. But it gets worse. My parents have frozen my bank accounts and my credit card. Midori paid me in cash for last weekend, but I deposited all but $40 of it yesterday. How much money do you have left from earlier?"

"Almost $500. I spent some of it."

"Plan B. We take a Greyhound bus to Los Angeles and then Uber to the audition and back. We'll have to find a super cheap hotel and share a room." When Jonah makes a noise, Egg adds,

"We're desperate here, Jonah. Compromises need to be made. We'll eat one good meal right before the audition for fuel, but otherwise we're gonna be living off protein bars since I just bought a huge box of them at Costco."

Mack digs her wallet out of her bag and pulls out the hundred-dollar bonus Mom gave her. She throws the twenties on top of Egg's wallet plus seventeen more dollars.

"I can't take your money, Mack." Egg pushes the pile of money back toward her.

"Yes, you can." Mack pushes it back.

"But Fiona is low on formula and diapers."

"Then I guess her *father* is going to have to do a better job of providing for her. In fact . . ." Mack digs in her bag again and then slaps her car keys in Egg's hand. "It's time for Tyler to help me out. Including giving me a ride to and from work for a few days. I'm tired of being a single parent. He needs to man up and do his share."

I put my hand out for Mack to high-five. It's about damn time.

"Are you sure, Mack?" Egg says. "I'm asking a lot of you. Maybe too much."

"No, Stu. You have been such a huge help to Gran and Fiona and me these last two weeks. Cooking dinner for us and mowing the lawn and cleaning the grout in the kitchen. I know you were bored, but still. We owe you."

"But your car."

"Yeah, you wreck it and my dad will kill you, but otherwise, enjoy."

"I promise to pay you back. Both of you."

"Wait." Jonah runs to grab his wallet. He adds thirty-seven dollars, a ten-dollar gift card for Subway, and a fifty-dollar pre-paid credit card to the pile. "Good luck."

"Go chase your dream." Mack looks at Egg and then me. "Even if it takes you both away from us, I know we need to let you fly."

Jonah laces his fingers through mine. Worry etches his face.

"I need to go home and pack," I say.

"Yeah, let's leave early tomorrow morning to give us plenty of time to rest up." Egg gathers up all the cash and cards and puts them in his wallet. "Make sure you get the 'rents to sign off on this. Do you want me to ask Midori for you?"

"No, I'm sure she'll be fine with it. If there is a problem, I'll let you know."

"Seriously, I can come over and work the Stuart Trout charm. Moms love me." Egg gives me a boy-next-door smile.

"I'm not a baby, Egg. I can do this. See you tomorrow morning. Rest up."

"I'd give you a ride, but somebody needs to stay here with Choi," Mack says.

"I'll stay with him." Egg hands Mack her keys back. "I've been wanting to have a man-to-man chat with him for a while now, anyway."

"Play nice, boys." Mack points at one and then the other. "I'll be back in ten."

Jonah wraps his arms around me. "As my favorite figure skater of all time once said to me: Good luck, skate fast, and stay balanced."

My heart warms. I lean in closer to whisper in his ear, "I love you."

Before he can respond, the front door of Ice Dreams crashes open.

"JONAH JUNG HOON CHOI!" I can practically see the fire coming out of Mrs. Choi's ears.

"Looks like my skating time is over for today." Jonah kisses the top of my head before turning toward his mother. "Mom, I can explain."

"Outside! Right now!"

"Let me get my bag first, geez."

"You will watch your tone, mister."

"You're the one screaming at me."

None of us dare to make eye contact with Mrs. Choi as Jonah sprints to the barre area and grabs his bag. He stuffs his new Surly Gurlz T-shirt deep inside it.

When I come out the front door five minutes later, Jonah and his mom are still arguing in the car. He runs an agitated hand through his hair and then bangs his fist on the window. I catch Jonah's eye as I pass. His fist opens up until his hand is placed flat on the glass.

"I love you too," his lips say back.

I wait at Mack's car as she and Egg lock up Ice Dreams for the day.

Mack sighs when the three of us are tucked safely into her car. "Yeah, there's a snowball's chance in Phoenix that Mrs. Choi is going to let Jonah come to the bout on Saturday now."

Chapter 31

I wish there were something I could do to help Jonah, but I have mom problems of my own to deal with.

"Honey, I would love for you to go to the audition, even if it were just for the experience," Mom says as I settle in on the couch beside her. "But we don't have the extra money right now for travel expenses."

I knew this would be Issue #1. I dig the Altoids tin out of my purse, pop it open, and pull out a stack of bills with rubber bands around them.

"I have the money." I put it on the table.

"Where did you get this?" Mom looks from the pile of money to the bottles of high-quality, prescription-only pain pills on the coffee table.

"Egg hired me to make the audition video with him. I earned a $100 bonus because he got a callback."

"We can't take Stuart's money, Livy. He's like family."

"Yes, we can. I worked hard for that money."

"You did work hard. You were a true professional. Your dad would be very proud of you. But Olympians on Ice, even the corps, is a whole other level of skating."

The knot in my stomach reappears. "Mom, you saw the audition tape. You know my skills are solid."

"I know, honey, but you're not auditioning to be a principal skater. The judges aren't looking for triples from their corps skaters. They're looking for artistry."

This barb hurts worse than my mom thinking I'm a small-time drug dealer.

"Olympians on Ice *asked* me to audition, so they must see something special in me even if you don't."

"You are special, Olivia, but . . ." Mom digs around in the couch cushions until she finds her phone. "Where is your dad skating this week? Maybe he could use his frequent flier points to take you to LA? And use points for a nice hotel. Then it would be like a mini vacation. You said you wanted to go to Disneyland. Why don't you make a nice daddy-and-me vacation out of it?"

"Will you stop treating me like a five-year-old!" I explode, sounding exactly like one.

"Olivia Midori Kennedy!" Mom's voice is equally shrill.

I stand. "Do you want me to be the parent or the child in this relationship? One minute you're in my business twenty-four-seven. The next I feel like I'm invisible to you. Make up your mind!"

Mom stands too, a trail of electrical wires hanging off her back. She looks me dead in the eyes. "I am the parent. You are my child."

"Then why aren't you there for me?" The ice is ragged today, and even if Ernie busted through the wall right now with the Zamboni, there's no saving me from a complete meltdown.

"I'm sorry, honey. I know I messed up after the lockdown at school. Mack did such a great job calming you down, though. Some days, I think she's a better mom to you than I am."

"I'm not talking about the stupid lockdown. I'm talking about Nationals last year. And high-performance camp last summer. And let's not forget about the train wreck that was Skate Detroit when Stuart and I had our asses handed to us."

"Honey, you are comparing apples to oranges."

"Am I? Are you afraid to train me? Is that what it is? Maybe deep down you know I have the potential to be even *better* than you and Dad. Maybe I could win more than one gold medal before I retire. Have a bigger career. Have a longer career. Have a life."

"You're not good enough, Olivia." The venom spews out of Mom's mouth, burning us both. "There. Now it's finally out in the open. I've been training talented girls for twenty years. I'm always looking for that one-in-a-million skater. That one kid who might have a shot at the Olympics. None of my students have had it. Including you."

The air rips out of my lungs. I slump down on the couch. Hot tears prick my eyes.

"Does Jonah have it?" I have to know. Mom makes a noncommittal noise. "Does he, Mom? Does Ice Dreams' reigning prince have that one-in-a-million spark?"

After a moment, Mom says, "Yes. That still doesn't guarantee he's going to make it to the top, but he's got raw talent. Like you did."

"Did? Do! You know what? Stop talking to me." I snatch my money off the table. "Just stop talking to me altogether."

Mom calls after me, but I sprint up the stairs. It's not like she can come after me. My phone vibrates.

Sorry about all the drama today. It's not Mom apologizing. It's Mr. One-in-a-Million.

Turns out, Mom's performance today was only the opening act. If you'd stuck around five minutes more, you would have witnessed the Choi tag team smackdown when Dad arrived. It wasn't pretty.

Sorry I missed that. But it looks like you got your phone back.

Yes! It's so they can keep better tabs on
me, but I'll take it. For now. Mack says we
should give them a day or two to calm down
before bringing up the derby bout.

Good idea.

Are you okay?

Yes.

Are you sure?

Yes. I gotta go. I need to pack.

Oh, okay. Night. <3

I turn off my phone without responding. A true one-in-a-
million skater can't be distracted. Not by friends. Not by family
drama. Not by her heart. Skating has to be her #1. Especially when
she lives in a world of people who only look out for #1.

Don't even think about it, Mom's note on the front door says. She
tried to be the parent. She gets bonus points for sleeping while sitting straight up on the couch facing the door. But it's an automatic
deduction in parenting when I simply grab my keys and walk out
the kitchen door instead.

Hey, you created this monster.

"I thought Stu was picking you up at ten tomorrow morning?"
Mack says, with a sleepy Fiona in her arms, when I show up on
her doorstep with my backpack and carry-on suitcase.

I execute a perfect "kiss and cry" smile. "Change of plans. Can

I crash on your couch tonight instead? That way we won't have to disturb Mom tomorrow morning."

Mack lets me in, but she gives me a skeptical look.

"C'mon, you know how Mom is. She's going to micromanage us, and then it will be noon by the time Egg and I finally hit the road. It's easier this way."

"Hmm, true." Mack bounces Fiona as we walk into the cluttered living room. "Stu has already gone to bed. I was giving Fi her last bottle of the day."

Mack chucks a pile of toys and books into a basket next to the couch. She brushes off the seat cushions and puts down a tartan blanket for me.

"Your room is ready." Mack gestures with a flourish at the couch. "Only the best for our favorite auntie, right, Fi?"

Fiona lets out an impressive burp before spitting up all over Mack's shoulder.

"Maaaan." Mack looks at her shoulder. "This is my favorite GNR shirt too. Help yourself to towels and whatever while I get Fi down. You know where everything is."

I clear my throat to get rid of the lump in it. "Thanks, Mack. You're the best."

I don't even have my pajamas out of my suitcase before Mack is back, without Fiona. She plops down on the couch.

"Okay, I'm not buying it. What's going on with you tonight, Olivia? And don't you dare say 'nothing.' You can tell me to mind my own damn business if you want, but don't lie to me."

I sit on the couch next to her and tuck my legs up. "Do you think Jonah is that one-in-a-million skater?"

"Yes. I have never seen someone as driven as he is. Yes, Mr. Choi pushes him. And believe me, I'm an expert on pushy parents, but Jonah drives himself harder than anyone I've ever met."

"What about me?"

"What about you?"

"Do you think I'm a one-in-a-million skater too? And be honest with me."

Every second of Mack's silence causes my already low self-confidence to plummet even further.

"Maybe," Mack finally says.

I hug my knees tighter to my chest. Mack puts her hand on my upper arm until I look at her.

"Some people are born with talent and fly to the top. Others have to claw their way to the top, rung by rung. You had the first one when you were younger, just like Choi. Then you went to play with the big kids, and they kicked your ass. Things got hard for the first time ever, and you gave up. You could still have it, though, Olivia, but now you're going to have to do it the hard way. If you've got the guts."

The pressure in my rib cage increases until I'm afraid I'll implode. I whisper the truth that has been following me around since last season when everything started going south. "But what if after all that, I'm *still* not good enough?"

"Good enough for what? The US Olympic figure skating team? The Olympics themselves? A gold medal? Two gold medals? A multimillion-dollar endorsement deal? A commentator gig? Don't you see? The doubt is going to be never-ending. The only thing you can control, Liv, is yourself. Keep showing up. Keep doing the work. Even when it's hard. Even when it's still not enough to win. See how far you can go. No regrets."

I wipe my eyes. "Are you talking to me or yourself?"

Mack punches me in the arm. "Both of us. Also, I know Midori probably forgot, but I haven't—you have two midterm exams tomorrow. You can't blow those off, you know."

"Really? If you were in my shoes, you'd pick a geometry and a Japanese exam over an Olympians on Ice audition?"

Mack makes a noncommittal noise. "Go to bed. I'm getting you up at six thirty so we can go for a training run before you leave for California."

"Who are you?" I whack Mack with a throw pillow and she whacks me back.

Chapter 32

On a good day, it takes about six hours to go across the desert to Los Angeles. Today is not that day. Between traffic jams, Egg's nervous stomach, and a flat tire in Cabazon, it feels like the universe is conspiring against us. And just when I think things can't possibly get worse, Mom calls Egg.

"I'm sorry, Midori. What can I say? Teenagers are a pain in the ass," Egg yells back at her as we sit underneath the giant T. rex waiting for AAA to arrive. "Look, we're almost to Los Angeles. Let us focus on our audition. When we get back to Phoenix, you can ground Olivia until she's forty, okay? I gotta go. I'm running out of battery."

I can still hear Mom yelling when Egg hangs up on her. The vein in Egg's temple looks ready to burst.

Egg growls. "You are in so much trouble. *We* are in so much trouble. Like, beyond normal teenage shenanigans trouble."

"I don't care," I lie.

"Fine, but *I* do. You know your mom could have me arrested? Remember." Egg points at himself. "I'm the adult here. My whole career could be over before it even begins because of this." Egg bangs his fists on the ground a few times before he takes a cleansing breath. "Why didn't you tell me your parents weren't on board with this?"

"Because I didn't want to let you down."

"Missing the audition would suck. Going to jail would suck a thousand times worse, though."

"You are not going to jail, Egg. We're not runaways. We're partners going to an audition. Any cop would understand that."

"No, they wouldn't. This is the real world, Olivia. Not the Skater Bubble you've always lived in. Do you know what this looks like? Human trafficking. My God, I have just used Sociology 101 in a real-life setting. Too bad my life is over."

I grab Egg's bicep and shake him. "Get a grip, Stuart Trout. We are *not* going to blow this audition because of a few, okay, a lot of setbacks. I need this job and am not going down without a fight. So, you better man up and do your part."

Egg groans. "What if it's not enough?"

"Then let's see how far we can go."

"You gotta give me a hundred and ten percent tomorrow. There is no room for error now."

"Only if you do the same."

"No regrets?"

"No regrets."

Chapter 33

I don't turn my phone on Friday morning either. I need to focus. I need to stay in my Skater Bubble. I can't let Egg down. I can't let myself down either. Unfortunately, Egg's crappy driving is letting me down. I know normal teens go on road trips. It seems so much more fun in the movies. Surely, normal teen road trips don't involve the amount of swearing ours has. I do my hair and makeup as we make confused loops around LA, and that's with the GPS on Egg's phone.

Our ninety minutes of scheduled stretch and prep time is cut down to all of five minutes by the time we finally arrive. We run full-out across the parking lot and down the street. We skid into the Olympians on Ice building one minute after nine.

"I'm sorry, we've already sent the applicants back for warm-up," a middle-aged white lady with a severe bun and scarlet lips says when Egg and I finally get to the front desk.

"Please. Let us back. We drove. All the way. From Arizona." Egg heaves while holding out the new headshots Mack made for us.

"Young man, if you're going to work in this industry, then you need to start acting like a professional." The lady doesn't even look up from the stack of headshots in front of her.

"But, but, but . . ."

"Do I need to call security?"

My stomach drops. I can't go back to Phoenix like this. I can't lose the rink over something so stupid. I can't give up. No regrets.

"Excuse me, Ms. Pavlovich," I say, reading her name tag. "My father, Michael Kennedy, skates on your current tour. And I was wondering if—"

The woman takes off her bedazzled purple reading glasses and looks up at me. "You're Mike and Midori's daughter?"

"Yes, ma'am. I'm Olivia Kennedy. I apologize for this morning. I swear, we aren't usually this unprofessional. Could you bend the rules just this once as a favor to my father?" I take our headshots from Egg and hold them out to her. "We can be on the ice in five. Goodness knows we are warmed up from the sprint we did from the parking lot."

"Ah, golden boy Michael." Ms. Pavlovich lets out a little sigh as she accepts our headshots. "Please tell him that his, hmmm, friend Faina sends her regards. That I remember Sarajevo fondly, and he still owes me a bottle of Dom Pérignon. Here. Take these." Dad's *friend* Faina hands me our numbers. "This is good enough for now, but come back at the break and do your paperwork correctly before we all get in trouble. Now go, quickly. Break a leg, Olivia."

The story behind why my dad owes this woman a bottle of something very expensive-sounding will have to wait for another time. I grab our audition numbers and pull Egg—who stands there slack-jawed after my gold-medal ass-kissing performance—through the double doors.

"Skaters may now take the ice to warm up," a man's voice echoes around the rink.

Egg swears. I'm lucky. I have my new skate outfit on underneath my warm-ups, so I only need a minute to strip down and get my skates on. Egg, with no time to make it to the locker room and back, drops his bag on the nearest bench and takes his sweatshirt off. He slides a simple black skate shirt with a little red piping over his head.

"Egg!" I say when I realize his skate pants are on the bench too.

"Turn your head if it bothers you." Egg drops his jeans and someone whistles.

We are on the ice in record time. Couples in coordinating outfits whiz by us. Egg jerks me into him half a second before a woman nearly lands her throw double toe loop on top of me.

"Thanks," I say, squished up against Egg.

"Rule Number One." Egg doesn't let me go. "And thank you for back there. I have no idea how you made that happen, but thanks. I know I don't give you enough credit sometimes."

"Sometimes?"

"A lot of the time, but I'll try harder from now on." Egg is quivering and dripping sweat on me already. "I can't believe I'm finally here. I may throw up."

I wince and try to pull away. Egg laughs and holds me tighter.

"Let me stand here and breathe for a second. The nausea will pass."

I take a moment to absorb the experience too, because there is no guarantee that it will ever happen again. The training rink is filled with giant posters of previous and current skaters out on tour with Olympians on Ice. A giant vintage poster of my parents hangs above the bench we crammed our gear under. Mom and Dad, in coordinating lemon-yellow, sparkly costumes, fly around the rink in matching sky-high arabesques. Mom's arms stretch out to the sides like wings. Back when my parents were young. Back when my mom was healthy. Back when the pair of underdog teenagers from America stunned the world with their electrifying performance and snatched the Olympic gold medal from the Russians. Back when they did commercials for car companies and had their faces plastered on boxes of cereal.

"Skaters, line up in numerical order, please," the man's voice echoes around the rink.

Britney Xiao flies by us. She gives me side-eye as she and her partner-of-the-day line up three couples down from us.

I give Egg a tight hug. "Stuart, whatever happens today, happens. We're going to leave it all on the ice. Even if we crash and burn like Skate Detroit."

"We are *not* going to crash and burn. We are back and better than we've ever been. Now, let's go kick some ass."

I look over at my parents' poster one last time. "No regrets."

"May we have all pairs on the ice," the announcer says at the end of the first section.

Egg grabs my hand, and we skate to the line. Blood rushes through my ears. We have to make it. We have no plan B.

"Couple number four. Couple number eight. Couple number ten. Couple number twelve. And couple number seventeen," the announcer says. Egg and I jump around like a pair of five-year-olds for about three seconds before we remember ourselves. "Thank you to all the couples who skated today. We wish we could offer contracts to all of you. Please consider auditioning for us again in the future."

Egg clears his throat and smooths out his skate shirt. "Good job, Olivia. All your blood, sweat, and tears paid off."

"Don't jinx us. We're not there yet."

"We will now take a lunch break," the announcer continues. "Returning couples need to be warmed up and on the ice in one hour. Dismissed."

We follow a herd of dejected skaters off the ice—some too old, some too inexperienced, some without enough training, and some without enough passion. I may be the youngest person in this rink today, but the ice rink has been my home literally since birth. This is my normal. But now is the time to be extra.

When we come off the ice, Egg says, "You change, and I'll go get the paperwork from Ms. I'll-Always-Remember-Sarajevo-Fondly."

I'm pleased to find that our bags are where we left them. That, unfortunately, wasn't a given. Or maybe it was. To sabotage another skater under the watchful gaze of Skate Gods Midori Nakashima and Michael Kennedy would surely result in bad skate karma of unprecedented levels. Even though I'm still mad at them, I'm also grateful to them. I bring my fingertips to my lips and slap a kiss on Mom and Dad's poster before I leave for the locker room.

As I slide into my phoenix costume, I size up my competition. And they size me up. I feel naked. Even after I have my costume securely on, I still feel exposed. They may remember this costume from last season, but they're about to see something completely new.

Nobody talks to one another as we do our makeup. I recognize a couple of the girls I used to compete against when we were juniors. We give one another nods, but we don't engage. Nobody wants a competitor in their Skater Bubble when preparing for competition.

"Oh, hey." Britney Xiao sits at the makeup station next to me, even though there are plenty of open stations around the room.

Of course she does. I nod in her direction.

"I was so surprised to see you and Stuart here this morning." Britney side-eyes me while I line my lids with Mack's glittery eyeliner. "I heard you two quit skating after Skate Detroit. 'Cause, you know, that last performance." Britney adds a dramatic cringe. "Ouch."

Not today, Satan.

"You, of all people, should know better than to listen to the gossip." I tap a little red glitter over top of my blood-red lipstick. "Don't worry. Team Kennedy/Trout is stronger than ever. You'll see."

"You know Stuart texted me about being his partner."

"Yep. But you were in London and couldn't get back in time to film with him. It's okay. We worked out the problem, fixed the choreography, and here we are."

"I didn't get a text while I was in London." The corner of Britney's mouth pulls up in a sneer. "But Stuart and I have been texting each other off and on since Skate Detroit." Some people club their opponent in the knee, Britney's preferred technique is a knife to the back. "Stuart is the one who suggested I audition for Olympians on Ice."

I clasp my hands together to keep them from strangling Britney. And then Egg.

"What can I say? Washed-up skaters don't have a lot of career choices." I keep my words measured, but everybody is looking at us, their phones at the ready in case a good catfight breaks out. "I'm just here to support my partner and make him look good. Then it's back to training for the Olympics for me." I hop off my stool and throw my gear into a locker. "I hope you have a good audition, Britney. Who are you skating with again? I can't keep up with all your partner changes."

"Nathan Vedders."

I do a dramatic cringe. "Ow."

More than one person in the room snickers. I hold my head high and own this performance. I slam my locker closed and strut out the door in all my glittery extra-ness.

Egg intercepts me outside of the women's locker room.

"Sign this." Egg is channeling his inner chipmunk with the amount of protein bar crammed in his cheeks.

He points to a couple of specific places on the paperwork that he already filled out for me. Before he can race back off, I grab his arm.

"Since when are you and Britney BFFs?" I say, and Egg gives me a puzzled look. "According to her, you two have 'been texting each other off and on since Skate Detroit.'"

Egg snorts.

"It was three texts and a quickly deleted inappropriate drunk text selfie. Her selfie. Not mine." He shakes his head in disbelief. "I can't believe you fell for the oldest trick in the book. Your performance earlier must have rocked Britney to her very shallow core for her to overcompensate so much and drill down into your insecurities. My God, I just used my Psychology 101 class in real life too! I guess I did learn stuff at college."

Egg throws an arm across my shoulders. "So, though I am flattered to have two lovely ladies fighting over me, I'm happy with the partner I have. Also, I would partner Mr. Egotistical Choi before I would partner Britney Xiao."

"Thanks." I wrap my arm around Egg's waist and close my eyes. "I gotta get back into the Skater Bubble with you. No distractions. No drama. No regrets."

"And we will do that." Egg peels me off him. "After I deliver these papers back to your new BFF Faina."

I clap politely after Britney and Nathan's performance. It's not bad. Especially for someone who has a stick up her butt. It's not gold medal material, though.

"Couple number seventeen, you may take the ice," the announcer says as Britney and Nathan do a cooldown lap.

I don't care if maybe ten people, including the judges, are watching me. I pretend like I'm at the Olympics.

"Grab it and growl, tiger," I say, kissing my fingertips, and smack Mom and Dad's poster for good luck. Egg does the same.

"One last request," Egg whispers as we walk hand in clammy hand to the boards. "I want you to kiss me at the end. For real." I recoil. "Hear me out. I want you to kiss me so that one day when somebody does kiss me for real, I'll know exactly what it's *not* supposed to feel like."

"Hey, I haven't had any technique complaints from Jonah." I remove my skate guards.

"Just like today, Short Stuff, it's not about technique." Egg grabs my hand, and we skate out to the middle of the rink. "It's about the passion and the commitment behind it."

"You got it. Now let's get it."

We take our opening pose. Britney Freakin' Xiao yawns. My heart pounds though I'm standing still. My whole body buzzes with adrenaline. I will my hands to stop shaking. I look at the judges. It's do or die. No regrets.

When the music starts, I hear an "oh" echo around the rink. It causes a genuine smile on my face. They were expecting Alexei's phoenix number. They have no idea what is about to come out of the ashes of our previous skating life.

The music fills my heart and vibrates every cell in my body. I let it all go, allowing my body to move around the space with no limitations. I skate my love letter to Jonah. *And. We. Nail. It.* Every lift. Every jump. Every spin. Egg and I are in perfect synchronization. Egg loops me around him in the lowest death spiral of all the couples today. When I come back up, we press together for our final spin combo. Three . . . two . . . one. Egg jams his toe pick into the ice to slow our rotation. I close my eyes and picture Jonah's face as Egg dips me back for our final pose. Egg's lips press into mine with passion and commitment. Someone in the rink whoops as we sell it to the cheap seats. When Egg rights me, I glance over at Britney. She puts down her phone after probably recording the whole thing. Good. I want her to remember that skate.

"Annnnnnd?" I say under my breath as Egg and I take a bow.

"Nope. Nothing. But your skating was awesome." Egg's now red, glittery lips part in a triumphant smile.

"Fair enough. Wipe your mouth."

"Couple number seventeen, approach the judges' table, please."

Egg laces his fingers through mine, and we skate in front of the judges' table. We have so got this. Especially since the old man in the middle of the table—who looks suspiciously like Stan Lee—is smiling at us.

"You are Mike and Midori's daughter?" the man says.

"Yes, sir."

"I thought so. I'm sorry." The man rips my headshot in half.

My yelp echoes around the silent rink.

"Olivia," the man continues, "I would sign you up in a heartbeat. I *will* sign you up in a heartbeat. When you are out of high school."

"Please. I can do this. My parents will sign off on anything. I don't care about school. I can get my GED or do online school or whatever," I say, but the man continues to shake his head. "Send us out on my dad's tour so he can be legally responsible for me. I'll skate in the corps. I'll be the giant snowman. I'll deodorize all the skates. I'll carry luggage. Please let me do this. Please."

"I'm sorry, Olivia. Honestly, I am. If you had an Olympic medal, I might be able to work something out, but you don't." The man pulls out a small golden case from his pocket and slides one of his business cards across the table to me. "If you want to be in the corps, come back and audition again after you've finished high school." When I reach out for the business card, he puts his fingertips on top of the card and looks me in the eye. "Or, if you want to be a headliner, go after that Olympic medal first. I know that's not what you want to hear today, but one day, you'll thank me." He removes his fingertips so I can take the card. "Now then, Mister . . . um . . . Trout, I presume you've already graduated from high school."

"Yes, sir." Egg squeezes my hand tightly.

"Then you may stay," the man says. "Are you interested in auditioning for a swing position since Olivia won't be able to partner with you? We always need more men for our show."

Egg looks at me and then at the judges and then back at me.

"Mr. Trout? We need to move on."

Egg's fingers slide away from mine. "Yes, sir."

"Moving on, then," the man says. "Thank you for your time, Miss Kennedy. Give Midori my best."

Tears well up in my eyes, but I refuse to let them out. The phoenix burning in my chest lets out one last triumphant screech before plummeting back to earth in a ball of fire. My new career is officially over before it has even started.

"Couple number eight, please take the ice," the voice booms over the rink speaker.

I skate like an Olympic short track skater off the ice.

"Olivia, wait." Egg skates after me.

I slip my skate guards on and step off the ice. I don't turn around. I make a beeline toward the women's locker room.

"Wait." Egg grabs my arm and makes me face him. "You know I have to do this."

"Yeah, I know. Feel free to take your knife out of my back before you go."

"Don't give me that, Olivia. This has always been about me, not us. I thought you understood that. You getting an invitation to audition was an unexpected bonus, but this has always been my audition, not yours."

"Got it, Stuart. It's all about you. All about being number one.

Well, good luck. Because our partnership is now officially over whether you get this gig or not. Like, for forever."

"Grow up, Olivia. You know this is the business. Partnerships are made and dissolved all the time." Egg looks around. Our cutting exchange has brought out the sharks, including Britney Xiao, who can smell my blood in the water. Egg drags me toward a dark corner.

"Get your hands off me." I yank my arm out of Egg's hand.

"Then get over here and talk to me like an adult before I have to go."

I want to smack the smirk off Britney's face. Instead, as I pass her, I mumble, "At least I landed *my* triple-double-double."

One shark swims quickly away.

"What am I supposed to do now, Stuart? I'm stuck here in LA while you skate off into never-never land."

Egg runs a hand through his hair and puffs air out of his cheeks. "I don't know. And honestly, I don't have time to deal with this right now."

"At least drive me back to the hotel. I'll hang out by the pool or something."

"I don't have time to do that. I need to prepare for the callbacks. I need to meet some of my new potential partners."

"Wow. Just wow."

"I know. This sucks. I suck. I'm the worst friend ever. Got it." Egg's face hardens. "And you know what? You would do *exactly* the same thing if our roles were reversed."

I open my mouth to argue, but nothing comes out. Because Egg is right. I would drop him like a hot potato in the same situation. That's the cost of being a one-in-a-million skater. You always put yourself first, even when it hurts the people you claim to love.

I stomp off to the women's locker room and hide in the toilet stall for the next hour. I cram the sleeve of my warm-up jacket into

my mouth to muffle my sobs. When I emerge again, the phoenix is dead. All that is left is a pile of ashes. I change back into
normal high school sophomore Olivia Kennedy—the one without
makeup and wearing jeans, a T-shirt, Chucks, and Mack's oversize hoodie. I stop at the door. My heart might be breaking, but
I can't show them that. I lift my head high and step out of the
women's locker room. Just to screw with me, the world continues to turn like everything's still fine. Like the gold medal wasn't
snatched away from me today. I finger the edge of the business
card crammed in the pocket of my hoodie. The gold medal might
be gone, but I know I earned it. Everybody knows I earned it. And
I will be back.

My stomach clenches when I see Egg at our bench, chatting
and joking with a petite blonde. Mom and Dad smile down from
the poster behind him, giving Stuart their blessing for his new life
without me. I am completely disposable. Nothing like being #2
in a world of people who only look out for #1. I pull my backpack
higher on my shoulders and walk out the double doors back to
real life.

Chapter 34

Real life outside the Skater Bubble is scary. And when the sun starts to go down, this part of Los Angeles becomes extremely scary. My heart pounds worse than after my audition, especially when a feral-looking man grabs at my arm after trying to talk to me for the last two blocks. I drop my smoothie and break into a run. Shooting pain surges up my back as the skate boots in my backpack collide with my spine. Though I had no intention of going back inside the Olympians on Ice building, necessity makes me tuck tail and do it anyway.

And of course, Britney Freakin' Xiao is in the lobby chatting loudly on her cell phone, because the universe hates me today. I pull my hoodie over my head, duck my chin, and slink off to a corner with my overpriced sandwich. When I slide down the wall to wait, the knees of my jeans decide they don't want to cooperate with me today either. I duck my covered head when Britney looks over to see what the ripping sound is.

"Do you know how much money I spent to train with Nathan?" Britney whines. "Thousands. And that's not even including the new Mustang we leased for him. Such a waste. And now I have to switch partners *again*."

Whatever. I'd gladly skate with Nathan at this point.

"With my luck, I'm going to get stuck with Stuart Trout as my partner." Britney sighs dramatically. "He's, like, obsessed with me. And I'm all, 'Back off, dude.'"

I wish Egg still had the drunk text selfie she sent him. Then again, that would require me to talk to him again.

"She was! It was okay. All right, it was better than okay. She made it to the couples' audition, but then they kicked her out. Like ripped up her headshot and said, 'Bye, Felicia.' I felt bad for her. It was embarrassing."

It takes all my self-control not to throw my overpriced sandwich at Britney's head.

"You better watch out. I hear she's making a comeback. And now that her pride is completely shredded, she's going to be even harder to beat. Yeah. Maybe you'll luck out, and nobody will agree to move to Phoenix to skate with her. 'Cause I mean, Phoenix, why?" Somebody pokes their head out the door and flags Britney. "Anyhoo, that's the tea, sis. Let's do lunch when I get back. Love you, babe! Ciao."

After Britney leaves, I pull the business card out of my hoodie pocket. I flip it through my fingers. *Walter Hale, owner and artistic director of Olympians on Ice.* What a roller-coaster ride today has been.

"Hey, you can't squat here. This is private property." Faina's high heels tap across the polished floor. "There's a homeless shelter four streets west over on Elm. You can get a hot meal and escape the cold there. Do you want a bus pass?"

I look around the empty lobby and then down at my clothes. Large and small splotches of oxidizing smoothie mark my right foot and up the right leg of my now ripped jeans. I push my hoodie back.

"I'm waiting on my partner . . . former partner . . . I'm waiting on Stuart Trout to finish his audition."

Faina nearly drops her phone. "Oh my goodness, Olivia. I am so sorry."

"It's okay. He deserved it. His audition was flawless today."

"That's not what I meant." Faina sits on the bench closest to me. "We unfortunately get a lot of broken souls on our stoop. And sometimes we're the ones who have done the breaking. This is LA after all, where dreams are both made and crushed. Hence my attempt to balance the karmic scales when I can with a bus pass or a few bucks. I heard you had a rough day."

The lump in my throat threatens to choke me. I nod at her.

"I'm sorry. This business is so hard. Are you flying back to Phoenix tonight?"

I push the lump down. "No. I'm stuck here until Stuart can drive us back across the desert."

"That's going to be a long wait, I'm afraid." Faina tucks an errant lock of graying hair back into her bun. "Insider secret: They're going to ask Stuart to come back tomorrow. The judges were so impressed by you two."

I snort and wave Mr. Hale's card at her.

"Olivia, I've been working with Mr. Hale for over a decade. I can count on one hand how many people he's given his card to and told them to come back later. Normally, he wants you now, or he doesn't want you at all. Mr. Hale couldn't land a single toe loop if his life depended on it, but that man has an eye for talent." Faina picks up her phone and scrolls through it. "That card isn't a no. It's a not now."

"I've been thinking about going back to being a single skater. It's not like I have a lot of partner choices in Phoenix." If we can barely afford to keep the rink open right now, leasing a car for some drama king like Nathan isn't an option.

"How do you feel about Colorado?" Faina's green eyes have a spark in them.

"It's . . . a lot colder than Phoenix?"

"Yes, it is. How do you feel about going to Colorado Springs to meet with a friend of mine?" Faina waves her phone at me.

I sit up straight. "You mean at the Broadmoor Skating Club, don't you?"

"I do." Faina's scarlet lips pull back into a smile. "I'm not promising you anything, of course. But they do have a long history of coaching elite skaters, including several Olympians. If you ever find yourself in the Colorado Springs area, let me know. I can set something up for you."

I throw my arms around Faina and then remember myself. "Sorry."

Faina tips my chin up with her immaculately manicured nails. "I can open the door for you, Olivia, but only you can walk through it."

"Thank you."

Faina stands and smooths down her skirt. "Now then, are you ready to go? I can arrange a ride to take you back to your hotel if you want to stay in LA this weekend. Or there's an overnight bus that runs from downtown LA to Phoenix Sky Harbor Airport if you want to go home tonight."

I pull out my phone and turn it on. There are so many missed calls, voice mails, texts, emails, and instant messages that I'm afraid my phone is going to explode.

"I want to go home. Tonight."

"Consider it done."

I text Dad from the bus station. I'm headed home. Solo. I'm coming by bus. I'll text you when I get back to Phoenix. BTW, your *friend* Faina says you now owe her two bottles of Dom Perignon.

Dad texts me back. I know. I just got off the phone with her. Now I owe her two bottles of Dom Perignon and a bottle of Tums.

Tums?

Yeah. Because she gets to deliver my res-
ignation letter to Mr. Hale. And all Hale is
going to break loose because of it.

Groan Dad, it was one semi-stupid
road trip. You don't have to give up
the limelight because of me. I promise
to get permission next time.

Thank you, you're still grounded for a
month, and I was planning to come off the
road anyway. It's time for Mom to have surgery. There's no other way around it according to the specialist. I'm coming home.

Despite the grounding, I'm glad Dad is coming home, and I
don't want Mom to be in so much pain all the time. But what
about all the past-due envelopes already piled up in the basket at
our front door? My heart clenches.

How are we going to pay for it though?

Let me worry about that.

You're selling the rink, aren't you? I'm afraid of Dad's answer, but
I have to know.

Gold Medal Ice made me an offer yesterday. They want to open a second location
in Phoenix.

DAD. NO!

They offered to let me stay on for the first six
months to help with the transition. I would
only be a coach, but at least I would have
a job for a little while longer. They wanted
Stuart too, but Faina tells me that there's a
95% chance he's going out on tour soon.

And me? The thought of teaching for the enemy makes my
stomach burn.

The contract is only for me. Otherwise they
want to clean house and bring in their own
people.

Oh, Mack. I wipe my eyes on my sleeve. And the Chois?

Will have to renegotiate their contract or
find a different rink. Gold Medal Ice says
they can't have one person taking up so
much premium ice time.

The joke's on them because Jonah
was invited to skate with future Olympians in Utah. He's leaving soon anyway.

Oh! That's news I hadn't heard.

And if *I* want to train?

We would get a discount on ice time. You
would have to audition for their coaches to
see if any of them would want to take you
on. Most aren't even taking new skaters
right now because the ice time is so limited.
Which is why they want Ice Dreams.

Losing the rink to Gold Medal Ice is one thing, but not even being allowed to skate at my own rink pushes me over the edge.

> Don't do it, Dad! I'm begging you.
> Please don't do it. It would kill me.

I love you with all my heart, Olivia, but you know we have to do this. I hope one day you'll understand.

> I HATE YOU!!!!

Dad doesn't text me anymore. Not that I would have texted him back anyway. Next up is Jonah. I'm not surprised the seventeen texts he sent on Friday got shorter and sharper as the day wore on. He's Ice Dreams' reigning prince. He's not used to being ignored. He's not used to being #2 in anybody's life.

His last text is Where are you? Tell me you are okay.

"I'm not okay," I whisper. My mind is a whirlwind of desperate ideas. I can't give in to my heart right now. I have to focus on the #1 problem.

Chapter 35

Thankfully, my seatmate—a young woman who still thinks she's going to be the next big thing in Hollywood despite being on this bus with me—goes to sleep once we pass the Cabazon dinosaurs. Though my body feels like it has weights attached to it, my mind won't shut down. All through the night, I pitch one outrageous, desperate idea to Mack after another. She shoots down the stupid ideas and weaves the well-that-idea-doesn't-completely-suck ones into a loose plan. At 4:00 a.m. Mack sends me a picture of her slightly burnt pancakes, even though it isn't a Tuesday. My empty stomach growls.

A little after seven, my bus rolls into Phoenix. I take a picture of the sunrise and text it to Jonah.

> I'm back in Phoenix. Things are a dumpster fire. You should move to Utah.

To my surprise, Jonah is awake. What? Why?

> Because Dad is selling Ice Dreams.

I've been plotting with Mack all night, but if none of our ideas work, we're going to lose Ice Dreams. So go to Utah. Chase your dreams. I'm not pushing you away. I'm letting you fly free.

Can we at least talk about this?

Yes, but not now. I haven't slept in 24 hours and my battery is at 5%.

I'm not surprised to see Mack with Fiona in her arms waiting for me at the bus station, even though I told her she didn't have to come. Tyler, however, is a surprise. We all pile into his four-door truck. I am grateful for the ride, but I still don't like him. He does earn points for insisting we stop for biscuits and hash browns since we're up so early on a Saturday morning. Mack makes small talk with Tyler, but they thankfully leave me alone in my thoughts.

"What are your cross streets, Olivia?" Tyler says.

I can't go home. I can't face Mom right now. I can't break her heart with Dad's betrayal. Ice Dreams is as much her baby as I am.

As if Mack can read my mind, she says, "Drop us off at Ice Dreams."

"It's not even nine o'clock yet," Tyler says.

"I know," Mack says, ending the conversation.

When Tyler pulls into Ice Dreams fifteen minutes later, Mack unhooks her seat belt and leans over the seat to kiss a sleeping Fiona's head.

"Your grandmother isn't coming back until tomorrow night, and Stuart is still in Los Angeles, right?" Tyler says.

"Yes. So, if you'd like to pick up some beef and broccoli on your way back to my house with Fiona tonight, maybe we could attempt family dinner."

"I could do that." Tyler leans in to kiss her goodbye.

Mack leans away. "We aren't there yet, Tyler. Let's see how family dinner goes first."

To his credit, Tyler says, "You got it. One step at a time. And we still need to talk about how to handle the holidays. My parents want Fiona for Christmas morning."

"Yeaaaaaah, not sure that's going to happen. We'll talk more about that later." Mack slides her computer bag over her shoulder. "Right now, I have a job to do."

I still think Mack can do better, but I slide my backpack on and keep my mouth closed. Mack and I trudge up the sidewalk. I'm just putting my keys in the lock when Mack yelps.

"Sorry." Jonah dodges around a Mercedes parked on the dumpster side of the building with his in-lines in his hands. "Didn't mean to sneak up on you."

"Damn it, Choi, don't tell me you snuck out again. Your parents hate me enough as it is," Mack says.

"I didn't sneak out. I told them where I was going."

"And they were okay with it?"

"Not exactly." Jonah winces. "But I reminded Mom that she's the one who wanted me to be more normal. Part of that means being there for your friends. She agreed with that, but then she reminded me that she owns my phone and can ping it for my exact location at any time. So, progress? Maybe?"

"Maybe. I'm glad you're here." Mack pats Jonah on the back. "I'm going to go boot up my computer. I'll give you two a moment."

Jonah gives Mack a nod of thanks. Mack pulls my keys out of the lock and tosses them back to me. After she goes inside, I sit on the step and wrap my arms around my knees. Jonah sits beside me. After a moment, his arm reaches around my back and he gently pulls me toward him until my head rests on his shoulder. His hoodie is soft against my cheek. His lips brush the top of my head.

"I'm guessing your audition didn't go so well if you are back in Phoenix solo," Jonah whispers.

I sit up straight and plunge my hand into the pocket of my hoodie. I flick Mr. Hale's business card in front of Jonah's face. He tips his head to the side. A confused look crosses his face as he reads it.

"Olympians on Ice wants me, but with either an Olympic medal around my neck or a high school diploma in my hand." I tuck the card back in my pocket. "But Faina said she could get me in the door at the prestigious Broadmoor Skating Club in Colorado Springs right now if I want."

"Oh, wow. I knew you were good, but not that good," Jonah says, and I scowl. "That didn't come out right. What I mean is that I always see Ice Dreams and Olivia Kennedy as a matching set. I don't know how one can exist without the other."

"Me neither." I stand and pull Jonah to his feet. "Which is why we have to convince my parents not to sell the rink. Mack and I have been up all night thinking about it."

"Show me what you've come up with and I'll give you my two cents." Jonah laces his fingers through mine. "I've become a skilled negotiator lately—or just an argumentative teenager if you ask Mom. I might be able to help you come up with something to change their minds."

The weight on my chest lightens some. Jonah can't solve my problems, but his presence on and off the ice helps balance me.

"Put your hands together for ANNABELLE 'MACK TRUCK' MACINTOOOOOSH!" I yell as Jonah and I enter Ice Dreams.

Mack stands in the snack bar with her laptop open on the counter. She doesn't even break into a smile at my intro. Then I see why. Over near Table #1 stands a middle-aged white woman with platinum-blond hair wearing tailored clothes and dripping in gold jewelry.

"Livy?" Dad steps out from behind her, a bunch of papers and a pen in his hand.

My heart sinks.

"Please, don't sell Ice Dreams, Dad. Give us six months . . . three months to get things turned around. I know we can do it."

"You are very sweet," the woman says, her gold bracelets jingling together. "I appreciate your enthusiasm, I do, but this is business."

"No, this is Ice *Dreams* not Ice *Business*. We follow Coach Kennedy's Rule Number One here. We look out for our partner." I look at Jonah and then Mack. "And our family."

Dad puts the paperwork down on the table. "Thank you so much for the ride from the airport this morning, Ms. Ormand. I will look over your generous offer again and get back to you soon."

"Mr. Kennedy, I can wait." Ms. Ormand dips her gold-tipped manicured hands into her designer purse and pulls out her car keys. "In three months, or even six, when your rink goes under—and it will—I'll be back. And next time, my offer will be half what it is today. Think about that and then get back to me."

Ms. Ormand jingles in front of the snack bar on her way out the door.

"Don't let the door hit you in the ass on your way out!" Mack yells after her.

"Annabelle!" Dad says.

"What? If she gets the rink, I'm going to be out of a job anyway."

Ms. Ormand snorts, puts her nose in the air, and retreats to her Mercedes outside. Dad runs his hand through his hair and lets out a frustrated sigh.

"Livy, what have you done?" Dad says.

"I've stood up for every skater who *isn't* number one. Who maybe doesn't even care about being number one. Ms. Ormand can have all the Hannahs and the people who suck the joy out of skating. I want us to do what we're best at."

"So, you are willing to gamble everything on one last-ditch effort to turn this rink around?" Dad comes to stand in front of me. He looks down at Jonah's and my hands, but neither of us let go. "What about your dream?"

"I haven't given up on *my* dream, but I'm willing to be number two for a while to keep Ice Dreams open."

"You would rather we sell our house than the rink." Mom's voice echoes in the empty rink as she shuffles across the floor to us.

"Yes. I would sleep on a cot in your office and shower at school if it meant we could keep Ice Dreams open a little longer."

"What do you think, Midori?" Dad takes Mom's hand. "Ice Dreams has always been your baby more than mine."

"But maybe it's time to let my babies grow up and fly away from the nest." Mom looks from me to Mack to Jonah, tears welling up in her eyes.

An awkward silence falls across the rink. My heart pounds in my ears. We all stand at a crossroads. Each of us with a different path to take.

"Maybe we should—" Mom says, as Axl Rose suddenly screams from Jonah's pocket.

"I am so sorry. That's my mom." Jonah scrambles to free his phone from his pocket and puts it up to his ear. "Hey, Mom. Hold on a sec, please." He looks at my parents. "I know I don't get a vote here, but I want to thank you for this. All of this. If you need to sell the rink, I understand, but I—" Jonah's voice cracks. "I . . . Thanks. Just. Thanks."

As Jonah rushes out the door, talking to his mom on the phone, Mack packs up her laptop.

"I know I don't get a vote either, but . . . what the kid said." Mack clears her throat and backs up. "All of it."

"Come. Sit down. We need to talk. The three of us." Dad gently ushers Mom to Table #1. "I'll make us some tea."

I slide in across the table from Mom. She looks as bad as I feel. We sit in silence. The last heated words we exchanged hang between us. Dad delivers a round of tea and slides into the table. He looks at Mom and then me.

"I've obviously missed something here." Dad blows on his tea. "Anybody care to clue me in?"

"Our daughter is mad because I didn't give her permission to go to LA with Stuart. Now she's going to be even madder because she's grounded for the next month for disobeying me."

"You still don't get it!" I slap my palms down on the table, making my hot tea slosh out of the cup. "I went to LA to prove you wrong. To prove my inner critic wrong too. That I'm not a washed-up has-been at sixteen. And guess what?" I pull Mr. Hale's business card out of my pocket and smack it in the middle of the table. "Mr. Hale thinks I'm a one-in-a-million skater, even if you two don't."

"So I heard at seven thirty this morning when Walter called to tell me all about the new idea that had kept him up all night." Mom picks up the business card and flips it through her fingers. "He also doesn't want to lose his headliner, Mike. And since Walter thinks Olivia has given up on her dream of being an Olympian, he's changed his mind and wants to create a Father-Daughter number. 'We'll even create a special promo for the whole month of June to celebrate Father's Day. His fans will eat it up, Midori—and buy the T-shirt!'" Mom sighs. "Maybe after I have this surgery, I should hang up my skates for good and close the rink. Maybe it's time for my dream to come to an end. I know I sound like a washed-up has-been. And there is a truth to that too, as ugly as it is. Maybe it's time to free you two from the burden that comes with living my dream instead of yours."

"Midori, this is not a burden. *You* are not a burden. My dream at nineteen years old was to win a gold medal at the Olympics, buy a bangin' BMW with a sweet sound system, and get my face on a box of Wheaties." Dad reaches his hand across the table to take Mom's. "And talk my best friend into marrying me one day. Check, check, check, and . . ." Dad points at the box of Wheaties in the snack bar with his free hand. "Check. Everything else that has come with this roller coaster of a life has been icing on the cake. Well, except the part about trading in my bangin' BMW for a minivan." Dad laughs at his own joke, though nobody else does. Dad takes one of my hands too. "So, if you want to sell the rink and officially retire or keep the rink and send us out on the road for a while, I'll do whatever it takes to keep our little family going. I'm all yours. I've always been all yours."

Mom's exterior begins to melt, but then it immediately hardens again. "Then why is Faina texting me all of a sudden after twenty years saying she wants to talk to me? And who gave her my number?"

"I did," I say. "I put you down as my emergency contact out of habit."

Something telegraphs between my parents. Something that makes my mom's eyebrows furrow.

"She wants to talk about Olivia," Dad says. "That's it."

"Faina says she can open the door for me at the Broadmoor

Skating Club in Colorado Springs," I say. "If I have the courage to walk through it."

Mom looks at me. "And do you? Because if you've got the guts to back up the raw talent that Walter and Faina can clearly see—even if I've been blind to it—then it's definitely time to let go of my dream so our family can pursue yours."

"And an Olympic run is going to be an all-hands-on-deck kind of commitment, Livy. For years. Just so you know what you are getting yourself—and us—into."

"And then there's the problem of finding a new partner. Walter told me Stuart is definitely going out on tour with them in the new year."

"I don't need a partner. I want to go back to being a single skater. But I want to save the rink first," I say.

"Honey, you don't have to do that for me," Mom says.

"I am and I'm not. I'm doing it for me too. And for Mack. And for Jonah. For all the people who believe in Ice *Dreams* over Ice *Business*. Whether they are the Red Hat ladies doing Zumba or derby girls dry-land training with our favorite speedy boi or first graders who just want to skate for the fun of it. We can't compete against Gold Medal Ice. And I don't want to. I want to do what we do best."

"YES!" Mack's voice echoes across the rink. "Sorry. I'm not eavesdropping. I just left my phone in the snack bar. I'll be out of your business in a sec."

"Annabelle." Mom pats the empty seat in our square.

"No, I couldn't."

"Yes, you could," I say. "I need a wingwoman on this."

"Go get your laptop and I'll make you some tea." Dad heads toward the snack bar. "I want to see the presentation you created that Ms. Ormand so rudely dismissed."

"You got it, boss." Mack's lip ring clinks against her bottom teeth as a huge smile lights up her face. "Also, I should give you guys a heads-up that the Chois—all of 'em—are in the parking lot. They're having a spirited debate about whether Jonah is going to Utah this year or not." When Mom turns her whole body to look at her, Mack says, "Totally not eavesdropping. They left their windows cracked."

"I'm not chastising you, Annabelle," Mom says. "I want to know how it's looking."

"Mr. Choi is a go. Mrs. Choi is a stay. Jonah can't get a word in edgewise. If they would just let Jonah talk, maybe they'd— Oh hey, Mr. Choi."

Jonah follows his parents into Ice Dreams, looking exasperated. "All I'm saying, Dad, is let's ask and see if it's even a possibility before we make a decision."

Mr. Choi gives the big white guy standing in the snack bar with a cup of tea in his hand a confused look before asking, "Midori, is there even the remotest chance we could build a short track program here?"

"A program? Maybe, if you recruit from the hockey rink across town," Mom says. "A program at Jonah's level? No. Your son is a one-in-a-million skater."

Mrs. Choi beams. Normally, I would be jealous, but I can see the crack forming in Mr. Choi's resolve.

"Midori and I have contacts in the Olympic community." Dad comes out of the snack bar to shake the Chois' hands and introduce himself. "We can help put feelers out for you for a new coach."

I stand and look Dad in the eye. "Tell them the whole truth, Dad."

"Olivia," Dad's voice has a warning tone.

"No, they need to know. If we lose Jonah to Utah now, then we will probably lose the rink in a few months." I look at Jonah. He nods at me. "If Jonah changes his mind and comes back to

Arizona, Gold Medal Ice's new Phoenix location isn't going to give you the whole rink, especially not during premium ice times. Jonah won't be the reigning Ice Prince at Gold Medal Ice. He will be just another talented skater fighting for ice time." I take Jonah's hand. "But that's not how we do things here. Ice Dreams is a family."

"The choice is yours, of course," Dad says diplomatically.

"Dad, I want to go to Utah," Jonah says. "But not yet. Do I think I have a shot at a medal at the Junior Championships in two weeks? Honestly, no. Am I a stronger, more consistent skater since moving to Phoenix, though? Definitely yes. And I've got the hardware to back that up. Let's double down, Dad. Let's stay in Phoenix together as a family a little longer."

Mack comes to stand behind us. She places a hand on each of our shoulders. "If he can whip a bunch of sassy derby girls into shape, just imagine what Jonah could do with a bunch of little kids."

"Ehhhh." Jonah shrugs. "I'm not sure about the little kid part, but I would be willing to assist the short track coach during group classes to help lower the cost of my private coaching. I know my dream is a financial burden on our family. I want to do my part."

"What do you think?" Mrs. Choi says to her husband.

"How about a trial period? Six months?" Mr. Choi says.

"Yaaaaaaasssss!" Mack grabs Jonah and me in a bone-crushing group hug.

"Mack has something she's been wanting to show us." Dad nods at Mack. "Now might be a good time to see it."

Dad makes another round of tea for everybody as Mack sets up her laptop on a stool in front of Table #1. Jonah straddles the bench seat behind me and wraps his arms around my waist. He leans in until his chin rests on my shoulder.

"Call me delusional, but I think we might be able to pull this off," Jonah whispers in my ear.

"Delusional." I fold my hands over Jonah's and give them a squeeze. "Since we can't figure out how to be normal teens, let's lean in to being extra. That's what we do best, after all."

"Speaking of being extra." Jonah nods at Mack.

"So, it's a little rough." Mack shuffles from foot to foot. "I can definitely make something more professional with a little more time and a lot more sleep, but here you go."

Mack pushes a button and steps out of the way. A montage of pictures flows across the screen to an upbeat instrumental soundtrack. Me doing a Biellmann spin. Jonah in a deep angle, his gloved fingers grazing the ice. Egg defying gravity, hovering over the ice in a butterfly jump. Egg and me doing a death spiral.

Mack's adulting voice narrates as the picture changes. *Here at Ice Dreams, we're more than just gold medals.*

A montage of old pictures of Mom and Dad from the Olympics mixes with Egg and me waving to the crowd with gold medals around our necks and Jonah with his newer medal pictures.

We're family.

Mom gasps when a picture comes on the screen of me kneeling down, tying a laughing Lina Kitagawa's skate boot. It's Mrs. Choi's turn when a picture of Jonah demonstrating a deep squat to a crowd of derby girls in the park comes up. She puts a hand on Mom's arm when a still of Jonah and me doing our hydroblade stunt slides across the screen.

So whether you aspire to go for the gold or are just looking for a fun new way to exercise, why don't you come dream with us today?

The last shot melts into the Ice Dreams logo with our address and social media handles.

"Wow . . . just . . . wow, Annabelle." Dad runs a hand through his hair. His eyes glisten.

Mom straight-up wipes her eyes with her fingertips. "Annabelle, you're fired."

"Wait, what?" Mack says.

"You need to go back to school or at least apply for a job with a PR firm. I love you like a daughter, but this is me pushing you out of the nest."

"I want to, but not yet." Mack gives me a nod. "Give us a chance to save the rink."

"It's going to take a group effort," I say.

"I'm game." Jonah puts his hand in the middle of the table. "Who's in?"

"I am." I put my hand on top of Jonah's.

One by one, everyone else at the table adds their hand. Mack puts her hand in last.

"Let's make this dream a reality." I look around the table and stop at Jonah.

"No regrets," Jonah says.

"No regrets."

Chapter 36

"Move it a little to the left. No, my left. Higher. Higher. Now it's too high."

"Mom, it's fine." I smack the pushpin into the wall and climb down off the chair. "The doors are opening soon, and we're still futzing around with the banner. Plus, you promised Tera Lynn that you wouldn't overdo it tonight."

"I'm not overdoing it. I feel better than I have in months." Mom leans in and tugs on the corner of the banner anyway. "Plus, Tera Lynn says I get a bonus massage tomorrow after our PT session for meeting my exercise goals this month. So bring me the balloons and then go get changed. Michael!"

"I'm doing a taste test for Mr. Sato," Dad says, his cheeks puffed out with rice and pork cutlet. "Excellent as always."

Dad slips a twenty-dollar bill in the donation jar that has my picture and "Go for the Gold, Olivia!" on the front of it and takes his paper bowl of katsudon with him to his assigned station over in what's become the short track speed skaters' dry land training area with Coach Phillips. We dance around each other as I bring Mom the swarm of gold balloons.

"Move it a little more to the right, Mike," Mom yells as I hand her the balloons.

Dad realigns the white podium in front of the crowd background and puts the realistic—but totally fake—gold medal on top of the highest spot in the center for people to take their picture with. Yet another one of Ice Dreams' PR manager Annabelle MacIntosh's brilliant ideas.

I take a quick detour on my way to the locker room.

"I will be back for one of those later." I point at the melon pan Lina's big sister, Skyler, arranges on the bake sale table next to Brandon's pastel macarons and his girlfriend, Naomi's, German chocolate and coconut brownies. Erika's marshmallow treats come in highly decorated individual baggies. "And one of those. And probably one of those."

"I'll put one of each back here for you," Skyler says with a smile.

"Olivia!" Mom yells across the rink.

"I'm going!" I race into the locker room and pull my first costume of three in tonight's student showcase out of my bag. I can't wait for everybody to see the number I choreographed for my Tuesday-night class. Sassy Lina Kitagawa is going to steal the show. I slide on my phoenix costume for one last outing. I wish Egg could have made it back from London in time for tonight's grand reopening extravaganza to skate with me. I do appreciate the two front-row tickets he talked Mr. Hale into donating for the raffle. I still expect comp tickets for their Phoenix performance next month, though. And a personal introduction to whoever is eating up all of Egg's free time since he can't seem to text me back in a reasonable amount of time anymore.

I line my eyes and tap a little bit of glitter on my bloodred lips for old time's sake. The derby girls are here. I can hear them in the barre area—which now doubles as the dry land training area— razzing Mack about her new man. I retie my laces and check my costume one last time in the mirror.

"Is she coming?" someone says, and another woman shushes her.

I walk out of the locker room to find the Surly Gurlz in an arc with their left hands extended. Starting with Barnacle Barb and ending with Mack, I travel the arc high-fiving each of the Gurlz. I even tap Fiona's outstretched hand.

"Give Auntie Olivia her present," Mack says, adjusting Fiona's Santa hat.

I squat down to take the gift bag from Fiona, but she doesn't want to give it up. I dip my hand in the bag anyway and pull out a bundle of black fabric with the Surly Gurlz logo on it.

"Put your hands together for OLIVIAAAAA 'PHOENIX' KENNEDYYYYY!" Mack yells when I flip the T-shirt over. Sure enough, PHOENIX in large red glitter letters decorates the back.

"I love it." I give Mack a hug, and she squeezes me so hard that my skates leave the floor.

"We'll have to wear our shirts to the bout next weekend." Jonah's voice floats over the crowd.

"Quick Silver!" Barnacle Barb messes up Jonah's hair as he passes by her. "Our boy cleans up nice, don't he?"

Mack backs up until Jonah—in a royal-blue button-down and charcoal dress pants—stands in front of me. My heart flutters.

"You made it," I say.

"You know I wouldn't have missed it."

"How was your weekend?"

When Jonah starts unbuttoning his shirt, Barnacle Barb covers her eyes and teases, "Hey now, this is a family-friendly event!"

Jonah pulls a gold medal out. And then a second one. "I know it's pretentious."

"Not pretentious. Maybe a little extra, though."

"Says the girl wearing basically a sparkly bikini." And even though everybody is looking at us, Jonah leans down and kisses me. When we break apart a moment later, he whispers, "Colorado Springs isn't going to know what hit 'em."

Acknowledgments

There are many people who helped me take this nugget of an idea and flesh it out into the finished form.

Thank you to the immediate and extended members of the Francis-Fujimura family. Without you all I wouldn't be inspired to write the stories that I write.

Kimber "Killer Queen" Thompson for practicing roller derby–worthy defense skills with me during the countless elementary school fundraisers we did at Skateland with our kids. If we hadn't done these events, I wouldn't have seen the roller derby mamas coming in afterward to practice, and this whole project would have never gotten off the ground.

Katie Van Ark for her ice skating expertise and gifting me with Olivia and Jonah's signature move.

Thank you to Mark from the West Michigan Speedskating Club for his technical help. You helped me bring Jonah to life.

Roller derby queen Whitney Frazier for helping me tighten up my roller derby scenes.

Apolo Ohno for writing his autobiography, *Zero Regrets: Be Greater Than Yesterday*. Though I haven't met Apolo (yet!), his account of his teenage years very much informed and inspired the creation of Jonah Choi.

Mirko Goolsbey for letting me pick the mind of a retired

Olympic pairs figure skater over lunch and my college roommate Marcia Walker for introducing us.

Erina and Kylee (and your wonderful mothers) for letting me peek inside the life of a one-in-a-million teen and watching you take on the world in your own unique ways.

Diana Gill, Kristin Temple, and the whole team at Tor Teen for taking a chance on a little indie-pubbed YA author who wanted to create more stories for families who look like hers and the teens/young adults in her life. Thank you!

Isabel Ngo, Christa Desir, Sydney Jeon, Akemi Johnson, and Lauren Nicolle Taylor for challenging me and inspiring me to take this book to the next level.

Courtney Milan for seeing straight into the heart of this story, for her words of encouragement, and for her ridiculous depth of knowledge of figure skating. You deserve a gold medal for all your help.

And finally my agent, Rebecca Angus, at Golden Wheat Literary for hearting my tweet during #PitMad and starting the domino effect which brings us to today. Here's to even more creative adventures together.

With love and gratitude,
Sara "Poison Pen" Fujimura

Author's Note

I've been going to Japan every summer with my now-adult children for the last fifteen years. So it is no surprise that I've been writing about bicultural families and, specifically, mixed Japanese American family life for almost twenty years now and in many different forms. As the American half of our Japanese American family and the mom of two biracial children, I looked for books that my kids could see themselves in at all stages of their lives. I am an avid YA reader, so there has never been a shortage of YA books in my house, but my son in particular rarely saw Asian or half-Asian boys as the main character or love interest in them. My kids quickly turned to anime, manga, and Japanese TV instead— places where they could see themselves as the hero, the villain, the love interest, and not just the sidekick or tech guy. So I wrote this for them, first and foremost.

Food also plays an important part in all of my work. If you've read any of my books, you've probably realized by now that I have a notorious sweet tooth. So, if you suddenly crave hotteok or melon pan or brownies while reading this book, I'm sorry. I can't help myself. I've always connected to Japanese culture through food, and I enjoy learning new recipes from my mother-in-law every time I go to Japan for a visit. I specifically love obento. So much so that if you go to anime cons in Arizona you may see me in Artist Alley as my alter ego, The Obento Lady. I made obento for my kids every day for thirteen years straight, so I am more than happy to give your lunch a makeover. Let's play with our food!

Every Reason We Shouldn't is a book for the next generation of biracial Asian teens in the US and around the globe looking to see themselves represented more in YA books. My books are only one specific lens on the bigger experience of being a multiracial Asian teen. You may see your family life portrayed in my books. You may not. If you don't, I encourage you to take a look at the running list I keep on my website (www.sarafujimura.com) of other YA books featuring biracial Asian main characters or love interests. It is still an incredibly short list. Please help me add to it.

Finally, though I take my research very seriously, I occasionally bend some of the facts to make my fiction flow better or as a wink to certain people in my life. For example, the date and location of the Japanese NHK Trophy Olivia and Jonah watch after his birthday party. I have a gold medal from Sapporo too. Granted, I bought mine at the gift shop next to the Sapporo Olympic Museum when I went to Hokkaido in the summer of 2019 with my husband, but there you go.

I hope this book brings you joy and inspiration as you dream big too.

Sara Fujimura

Turn the page for a sneak peek at
Sara Fujimura's next novel

Available July 2021

Chapter 1

"Can I get you anything else?" My favorite waiter at Matsuda puts down a bowl of edamame still in the pods and a steaming cup of green tea in front of me.

I slide my shades off and let my guard down. I can be myself again because the cameras aren't allowed to follow me in here—or at school.

"You could join me." I give him a flirty smile.

"Duh, it's Wednesday. My future girlfriend is on TV. Like I'm going to miss that."

As I set up my tablet, Leo grabs a tray filled with all the decorative shōyu bottles from the restaurant's tables and a giant jug of soy sauce to refill them. I scooch over in my favorite booth so that Leo and his tray can join me. The opening strains of *Kitsune Mask*'s wailing guitar echoes around the otherwise empty restaurant. Leo and I do our usual dance, which includes flailing arm movements—at least until my hand hits the tray and knocks over one of the decorative bottles, spilling shōyu everywhere.

"Dakota!" Leo lightly chastises me before jumping up to get a rag. "Pause it. I'll be right back."

My eyes follow after him. Leo Matsuda. My best friend for over a decade. The person whose lips send arcs of electricity through my body. Well, at least in my dreams, they do. In reality? I don't know. I'd be happy to take one for the team and find out though.

I shake last night's version—which included some intense action on the Matsudas' living room couch—from my brain and return to the Friend Zone as Leo comes back with a rag and a plate of karaage.

"Ojiichan said to give these to you." Leo puts the plate filled with five Japanese-style chicken nuggets in front of me and mops up the spilled shōyu.

"Dōmo arigatō gozaimashita, Ojiichan!" I yell a thanks toward the kitchen door. "Put it on my tab!"

"Hai, hai," *Yes. Yes.* Leo's grandfather yells back, though we both know he isn't keeping a running total of all the times the Matsudas have fed me for free.

"If we suddenly get busy in the next hour, can you run the cash register? Mom and Dad are at the bank, and Aurora has marching band until seven." Leo sits back down beside me and wipes his hands on his waist apron.

"So the karaage is a bribe, then?"

"Pretty much."

I take a bite of the lightly spiced, deep-fried chicken. "Totally working."

"Now then. My future girlfriend. Jay Yoshikawa."

"Leo, Jay Yoshikawa isn't a real person, and Ava Takahashi who plays her is married. Not to mention that she's twenty-five and you're sixteen. So, ew."

"Shut up and let me dream."

"Wait, I forgot to put the subtitles on."

Leo doesn't need subtitles for the Japanese parts, but I do. His lack of Japanese writing skills got him stuck back in Japanese II with me learning the basics, but Leo's Japanese speaking skills are advanced, especially when he talks about food. Though I guess that's a given when you work in your Japanese grandfather's restaurant. Meanwhile, Ojiichan talks to Mrs. Matsuda in English—though he doesn't need to—to work on his language skills. Her years teaching English in Japan with the JET program after college have given her some mad skills. I aspire to get to that level. Maybe I could go to Japan on the JET program one day, too?

I'm not going anywhere until my contract with HGTV is up though. They own me for the rest of this season. Then I will be free. Free to be me. Free to do whatever I want without having it possibly documented on film. I can leave my sunglasses off and my barriers down all the time. I can tell Leo how I feel about him.

"You okay, Koty?" Leo tips his head to the side and gives me a quizzical look.

"Yeah, sorry." I push play and let Leo slip away into his favorite show. One of the few things that is just for him in his overcrowded life.

As we watch the show, I cut my eyes to the side occasionally to watch Leo. Yeah, he has it bad for Jay Yoshikawa. Maybe one day he'll look at me that way, too.

"Can I have some edamame?" Leo says when the show breaks for a commercial. He opens his mouth. I shoot a couple of soybeans into his mouth. One pings off his upper lip and onto the table. "Hey, in my mouth and not up my nose, please."

"Learned your lesson from the last time?"

"I was four. Give me a break."

Our favorite show comes back on, and Leo's attention goes back to it. Jay is just about ready to crush this week's creeptastic yōkai as her secret identity Kitsune Mask when Mr. and Mrs. Matsuda burst through the front door of the restaurant.

"It's fine, honey," Mrs. Matsuda says. "Everything is going to work out fine. We'll swap things around a bit. That will help boost traffic."

"Hey, kids." Mr. Matsuda looks over his shoulder and gives his wife a pointed look. She drops the conversation.

"Hey, Mr. Matsuda. Mrs. Matsuda," I say as Leo refills the last of the shōyu bottles.

"Anything else you guys want done before what I hope will be the dinner rush?" Leo slides to his feet and balances the tray on his arm with his usual grace.

"No, honey. I'll call you if I need you." Mrs. Matsuda kisses the top of Leo's closely cropped head. "Do some homework so you won't have to stay up so late again tonight." Leo groans. "Okay, you can finish your show first."

Leo flits around the restaurant putting all the shōyu bottles back on their tables while humming our latest jam. I nod along, as YouTube sensation Rayne Lee's song "One Last Kiss" has been on my mental radio all day long, too. After depositing the tray on the counter, Leo over-sings the chorus while doing a dance-y walk across the restaurant. He pauses in the middle of the floor to do the video's signature four finger snaps before finishing his strut to our table. I laugh. Nobody at school gets to see this side of Leo. These one-man shows are only for me.

"You are such a dork," I say as Leo slides back into the booth with me.

"Can't help it. Rayne's song has been stuck in my head all day long."

As soon as I push play again, a couple comes into the restaurant. Followed by a family of six. Leo's free time is over for today. It's time for him to do his part in the family machine. My heart hurts for him. And for me.

"Tell you what. After I'm done, I'll leave my tablet in the back with Ojiichan. You can watch the last ten minutes tonight when you get home or if you have a slow spot during dinner."

"Thanks." Leo's dimpled smile makes my heart melt.

I clear my throat. *Get back in the Friend Zone, Dakota.* "Any time."

"This is awesome, Patrick," Mom says to her college friend—and frequent guest expert on the show—via Skype. "I knew you would know. You were always Dr. Henderson's favorite for a reason." Mom waves at me over the top of her computer monitor. "Let's do this all again on . . ." Mom looks at Stephanie, our show's talent coordinator, who gives her the answer. "Tuesday at 1:30 p.m. Same convo without the personal stuff. And be sure to move to your left about six inches more so we can get your business logo in the background. Great. See you soon."

Mom takes off her headset and swivels her chair around. "How was school today, Koty?"

"Eh." I shrug.

Stephanie moves a pile of Mom's research books off the only other chair in Mom's cramped home office and pats it until I sit down. Ugh. There will be work-work coming any second now.

"Tea break?" Stephanie says, confirming my suspicions.

"Yes, please, Steph." Mom slides off her reading glasses and rubs her eyes. "Let's break open that goodie box from Cadbury's."

While Stephanie heads to the kitchen, Mom rolls her chair over to the circular table and peers at Stephanie's open laptop.

"So next Monday, break out the flannels. We're going up to McGuthrie Farms to pick out our Christmas tree for the holiday special."

Sweat pools in the back of my tank top from my short skateboard ride home from Matsuda. "Do I have to wear a winter coat? All that faux fur around my sweaty face is going to be itchy."

"Yes."

"C'mon, Mom. It's still eighty degrees up north, I bet."

"Seventy-five," Mom corrects me. "But we're going to wear the coats and enjoy McGuthrie's famous hot chocolate and think cool thoughts. After all, we are professionals. Unless, of course, you've changed your mind about buying a car."

"Hot chocolate and winter coats in August it is."

"That's my girl."

Leo refers to the way my family lives four or more months in the future because of our shooting schedule as the "McDonalds' Alternate Universe." For example, we filmed our traditional Mc-Donald Family Thanksgiving with turkey, matching sweaters, and the air conditioner turned down to arctic levels before heading over to the Matsudas' house for a belated Independence Day barbecue.

"Can't we go on Saturday or Sunday instead?" I say. "I don't want to miss school."

Mom raises an eyebrow. "Because of school or because Leo's only day off is Monday?"

"School." But when Mom's laser stare penetrates me, I add, "And it's Leo's only *afternoon/evening* off. We still have to go to school. We wanted to watch a movie after our JCC meeting."

"I'll see if Stephanie can move it back to the weekend, but you know that comes with the extra crowds. Which is more important to you? Your personal space while filming or an afternoon with Leo?"

Hands down, a free afternoon with Leo, but I pretend to think it over. "I'm getting better with the crowds. Just promise that if someone brings up last year's Homecoming that we are out."

"Of course. I know that's still a sore spot for you."

That's the understatement of the century. A sore spot is an embarrassing moment that your friends rag you about for a few months. A sore spot isn't having your social blunders made into gifs and memes that circulate the internet. And then there's the

SNL skit that cemented the moment into pop-cultural history. My heart rate doubles, and the prickling sensation returns to my chest.

"Dakota. Deepen your breaths." Mom's hand on my arm slows my downward spiral. "We are *not* going there. Not today. Not ever again. Come back to today. Tell me about what you did after school. Tell me about Leo. What was he wearing?"

In any other context, that last statement would be somewhere between wildly inappropriate and completely gross, but I know what Mom is doing. I picture us sitting in the booth. Leo wears a T-shirt the same color as the cooked edamame shells. I focus the lens on Leo's face as the bean misses his open mouth and ricochets off his upper lip. The lips that keep ending up on mine in my dreams. When I open my eyes, Stephanie stands next to us with the tea tray and a concerned look on her face.

"How are you doing now?" Mom says.

"A little better. Dr. Berger's techniques help," I say.

Stephanie puts the tray on the table and serves us like she's a waitress in a cluttered, nerdy tea house. "Try the square ones. They have dark chocolate in the center."

I'm convinced this is why Mom *gently persuaded* the production company to pick Stephanie as our new talent coordinator several years ago. Stephanie and Mom share a mutual love of afternoon tea. They dissect PBS's *Masterpiece Theatre* on Monday mornings like other people discuss *The Bachelor*. They are also both graduates of Oxford University, though a good twenty-plus years apart. You want to push either of their buttons? Put a tea bag in a coffee cup of water, nuke it in the microwave, and refer to it as tea.

"Steph, can we see if McGuthrie Farms is willing to move our shooting date to the weekend instead of Monday?" Mom helps herself to one of the heaping pile of chocolate-covered biscuits— "Do not call them cookies"—in the center of the table.

Stephanie raises a quizzical eyebrow. "Are you sure you want to do that, Dakota?"

"Yes," I say.

"Okay then. I'll make it happen." Stephanie taps a quick note on her laptop before placing it on the bookshelf next to some antique-looking fabric samples.

I thought my contented sigh was Mr. Inside Voice, but apparently it wasn't because Stephanie says, "Are you ever going to ask Leo out on a real date?"

"No." I nibble on a biscuit. "At least, not until my contract is up and the cameras are gone."

"Good plan," Mom says. It's one thing for people to make a bingo game out of your unintentionally overused catchphrases, but the Great Homecoming Disaster cut my parents—especially Mom—deeply, too. "One last season, then we can all try something new. In fact, I was thinking about going back to Oxford for a visit this summer while Dakota is in Japan on her school trip. Solo."

My face must telegraph my concern because Mom adds, "It's fine. Your dad and Uncle Ted are already talking about some big fishing trip up in Alaska around the same time. It will be a great chance for everybody to disconnect from our previous life and try something new. Maybe grow a little bit. Definitely a chance to refresh and recharge."

"If you need someone to carry your luggage while you're at Oxford." Stephanie raises her hand. "I volunteer as tribute."

"Tell you what, Steph. You decide where you want to go after we wrap the show, and I will make it happen. Airfare, hotel, the whole nine yards. You deserve it after all the network nonsense you've helped us navigate these last few years."

"I would love that, Tamlyn. Where to go, though?" Stephanie taps her lips with her index finger.

Mom's phone pings. "Doug is finished. He wants us to come next door and see it."

"He couldn't take a picture and show us?" I shake my head and chug the last of my tea.

"Humor him." Mom puts a few cookies on a decorative napkin. "Here, bring your dad some biscuits."

"Wait. Before you two go." Stephanie quickly tidies the table and rearranges it a bit. She takes a bite out of one of the cookies and places it back on the plate. She opens up the camera app on her work phone and frames the shot.

"Please don't put me in it," I beg. "I've got a huge zit on my forehead."

Stephanie shuffles the teaware around. "Both of you *caress* the fine bone china teacups. Yep, that looks good. I'll load it up and tag Cadbury and Noritake in thanks. Don't forget, Koty, you need to post today, too. Got to keep The Network happy."

"Can you send me a picture and caption? I have a ton of homework tonight."

"It's supposed to be your feed, Dakota. Phil wants authenticity. And *spark*." Mom mocks Phil's jazz hands "spark."

Stephanie and I look at each other and let out a derisive snort.

"Tomorrow, we talk about the spin-off digital series, okay?" Stephanie says and I groan. She ignores me and loads our tea stuff back onto the tray. "Tamara Weatherbee is pressing Phil about this. He's not a fan of our new EP but he has to play nice with her. At least until he either takes her job or lands an executive producer job at another production company. Tell me what *you* want, Dakota, and I'll see if we can get The Network to give a little more with their take."

I don't know what to ask for in return for doing their stupid YouTube-wannabe show. Thanks to my generous contract with HGTV, I can buy anything I want. . . .

Okay, there are two things my money can't buy: A car and my way out of Leo's Friend Zone. At least, the first one I can solve after I pass Driver's Ed at school and receive a full driver's license issued by the state of Arizona.

Dad slides his safety glasses up when we come through the door a minute later. His salt-and-pepper hair sticks up at a bunch of weird angles.

Dad throws his hands out wide. "Tah-dah!"

"They're just fancy cookies, Dad."

"I was referring to the state of the newly refurbished and installed banister behind me." Dad pats the banister proudly. "But, I am equally excited that you brought me a snack."

"Patrick said the beat-up refrigerator we found down in Tucson was mid-1930s like I thought." Mom pats some of Dad's silver horns down. "I'm going to research it a bit more before we film on Tuesday. Let's pull out the icebox vs. high-tech—at least by 1930s standards—refrigerator angle in the next episode. It's unique, plus it will give Patrick's business a bump. He and Phoebe are expecting their third grandchild in the spring, so they could use the extra cash."

"Well now I feel old." Dad double fists the cookies.

"Whoa, slow down there, Santa," I say, and Dad winces at his latest internet nickname.

"Hey, Santa is fine." Mom plants a kiss on Dad's cheek above his now fully white beard. "Santa is a positive thing."

"So, you're saying that I can now refer to you as Mrs. Claus?" Dad says.

"Absolutely not." Mom pats at her hair. "Why? Are my roots showing?"

People routinely think my parents, who are both 62, are my grandparents. Nope. Go back to Season 4, Episode 12, "A Christmas Miracle." It's the episode where Mom revealed that at 46, she was going to be a first-time mom. She had planned on being quiet about it. After the tabloids kept mistaking Mom's horrible morning sickness—which made her look gaunt and pale on-screen—as cancer, they decided to put the rumors to rest.

Producers couldn't have scripted a more emotionally charged plot arc than Mom collapsing at a book signing and going into premature labor. Me being born eight hours later and spending an overly complicated three months in the NICU was ratings gold. As fans helped pay for my outrageous medical bills—by watching our show and coming to in-person events—my parents still feel an obligation to put more of themselves out there for their True Fans than most people would. That's why they agreed for me to be on TV with them. So I could play the role of the Miracle Baby. Then the Miracle Child. Then the Awkward Adolescent. And, thanks to last year about this time, the Angsty Teenager.

Now I'm ready for this role to be over. I want to be Just Dakota. I don't know who she is or what she wants, though.

Strike that. There is one thing I definitely want. Only I can't have him. Yet.

"Let me prep for shooting tomorrow, and then I'll go shower." Dad slides "Mjölnir," a.k.a. his favorite hammer, back into the loop on his tool belt. "Since it's my night to cook, I vote we get takeout from Matsuda and binge-watch something."

Never one to turn down dinner from Matsuda, I say, "Or we could eat at the restaurant and then come home. I have a kanji test tomorrow in Japanese to study for and an essay due, too."

"Do you want me to quiz you on the kanji? That way I can practice, too. I wish I would have started studying Japanese *before* I was an adult, but my mother—and especially my grandmother—didn't want us to. She wanted us to leave our Japanese side behind and become 100 percent American."

"Well, that's biting me in the butt right now." Granted, I barely squeak under the Asian bar at only one-quarter Japanese, but it's still a part of me. A part of my history. "If we eat in at Matsuda, then I can ask Mrs. Matsuda to check my Japanese essay at the same time."

"Dakota, we are not asking Jen to check your essay while she's working," Mom says.

Part of me wonders if Mom's resistance to her closest friend checking my work has more to do with the fact that a 0 percent Japanese person knows more about Japanese language, culture, and food than her 50 percent Japanese self does. But Mom has never lived in Japan, and Mrs. Matsuda did for years.

"Only if they're not that busy," I say.

"Fine. I have a couple of more emails to do, but I'll be ready to go by six, Doug." Mom kisses Dad's cheek again. "I love it when it's your night to cook."

"I'm not that bad!" Dad says.

"Weren't you the person Food TV specifically called to be on their *Worst Cooks in America* show, the celebrity charity edition?" I say.

"Maaaaybe. By the way, I see right through you, Dakota Rae. You want to go to Matsuda so you can see Leo," Dad says and my heart trips. "I know we've been working a lot lately. You miss your friends. Why don't you invite Leo over? Order some pizzas. Spend some quality couch potato time together."

I guarantee that the version of couch potato time with Leo that passes through my brain is 100 percent different than what Dad's thinking.

"Yeah, I'd like that. A lot."

About the Author

SARA FUJIMURA is an award-winning young adult author and creative writing teacher. She is the American half of her Japanese American family, and she has written about Japanese culture and raising bicultural children for such magazines as *AppleSeeds, Learning Through History, East West,* and *Mothering,* as well as travel-related articles for *To Japan with Love.* Her self-published young adult novels include *Tanabata Wish* and *Breathe.* She lives in Phoenix with her husband and children.

sarafujimura.com
Facebook: sarafujimura
Twitter: @SaraFujimura
Instagram: saraffujimura